P9-DEO-181

The Tobacco Men

A novel

based on notes by

Theodore Dreiser

and Hy Kraft.

With a foreword

by Hy Kraft.

Holt, Rinehart

and Winston.

New York Chicago

San Francisco

The Tobacco Men

Borden Deal

Published simultaneously in Canada by Holt,
Rinehart and Winston of Canada, Limited.
Library of Congress Catalog Card Number: 65-12002
First Edition

Designer: Ernst Reichl
81772-0115
Printed in the United States of America

For Babs,
Again

CERTAIN of the events in this book belong to our history; however, the characters and places are entirely fictitious and any resemblance to actual places or characters, living or dead, is purely coincidental.

PUBLISHER'S NOTE In 1932, Theodore Dreiser and Hy Kraft traveled to Kentucky to investigate an important and dramatic episode of American history which had never fully been treated in fiction, the Tobacco Wars of the turn of this century. The results were some twenty pages of notes on the tobacco industry between 1860 and 1910 and a preliminary script for a motion picture. Dreiser never made further use of this material. Recently, after reading these notes, Borden Deal wrote THE TOBACCO MEN, a new, entirely original work of fiction.

Foreword

On March 10, 1931, Theodore Dreiser, after having read the screenplay of *The American Tragedy,* wrote Jesse Lasky a letter detailing his criticisms and suggestions. Among the latter was Dreiser's demand that he go to Hollywood accompanied by a writer of his choice: "For this I would like to engage Hy Kraft who is known to you." A few days later Lasky and Dreiser met at the home of Will Hays, the first "czar" of the picture industry. Dreiser telephoned me from this meeting and for the first time told me of this proposal and Lasky's agreement, and he asked me if I could fly to Hollywood: the picture was already in production. The next day Dreiser and I flew to California.

This was the first time that a motion picture company had been defied by an author. "I feel in a way that I am acting for the thousands of authors who haven't had a square deal in having their works belittled for screen exploitation," said Dreiser in a public statement. Needless to say we weren't warmly welcomed but we did manage a few small but important changes. I recount this experience because it was Dreiser's first joust with the techniques and machinery of picture making. This challenged and impelled him to attempt the writing of a novel directly for the screen.

Late in 1932, Dreiser started to collect notes and do research on tobacco tycoons. Self-made robber barons and monopolists of all kinds had a real fascination for Dreiser. He dissected and examined these specimens with the persistence and concentration one ordinarily associates with a microbe hunter. In the process of this exhaustive research Dreiser came upon the incident of the bloody Tobacco Wars of 1905. With this as his climax, Dreiser composed a detailed outline of his film novel. The intention of the project was expressed in the following foreword.

> This motion picture will present the natural drama of one interesting phase of American life and its commercial development. It will involve not only what is common in American life—the aggressive and dynamic plans and actions of a certain group of American industrial leaders, practical and of course ruthless in their approach toward the lesser individual and his life—but what is rarer: the sudden and very dynamic reaction of these same minor and oppressed individuals who, finding themselves inequitably treated, proceed to fight and in such a way as to involve them in civil war.
>
> The cause, the progress and the conclusions of this social war will be shown, and in the end, and for the time being at least, a better social and economic condition for the growers and farmers.

Dreiser took me on as collaborator and in order to verify the background and locale, Dreiser and I motored from New York to the tobacco producing and manufacturing centers of the South. (Joe Rothman, a director, was with us for part of this trip.) In sub-zero weather Dreiser and I trudged the icy roads in and around Hopkinsville, Kentucky, the scene of the pitched battle between the tobacco farmers and the trust's mercenaries. I can still see Dreiser, a towering figure, indifferent to the wind and whirling snow, standing in front of the cabin where the doctor-hero of the scenario was born. We walked the railroad tracks, stood in front of the court house, examined the files of old newspapers, talked to surviving witnesses. Dreiser was taking a chance by going into Kentucky, for only a few months earlier he had led a writers' delegation to Harlan, Kentucky, thus focusing national attention on the miners' strike. As a consequence of his presence and subsequent statements, he was twice indicted—once on the charge of criminal syndicalism and then on the ludicrous charge of adultery. Had he been recognized in Kentucky he could have been arrested and held; fortunately his frame and his fame hadn't reached Hopkinsville but we did spend a slightly nervous day and night there. This wasn't bravado on Dreiser's part, it was in line with his approach to his work—he had to see and feel the countryside that he intended to depict. We went everywhere—tobacco auctions, farms, cottages; we observed the processes of tobacco from the growing to the burning, the storing, the sorting, the selling. And when we returned from the South, Dreiser, still searching for further firsthand knowledge, took me on a field trip to Connecticut where a type of cigar wrapper is grown.

Once we assembled this material, I stayed at his house in Mt. Kisco where we wrote the screen play. But 1933 was hardly the appropriate time to sell or to obtain finances for a moving picture of this so-called controversial (!) nature. Nor were the ensuing years more opportune. However, in 1961, Roger Lewis read the Dreiser-Kraft material and suggested that the screen play we wrote be turned over to a sympathetic novelist who would use this as the basis of a new work of fiction. With the generous consent of the University of Pennsylvania and the cooperation of Miss Neda Westlake, Librarian, the rights were turned over to me. Then, jointly with Harold Dies, trustee for the Dreiser Estate, an arrangement was made giving Borden Deal the right to use the notes, screenplay and other material for the purposes of this novel.

It was my privilege to work with Theodore Dreiser and it is my privilege to write this foreword in memory of a truly compassionate writer.

—Hy Kraft

Book One: Force

Chapter One

THE year was 1872, the town was Manchester, North Carolina, and the boy was fourteen years old. His name was Oren Knox. He was hungry.

For more than food. His stomach had been queasy with the before-daylight breakfast; not from the food, but from that larger appetite. It was now two o'clock in the afternoon, and he had been in town since early morning. Yet—the hunger remained. It would be difficult to say for what he hungered; he had thought, in the queasy thoughts of before-dawn, that the appetite was purely for the adventure of going-to-town. Now, his only remaining prospect the belated return of his uncle, followed by homeward departure, he knew only disappointment that the day in town had failed to fill his anticipation.

He was stocky and muscular, as tall now, five feet seven, as he would ever be. His legs were thick in the clumsy homemade jeans britches, his arms short, stubby, thick, too, with little taper from elbow to wrist. He wore a hickory-stripe shirt and was barefooted. His head had a German roundness, though there was no discernible German in his ancestry, the skull thick, rounded, as his body was thick and blocky. His hair was brown. His eyes were a washed blue, flat in the broad face that showed older than his age. The appearance of maturity came from his eyes, from his mouth. His lips, hiding from view the strong, short teeth, were held so firmly that one could not imagine them slacking even in sleep.

Oren Knox was not a handsome boy. His face was nondescript, except for the appearance of being older than his years. He was too short for his stockiness, his arms too short for the size of his body. He seemed slow, thick, even dull-witted. But cradled inside the protective thickness of his round skull lay the brain that had observed for fourteen years. Within the brain prowled the hunger that he did not know how to satisfy.

These were the first auction days for the new crop of tobacco. Still September, there was a midday warmth in the air, though this morning on the wagon coming into town Oren's bare feet had been chilled. The street before the auction warehouses was jammed with buggies and Nissen wagons. People swirled in slow eddies. The air was stained by the equally pungent odors of horse manure and of tobacco, by a plangent sense of excitement, of money, of the year's completion. Inside the warehouses Oren could see, through the great entering ramps, men moving in the slow, orderly movement of bid and buy, circumscribed by the piles of yellow leaf. The sound of the auctioneer's voice rose like an incantation, embodying the anticipation of the day. Near him a cluster of men laughed at a joke told by a man smoking a cigar and wearing an imitation-gold watch chain across the broad expanse of his stomach. The joke-teller tucked his thumbs into his vest pockets and reared back, pleased with himself. In the street a daring Rhode Island Red rooster, thin-bodied, active, picked with immunity from pile to pile of droppings about the feet of the horses. A satellite swarm of immigrant English sparrows profited from his scattering of the steaming clods.

All day the street had been jammed with the light Nissen wagons, inching toward the two warehouses, one on each side of the street not quite opposite each other. With so many waiting to sell, there was no purpose in the ritual calls of the outside man whose job it was to coax the tobacco into his employer's warehouse. The waiting farmers would have heeded either call if it had been possible.

Oren had moved in and about the excitement ever since his uncle, after selling their own small load, had disappeared in the direction of Main Street, warning Oren sternly not to wander far from the wagon, for he intended to leave early today. For a long time Oren had remained inside, keenly interested in the process of selling. Then he had come outside to watch the peripheral activities: the crap game up an alley beside the warehouse, the man selling Seth Thomas clocks from the back end of a buggy, the shell game operating under the shade of a hardware-store awning across the street until the store owner came out and shooed away the operator because such a large crowd was congregating that his customers' entrance was completely blocked.

It was the first time his uncle had allowed Oren to come to town on an auction day. At first his senses had been stuffed with sensation, but now he was beginning to tire. He knew that somewhere in Manchester was his mother. He had not seen her since the spring, when she had visited for one Sunday. But he did not know how to find her and he feared to venture out of the small area of known territory into the strangeness of the town.

He found no comfort in thinking of his mother. That time had been so long ago he did not even try to remember it. He did not want to remember . . . because of his father.

Two years old when his father had gone away to the war, Oren could only sense his absence, without understanding the reason for it. He was seven when, the war ended, he understood at last the truth of what his mother had told him about his father never returning. For an entire year, from his father's death until the other men began coming home, he had believed, without needing to talk about it to anyone, that his mother simply did not understand these things. His father was away because the other men were away; when they returned his father would also return, from death as the other men would return from war. When his father failed to fulfill Oren's conviction, Oren decided that the continued absence stemmed from his father's wish to remain dead, rather than by the simple circumstance of death itself. He could find no forgiveness for his father. The gun came home, the gray uniform stained by mud and blood, the ivory toothpick, the gold watch. Why should his father send these relics, while withholding himself?

Oren was too young to understand the details of difference between prewar and postwar; but he could sense the change, suffer its consequences. Edward Knox, his father, had been a prosperous and respected man. He owned an excellent farm, careful always to plant corn and wheat as well as tobacco. He had owned two slaves, a house-girl and a field-hand. The field-hand, Toby, an excellent curer of tobacco, was in demand throughout the countryside during the season. Mr. Knox took his pay in tobacco, adding it to his own crop, and Toby was allowed to choose those for whom he wished to work and to arrange his perquisites on the side. Toby knew his value; his perquisites were substantial, always part, at least, in cash money, which he was saving toward the purchase of his own freedom. Unfortunately his talent made him a valuable property.

Edward Knox wore black broadcloth on Sundays and the step of his foot, the sound of his voice, was grave, as befitted a man of his standing. Men came to him for advice on weather and tobacco-raising and politics. He, like many others, was experimenting with the new bright tobacco, striving each year for the golden wrapper leaf that brought the highest prices. He had himself taken the long journey to Caswell County to talk to Abisha Slade about charcoal firing. He was, therefore, the foremost authority on gold leaf in his neighborhood.

He rode away to war on their best buggy horse, carrying his own Sharps breech-loading rifle; not in the euphoria of gallantry but with a firm sense of duty. His example served well the Confederate recruiting among his neighbors.

War brought no outward physical change. The farm remained, the substantial two-story frame house with the deep porch, the respect of the neighbors, the standing in the community. But food became scarcer, the work more tedious and unrewarding. When emancipation came, Toby and Caroline disappeared toward town between the dark and the daylight. Oren's mother carried the burden uncomplainingly, working doggedly to feed them out of the garden, to clothe them by her own efforts. But she became pale, thin, silent, where before she had been a buxom, happy woman. Lines etched themselves in her face and her hair began to turn gray.

Once or twice troops passed through the countryside; only small bands, but large enough for mischief. Whether of blue or of gray, chickens disappeared, horses were taken, food demanded. A small quantity of tobacco had remained from the last crop; it was soon gone under the ravaging bands. One night the barn went up in flames, not a casualty of war but only of accident, for some Yankee soldiers had been sleeping in the hayloft. One had gone to sleep with a pipe in his hand, loaded with shredded gold leaf from the tobacco barn.

The year that Oren was seven, the year that his father did not return from the war, they were virtually destitute. William, at eleven the oldest of the three boys, proposed a tobacco crop. The tobacco fly got into the plant bed and their seedlings did not survive. A neighbor gave them a small quantity of seedlings, which they set out in a portion of the prepared ground. The cutworm got them before they had scarcely been pegged into the earth. Out of their effort one solitary stalk of tobacco reared itself splendidly from their labor. They allowed the tobacco worm this solitary fruit of their endeavor.

While others about them were beginning to prosper themselves out of the debacle of war, the Knoxes were in worse shape than ever. The countryside recovered quickly, unlike the rest of the South. There was a rising demand for the bright leaf of this region that made the best smoking tobacco, the best wrappers for plug. The dream of the golden wrapper, with its phenomenal prices, was nearer to realization with the advance in curing techniques. The golden wrapper was elusive, but, given luck and knowledge, it was possible.

They became "those poor Knoxes"; that "widder-woman with them three boys and the oldest just eleven." Mrs. Knox shamefully accepted cornbread wrapped in a soft concealing cloth and brought by neighbor-women to the back door; a small sack of flour was left by an inarticulate man who said, "Well, we just happened to have more than we needed and you know how the weevils will get into it if you try to keep it too long."

Mrs. Knox could not live indefinitely on the charity of her neighbors. That spring William tried for another planting of tobacco. When the fly got into the bed once again, they knew they could continue no longer without a drastic change in their fortunes.

Oren was only eight. He did not understand how a stranger could suddenly own their farm. But he was old enough to know what was happening the day the neighbor-men clustered in the front yard.

"What am I bid for this fine old Napoleon bed?" the auctioneer cried. "What am I bid?"

"A dollar," a voice said. "A dollar and a half," another voice said. "Two dollars." "Two dollars and a half."

"What am I bid?" the auctioneer cried. "Remember, folks, it's a widder-woman here. I've got two dollars and a half. Who'll say three?"

No one would say three.

Oren stood on the edge of the porch as item by item the furniture of their lives was dragged out into the violating daylight and sold for pennies. His heart was like a stone inside his chest as he watched the men's faces, avid for bargains.

His father's uniform was put up for sale. A woman fingered the material critically and offered two bits. Oren turned, went inside the house. The rooms, with their bareness, seemed bigger than before. His footsteps echoed in the emptiness. In the corners where the beds had been were rat-curls of dust. He entered the kitchen, where two men were dismantling the stovepipe. Remembering the jar in which his mother had kept the small money that came into her hands, he climbed up and got it. A solitary dime remained.

He looked closely at the date, 1858, under the seated Liberty with the head turned looking over her shoulder as though danger were coming up from behind. He counted the thirteen stars around the upper half of the coin. On the reverse was the legend,

ONE DIME, surrounded by a laurel wreath, around which were the words, UNITED STATES OF AMERICA.

The year of his birth was 1858. He thought on that for a moment, marveling that the coin should be exactly his own age. It seemed as though that should mean something. He did not know what; but, surely, something.

His heart lifted, he returned to the porch, the dime sweating in the tightly gripped hand plunged into the safety of his britches pocket.

The auctioneer was holding the Sharps rifle in his hand. "Now, men," he was saying. "Here it is. A fine old Sharps rifle. It's been to the war, but it's still a fine gun. You won't find yourselves no better gun than this gun I'm holding right here in my hand. Now I want to hear from you sporting men out there. What am I bid?"

"Ten cents," Oren said.

The high, clear penetration of his voice cut a pause in the sounds of the day. The men turned toward him. His body was rigid, his hand thrust into his pocket gripping the dime. He stared into their faces, his body blocky, his face tight-lipped, the blue eyes direct and seeing. He took his hand from the pocket, thrusting it away from his body, holding the small dime in the opened palm.

"I got the dime," he said.

The auctioneer threw back his head, laughing. "I got a dime," he said in a rapid, sing-song voice. "I got a dime. I got a dime. Where's fifteen cents? Where's two bits?"

"A dollar," a voice said from the crowd.

The gun brought a good price. The bidding became more spirited and competitive than at any time throughout the morning. Oren stood watching as the Sharps rifle was knocked down to the highest bidder. The dime was again in his pocket, his hand closed tightly over it. His eyes followed the gun as it was passed out into the crowd. It brought my daddy no good, anyway, he told himself. He did not weep.

It was an ending, a beginning. After the sale, Oren sat crouched in the back of his uncle's surrey, his right elbow gripping him to the flimsy side, and looked at his mother standing on the steps of the empty house. Already the house seemed deserted, though his mother was still there. Her buggy waited also, while she stood empty on the steps, her hand pressed against her lips. His two brothers had already departed with the other kin who had offered to take them.

"You be a good boy, now, Oren," his mother called. "You hear?"

She was going into Manchester to find work. She had said that after she had found work they would all be together again. There was employment to be had in the new tobacco factories springing from the war-torn earth. She had said all this, holding the three boys close against her long skirts. Oren had put his face against her thigh, not listening to the soothing words. He had never been to town in his life; for him a place called Town existed in a limbo a million miles away from anything he had ever known. She might as well have decided to die, as his father had done.

He sat on the floor of the surrey, his elbow gripping him against its side, and when she said, "You be a good boy. You hear?" he did not answer, but only kept looking at her as the surrey began to move, one wheel jolting over a hard clod of earth and dropping, the shock transmitting itself through the wheels into the body of the surrey and on into his spine as though he himself were a part of the structure. His uncle spoke to the team, slapping them with the reins, and their pace briskened. Oren sat watching as the house, his mother standing on the steps of the house, receded into remoteness. Before they had lessened into nothingness his mother had left the steps, mounting into the waiting buggy for her own departure.

Oren was not alone in the back of the surrey. His uncle had fattened himself on the sale, as the neighbors had done; he had purchased a kitchen safe and a stone churn. Oren still had the dime dated with the year of his birth in his pocket. The dime was all he brought away from his first eight years of life.

It was dark by the time they reached his uncle's house. His uncle stopped the team in the back yard alongside the lot fence.

He climbed down stiffly over the wheel. Oren had still not moved, sitting in exactly the same position as when he had first climbed obediently into the surrey. His uncle did not look at him.

"Take out that team and feed and water them. Five ears of corn apiece and a hefty fork of hay. Then come on in the house. Supper will be on the table."

Uncle Mark was a tall, dour, childless man. All the lines in his face moved downward and he walked in a bent-kneed loping stride. Oren forever remembered that the knees of his pants, even his Sunday pants, were bagged from the curve of his bony legs inside them. He was a Methodist layman, high in church affairs, and he called every man "Brother," as though he were actually the preacher he had wanted to be.

Aunt Kate, his wife, was tall too, thin as a rail, her hands spare, bony-knuckled. She had a voice as sharp as her kitchen knife and little patience for a growing boy. When Oren came into the house they were sitting at the round kitchen table. There was a place laid for him in the middle, halfway between them.

"Wash your hands and come to the table," Aunt Kate said in her sharp voice.

They waited, not speaking, while he went to the wash bench against one wall of the back porch. He dipped water from the cedar bucket into the washpan and washed his face and hands. With his fingers he smoothed his hair. It was dark on the porch and he could look in at their faces, lighted by the coal-oil lamp.

"Well, don't take all night about it!" Aunt Kate said.

He came on into the kitchen, slid into his chair between them. Uncle Mark bent his eyebrows at him.

"Can you say grace, boy?"

Oren did not look at either of them. "I reckon I don't know how," he said.

"He's your sister's boy," Aunt Kate said.

"Tomorrow night you will say grace," Uncle Mark said.

He bowed his head. Oren tried to listen to the quick mumbled words. He could not make any sense out of them.

His uncle owned a good-sized farm, with two Negro sharecroppers raising tobacco for him in addition to the land he reserved for his own use. Occasionally he bought small lots of tobacco from neighboring farmers in need of immediate cash. Oren watched this procedure the very next morning. The seller would arrive with a few baskets of tobacco. His uncle would gravely inspect the tobacco, name his price, wait for the hesitation of the farmer to wear itself out against the need for the money. Then his uncle would go inside the house, lift a corner of the feather bed on which he slept, pull out the worn leather bag, and untie the rawhide string that looped around the throat of the bag. He would count out the necessary bills and silver, thrust the bag under the ticking, after carefully re-tying the string, and emerge from the house to pay the waiting farmer.

In his own lights, Uncle Mark was good to Oren. Though Oren worked from daylight until dark, at all the tasks of the farm from feeding the horses to worming the tobacco, he also permitted Oren to attend the grammar school, three miles up the road, without ever keeping him out because of pressing work at home. He never laid a hand on the boy, never raised his voice to chastise him. Aunt Kate upbraided Oren at times in an habitual hectoring tone, just as she did her husband. There was no malice in it, only her nervous nature, and only once did she lift her hand to him. That one time, she stopped the blow before it touched his cheek.

"If you was my own boy, I'd whale the tar out of you," she said. "But you're his sister's son."

Oren did not mind the work. All the boys he knew at school worked. He was a valued hand on the farm. He liked working in the tobacco, especially when it was taken out of the curing barns to be graded. He rapidly became the best grader on the farm, his eye able to distinguish subtle shades of difference in the leaf. His uncle quickly came to depend on him. Oren still remembered the first time his uncle had called him from the barn to inspect a load of tobacco he was preparing to buy from a neighboring farmer.

"What do you think, boy?" he had said. "You think I ought to buy this leaf?"

It was a loveless household. There was no laughter in either his uncle or his aunt. After supper his uncle would sit with his Bible or his newspaper close to the coal-oil lamp, holding the page high to catch the full light, while his aunt sat quietly with her mending, or rose to wash the dishes with water warmed on the back of the stove. On Wednesday night, on Sunday morning and Sunday night, they went to the little Methodist church three miles down the road, opposite the school. Every Sunday morning it was his task to wash the surrey, harness the team of horses, and drive it to the front of the house, waiting there until his uncle and aunt emerged. The prayers were long, the sermons interminable, and every night at supper Oren made the same cadenced rise and fall of mumbled words that his uncle called grace, without ever understanding what it was he was meant to say.

None of it touched him. He kept the dime in a cloth tobacco sack under the cornshuck mattress of his bed, just as his uncle kept his deerskin money pouch in his mattress, and the dime spoke more to him than all the interminable sermons he had heard in his short life.

Now, in 1872, Oren Knox, fourteen years old, waited for Uncle Mark to finish his business so they could go home. Oren thought about how they would arrive after dark, the night work yet to be done by lantern light, making it slower, more tedious, than ever. He only wished that his uncle would come on, so they could get started. Besides, he was hungry.

A man on one of the nearby wagons waved to him. "Hey, boy, come here."

Oren went obediently to the side of the wagon. "Yes sir?" he said.

"Hold this-here team for me while I go find me a place to take a leak," the farmer said.

Oren climbed up on the wagon and took the reins. The farmer disappeared behind the warehouse. The team was quiet, their heads drooping. Oren turned in the seat to look at the tobacco, thinking, Some of these folks never will learn how to cure tobacco.

It was a bad curing, all right. Badly graded, too. There was some good tobacco mixed with the trash. A lot of people were trying to raise tobacco who didn't know the first thing about it. Why, if he graded tobacco like that, Uncle Mark would . . .

"Thankee, boy," the farmer said, climbing up on the wheel. "Thought I was gonna bust if I didn't find me some relief. I wouldn't even have come if I'd knowed every other leaf of tobacco in the county was aiming to cross the breaks today."

"You been waiting a long time?" Oren said politely, relinquishing the reins.

"Son, my children will call me granddaddy by the time I get home," the farmer said. "If I could find me one of them pinhookers, darned if I wouldn't sell him my load and go home. Here since daylight and my old woman at home so down in the back she can't hardly move."

Oren looked at him. His face was thin, his teeth stained by tobacco juice. He wore ragged cottonade pants and a dirty shirt, even for coming to town to sell his tobacco. The wagon was ramshackle, the mules ill-fed.

"How much you want for it?" Oren said.

The man turned toward him, laughing. "You aiming to buy it, boy?"

"I buy for my uncle," Oren said without hesitation.

The man studied him. "You ain't got your growth yet, son," he said candidly. "And you talking about buying tobacco?"

"I been buying," Oren said. "Of course, if you rather keep on waiting . . ."

"You got any money on you?"

"I'd have to wait an hour or two to pay you," Oren said. "My uncle's got the money. But I'll guarantee you you'll be paid inside of two hours and on your way home."

The farmer lifted his head to stare down the street. It had been a long time since any of the wagons had moved.

Oren watched him. "How much did you figure on getting?"

he said. "I taken a look at it while you were gone. It ain't very good tobacco."

"I had bad luck with my curing," the man said. "How much you figure on paying?"

"You name the price."

"Well now." The farmer paused, considering. "I was counting on a round price of eleven cents, anyway."

"It ain't that good," Oren said.

"If I didn't have to wait, I reckon I could take a little less," the farmer said. "Say ten cents a pound."

Oren turned his head, surveying the tobacco. He picked up a leaf, studied it. He shook his head.

"I don't think you know how bad a curing you did get," he said.

"I'd have to see ten cents a pound," the farmer said.

Oren jumped down from the wagon. "I hope you get it inside," he said. "They say so much tobacco in town, prices ain't holding any too good."

He began walking away. He did not look back.

"Hey, wait a minute!"

He stopped, turned. "Yes sir?" he said politely.

The man stared down at him. "How much you figure on paying?"

"I'll tell you the truth," Oren said. "That tobacco ain't worth a round price of six cents. They might even laugh at a man for putting it on the floor."

"Folks been getting upwards of eleven cents. I talked to a man not a hour ago said his tobacco went for fifteen cents a pound."

"Folks always talk about their best tobacco. You ain't *got* no best on that wagon, mister."

They haggled over the quality, finally settling on seven cents a pound. The man claimed three hundred pounds on the wagon. Oren, weighing with his eye, knew the estimate was close and accepted it.

"Now you just take your wagon out of line, help me unload,

and then find you some shade," Oren said. "Soon as my uncle comes, you'll get paid."

They unloaded the tobacco behind the warehouse. Oren waited until the man had driven out of sight down the alley, toward some horse-chestnut trees where he intended to wait. Then, feverishly, he began to regrade the tobacco.

He had to work faster than he ever had before. He was sweating with the work. Most of the tobacco was poor stuff. But he kept finding an occasional fair wrapper leaf, golden-yellow in tone.

Working at top speed, it took more than an hour to finish the job. He glanced up at the sun, fearful that the man would return, that his uncle would come. If his uncle appeared, Oren would have to let him pay the man and take the profits.

Finished with regrading, he went to the back of the warehouse. The little door there was closed. He banged on it imperiously until a Negro worker came.

"What you want, boy?" he said.

"I got me just a little tad of tobacco out here," Oren said. "I been waiting all day. Let me slip it in the back door and get it sold. My mama's gonna swear I done run off."

"You know you can't enter no tobacco through the back door," the Negro said. "Take it in the front door like all them other folks."

"My mother's sick at home," Oren said desperately. "I've been here the livelong day. I've got to sell this tobacco and buy some medicine for her."

"Sorry, boy. You don't know the tales I've heard today at this back door."

Oren straightened. "I'll give you a dime," he said.

The Negro hesitated. Oren dug into his pocket, held out the coin.

"Won't nobody know," he said. "Come on."

The Negro looked over his shoulder. He took the dime. Oren did not feel even a twinge at its loss, he was so rapt by the necessity of speed.

"All right. Let's get it weighed and on the floor. Hurry now before somebody sees us," the Negro said.

They worked rapidly, weighing the tobacco and placing it at one end of a long row. Everyone was clustered about the point of sale and they were not noticed in their surreptitious movements.

The Negro man drifted away unobtrusively, leaving Oren to stand stiffly behind his piles of tobacco. Before he was ready, it seemed, they were upon him.

The auctioneer glanced at him. "This your tobacco, boy?"

"Yes sir," Oren said.

"Where's your daddy?"

"I ain't got no daddy."

"Where's your mammy?"

"She's home sick," Oren said. "I got to sell the tobacco to buy her some medicine."

They looked at him. He stood behind the four piles of his tobacco—a handful of wrapper leaf, a pile of fair cutters, the other two piles of poor fillers and smokers—and looked back at them. He tried to think about his mother being sick at home, about how he needed medicine for her, about how his daddy was dead.

"Now, folks, let's do right by the orphan boy," the auctioneer said, beginning to swing into the chant of selling. "Bid from the heart, now, not from the pocketbook. What do I hear for this little tad of wrappers he's got here? I got a ten, a ten, a ten-and-a-half, I got eleven, eleven, I got twelve . . ."

The music of the prices soared in Oren's heart. The twenty pounds of wrappers brought forty cents a pound, the eighty pounds of cutters went out at seventeen, while the one hundred pounds each of fillers and smokers brought eleven and eight cents respectively. It went so quickly he was breathless. The bidding was brisk at the sentimental urging of the auctioneer and before he knew it the slips were dropped on his small piles and the sale had moved on.

He went to the window to collect his money. It came to forty dollars and sixty cents, less seven dollars and six cents warehouse, weighing and auctioneer's charges. He had cleared twelve dollars and fifty-four cents for an hour's work in grading the tobacco properly and bringing it quickly to the breaks. There was his dime, too, used for a bribe.

He left the warehouse by the front door and sought out the farmer in the shade of the horse-chestnut trees.

"Here's your money," he said, paying the farmer his twenty-one dollars.

"You taken your time," the farmer said sourly, half sorry, now that the tobacco was sold, that he had agreed to the deal.

"My uncle was a time in coming," Oren said.

"How did he make out on the breaks?"

"He just about evened out after them charges in there," Oren said. "They take the skin offen your teeth to sell your tobacco for you."

The farmer looked mollified. "Well, I reckon I better hit for home," he said. "The old lady been looking for me since the midday sun."

Oren stood still, watching him drive off. His hand clutched the money in his pocket. Twelve dollars and fifty-four cents. He turned, then, and made his way to the place where he had waited, an unfathomable time ago, for his uncle. His uncle was standing impatiently on the corner.

"Where you been, boy?" he said.

Without waiting for an answer, he plunged away in his long, bent-kneed stride, without pausing to look whether Oren could keep up or not. Oren panted after him. Uncle Mark stopped where the horses were tied, undid the bridle reins, stepped up into the wagon seat.

"Get in," he said. "It'll be black dark before the night work's done."

Oren looked up at him. "I ain't going home," he said.

His uncle peered down over the side of the wagon. "What's that?"

Oren clutched the money inside his pocket.

"I ain't going," he said.

"How you figure on keeping from starving to death?"

Chapter Two

DURING the week that Oren had been in town he had made several more pinhooker deals, had brought the tobacco to the breaks in one of the two auction warehouses, had pocketed his profits. Every day, in his wrinkled gray jeans pants, lined with unbleached domestic, his hickory-stripe shirt, and bare feet, he haunted the warehouse district. He watched the handling of the tobacco, followed with intense interest the process of prices on each succeeding day; he even found an opportunity to visit a redrying factory to see how the tobacco was put into order for long keeping.

He was deeply awed, at first, by the men he moved among, believing like gospel their knowledgeable talk about tobacco, admiring their vests and watch chains and fancy shoes. They were expansive men, easy with laughter, full with jokes, words as ready to their use as land to a farmer's hand. They lighted great cigars, carelessly throwing them away half-smoked, and they met no man who was not a friend. Oren was not visible in their sight; to them he was just another country boy come to town to spend one awed day among their grandeur. He could stand close and listen to their words without interference.

He remained in awe until he saw a buyer make a mistake in

"I figure to make out."

His uncle sat still, staring down at him. Oren did
under the weight of his gaze but stood quietly, waiting.

"You're fourteen years old," his uncle said then.
you're old enough to make up your own mind." He
the horses. "Giddap out there."

Oren watched him drive away down the street. O
have waved a goodbye if his uncle had looked bac
uncle did not turn his head.

Oren wavered uncertainly for a moment. Then, t
his dime, he sought out the Negro who had sneaked h
through the back door.

"That dime I gave you," he said carelessly. "Let
you another one for it."

He had thought first to offer fifteen cents. He
gesture for a last resort instead.

The Negro stopped in his work. "What you want
for?" he said. "A dime is a dime, ain't it?"

Oren took out the newest, shiniest dime earned in
profits. "Swap you," he said.

"Did I get yo' lucky piece, boy?" the Negro said.
some to git back a lucky piece."

"It ain't my lucky piece," Oren said seriously. "Bu
dime has been used to stop a dead man's eye. I didn'
that at the time because it was the onliest dime I had.
owe you a good dime, not a dime that's stopped a d
eye."

With his talisman recovered, Oren left the warehou
to look for a place to sleep that night. He was alone in
It was the way he wanted to be.

judging a pile of tobacco. After that, he watched more critically and came to realize that he knew tobacco quite as well as they did—better than most. Why, he could go right on the floor with them and hold his own! With that knowledge, his awe diminished; but not his interest. The difference between Oren and the adult pinhookers lay not in knowledge of tobacco, not in shrewdness, but merely in money. Where Oren had to scrounge a small parcel of tobacco by talking the farmer into waiting for his pay until he had had time to regrade it and sell it, they bought grand lots in a grand manner. They often went to the country and bought right out of the barn, hiring a team from the warehouse to fetch the tobacco to the breaks. They bought in the streets with a combination of shrewdness and blandishment, whispering tales of jammed breaks and falling prices. They bought on the breaks themselves, bidding against the legitimate buyers for factory or export, had their tobacco redried and held it for two months or three months or a year until the price rose. Some of them owned their own redrying houses and bought not only for speculation but on order for distant customers. These were no longer called pinhookers, but leaf dealers, and they were substantial men in the community of Manchester.

He saw also how the owners of the auction warehouses bought and sold tobacco for their own account. They did it partly to keep up prices in moments of weakness, or to get a good price for a favored farmer. But they were also speculators and they were not above taking unfair advantage of their most immediate customer, the farmer. More than once Oren saw a warehouse owner bid in a lot of tobacco at a low price, when it could have been driven higher, while the farmer stood by helplessly.

It was a strange world, in which the evil weed was king. Farmers came smiling from the breaks, and farmers came ready to weep. Each planter stood behind his tobacco, half-suppliant, half-arrogant, both hating and loving the men who clustered about him, in thirty seconds disposing of his year's labor. The buyers would scarcely notice the planter, only his tobacco; yet giving it no more than a glance at best, pulling a hand, looking at it, tossing it back on the pile.

They bid, not with words but with obscure gestures, one man by tugging on his ear, another by clearing his throat, another by the twiddle of his fingers. It was cabalistic, secretive, so that often the farmer did not know how much he had been paid until he had studied the tag dropped on his piles of tobacco. He would stand looking after the buyers and the auctioneer as they moved on down the row, baffled, unfulfilled, half-angry, his mind remembering all too clearly the prices trumpeted in the advertisements of the warehouse, remembering the glib talk of the drummer who had called on him with great tales of the crowd of buyers, of the excessive competition between them that was driving prices to untold highs.

Occasionally, only occasionally, it would come true. The tobacco would be good, the buyers brisk, and the price on those particular piles would soar with bewildering rapidity while the farmer gasped under the sudden shock of fortune. The news of the sale would spread throughout the district, begetting excitement and creating grist for the drummer's blandishment, finally becoming immortalized in the warehouse's next advertisement.

Wrapper leaf always brought excitement with its appearance on the breaks. The wrapper leaf, rare and much-prized, was the ultimate in bright tobacco. Few farmers had the fortune, the knowledge, necessary to bring it to market. Deep gold in color, brought to perfection by perfect firing, it was used to wrap the plugs of chewing tobacco. The chewing-tobacco factories could never find enough of it, for good wrapper leaf was the secret of success in their highly competitive business. A good wrapper dressed the plug with the promise of hidden delights, led the demonstration of the salesmen, made the display an attraction instead of a deterrent. When the arrival of a quantity of wrapper was rumored, the population of the warehouse district flocked to watch its display and sale. It was admired with envy, the bidding was witnessed with absorbing interest by all concerned. The fortunate farmer was the center of attention. The owner of the warehouse would meet him at the ramp, shake his hand, and urge upon him a drink of whiskey. He was introduced to the buyers and generally regarded as a great man. One farmer,

Lee Harrington by name, was so consistently successful with the production of good wrapper that he would announce beforehand the day and the hour of his tobacco sale. At the appointed time he would drive past all the waiting teams to receive his royal welcome, his royal prices.

With the recent burgeoning of smoking tobacco, high grades of cutters and smokers were beginning to gain a certain amount of attention also; but the wrapper was king, enrobed not only in actuality but in legend. It remained so even after the smokers and cutters had far exceeded the immediate importance of wrapper leaf.

Oren saw it all, absorbed it, knew it immediately through his five natural senses and that sixth sense that dealt most directly with the leaf. This was his world; here he would make his mark, if there was a mark to be made. He knew it was an imperfect world; he would not have wished it otherwise. If these men were indeed as grand, as all-wise in the intricacies of tobacco, as they seemed to be, there would be no place for a fourteen-year-old boy named Oren Knox.

That first night, he had slept in the loft of the barn that housed the warehouse teams. The teams were used to haul the tobacco for redrying or to send out into the country, when the roads were bad, to double-team the farmers' wagons into town; and, incidentally, to fetch them to the right warehouse.

Next day, he found a place to sleep. It was a small room, independent of the main building, in the backyard of a boardinghouse. He stood in the doorway and told the lies into Mrs. Thompson's shrewd face about how he was an orphan boy who needed a place to stay, how he didn't have money or a job and could only offer work for two meals a day and a place to sleep. The room was too small and dingy to rent for money, so she consented to the room and one meal a day for his services in rising early and lighting the fires, for bringing in the wood and taking out the ashes.

The room was barely big enough to swing a cat in. There was a low, rickety bed with a ratty coverlet, a small heater with its pipe exiting through the tinned-over space where a windowpane should have been. There was a bureau which had once been painted blue. He opened the bureau drawers and looked inside them, though he had nothing to place in them. He owned only the clothes he stood up in.

Two days later, after he had made his second profit, he made the grave purchase of a pair of brogans, for it was cold in the mornings on his bare feet. They were made of split leather, with buckles instead of strings. The seams were bound with heavy harness brads and the soles were bound to the straight-lasted uppers with untrimmed hardwood pegs. He was now set for the winter. Though he admired the suits of the men, and wondered at the enormous prices they must have paid for them, he knew his own strength lay in the innocuousness of his jeans britches and hickory shirt.

He lay that night in the small room, the darkness flickered by rays of light from the dying fire in the heater. He was alone, but he did not feel alone. It seemed as though his whole life had been trending toward this time, this place; from that first memory of how he had felt about his father's decision not to return from death, until he had watched the Sharps rifle sold, until he had sat in Uncle Mark's surrey and watched his mother receding into the distance, until this precise, fire-flickered moment of supreme loneliness and achievement.

His mother was here in Manchester. He was not yet ready to seek her out. The time would come, he knew, when he must go back at least that far, know her once again in this limbo of town into which she had receded as his father had receded into death. There was no seeking of his father. His mother was here and he must eventually look into her face. But not yet.

He thought, then, of the money he had earned. Tomorrow, for the first time, he could buy outright, if he could find a small lot of tobacco, instead of facing the necessity of talking the farmer into waiting for his money. Of course, if he should have to continue, he was confident he could manage. It was astonishing how easily men could be talked into doing precisely what you wanted them to do. He already knew the mechanism to employ;

his purpose could be accomplished when one's opponent had no set purpose of his own. A man needed a direction; if he did not own a direction of his own, he was grateful if you showed him one he could follow. He did not particularly care whether or not it was profitable, as long as he was relieved of the necessity for thought. Not all men were like that; but, he thought contentedly, enough, at least, for his slowly shaping plan. He wondered if his father had been a man of that stripe, if death had led him easily into death's country.

He was a man of fourteen who owned his direction so surely nothing could lead him astray. Lying in the light-flickered darkness, he tasted the appetite as palpable in his mind as the belly's hunger for food. It stirred in him like a restless animal, anxious to be afoot, impatient at the delay of night that held tomorrow distant. He could not see the far reaches of the direction, only dimly its nearness; but he knew it took on the shape of the leaf, the smell of the nicotine.

Yet, oddly, he had no taste for its use. He had once crushed between his teeth a mouthful of twist. The rich juices had gagged him, drawn his throat tight, retched his stomach so that he had ejected the chaw with spasmic vigor. His stomach had quivered for a day afterward. He liked the smell of tobacco in the air, especially in the barn while it was being cured, but he could not bear it in his own body. He had tried smoking a pipe, a cigar, even a hand-rolled cigarette. The smoke had been acrid and dry in his mouth, it had gripped his lungs like a rough hand. His mouth had boiled with spit while his brain had dizzied in his head.

All the men he knew used tobacco. They smoked it, chewed it, snuffed it, they spattered the earth with its use, their jaws moving in long slow motions like cattle, they took pride in the range and accuracy of their expectoration. Even Uncle Mark had smoked a pipe, crumbling in his own leaf or shaving off the end of a twist of pigtail.

It remained a profound mystery that mankind would pay good money for the satisfaction of an acquired taste. Mankind had thronged to buy tobacco from the moment of its introduction into their society. The explorers caught the habit from the Indians of the new world, had passed it to their kings and queens and from the kings and queens to the aristocracy, from the aristocracy to the common man. Once acquired, the habit was irresistible. Oren could not learn the habit of tobacco, nor could he understand the necessity that dwelt in men for its constant use. But he needed only to know that the universal vice existed, not the why of it.

He rose early each morning to start the morning fires. Some of the tobacco buyers lived in the boardinghouse, but he was not privileged to listen to their breakfast talk. He elected the most substantial meal of the day, supper, both because of its substance and because, eating late, he need not go to bed hungry. Even at supper he was not permitted to eat at the table with the paying boarders, but took his sustenance in the kitchen with the Negro cook.

The fourth time he appeared on the breaks with tobacco for sale, the auctioneer, as he approached, cried out, "Here's our orphan boy again, men. Let's get him a good price, now."

The men laughed. Oren looked sharply at the auctioneer, but held his tongue.

"How's your mama, boy?" the auctioneer said in his booming voice that could be heard throughout the great floor.

"She's still sick," Oren said in a stiff voice.

"You must have raised a pretty good crop anyway," the auctioneer said, glancing slyly at the men.

"I bought this tobacco," Oren said, knowing he couldn't work the orphan boy any longer. "I've gone into business for myself."

The men laughed again, all together.

"You mean you're a pinhooker, son?" one of them said.

"Yes sir," Oren said. "I've taken up the trade."

"You know we don't like pinhookers in here," another man said. "They get under our feet and when they get under our feet they're likely to get stomped on."

"Looks to me like every man on this floor is pinhooking in one way or another," Oren said. "I seen you buy and sell in the same day, mister. Just yesterday—and with your company's money."

The man's face reddened. The other buyers shouted with laughter at his expense.

"All right," the auctioneer said briskly. "What am I bid on this fine tobacco? We all know he knows how to grade it right. Give me a figure now. Give me a figure."

"I wouldn't pay him four cents a pound," the angry man said, walking away from the group.

The tobacco sold for nearly as good a price as his other lots. Oren took his slip to the cashier's window to get his money. As he left the warehouse a man spoke to him.

"I want to see you, boy," he said.

Oren stopped, looking back. It was the warehouse owner. Oren's stomach tightened. He returned to the man, slowly, trying to anticipate the trouble this summons could cause him.

"Yes sir?" he said.

Wilbur Clark was a big man, with an open, ruddy face. His head seemed small for the size of his body, but he smiled so much that no one noticed it. His eyebrows were so pale that his face seemed hairless. Unlike most of the men, he went bareheaded all the time, winter and summer.

"How come you to take up pinhooking in my warehouse?" he said, staring at Oren down the length of his body.

"To make a living," Oren said.

"Didn't I see you in here with Mr. Mark Lester?"

"Yes sir. He's my uncle."

"Why ain't you with him now?"

"I ain't staying with him no more," Oren said.

"Does he know that?"

"Yes sir. He didn't raise no fuss about it, neither."

"Looks like he'd hate to lose a fine good-sized boy. Especially if that boy knew tobacco like you know it."

"Don't think I run away," Oren said stubbornly. "He taken

me when we had to break up housekeeping, after my mother lost our place. I worked my way with him. So when I told him I aimed to stay in town, he didn't raise a word agin it."

Wilbur Clark stared down at him for a long, thoughtful moment.

"What are you doing for money to buy and sell with?" he said.

"That's the hard part," Oren admitted. "I can handle so little at a time your warehouse charges just about eat me up."

"But you're still making a living."

"Yes sir."

"How much money you got?"

Oren drew back his head. "I don't reckon that's anybody's business but my own," he said.

"Don't get stiff with me, boy," Mr. Clark said. "I got a reason for it, or I wouldn't be asking. Now tell me. How much you got on you right this minute?"

Oren hesitated. He mentally halved the money in his pocket. "One hundred dollars," he said.

"How much did you open up with? That day you come to town?"

"I had one dime on me," Oren said.

Wilbur Clark laughed. There was astonishment in the sound. "Boy, that's hard to believe. Show me that hundred."

"No sir. I don't aim to be flashing no bills around here. There's too many folks apt to be ready to take it away from me."

"You wouldn't lie to me, would you?"

Oren watched him. "I reckon I would, if it come down to had-to," he said. "But I don't see no cause for lying."

Wilbur Clark laughed again. Then he sobered. "Listen, boy," he said. "I got a proposition."

Oren's voice was wary. "What you got in mind?"

"It's going to take a while to make your pile with no more money than that to operate on," Mr. Clark said. "You ain't gonna be able to keep up the pace you've set for yourself, you know. Folks are getting onto you. That orphan boy you been working has just about played out already."

"I'll make out," Oren said.

"How would you like to work for me?"

"I don't want to work for no man."

"I don't mean on salary. I mean on my money."

"What you got in mind?"

"Well, you know I need a man on the side once in a while," Mr. Clark said. "Somebody nobody would suspect was working for the warehouse. You can buy and sell for me as well as for yourself. I furnish the money, you furnish the rest. From time to time I'll have little things for you to do, buying for the house, maybe running up the bidding, things like that."

"What's in it for me?" Oren said bluntly.

"Fifty-fifty. We'll split the profits right down the middle."

"Sixty-forty," Oren said. "With me on the long end."

"Fifty-fifty."

"Sixty-forty. I don't need you, Mr. Clark. I been doing all right."

He started to walk away.

"What will you do if I bar you from my floor?" Mr. Clark said to his back.

Oren turned. "There's always the other warehouse across the street, if you don't like my business," he said.

"You think I can't tell them about you, get you barred over there, too?"

"All right," Oren said. "Make it fifty-fifty. But I don't have to pay any charges on my tobacco."

Mr. Clark shook his head. "That would lead to nothing but trouble," he said. "Can't make any exceptions there. Too many people would come to know about it."

"All right, then," Oren said. "I'll split the difference with you. Forty-five—fifty-five."

Mr. Clark laughed. "You're a hard bargainer, son."

"I wouldn't be the man you want, if I wasn't," Oren said, the shadow of a grin appearing for the first time on his face.

"I reckon you're right, at that," Mr. Clark said. "All right. You can draw up to a thousand dollars to start with. We'll raise the limit as time goes on and we see how it works out." He paused, looking down at Oren. "Now, I know you're going to try it," he said. "Just don't let me catch you. If I ever find out you're taking one penny over your due, I'll ruin you in this tobacco town. You hear me?"

"You be honest with me, I'll be honest with you."

Mr. Clark abruptly thrust out his hand. "Now, that sounds like a square deal," he said. "I'll shake on that."

They shook hands, solemnly.

Oren left the warehouse, his soul singing. He could feel the strength of the thousand dollars inside him right now. The street itself had changed with this new power. He belonged here, where before he had existed only because he was invisible. There was not a load of tobacco in the street that he could not buy. He could buy tobacco and wait for a week to resell it. It would even be possible to redry his purchases and store it for the slack season. Prices always went up when the auctions had ended. He looked back at the warehouse he had just left. It was a huge building, with a vast floor space, great entering ramps and skylights in the roof to give a uniform light for the judging of the leaf. It was solid, substantial, made of brick so that it would last. And he was a part of it.

Down the street, he hesitated before a clothing store. He had never bought clothes for himself, had, indeed, never worn anything but homemade jeans britches. The jeans, however, would no longer do. He went inside.

When he emerged, an hour later, he carried under his arm a large bundle. It contained a two-piece mohair suit of a lustrous finish, black, with birdseye-weave stripes of the same color. He had paid nine dollars and ninety cents for it. It was light-weight for the winter that was coming on. But the woolen worsted suits ran considerably more and he could not bring himself to meet the price. He could make out through the winter and then it would be just right for the spring and summer. The coat was single breasted, with three buttons, the corners slightly cut away to give a subtle suggestion of the Prince Albert style, although the coat was short. The pants were peg-top, with two-and-a-half inch cuffs. The coat was half-lined with alpaca.

He also carried in the package a pair of two-dollar patent colt shoes with perforated wing tips and broad, ribbon-like laces. He had needed them because the other shoes he had bought had been brogans, to go with his jeans britches and hickory shirt. He had also bought three shirts, two cream white for seventy-nine cents each, one cream white with black stripes for a dollar and nineteen cents. He had paid sixty-five cents for a Turkish Morocco braided leather belt, fifty-nine cents for six extra detachable collars, a nickel for a black silk bow tie.

All in all, he had laid out fifteen dollars and ninety-six cents and as he walked toward the boardinghouse he felt both impoverished and incredibly rich. Once home, he took a careful bath—his facilities a tub standing in a side room, to which he brought several buckets of water warmed on the kitchen stove by grace of the Negro cook—before he dressed himself in the new clothes.

There was no mirror in which to see himself. He found it hard to imagine how he must look. He remembered a long mirror in the hall of the boardinghouse. In order to avoid the Negro cook, he went around and let himself in the front way. The deserted hallway was rather dark, but the mirror was full length. Cautiously he ranged himself in full view.

It was like looking at a stranger. He stood first full-face, then sideways, trying to see himself in profile. The clothes made him seem stockier, broader, older. To him, they bore an intolerable elegance. They felt heavy on his body, stiff and cumbersome.

The landlady came upon him unawares. "Can I help you, sir?" she said, approaching him as a stranger. Then she stopped, open-mouthed. "Why, it's you, Oren!"

Oren was both flattered and abashed. "Yes'm," he said. "It's me."

"Well, ain't you diked out to beat the band!" Mrs. Thompson exclaimed, taking a backward pace to view him entire.

He fled from her scrutiny into the street.

He was ready to visit his mother. He had not known why he

had waited to do so. Her infrequent visits to Uncle Mark's farm had been occasions of excitement. He had thought about her every day since he had been in Manchester, knowing he should seek her out. Something had held him back from the venture. Now, at least, he had one visible sign of success, and the time had come.

She worked at the Fuller Tobacco factory. He knew vaguely where it was located. He felt strange, moving through the streets in his elegant new clothes. It seemed as though people saw him with intensity, knowing the uncomfortable newness of his wear.

The factory was a tall three-story building of dingy brick, with white tin cornices. The windows were drab, dust-covered. For a block, as he approached, the smell of massed tobacco strengthened in the air. It was a smell to which he was accustomed.

There was a guard at the door. "Can I help you?" he said, properly respectful toward the new suit.

"Could you tell me where Mrs. Knox works?" Oren said.

"There's two hundred hands here," the guard said. "How do you expect me to know something like that?"

"How can I find out where she works?" Oren said patiently.

"Go through to the sacking room. Ask the foreman. If she's not there, try the stamp-and-label department."

He entered the factory, passing through a heavy door into bedlam. The floor was large, lighted by rows of tobacco-dusty windows, populated by workers pursuing their mysterious tasks with intent interest. Oren stopped to watch, trying to sort out the varied activities into a pattern.

The tobacco leaves, dried but unstemmed, came from chutes that led, he supposed, to an upper floor. The three steam-driven Smith cutting machines, the center of interest and labor here, threshed away at the tobacco, beating it into fragments. Men, wearing cloths over the lower half of their faces as protection against the tobacco dust in the air, fed the machines in a harried pattern of effort, while other men took the granulated tobacco from the other end, dumping it down a chute to the basement. While he watched, a belt slipped whirling from a driving wheel, twisting wildly as it slapped sideways. The men yelled, ducking, as the cutting machine chattered to a stop. The men rushed to replace and tighten the belt. In a few minutes the work flow had continued over the interruption.

This was an all-male department, he saw, so when the foreman approached him, he inquired his way to the sacking department. He was directed to the second floor. He climbed the stairs and opened the door upon another scene of work.

This room was long, too, lighted by the dusty windows. The first half of the room consisted of serried ranks of narrow tables, each attended by a woman. The tables stood as close together as possible, leaving little space to walk between. Mounted on each table was an iron cylinder, the name, MAYO, embossed on it in large iron letters. White and Negro boys scurried back and forth, keeping the Mayo presses filled with granulated tobacco. The women deftly slipped cloth bags over a cylinder, at the same time working a treadle to pack the cylinder full of tobacco. The cylinder was withdrawn, leaving the closely packed tobacco in the bag. More boys carried away the bags to the stamp-and-label department, at the other end of the floor.

The work was quieter here, even the boys intent and hurried. The air was moted with tobacco dust. There was no chatter among the women operatives as each one bent to her task.

Oren walked toward the one visible man, seated on a platform so he could oversee the entire floor.

"Can you tell me where I can find a Mrs. Knox?" he said.

The man frowned down at him. "Who let you in here?" he said.

"The guard at the gate."

"He knows we don't allow strangers to wander around the factory," the foreman said.

"Mrs. Knox is my mother," Oren said.

"No Mrs. Knox in my department," the foreman said. "Try down yonder at the other end."

"Thank you," Oren said, passing on.

"Hey, you want a job?" the foreman called after him. "Good wages here, you know. Good piecework."

"I have a job," Oren said politely.

He found a path through the Mayo presses to the other end of the building. Here the women were busily putting labels and tags on the tobacco sacks, while their attendant army of white and Negro boys—and some girls, too, Oren saw—packed the finished bags into cartons. The foreman here was mounted high, also, to oversee the whole operation in one glance.

He asked his question once again. The foreman frowned down at him, as the other had, instinctively disliking Oren's presence in his department.

"She was here," he said. "She hasn't been to work for a week, though. So I guess maybe she quit. That's the way they'll do you; not give you word one, just quit coming one day and you don't know whether you've got a hand or not. And me supposed to keep up with them devilish machines down there."

"Do you have any idea where she lives?"

"Try that woman over there," the foreman said, pointing. "I seen the two of them coming and going together."

His approach frightened the woman. She paused in her work, glancing quickly at the foreman, one hand pushing back the hair from her face.

"Law, you her boy?" she said.

"Yes'm," Oren said. "I'm Oren."

"She's been sick," the woman said. "Just couldn't make it to work. You'll find her at home."

The foreman watched them impatiently as she gave him quick directions. Oren left as quickly as he could, the woman turning to her work with increased speed to make up the lost minutes.

Once on the street, Oren paused, looking back thoughtfully. Maybe some of the tobacco he had handled had come here to be made into smoking tobacco, dried and threshed and packed into the bags with the gaudy labels.

It was only a few blocks to the house where his mother lived. The neighborhood was shabby, the houses unpainted, crowded in tight rows. They were shotgun houses, built straight through from front to rear. The yards were bare of grass, worn down by the constant moil of children chasing each other in play.

There were no numbers on the houses. He picked one by instinct because in the yard someone had attempted to grow flowers, the scraped-together beds now bare with dry stalks. It had, apparently, been a futile attempt in the sterile soil.

Followed by a tag of children, attracted by his strangeness in the neighborhood, Oren went up the walk outlined by the old flowerbeds. The porch creaked when he stepped on it. He knocked at the door, listened, knocked again more loudly.

A feeble voice answered from within. "Come in. Come on in."

He hesitated, wanting to flee instead of pushing open the door. He stepped directly from outside into the living room. It was darker here, after the blaze of sun without, and for a moment he could not see. As his eyes adjusted, he could see the quilted bed in a corner of the living room. His mother was propped up on one elbow, turned inquiringly toward the door.

"Yes?" she said in a voice that did not recognize him. Then, uncertainly, "Oren?"

"It's me, Mama," he said, coming close to her.

"Why, Oren," she said, her eyes taking in his unaccustomed dress. "What are you doing here, Oren? And in those clothes?"

"I've left Uncle Mark," he said. "I'm working in town now."

She lay back on the pillow. He could see her plainly now. Her face was pale, thin, white. Her hair had gone completely gray and in her face were new lines, making her something of a stranger. There was a pinched look about her nose and mouth, too, that he did not recognize. She was so thin she made scarcely a hump under the bedclothes.

"Oren, you shouldn't have done that," she said. "Your Uncle Mark was good to you."

"I had to get out on my own," he said. "I'm fourteen now, Mama. It's time I made my own way."

Now that he was somewhat accustomed, he could approach

her more nearly. He leaned over the bed. As he started to kiss her she turned her head so that his lips brushed her cheek. He drew back, looking down at her. She had tried, without success, to make the gesture casual.

"Mama," he said. "What are you sick of? Have you got the consumption?"

"Consumption? Why, what an idea! I'm just feeling a little poorly, that's all. A few days in bed . . ."

She coughed. The spasm racked her body until Oren ached with the pain of it.

"I'll be back in the factory next week."

"Mama . . ." he said.

"If you're living in town, you just move right in with me," she said with determined briskness. "Both of us working, we can bring your brothers home, too. I told you when you went to your Uncle Mark it wouldn't be no time atall till we're all together again. Now it's beginning to happen, you coming to town and all . . ."

"I can't, Mama," he said, cutting across the flow of her words. "I have to live close to my work."

"What are you doing, son?"

"I'm buying and selling tobacco," he said. "I started on my own, but I'm working with the owner of the warehouse now."

"But there's no reason you shouldn't live here. You can . . ."

He looked about the room. His heart ached for her. Yet he could feel only revulsion for the conditions of her life. He felt as though she were trying to drag him downward from what he had become. She wanted to keep him that boy whose father had not wanted to come home, whose father's rifle had been sold at public auction. It was like a tide and he a poor swimmer, trying feebly to breast the undertow, fighting the undertow for the sake of a dimly seen shore.

"I can't, Mama," he said. "I have to live with my business."

She looked at him with wet eyes. "I wish you could," she said, her voice sighing in defeat. "It's so lonesome here by myself. A woman finds it hard to live alone when she's had a family." She coughed again.

"Mama. Have you seen a doctor?"

"No need. It's just that tobacco dust gets into a person's lungs something awful. And the smell of it . . ."

"Tobacco wouldn't make you cough like that."

"Don't fret yourself, son. I'll be back at work next week."

He stared down at her, knowing, as he knew the quality of a tobacco leaf, that within a year she would be dead. The mark of death lay already in the cold ivory of her flesh, the knowledge of it deep as wisdom in her eyes. There was nothing he could do; if he should try to save her from drowning, he would only drown himself.

"Do you need any money?" he said.

"I still have some left from my last pay," she said, her voice more feeble now, as though his visit had drained whatever strength remained.

He found a ten-dollar bill, placed it in her hand.

"That's all I can spare now," he said. "But next week I can bring you another ten. Can you get along on ten dollars a week?"

Her breath gasped. "Why, I don't need that much. That's nearly three times what I make. It's hard to make more'n fifty cents a day. I ain't done that good since I started being so weakified all the time."

"All right. I'll bring you five dollars a week from now on. And don't you go back to that factory. You hear?"

Her eyes filled with tears. "I knew I had good boys," she said. Her hand grasped the ten-dollar bill, holding it crumpled against her cheek. "It won't be any time atall until we're all together again, like a family ought to be."

"I got to go now," Oren said. "They'll be looking for me at the warehouse. I'm staying at Miz Thompson's boardinghouse. Now if you get to feeling worse, you send for me. You hear?"

"I'll be all right. There's a woman next door does for me, time she ain't working."

"Goodbye, Mama," he said, escaping toward the door. He stopped. "What's the name of the man who owns the place where you work?" he said.

"I don't know his name."

"Is it the same name as the factory?"

"Fuller Tobacco Factory. I reckon it's owned by a Mr. Fuller."

He nodded. "I just wanted to know," he said.

He went on. Once in the street he felt released, free of the danger that had welled up around him like a catching wave. He hurried toward the part of town that contained his new self. The five dollars a week he had promised was a ransom gladly paid for the possession of his soul.

VISTA: I

Amos: The Discontented Heart

THE barn stood tall against the Tennessee sky. The logs that had been raised in its making had silvered through slow years of sun and weather. It stood on a slight rise, two hundred yards from the ramshackle house that hid around the shoulder of the hill. The double doors were held closed by prop poles, shutting in the five tiers of cured tobacco.

They came to the barn in the early morning. The day was low, cloudy, and a wet wind blew. Yesterday had been the same, and perhaps it would continue tomorrow.

"Hit *ought* to be in order," Art Haines said, lifting the prop poles and swinging wide the doors. "If it ain't come into case by now, it never will."

Amos watched his father reach up one hand to gauge the nearest stalk of tobacco, hanging from the lowest tier. The tobacco hung in tight rows all the way to the back of the barn. On the hard dirt floor were parallel rows of feathery gray ashes, where the hardwood fires had burned to cure the leaf. The strong odor of the tobacco crept into his nostrils.

"It's in order," Art said, and with the words Amos knew that all day the smell of the tobacco would be in his nostrils as they began the final work of stripping, sorting and grading.

Amos saw that the faces of the others, like his father's, were full with accomplishment. Here was the culmination of their year's work. The crop, at last beyond the danger of fly, cutworm and hail, had passed successfully through cutting, bulking and fire-curing. The tobacco had not molded, the barn had not caught fire. In this barn a year of their lives was embodied in the five tiers of stalks.

Amos, looking into their faces, searched within himself for the fulfillment the others knew. He found nothing. He had known there was nothing before he had looked. He was envious of his brothers, his father, gathered so eagerly to see if the tobacco was in case for handling. They were happy, because tobacco was their lives.

Tobacco had never been his life. It never would be. He stood among them, seemingly of them but entirely a stranger. He had upon his body, in the shape of his face, the stamp of kinship. Like his father he was tall, his skin dark beyond the tanning of the sun, his hair lanky and black. At sixteen there were lines in his face, making crowsfeet, marking his forehead. His eyes were somber black, his nose high and straight as the blade of a plow. The discontent of his heart did not show in his face, but the thinking that set him apart did show. He wore the same clothes as they, the ragged jean pants, the work shirt, the clumsy brogans. His pants legs and shirt sleeves were too short and his big feet and hands stuck out awkwardly. There was guilt in his discontented heart that he was not like them.

"I reckon we got us a good crop," Mr. Staines said with satisfaction. "You boys get on in there now, and go to work."

Amos turned his head to look at Mr. Staines. He was the owner of the land on which the Haines family made their living. "Haineses has always worked for Staineses," his father said often, with satisfaction equally in the fact and in the alliteration.

It was called working on the thirds and the fourths. Mr. Staines furnished the land and an advance of credit. The Haines furnished their work stock, their plow tools, and their entire lives. For his contribution, Mr. Staines received one third of the tobacco and one fourth of the other crops. He usually got most of the rest in payment of their yearly debt. Mr. Staines now lived in a white house in Jamestown. His father had lived in a farm house three miles down the dirt road toward town but Mr. Staines only visited now, instead of spending his life here. The Haines family lived in the same house they had lived in ever since Haineses had worked for Staineses.

They began the work. Amos entered the barn and began handing down the sticks of tobacco. The scent of the tobacco, stirred by the movement, assailed his nostrils. It was pungent with the damp case it had taken from the weather. Only on damp days could the cured leaf be handled; in dry weather it was brittle, easily shattered.

Amos was soon sweating in the closeness of the barn. His brothers in turn took the sticks from him and carried them into the lean-to that was the sorting room. Sometimes it was necessary to bulk down the tobacco on the sticks but, on due consideration, Art and Mr. Staines decided that they could proceed immediately to the stripping and grading, after which the leaves would be bound into hands. Then the hands, graded into trash, lugs and leaf, would be prized into hogsheads ready for sale.

Amos was the second oldest of three brothers and four sisters. The others were the children of his father; he was, too, except for his mind. He had learned, without ever knowing how he had learned it, that there are those who are content in their life and there are those who are discontent. Everyone he knew seemed content—most of all, his own family. He did not know why he should be burdened with a difference. But the discontented heart is not an answer; it is only a question. All his life he had lived with the question. Because he knew no one like him, he thought there must be something wrong with him.

His differentness was ever-present. It hurt Amos when his brothers, with other boys, rubbed a dog's behind with turpentine on a corncob, in order to watch gleefully the dog's yelping run, at intervals dropping his frantic rump to the earth in an attempt to ease the unquenchable burn. He had never hunted rabbits with sticks in the winter snow, as his brothers so often did. He did not like to see the bright blood on the white snow.

He had once found a blue jay with a broken wing. Holding the bird tenderly in his two hands and soothing its frantic cries, he was trying to decide how to go about helping it when his older brother John had come out of the house to see what was going on.

"I wonder how you can mend a broken wing," Amos said.

"Here, let me show you," John said.

Trusting his elderness, Amos yielded the blue jay into his brother's hands. With a quick, fatal movement, John grasped the bird by the narrow head and jerked his hand, twisting the bird's neck. He dropped the limp body to the ground at their feet and said, "See? I fixed his wing for him. It won't never bother him no more."

Amos looked into his brother's face and saw, in the gleam of his eyes, the mischief of his mouth, pleasure he himself could never possibly understand. He did not say anything; he only turned away into himself.

"Haineses has always worked for Staineses." The Haines were tobacco men. Tobacco was not a crop, a living, but a way of life. Amos sweated as he worked higher and higher into the tiers. He could cast his mind back over the year from the day the plant bed had been prepared. He had lived it, as well as they; but it had not touched him as it had touched the others.

Mr. Staines had left, now that the work was well under way, mounting into his buggy and returning to his white house in Jamestown. He would take his next interest in the tobacco on the day it was sold. The work did not come from his hands.

The tobacco year began in January. A spell of bright, warm weather would come, the nights frosty but with a sufficient thawing of the woods earth. Snow might lie still along the north side of the fence rows; but on one of these warm days his father would say at breakfast, "Today we burn the first plant bed."

The faces around the table would brighten as though brightened by the warm sun. They all, except Amos, loved the burning time. His father would already have picked a spot of rich, loamy soil in the woods, slanted for drainage and lying fair to the sun. From time to time they would have piled great piles of dead logs and trash there. They began by cutting green logs to mix with the dry wood.

They worked feverishly, placing the wood for burning evenly over the bed so that, however the wind blew, the fire would catch it. They waited for night to apply the torch, though it was not necessary—except that a bonfire was more soul-satisfying in the dark. Men and boys came from neighboring farms to participate, as Amos' father and brothers would attend the neighbors' burnings. All night they lived with the fire. The men, allowing the eager boys to do most of the work, sat close to the warmth and spun stories of ghosts and old huntings while the boys romped around the edges of the bonfire in a great excitement for which they had no words, only shouts and laughter.

Going to the house for an hour or two of sleep, by dawn they were again at the plant bed, drawing the remnants of smoky logs. As they dug up the burned earth, it expired wisps of steamy vapor. After the plant bed was raked to remove clods and roots, everyone stood around the edges, watching Art Haines as he mixed the incredibly tiny tobacco seeds with ashes and sowed them with careful precision over the prepared earth.

Then they tromped the bed, being careful to perform the task evenly in order to bury the seed. Good straight brush limbs would have been laid aside from the cutting of the green logs and these were now placed uniformly over the bed, like shingling a roof.

The task was finished. Later, all the way up into April, new plant beds would be made. But the first one was the beginning of the tobacco year and their hearts were full to bursting with the hope of spring and first planting.

In May came the first season. The land would already have been broken and plowed, harrowed and reharrowed, laid off into rows and checked, and the hills painstakingly made with a hoe. But they had to wait for the season. The season often announced itself at night, in the sound of a gentle rain on the roof. They turned over in bed, comfortable with sleep, aware in the midst of comfort that tomorrow the planting would begin.

The day was warm and wet even at sunrise as they began

drawing plants from the plant bed and placing them gently into baskets. Amos walked along the rows, dropping one tobacco plant at each hill. There was one setter for each dropper. The setter took up the plant gently in his left hand as his right hand drove the setting peg into the loose earth. By the time his fingers had pressed the earth around the roots thrust into the peg hole, he would already be moving forward half-bent to the next hill.

They worked at setting the plants from first sun until dark closed in, for one never knew how long the season would last or when the next would come. At the end of the day the setters could hardly stand erect. Amos watched his father lie groaning face down on the front porch as his mother treaded the stiffness out of his tired and twisted back with her bare feet.

The tobacco crop, at this stage, was always perfect. The time of anxious combat against all the ills and enemies that tobacco is heir to had not yet come. But the labor of the crop began soon enough.

Day after endless hot day, they plowed and hoed and primed and topped and suckered. Amos would wear engraved lifelong on his mind the endless crawling of the rows, carefully turning each individual leaf, searching for tobacco worms, for the eggs of the tobacco fly from which the voracious worms were hatched. It was a tedious, exasperating task. The juice of the plants got on your hands; if you touched your face your eyes would burn for hours afterward. Perfection was demanded; once Art had found a worm that John had missed on his rounds. As an unforgettable lesson in perfectionism for all his sons, Art had forced John to bite the worm in two with his teeth.

The cutting season began the last of August, after a short laying-by period. It was an anxious time. Every day that the tobacco stood in the field was an additional danger. The great leaves, dark green and gummy, were a hostage to fortune. At first it was storm and hail; later the danger of frost. An early frost could take the whole crop, every single leaf. Yet one could not cut while the tobacco was still unripe.

Art Haines watched the weather signs; how the birds moved in the air, the very feel of the air in the early mornings, the sound the wind made at night around the corners of the house. When the day of decision came, they went all together into the fields with their tobacco knives. The cutter, with one stroke, would split each stalk nearly to the roots. His left hand would then take the stalk, bending it, and another stroke would sever the plant close to the ground. The stalk was then hung upside down on the tobacco stick to wilt before being taken to the curing barn.

Amos always drew the job of housing the tobacco. Standing spraddled on two tier poles four feet apart, he reached down with both hands to receive the heavy sticks of green tobacco. Then he reached up to place the stick on the tier above, starting with the highest and working down to his level. He then dropped down to a lower level, to repeat the process for what seemed an endless time.

He was smothered in the tobacco. The heavy, wilted leaves were gummy and the strong gum came off on his clothes, on his hands. He did not dare touch his face; yet he could not keep the gum out of his eyes. There was no fresh air in the tight barn. He sweated and itched and tried to wipe his eyes with the backs of his hands, only making matters worse. At the end of the day he would come out of the barn five pounds lighter, his clothes filthy, and every tender place burning. He bathed his eyes with a towel wrung in cold water, the cool comfort pressing gratefully against his flesh.

The tobacco was still not out of danger. If it were not hung properly, house burn, a kind of rot, would take the leaf. If too much heat were applied too quickly, while much sap remained in the leaf, the tobacco would be scalded. Later, after most of the sap had been sweated out, one leaf touching a flame could erupt a whoosh of fire, as irrevocable as an explosion, in the laden air. The barn, as well as the whole crop, would be lost.

Curing always began at night. The neighbors came again to the festivities, as to the burning of the plant bed. The slow fires were started under the tobacco and tended throughout the night, until everyone had left except for one guardian, who had to keep the fire hot but without flames. These nights would be frosty-cold and on his turns of duty Amos sat huddled in his coat, standing occasionally to stamp his feet and swing his arms.

These were the times for thinking and, alone tending the fires, he thought deeply. In his limited experience, it seemed that the world was populated by two kinds of people; the many who added to the world's pain, the few who took away from it. He wanted to be one of those few who took pain away, in spite of the fact that he had known only the other kind.

Only one man had ever been on his side. Amos remembered vividly the birth of his youngest sister. He had been eight years old in 1866 when Vivian had been born, the daughter of his father's return from the war. The birth had been hard, for his mother was already old beyond her time from having borne six previous children.

For three days, attended by the midwife, she had stayed in labor, until his father, annoyed beyond endurance by the constant sound of her voice in pain, had sent reluctantly for the doctor.

Amos had ached throughout the protracted birthing. Every sound his mother made cut him like a knife. So when Dr. Allgood came from his buggy with a long stride, swinging his black bag at his side, Amos watched him with large and hopeful eyes. He lingered on the porch, fascinated and horrified, unable to move out of the range of her pain.

The pain had continued, had, indeed, increased, until she was screaming. Amos wanted to scream, too, to relieve his intolerable tension. He hoped desperately she would die, that the screaming might stop. He prayed that she might die.

The screaming did stop. His breath locked in his throat, he listened to the ominous shuffling sounds, the low voices, inside the house. He looked into the doctor's face as he emerged, certain that the doctor would announce death and that he, Amos, had willed it. Dr. Allgood had smiled, saying, "Well, son, you got you a little sister. That is, if you were in the need of one."

"The old lady all right?" Art Haines had asked from where he sat against a tree in the bare yard, unswept now for many days, littered with leaves and chicken droppings.

"She'll be all right," Dr. Allgood said. "She ought to take it easy for a while. It's been hard on her. I wouldn't recommend you try it again. You aim to pay me for my time?"

"I'll try to bring you some meat come hog-killing time," Art said.

Amos watched Dr. Allgood climb into his buggy and drive away. He was the only man Amos had ever known who could stop pain.

It did not seem fair that so many people can add to the world's pain, so few can diminish it. Another fear dwelt inside Amos; this, perhaps, was the prime reason for his discontented heart. He was afraid that, knowing only people who belonged to the great majority, he would become like them and so in the end add his inevitable mite to the cumulative burden of pain and hurt carried by the world.

Yet he was blood of their blood, flesh of their flesh; in this, the only world he knew, he carried his share of responsibility. He could not leave without abandoning his responsibilities. No longer could he take the load from his younger brothers, no longer could he help his mother with the washing of the clothes, the hoeing of the garden.

There was no way, except the one way. He must announce within his own soul his separateness and then make it a fact in his life. He could save only himself. If he did not save himself, he would save nothing.

When the tobacco was graded and prized into hogsheads, he knew that the time had come. There must be a first step away, and then another, and another. His discontented heart would not allow him the luxury of remaining. He must abandon Haineses in order to take the first step; utterly and completely, forever separate from Haineses as even a stranger is not separate.

There was no joy in his heart as he walked down the road to Temple's Store, only the guilt at taking the step he knew he must take. He kept stopping, and looking back, and wondering if there were another way he could not yet see. But he went on, his heart full with the guilt, the discontent, that would be his own special burden throughout his life.

At Temple's Store he entered, picked up a broom. He began by sweeping the floor, starting from the back and working busily toward the door.

"You there, boy. What do you think you're doing?" Mr. Temple said.

"I'm sweeping the floor for you," Amos said.

"Why are you sweeping my floor? I don't intend to furnish you any candy for the job, if that's what you've got on your mind. That floor don't need sweeping for another week, anyhow."

Amos straightened, looking at Mr. Temple. "I'm working for you, Mr. Temple," he said.

Mr. Temple snorted. "You may be working for me. But I ain't paying you one red cent for your labor. I ain't even *asked* you to work for me, boy. What's your name, anyway? Ain't you one of . . . ?"

"Amos Haines," Amos said. "I don't ask for no pay. I just ask for a place to sleep on them sacks back yonder and something to eat. I'll be worth it, Mr. Temple. I promise you I'll be worth it."

It was the first step.

Chapter Three

At sixteen Oren Knox was ready to make his move. During these two years he had plied his trade as if pinhooking were his lifework; buying and selling for the house, working both outside on the street and inside on the breaks. Occasionally he rented a buggy from the livery stable and made a foray into the countryside, visiting farmers, talking always tobacco and tobacco prices. At sixteen he was a respected man in the trade, known to be shrewd but whose words were the words of wisdom. He had developed an uncanny ability to forecast next week's and next month's prices on the breaks.

It was not intuition; it was diligent labor. He made a practice of touring the factories to determine their present stock and future needs. He knew which factories were making a success, which were getting along, which were failing in the competition that became fiercer with each passing year. On any given day he could tell you the approximate amount of tobacco in each redrying house in the district. He followed the auctions in other towns as well as his own; he discovered it was often worthwhile to haul tobacco from Manchester to the Durham or Danville markets to take advantage of a special price situation there.

Tobacco was his life. He loved the look of the weed in all its stages of growth and processing, he liked to stretch a leaf between his hands and study it, feeling the texture with his fingers as he judged the color with his eye. It seemed to him a magic weed, a boon to mankind though he personally could not use it in any form. He wondered what people had done, before tobacco had been discovered in the New World, to soothe their nerves and lighten their conversation.

During the second year he buried his mother. He had known, that first time he had visited her in Manchester, that this was a duty soon to come upon him. She lived almost exactly a year beyond that first visit, becoming paler with each passing day, thinner, at the end so near to transition that, still alive, she seemed already to bear death in her body like an incubus.

Oren did not see her often during her dying time; he could seldom bear to expose himself to the danger of being pulled backward, downward, into that bad time of his life. He knew he stood teetering on the brink, only barely escaped, and if he faltered just once, made just one backward step, he would be submerged, never again to escape. Once, twice, three times, he forced himself to go to her, restless and nervous in the barren little house that was her dying place; from the moment of his arrival he was desperate to depart, while she clung to him with a wordy yearning in which she talked incessantly of the time soon to come when they would all be together again, a normal family like all families. At times he got the feeling she believed that, if such a miracle could happen, a further miracle would bring also his father. Each visit would end with his abrupt, straining escape into his own world. The first man he dealt with upon his return to the warehouse was likely to find Oren particularly anxious to make a profit.

Each week he faithfully sent his mother the five dollars he had promised, putting the money in an envelope and paying one of the warehouse Negroes a nickel to take it to her, requiring the messenger to return the envelope to him with the signature of her receipt. When she died he bought the coffin and hired the hearse to take her to the burying ground at their old church in the country. He sent word to his aunt and uncle, to his two brothers, to the other relatives.

At the graveside he stood among them but he did not know them. His two brothers, both older than he, were country boys still, while he wore a town suit and shoes and a four-in-hand tie. They looked on him with awe, they wanted to draw close in the common grief. He could find nothing to say to them. They, like his mother, were a part of that world on which he had closed a door.

Returning to town in the rented buggy, he idly calculated the expenditures. Five dollars a week for fifty weeks, two hundred and fifty dollars; plus that original ten dollars, two sixty; the coffin, seventy-five dollars, three hundred and thirty-five; the hearse drawn by two black horses, with black plumes nodding on their heads, ten dollars; three hundred and forty-five dollars in all. He had dispensed with the services of the undertaker, except for the hearse. He had depended on the neighbor women to lay her out for burial, on the neighbors near the old church to dig the grave and lower her into the earth, on the old preacher of that church to deliver the graveside words. He had given the preacher three dollars and that made it three hundred and forty-eight dollars.

He had not begrudged one penny, though he could have turned the money over several times if it had been available for his activities. It had been a small ransom to pay for the privilege of departing alone from the burial, leaving his two brothers, his Uncle Mark and Aunt Kate, the other relatives, to scatter to their various ways. Once out of sight of the church, he slapped the horse into a brisk trot, anxious to get back to town. There would be no further ransoms to pay.

He was frugal in his living. Though his share of the proceeds from his trading was ample, he continued to put on his jeans britches and hickory-stripe shirt morning and night to tend the fires in the boardinghouse for his keep, he continued to eat in the kitchen with the Negro cook rather than at the long table in the dining room with the permanent and transient guests. Often, as he ate, he could hear their talk and laughter through the door that divided him from them; he felt no urge to join. He continued to live in the small house in the back yard, heating water on the kitchen stove twice a week for his bath, doing his own washing, ironing his shirts with a flatiron borrowed from the main house. He bought a brush and brushed each suit, three of them by now, each time he took it off. He pressed the suits, too, steaming through a damp cloth with the hot iron. He spot-cleaned the suits as they needed it.

Much of his free time was spent in these tasks. But he found time to enroll in the local business college to study bookkeeping and sundry other subjects—he paid special attention to an absorption of English grammar and social and business etiquette—paying his tuition by janitor work there, also. In six months he had absorbed all they could teach him.

He kept his increasing riches in a deerskin pouch under his mattress, as Uncle Mark had done. Each week, on Sunday night, he counted the money and added the week's getting to the accumulation.

The counting was a solemn time. He loved the silky feel of the bills, the massy gold eagles and double eagles, the silver dollars, the flow of small change in his hands. He stacked them into piles and sorted the bills into denominations, contemplating the accumulated hoard with a certain awe and disbelief before returning it to the deerskin pouch. Always, at the end, he took his lucky 1858 dime from his pocket and looked at it. He carried the dime in his empty watch pocket so he would not spend it by accident. Most men, he knew, would have pierced the coin and strung it on a chain. But he wanted to feel it in his pocket in negotiable form, not only as a keepsake. He had had to use it once; he felt, vaguely, that the time might come when the dime would again be needed.

One night he counted out ten dollars short. He counted again, and then the third time, with increasing dismay. The ten dollars had irrevocably vanished. He sat staring at the treasure, sick at his stomach, utterly devastated by the loss. He had not minded spending the money for his mother's final illness and death; this unaccounted loss hurt him deeply.

Next morning, the cook came to work in a new hat, a new pair of shoes. They had always been friendly with each other. He watched as she crossed the back yard and disappeared inside the door.

He knew she was wearing his ten dollars. He walked across the yard, opened the kitchen door. She was just taking off the hat, getting ready to start breakfast.

"I reckon you needed that new hat and them shoes," he said.

She paused, her hands up to her head. "What you talking about, boy?"

"You know what I am talking about."

She took down her hands, watching him as he turned to leave the kitchen. "What you gonna do?"

Without answering her, he kept going. He wanted her to worry. There was no way to recover the ten dollars; she would deny to the point of death that she had taken it. But she could, at least, worry for a while about his retaliation.

Her voice rose to a higher note. "Just count yo'self lucky," she said, the words lifting and pursuing him. "Somebody gonna knock you in the head one of these nights and take *all* that treasure. Just count yo'self lucky, that's all."

He returned to his room. He took out the deerskin pouch and once again counted the money carefully. He subtracted ten dollars from the total he carried in his mind. He divided the money into two equal piles and contemplated it. The ache of the loss was still within him, as though the ten dollars had been a child of his loins. There was a further pain in knowing he would never again sit on his bed on Sunday night and count his getting, the bills and coins as real to his touch as life.

Instinctively, profoundly, he distrusted banks. That morning, when the banks opened, he appeared first at the one and then at the other, depositing half his money in each place. The figures in his bankbooks totaled three thousand, twelve dollars and eighty-three cents. As he walked to the warehouse he carried the bankbooks in his hands, looking at the figures. They were unreal; they did not encompass the money at all.

Oren, during these two years, had paid special attention to

the Fuller Tobacco Factory. Foster Fuller occasionally appeared on the breaks himself to purchase tobacco and more than a year ago Oren had made his acquaintance by pointing out a particularly good pile of smokers.

"That's just the grade of leaf you need, Mr. Fuller," he had remarked. "Better snap it up."

Mr. Fuller had looked at him incuriously; but he had bought the tobacco. Mr. Fuller wore a heavy, slow-moving face. He seldom smiled, though he did not strike one as a gloomy man. He seemed placid, almost inert. Fifty years old, he stood rock-solid on his plodding feet. His voice, like his mind, moved at glacial speed. Watching him on his infrequent appearances on the breaks, Oren saw that he was only a fair judge of tobacco, occasionally overpaying on the grade. When he would find himself out front on a bid he would look slowly at the other buyers, as though wondering what had happened.

Oren found it difficult to refrain from classifying Mr. Fuller as a stupid man. But no man, Oren thought, could be completely stupid who owned, in his own name with no partners, a tobacco factory. He could only reach the conclusion that Mr. Fuller's placid slowness must be deceptive. It was certainly deceptive; if the lightning of calculation flashed behind the façade it remained well hidden.

One day Oren Knox called on Mr. Fuller in his office at the factory. It was a dingy room, wood-paneled, dark from the curtains drawn at the windows. Mr. Fuller worked at a rolltop desk, red mahogany in color, the pigeon holes stuffed with papers. A cigar burned in an ashtray to one side. In the anteroom to the office a male clerk, shirt-sleeved, with armbands holding up his sleeves and sateen cuff-protectors around his wrists, worked eyeshaded on a high, slanted-top writing desk.

"What can I do for you, Mr. Knox?" Mr. Fuller said in his slow-moving voice. With equal deliberation he picked the cigar from its ashtray, puffed on it.

"Well, Mr. Fuller, I've come to help you out."

"How are you planning to do that, Mr. Knox?"

"I've noticed that old Bull Durham has been giving you a

hard time. Every tobacco store I got into, I see lots of Bull Durham and mighty little of Fuller's Best."

"Everybody knows that Bull Durham is the best-selling smoking tobacco," Mr. Fuller said. "They've got an edge on all the other brands. Why, some folks say 'Bull Durham' when they mean smoking tobacco. Automatically, you might say."

Oren leaned forward. "That's no law of God, Mr. Fuller," he said. "Anything but a law of God can be changed."

"How you aim to change it?"

Oren sat still, watching Mr. Fuller's face. "We all know how Bull Durham got the head start," he said. "All them soldier boys bivouacked around Durham's while the generals talked surrender and spending their time scavenging food and tobacco. They raised particular Hades with the tobacco stored in John Ruffin Green's factory and they liked the taste of the bright leaf. So when they got home they wrote back to Durham's Station asking for some more of that good Durham smoking tobacco. Old John Ruffin Green knew a good thing when he seen it; he filled every one of them retail orders, scattering Bull Durham all over the country. It went on from there."

Oren paused. He could not gauge the impact the words were making on Mr. Fuller. He slowed his voice.

"Now, everybody's looked on that as happenstance ever since," he said. "But it ain't happenstance. It's distribution, Mr. Fuller. That's what it is—distribution."

"Distribution?" Mr. Fuller said, as though he had never heard the word.

"Distribution is what Bull Durham has got. That's the secret of success in this tobacco business. Mr. Fuller, if you had distribution, you wouldn't have your warehouse full of smoking tobacco sacked and labeled and stamped. It'd be in the stores across the country. Mr. Fuller, I can get you that distribution."

"With Bull Durham so far out in front, how you aim to do that?"

"Salesmanship. That's the secret of distribution, Mr. Fuller. Sheer old hard-down salesmanship. Green got his distribution through a stroke of luck . . . what a man calls luck anyway, which is no more than being in the right place at the right time with the right product. That can't happen again. But salesmanship can happen any time a good salesman comes along, Mr. Fuller."

"What you got in mind?"

"I want to take that tobacco out of your warehouse and put it in the stores. I want to go on the road and sell Fuller's Best for you, Mr. Fuller."

A slow look of skepticism worked its way across Mr. Fuller's face. "I thought you were a pinhooker."

"That's what I've been called. What I've been is a salesman, Mr. Fuller, when you get right down to it. You know I've made out on the breaks. I can do you the same kind of good."

"If you've made out, why do you want to quit and go into another line?"

"It's the same old line, Mr. Fuller. Tobacco. I know I can keep right on with what I'm doing now—doing well at it too. Right now, if I had a mind to, I could come close to setting up as a leaf dealer, with my own redrying facilities and all. But, to my mind, the future lies in manufacturing. There's where the tobacco trade is gonna grow."

"I do about the same amount of business year after year," Mr. Fuller said. "I don't see much growth in it. Folks gonna smoke about the same amount. I hold my same share of the market every year. So I'm satisfied."

"But you're *not* holding your same share. Listen, Mr. Fuller. The population of this country increases every year. Every year a bigger percentage of that population uses the weed, in one form or another. Here's something else; you walk down the street and count the people using tobacco in its different forms. If you had done that last year, you'd find that this year more people are using smoking tobacco than last year. When you hold your same sales year after year, that means you're losing out on three counts, Mr. Fuller. One, the growth of population; two, the increasing percentage of people using tobacco; and three, the increasing percentage of tobacco-users who use smoking tobacco." He leaned back, watching Mr. Fuller. "By holding your same rate of sales, Mr. Fuller, in five years you'll be out of business."

The last statement seemed to jar Mr. Fuller. He shifted in his chair, puffed on his cigar, looked at it, laid it in the ashtray.

"How you know all this?" he said.

"I been watching. I been figuring. I been thinking," Oren said. "You watch it a while, figure a little bit, and do some thinking about what you've found out—you'll see that I'm dead right. And salesmanship is the only thing that can change the picture."

"You're not going to be able to make people forget Bull Durham," Mr. Fuller said.

"I may not kill the Bull," Oren said confidently. "But I can cut him down to size. Just give me the chance. I'll show you."

"You're an independent man, Mr. Knox. How come you want to work for me?"

Oren frowned. "I told you. The growth is in manufacturing. I want to be in on it."

"You won't make the money you're making handling the leaf."

"I'm not asking for money. I'm asking for the chance."

"How much salary would you expect?"

"You put me on for twenty-five dollars a week plus a commission on sales—I'll pay my own road expenses—and I'll be satisfied."

"You'll be taking a cut."

"We'll see whether I will or not. And I'll guarantee you . . . I'll empty that warehouse for you."

Mr. Fuller looked troubled. "I don't know," he said. "Seems like I'm doing all right the way things are. Say you are lucky and you do raise our sales. Then I've got to step up production. That means more hands in the factory, more leaf-buying, bigger inventory, all that. Seems like nothing but trouble to me, Mr. Knox. Seems like I might as well leave well enough alone."

"But it's not well enough! In five years you'll be out of business at the rate you're going. You heard me outline the facts. One, the population is growing. Two, the percentage of tobacco-users is increasing. Three, the percentage of smokers within that percentage of tobacco-users is increasing. You can't ignore those facts, Mr. Fuller."

"I don't know," Mr. Fuller said doubtfully.

"I'll tell you something else," Oren said. "You're paying too much for your leaf. You let me handle your leaf-buying, during the time I'll be in town, and I'll cut your raw-product cost by ten per cent."

"You'll do that, too, for the twenty-five plus commission?"

"No. I'll tell you what. Twenty-five plus commission on the road, me paying my expenses. While I'm in town, I'll buy your leaf. You pay me five per cent and I'll guarantee to cut your cost by another five. If I don't, then it won't cost you anything. Now that's a square deal, Mr. Fuller. It'll do us both good."

"I still don't see why you want to quit your trade and go to work for me. For less money, at that."

Oren stood up. "You let me worry about that. You just think about whether I can do you any good. I told you, anyway—I'm going where the tobacco trade goes, and that's into manufacturing and selling. I came to you because you've got the factory."

"Why don't you go to Bull Durham?"

"They don't need me. They're successful. You need me because you're not successful." He leaned over Mr. Fuller. "There's another reason I came to you, a reason you don't even know about. My mother worked in your factory, Mr. Fuller. When she came to town, she got a job in your stamp-and-label department. You gave her a job when she needed one. Now, you probably didn't even know about that. But I did. So when I decided to make my move, I knew you were the man I wanted to help out, for that reason alone."

There was a pause.

"I'll have to think about it," Mr. Fuller said at last. He looked up at Oren. "While I'm thinking, you go ahead and buy my leaf on the breaks. I know I can put dependence on you there."

"I'll be glad to do that," Oren said. "But you don't need a

lot of leaf. Not till we move the smoking tobacco you've already got stacked up in boxes and unsold."

"I'll let you know."

"Don't take too long, Mr. Fuller. I've got to make my decision soon, now. If I don't come in with you, I'm going with another factory."

He put on his hat and walked out of the office, leaving Mr. Fuller staring after him.

Three days later, in Knoxville, Tennessee, Oren Knox made his first call in his new capacity as drummer for the Fuller Tobacco Factory. He had never been in Knoxville before. He had come in on the East Tennessee & Virginia Railroad through Bristol, Tennessee, by way of Danville, Virginia. He had wanted to get out of the immediate territory of the smoking-tobacco factories in North Carolina and Virginia, but not so far that his brand would be completely unknown. On this trip, among the several brands manufactured by Fuller, he intended to concentrate solely on Fuller's Best. The other brands sold even less than Fuller's leading label. On the same train on which he had traveled by day coach, he had shipped a quantity of Fuller's Best so he could fill orders on the day of purchase.

That first morning, he walked down Gay Street from his cheap boardinghouse, past the Cumberland Hotel where the more prosperous drummers had their lodgings, until he found the first tobacco shop. He entered confidently, without hesitation.

"Gentlemen," he said to the proprietor behind the counter, to the several men selecting cigars.

He waited patiently until the proprietor, finished with his trade, had turned expectantly.

"What can I do for you, sir?" the proprietor asked.

Oren held out his hand. "My name is Oren Knox," he said. "I'm traveling for the Fuller Tobacco Factory out of Manchester, North Carolina. I'm here to take your order for Fuller's Best."

He had made a quick glance over the display of smoking tobaccos, to see that his brand was not stocked here. He took a sample from his coat pocket and laid it on the counter. Mr.

Fuller's benign, placid countenance stared up at them from the gaudy label.

The owner shook his head. "Sorry," he said. "I don't get hardly any calls for Fuller's Best." The other men, listening, laughed. "I sell mostly Bull Durham."

"A lot of people make that same mistake," Oren said. He wanted the men to laugh on his side. "So many make that mistake that Mr. Durham can't keep enough bulls to supply the fertilizer that goes into his smoking tobacco. Why, he told me just last week that if he didn't watch out he'd have to start stretching his bull manure by adding tobacco to it—even if it was agin his principles."

They laughed, all right, one man slapping his thigh. The storekeeper himself chuckled.

"Now, gentlemen, I want to introduce you to Fuller's Best, the finest bright-leaf smoking tobacco made. We're just opening up this territory—I don't believe you gave me your name, sir . . ."

"Henry," the owner said. "George Henry."

"We're just opening up this territory, Mr. Henry, and I wouldn't want you to miss the opportunity to be the first in Knoxville to stock Fuller's Best. Everywhere we go we are driving the Bull right back to pasture. Give your customer just one pipe of Fuller's Best and he won't ask for anything else the rest of his life. Now, Mr. Henry, I want to put you down for a nice substantial order and tomorrow morning I will fix your display of Fuller's Best myself."

"I've had Fuller's Best in stock," Mr. Henry said. "It just wouldn't move. Sat right there until I had to take it off the shelf." He grinned. "Maybe folks like the taste of the Bull's manure, Mr. Knox. Whatever it is, I sell a mess of it."

Oren knew, immediately, it was no use. He picked up the sack of tobacco, put it into his pocket.

"Well I'm sure sorry to know that you feel that way, Mr. Henry," he said. "I think you're making a mistake. But I ain't going to argue with a man who thinks he knows his own mind. I wouldn't want you to stock my brand unless you were convinced it was the best brand in the world and would want to recommend it personally to every customer who walks in that door. Good day, gentlemen."

He exited into the street, holding his back straight. They did not laugh again, behind him, and he was relieved. He moved briskly until he was out of sight of the doorway. He slowed, then, thoughtfully shaking his head.

He kept on trying. All day he made his calls, plodding on his short, thick legs from store to store, patiently giving his best pitch again and again into the unconvinced faces. He did not take a single order. While Bull Durham did not hold total sway, there was no place for Fuller's Best. Time after time the owners told him, regretfully, that they had stocked the brand, at one time or another, without success.

All day his mind ran around the corners of his dilemma. He had talked big to Mr. Fuller, out of his own confidence. He had known, even then, the poor reception that Fuller's Best was getting from the trade. He had believed all that was needed was his own push behind it. Well, he thought moodily, one can beat a dead mule all day without making him get up into the traces.

In the middle of the afternoon, he stopped. His legs ached; he had walked more today than at any time since the last day he had spent plowing for his Uncle Mark. He took the sack of tobacco from his pocket and looked at the portrait of Foster Fuller on the label.

"Mr. Fuller, you're a dead mule," he said out loud. "Even I didn't know how dead."

He briskened his step, his mind made up. He went first to the tobacco warehouse district, where he mingled with the buyers, introducing himself and talking tobacco for a time, before casually inquiring where he could get some lithographing work done. It was late in the afternoon by the time he found the shop.

"I'd like to have some labels run off," he said. "I need them as quickly as possible."

"In the morning be all right?"

"Yes," he said. "If you can help me in the design."

"Be glad to do that."

They worked for an hour making up the design. It was based on his own name, Oren Knox, the O and the K printed very large, the "ren" and the "nox" so small one had to read it carefully. The word "Durham" showed as large as the "O.K."

They did sketch after sketch until Oren was satisfied.

"That'll do it, I reckon," he said at last. "I want my name on it, but I want people to see it as O.K. Durham Smoking Tobacco." He paused, considering. "I want to make folks look close, too, so they'll see the Oren Knox as well as the O.K. Durham." He turned away thoughtfully, staring out the window. "Let's put a little bitty woman on there," he said. "Sort of peeping out from behind that K, and as nekkid as the law allows. Make 'em wonder whether they really see her or not, so they'll look long and hard at my label."

The lithographer grinned. "You selling women or you selling tobacco?"

"Well, I figure if they'll buy my little bitty woman they'll have to purchase the tobacco to go along with her," Oren said.

The lithographer laughed. "I reckon you could sell anything in the world with a picture of a nekkid woman on it."

"Hell, look what Bull Durham is doing with nothing but a bull."

He left the shop, with the promise that he could pick up the first batch of labels early in the morning. He returned to the tobacco district, thinking there would be the best place to hire hands for pasting on the labels. He made an agreement with six Negro men to send their wives early the next morning to the railroad warehouse where he had stored his cartons of smoking tobacco.

He returned to his boardinghouse and ate supper. He was restless with the suspension of the day, with the uncertainty of success on tomorrow. He strolled down the street after supper and entered the lobby of the Cumberland. It was comfortably populated with successful traveling men, their vests as loud as their voices, their cigar smoke rich and pure in the air, their smiles hearty and well-met.

Oren found a place on a plush sofa. In a few minutes he had entered into conversation with another drummer.

"Nice place here," the man said. "I always stay at the Cumberland in Knoxville."

"Yes," Oren said noncommittally, thinking of his dingy boardinghouse up the street, of the undoubtedly lumpy mattress on which he would sleep tonight. "Very nice."

The man thrust out his hand. "My name is Taylor Tryon," he said. "Traveling in hardware for W. B. Belknap and Company, out of Louisville."

"Oren Knox," Oren said. "Smoking tobacco, out of Manchester, North Carolina."

"What's your brand?"

"O.K. Durham Smoking Tobacco. My own brand. O.K., Oren Knox."

"Clever, clever. I never heard of it. I'm a cigar man myself. Here, have a cigar. Can't beat a good Havana."

He took a cigar from his vest pocket, extending it to Oren. Oren shook his head.

"Thank you," he said politely. "I don't smoke."

Tryon threw back his head. "Now that's a laugh," he said. "A tobacco drummer that doesn't smoke."

"How's the hardware trade?" Oren said to change the subject.

"Couldn't be better," Tryon said. "I've got a great line of goods. Belknap puts out a catalogue every year, got everything you can think of in the hardware line. Here, let me show you a little item that's one of our most popular lines this year."

Oren watched as he pulled his huge sample case from around the end of the sofa, opened it. Taylor Tryon was a big man, with heavy, sloping shoulders. His face was as enthusiastic as his voice, flushed with vigor and conviction. His hair was sandy red. His skin, lightly blotched with freckles, looked delicate, susceptible to sun and weather. It was difficult to estimate his years—he could have been any age from twenty-five to forty-five.

"Look at that little Cottage Barometer," Tryon said enthusiastically. "Hang that up in your house and you know all about the weather. See there—fair, unsettled, stormy—and it's got your temperature right alongside. Zero, freezing, temperate, summer heat, and blood heat. Everybody ought to have one. Made by Taylor Brothers in Rochester, New York, and just look at that pretty cherry moulding so your wife won't care if you hang it in your parlor. Now how much you figure that little item goes for?"

"It'd be hard to say," Oren said cautiously.

"Three dollars a dozen. That's twenty-five cents apiece. Now, that's a two-dollar item if ever I've seen one. Mark it two, sell it for a dollar, and make your customer feel happy he walked into your store. Let me show you something else. Here's an item for the luxury trade. Ain't got it with me, got a picture of it. The Enterprise coffee mill, manufactured in Philadelphia, P. A. Nickel-plated hopper and two twenty-five-inch flywheels. They'll set you back twenty-five simoleons apiece. But just take a look. Why, you'll keep that coffee mill in your parlor for your guests to admire. And here's something else, the Little Star Apple Parer . . ."

"Let me see that Cottage Barometer again," Oren said, stopping the flow of talk that came as effortlessly from the man as cigar smoke.

Tryon stared at him. "You in the need of hardware?" he said. "If you're in the business, I can show you a complete line—and I mean complete . . ."

"I was just interested in that barometer," Oren said. "Got an idea in mind."

Tryon handed it to him. Oren studied it carefully.

"How much did you say this sold for?"

"Three dollars a dozen. Twenty-five cents apiece to the trade. It's a two-dollar item if ever I saw one."

"How long would it take you to make delivery on a few dozen of these?"

"I've got some at the local jobber's," Tryon said. "I don't know just how many dozen are left. What's a tobacco drummer need a stock of barometers for?"

"Well now," Oren said. "I figured they might be just the thing to stir up a little goodwill amongst my dealers. You know . . . they buy a certain quantity of O.K. Durham Smoking Tobacco, they get free, for their own use, a genuine two-dollar Cottage Barometer."

"Say, now, that's O.K., O.K.!" Tryon said, laughing and slapping Oren on the back. "How many you need?"

"Let me try out a dozen," Oren said cautiously. "I'll need to sample the sentiment. If it works, you can give me your home-office address and I'll place a substantial order with you."

"I'll say you're a live one," Tryon said admiringly. "You know a good thing when you see it."

"We'll see how it works out," Oren said. He rose. "If you can meet me here in the morning with the dozen, I think we might be in business."

"I'll do that."

"Good night," Oren said. "See you tomorrow."

He threaded his way through the lobby until Tryon had lost sight of him. Then he slipped out of a side door into the street and made his way to his boardinghouse. That night he slept the sleep of the just on a terrible bed. He was up at daylight to begin the new day.

He made his first call on Mr. Henry, the man on whom he had first called yesterday. He found Mr. Henry alone.

"Mr. Henry," he said. "My name is Oren Knox, the originator of O.K. Durham Smoking Tobacco. I am traveling to the trade myself to personally introduce this finest bright-leaf smoking tobacco. You won't find a better Durham District tobacco on the market today. I want you to be the first man in Knoxville to stock and sell O.K. Durham Smoking Tobacco. I'm told you're a man that other men follow. Well, the whole United States of America is going to follow you into O.K. Durham."

"Say, ain't you the fellow in here yesterday with that Fuller's Best?" Mr. Henry said suspiciously. "Seems to me like you're traveling for two companies."

"I want to tell you the truth about that," Oren said easily. "You were on trial yesterday. If I had written your order for

Fuller's Best, you'd never have had a chance at O.K. Durham."

"What do you mean?"

"I wanted to find out if you were a man who knew tobacco, or whether you were just passing articles of trade across the counter."

"That's a pretty shifty way of doing business, seems like to me. How would you have filled my order for Fuller's Best, if I'd given you one?"

"We have taken over the Fuller Factory," Oren said. "I have personally blended the new O.K. Durham." He took several sacks of the tobacco out of his pocket, gleaming with the bright new lithographed label. "I want you to take a good look at our new label. Study it close, now, and you'll find out why this is going to be your most popular item with your steadiest customers."

Mr. Henry took one of the sacks, his face puzzled. For a moment he looked without seeing. Then a delighted smile spread slowly across his face.

"Well, now, if that don't beat all!" he said. "She's a pretty thing, too, ain't she?"

"Just think of the pleasure you'll have watching your customers discover the secret of O.K. Durham Smoking Tobacco," Oren said, laughing. "Now, how many cartons do you want for a starter? Enough for a big display, I know."

"I don't know," Mr. Henry said, caution returning. "Folks like to smoke that old Bull Durham. I don't know how O.K. Durham will go. They'll look at it, and they'll laugh, but will they buy? It's hard to say."

"Let me show you something else," Oren said. He took the Cottage Barometer out of his coat pocket and placed it on the counter. "We want you personally, Mr. Henry, to be a friend of Oren Knox and of O.K. Durham. Upon the quantity purchase of O.K. Durham, we make you a free gift of this beautiful Taylor Brothers Cottage Barometer. Just look at that pretty cherry moulding—your wife won't care if you hang your Cottage Barometer right in your parlor. It'll add grace and distinction to any room in the house. Hang it up and you know all about the weather—fair, unsettled, stormy—and right alongside it you've got your thermometer. Now, you can't buy a Cottage Barometer in the stores for less than two dollars; it's yours free, to take home with you tonight and read tomorrow's weather from."

"Well, now, ain't that nice?" Mr. Henry said admiringly, picking it up and looking at it. "Always did want one of those dinged things but I never would lay out the money for it."

"It's yours," Oren said generously. "And I don't mind telling you, Mr. Henry, there are going to be other dealer gifts you can receive absolutely free of charge as you continue to stock and push O.K. Durham Smoking Tobacco. We are planning to get out a little catalogue that you can pick your free gifts from. Handy and beautiful little items for your home and your store, and they won't cost you one red cent."

He wrote the order. Every place he called on, that second day, he wrote the order. On his last call of the day, he visited the local tobacco jobber and introduced himself.

He gave the tobacco jobber a Cottage Barometer the moment he entered, ensuring his welcome. He told the jobber how every tobacconist in Knoxville was pushing O.K. Durham Smoking Tobacco, and so it behooved the jobber to buy his remaining stock so he could replenish the store stocks immediately, without having to wait for further shipments from the factory, which might take a week or more.

"They're going to be moving that O.K. Durham Smoking Tobacco," he said earnestly. "They'll be mighty disappointed when they call on you for new stock if you can't supply them."

The jobber took on the remaining supply without demur. Oren then hastened to the warehouse, to find that the new labels had all been affixed. He hired a wagon and dragooned the husband of one of the women to drive the wagon around town to deliver the orders. Oren went along and took in the money. They delivered the last of the tobacco to the jobber's warehouse and Oren collected the money due there.

It was late by the time he was through. He paid off the Negro man and ate supper at the boardinghouse. He inquired about trains, knowing he must return home immediately to arrange matters at the factory end. He had not thought about that aspect of his evolving plan until this moment.

He found an hour to spare and stopped in at the Cumberland, seeking out Tryon.

"The barometer premium worked even better than I thought," he said. "Now, if you can make us a price on it, I'm ready to do business. We need a nice line of items running somewhere around the same price, three dollars a dozen. Something that looks like two dollars worth of goods, just like that barometer."

"I'm glad to hear that," Tryon said eagerly. "If you will have dinner with me . . ."

"I have to return to Manchester tonight," Oren said. "You take a couple of days and work out your list. Now, I want a good price. I don't mind telling you that I'm going to explore other sources. But I'd like for you to have the business. You be in Manchester later on this week and we'll talk turkey. That suit you?"

"Suits me fine," Tryon said enthusiastically.

They shook hands, and Oren had ample time to catch his train.

Foster Fuller was a stubborn man, hard to convince. "Just what the Sam Hill do you think you've been up to?" he said, staring down at the bag of O.K. Durham Smoking Tobacco lying on his desk.

"I've been selling smoking tobacco," Oren said calmly. "That's more than anybody has been doing around this factory for some time."

"Who gave you the authority to make such decisions?"

"I took the authority, Mr. Fuller, " Oren said. "When I saw the reception your brand was getting, I knew I had to do something." He stood up. "Remember, I've got a lot in this, too. I quit the leaf trade, where I was making a good living. I'm spending my own money on traveling expenses."

"I don't know how you thought your own name on the label would be any better than my name."

"Take a good close look at that label."

Mr. Fuller picked up the sack. He peered at the label, for what seemed to Oren a long time.

"Humph," he said at last. He looked at Oren. "You're a pretty sneaky fellow, Mr. Knox. I didn't know how sneaky."

"I got around the Bull," Oren said. "Now, if you think what I did was wrong, I'll go back to the leaf trade. Because I can't sell Fuller's Best, Mr. Fuller. O.K. Durham I can sell. If you'd rather keep your tobacco in your warehouse with your picture on it . . ."

"So it's your idea that Fuller's Tobacco Factory is going to manufacture Oren Knox Tobacco."

"That's the only out I saw," Oren said. "I had to try, Mr. Fuller. I thought you wanted to sell tobacco. Well, I sold some for you." He turned away. "Thank you for giving me the trial, Mr. Fuller. I'm sorry it didn't work out."

"Sit down, sit down," Mr. Fuller growled.

Oren sat. Only then did he discover that his legs were trembling. The palms of his hands were cold, damp. He had not known he was frightened until the moment of tension was over.

"That's not all," he said. "You've not only got to get labels made and relabel all the stock in the warehouse. You've got to get a premium catalog printed and distributed to the jobbers and dealers. I've committed us to a dealer-premium campaign."

He took the remaining barometer from his pocket. "I placed ten orders in Knoxville, not counting the jobber taking the balance," he said. "I gave away eleven barometers. I wanted to go on through Tennessee. But I was out of stock on both the merchandise and the premium. Now, nobody is going to want more than one barometer. What we need is a line of premiums so they can make a choice. I've got a hardware drummer coming in here from Belknap and Company in Louisville to set us up in the premium business."

Mr. Fuller humphed again. "You've been a busy man in Knoxville," he said.

"I've been selling," Oren said. "That's what I left town to do." He leaned forward. "I can clean that warehouse out for you in a month. In two months you'll have to step up your production. You won't be able to keep up with the demand I'll create for O.K. Durham Smoking Tobacco."

"Well, who's stopping you?" Mr. Fuller said. "Not me."

Oren rose again. "I'll go see about those labels," he said quietly. "You want me to hire the extra hands to work the warehouse stock?"

"Sure, sure," Mr. Fuller said. "You handle it."

"I'll be proud to do that," Oren said.

He left the office. He went down the corridor, to the connecting door that led into the work area. He paused in the doorway, holding the door open with one hand, and looked at the men working about the cutting machines.

It was his factory now. They didn't know it yet, but they were making **O**ren **K**nox Durham Smoking Tobacco. One of these days he would own it in name as well.

Chapter Four

OREN KNOX proceeded to take a giant step. Because of his new responsibilities at the Fuller Tobacco Factory, he rearranged his private life. His first move was to relinquish his arrangement at the boardinghouse whereby he built fires and did other janitorial work in exchange for his room and board. He bargained with Mrs. Thompson for exclusive possession of a second-floor room at the front of the house. It was her best room, fortuitously vacant at the moment of his decision. Most of the boarders doubled up to cut expenses; Oren wanted a solitary place of his own.

He moved in that very day. It was an elegant room, in the corner so that he had windows on two sides. It was furnished with a matched bedroom suite of Circassian Walnut. The head and foot ends of the bed had a wide, graceful curve in the Napoleon style. The bed boasted heavy crossband veneered top rolls, highly figured. The dresser was broad, with a French bevel plate mirror; its mirror frame had the same crossband veneer as the bed. The chiffonier was high and narrow, with six drawers, furnished too with a smaller French bevel plate mirror. There was a matched commode, also. Instead of a mirror it had a harplike structure on the top, two curved supports and a cross-bar, providing a place to hang his towel. Each piece stood on heavy hand-carved claw feet.

"This was our own bedroom suite until my late husband passed away," Mrs. Thompson told him in a cautionary voice. "I know you'll take care of it, Mr. Knox."

There was also a quartered-oak, golden-finish rocking chair, with an extra-wide, curbed top panel, eleven fancy turned spindles in the back, a form-fitting roll veneer seat, and ornately carved continuous front posts. It was high-backed and massive and the only place in the room where he could sit, except for the bed and the chamberpot.

For his own use, he purchased a golden oak parlor desk, with a large drop leaf and shelves below for books, the shelves hidden by a small curtain. The top of the desk was ornamented with bracket shelves and another, tiny, French bevel mirror. With it he bought a Douglas chair made of seasoned Wisconsin hickory rock elm, the back-rest, arms, and seat neatly striped. Together they cost seven dollars and sixty-four cents.

He liked the room. It was more elegant than any place he had ever seen, so he moved in it as cautiously as Mrs. Thompson could have desired. His six-piece toilet set was white and gold, semi-porcelain, decorated with a band of bright gold and large bright gold medallions. There was a wash pitcher, a wash bowl, covered chamberpot, soap slab, and one mug. Instead of a dangling bulb, the room was lighted by a three-light fancy polished brass chandelier, with fancy star pattern glass shades, supplemented by an Ideal electric portable lamp made of satin brass with a tulip-leaf embossed base and twelve-inch straw opalescent shade. For emergencies, when the power should fail, as it often did, there was a coal-oil parlor lamp, made of genuine Kopp Cardinal glass with embossed pineapple body and a ten-inch globe to match. It had an embossed brass base, fancy brass crown, used a Number Two Rochester chimney and wick, and put out one hundred candlepower.

The room was wallpapered in a deep rich green with a coral fleur-de-lis pattern. The carpet was worn Wilton velvet, with a stylized Oriental design. The windows were curtained with white curtains, drawn back by ties decorated with large elaborate bows.

All in all, an elegant home for the rising young bachelor. Oren was impressed with this visible evidence of his achievement; sitting in the room, he could actually believe that he had talked Mr. Fuller into doing business according to Oren's plan. He could still remember the sweaty feel of his palms during that interview in Mr. Fuller's office. He had known that failure here meant a giant step backward instead of a giant step forward.

Oren Knox was sixteen years old. The world in which he had his being was a male world. He had not spoken to a girl of his own age since grammar school. Womankind had no place in his plans. Women were mysterious, an inexplicable irrationality in an ordered universe. He was not bothered by this hiatus in his life; even at night, lying awake in the Napoleon bed, he spent the half-waking moments thinking of tomorrow's business, not, as would be expected of a sixteen-year-old boy in the prime of his manhood, in half-furtive fantasies. He had never once in his life looked at a woman and, looking, felt a definite urge or thought or feeling, a definite emotion linking him even momentarily into a fleeting relationship.

He knew, of course, the function of a woman in a man's life. He knew that other men spent an inordinate amount of time thinking about women; feeling about women; loving women; wanting women; and in needing women's love. He classified it as he classified tobacco and whiskey and laughter; amiable vices on which other men spent time and money and attention in amounts which Oren, in his directioned frugality, could not afford. He was not puritanical about it. On the contrary; it pleased him that other men could not, would not, sustain the concentration upon essentials that he himself sustained, as a matter of course, every waking hour of the day.

In spite of his new extravagances, he spent little. Even with his reduced income, he banked each week a substantial portion of his pay. Instead of doing janitorial work for his keep, he paid in cash; instead of washing and ironing his own shirts, he sent them out with the Negro woman who called every Monday at the boardinghouse. He continued to brush his suits faithfully after each wearing, he blacked his shoes each night upon taking them off. But he spent nothing on tobacco or women or laughter or whiskey, he had never visited an opera house or traveling circus or minstrel show. He knew that for two dollars, in a certain house in town, he could initiate himself into the mysteries of sex. The two dollars was more important to him than the initiation.

Oren had, in fact, been inside the house; he had taken Taylor Tryon there when Tryon had made the call in Manchester to close the deal on the premium list. Oren had paid the madam for Tryon's passage through the upper regions while he himself had remained below, working through the list and calculating quantities and prices. When Tryon descended, flushed and satisfied, Oren showed him the list.

"That's how I'll do business," he said.

Tryon studied the figures. "You've cut it too deep," he said. "We can't do business on that basis. Why, it'd take an eagle eye to see my commission in those prices."

Oren leaned back, looking up at Tryon. His blue eyes were cold, seeing. "You ever thought of going into the tobacco trade?" he said.

"What are you talking about? I'm a hardware man."

"You're a salesman, Mr. Tryon. You're no more a hardware man than I am. You just happen to be in hardware."

"Well now," Tyron said. "You put it like that, I reckon you're right. What's on your mind?"

"We need salesmen. I'll be on the road myself. But I can't put in as much time on the road as I ought to. There's too much to do here. The factory must be organized for more production, cheaper production. I've got to do something about the buying of the leaf—we're losing money hand over fist with Mr. Fuller doing the buying. I need a steady man on the road."

"You think I'm the man?"

"You walked up to me in the lobby of the Cumberland Hotel in Knoxville. You didn't have no more idea than the man in the moon that I was in the least interested in hardware. But you started selling just as natural as you kept on breathing. That's the kind of man I call a salesman."

Tryon watched him doubtfully. "I don't know," he said. "From what I've seen since I've been here in Manchester, you're a pretty marginal operation. You're a small factory, with an off-brand, up against major competition from one of the best-established brands in the whole United States of America. You know what I'm talking about—Bull Durham. There isn't enough range in manufacturing cost to be able to underprice him. You can finagle around here and there with dealer premiums, and that nekkid woman you've got on the package is a red-hot idea; but you just don't have much room to maneuver in."

He stopped, watching Oren.

"Take a look at you, you're a grown man. Take another look, you're nothing but a boy. I'll bet you ain't eighteen years old. I was setting up in my room that night I met you in Knoxville, fixing to go to bed, and I suddenly realized that little fact. And me mistering you and handing you one of my best cigars."

Oren smiled. "What difference does my age make? I reckon you know I plastered Knoxville with O.K. Durham Smoking Tobacco."

"Let me sum it up. You're young. Fuller is a small factory, with major competition. You can't claim to be anything but a marginal operation. On the other hand, when you travel for Belknap, folks are glad to see you coming. You stay at the best hotels, where you're greeted with a smile. Belknap is one of the biggest and best hardware companies in the business. And hardware—this is a mechanical-minded nation. Americans like hardware, they like the heft of it in their hands, the ingenuity of it, its usefulness."

"With tobacco, you're selling a vice," Oren said. "You're satisfying a taste that mankind has acquired. Hardware will come and go with the economy, Mr. Tryon. Tobacco will go on as long as mankind goes on, boom or bust. Now listen to me. I'll grant that we're small and we've got tough competition. Bull Durham is a great big wall like the wall of China and I still don't see no way around it. All I can do is pick at it with a chisel here and there."

He paused. He looked straight into Taylor Tryon's eyes.

"I'm not asking you to hire out to the Fuller Tobacco Factory," he said. "I'm asking you to hire out to me. Fuller may not be going anywhere. Oren Knox is. Fuller will pay you your wages—for the time being—but it's me you'll be working for. You'll sell O.K. Durham right now, maybe for some time to come. But I'm moving in this tobacco trade and Fuller is just a way stop on the mainline I'm riding. Don't you think about Fuller, you think about me, and then you decide if you like my proposition."

"Will I make the money I'm making now? I noticed you were staying at the Cumberland, just like I was. So . . ."

"I was just visiting in the Cumberland lobby," Oren said. "I lived at a boardinghouse up the street. No. You won't make the money you're making now. Not at first. But you stay with me and you'll die a wealthy man. You'll be able to own Belknap for a play-pretty, if you're so inclined."

"Nobody's ever made that kind of money in the tobacco trade."

"I will," Oren said. "Are you game?"

"I'll be damned," Tryon said. "I don't doubt you'll do it, too. How old are you, anyway?"

"I'm sixteen," Oren said. "What's that got to do with it?"

"It's a sporting proposition, all right," Tryon said thoughtfully. He smiled. "I always was a sporting man."

Oren rose, holding out his hand. "It's a deal, then?"

Tryon took it. "It's a deal."

"Don't you want to talk salary and commission?"

"I'm not worrying about salary and commission. You tell a man he'll be wealthy one day and then expect him to worry about salary and commission?"

"All right," Oren said. "You spend the first week learning about tobacco. You start out in the field and you follow that tobacco right until it comes out of the factory. Next week you go on the road."

"What about this?" Tryon said, indicating the paper on which was written the order for premium items. "I can't put this through and then quit to go to work for you. It wouldn't be right."

"Put it through," Oren said brutally. "Then, in two weeks, turn in your resignation. Remember. You're working for me now, not Belknap. Save me some money. Shave those prices even more if you can make it stick."

"My God," Taylor Tryon said softly. "And you ain't but sixteen yet."

"Let's get out of here," Oren said. "Unless you want to go back upstairs."

Tryon glanced toward the stairs. He laughed.

"No," he said. "If I'm going to be around you from now on, I reckon I better learn to control my vices."

Oren was not given a title at the factory. In the following months, his activities were too varied to be encompassed by a title. With Taylor Tryon on the road, he began at the buying end, finding himself once again on the breaks purchasing tobacco. He bought, not for his own account, but for the factory. He regularized his buying so that one day a week, or at most two, would suffice. Once the buying was placed on an efficient, cost-cutting basis, he moved into the factory proper. There was, of course, the necessity of selling; he spent half his time on the road, ranging far and wide, becoming one with the multitude of drummers riding the coaches and parlor cars with their sample cases, their good laughter, their loud talk.

He moved among them, mostly silent but always ready to listen. A good listener was needed among such compulsive talkers and as a consequence he was well regarded. He, too, carried a sample case, though his only product was O.K. Durham Smoking Tobacco. In addition to a few bags of tobacco he carried premium samples, along with a premium catalogue to display the weightier items. He entertained respect and recognizance because his own name was on his product; besides, his label with the naked woman was always good for a laugh.

He lived as frugally on the road as at home. He traveled at night whenever he could to save buying a bed, sleeping sitting upright in the coach seat, his feet propped on the seat opposite. He developed the knack of dropping instantly into slumber, under whatever conditions. He stopped at boardinghouses instead of hotels, though he knew all the hotels popular with traveling men because he made it a practice to visit their lobbies, as he had done that first time in Knoxville.

Because of his habitual silence, because of his difference from the usual breed of drummers, the other salesmen tended to treat him with an unusual deference and respect. Where Taylor Tryon stepped immediately upon familiar ground, in whatever city he found himself, a certain distantness moved always with Oren, though he was younger than most of these men. There was a circle of unapproachability, an aura of introspection, they did not quite dare to breach. These were hearty and gregarious men; men accustomed to being accepted immediately on familiar, even intimate, terms by all and sundry. Occasionally one would encroach upon Oren Knox's reserve. He did nothing, ostensibly; but his quietness, his assumption of inviolability, repelled the presumption as effectively as if he had used harsh words.

Oren had no gaiety in his make-up. It puzzled him that the road, to these men, was a way of life. They dressed the part of the drummer, with expensive brocaded vests and fancy four-in-hand ties. They wore patent colt shoes with green inserts on the sides, expensive hats, pearl or diamond—or imitation-pearl and imitation-diamond—stickpins; they acted the part of the drummer, with flamboyant voices and hail-fellow-well-met manners, with an air of easy spending and intimate familiarity with women; they lived the part of the drummer, believing in their own legend of dress and manner so intensely one could not distinguish make-believe from reality.

In their more serious moments, they talked of the vital role played by the drummer in the economy of the nation. They considered themselves the creators of taste and demand.

"Why, if there wasn't a drummer to tell them, people wouldn't even have sense enough to know what to want," they told each other enthusiastically.

They considered themselves key men in the expansion of trade. They talked about the impact of the drummer upon the small towns and rural communities.

"Get your foot in the door? Hell, they see you coming, that door's wide open and the welcome mat is out. My customers had rather see me coming than old Santa Claus hisself! Take you home for supper and introduce you to their marriageable daughters. How many of you have talked your way through a chicken dinner in the past week, and had to dodge the parlor on the way out?"

Oren believed that many, if not most, of these men would have traveled whether or not they had anything to sell. The selling, to them, was only an excuse for their way of life, not the reason for it.

As for Oren, he remained conscious, every waking moment, of the reason behind his travels. He had a constant apprehension in the back of his mind of the factory in Manchester spewing forth the endless sacks of O.K. Durham Smoking Tobacco. He knew his most basic task was to place those sacks of smoking tobacco on the retail shelves, and move them from there into the hands of the consumer. He wore no flamboyant vests, but dressed soberly, inexpensively. He wasted no conversation, burdened himself with no friendships, unless his relationship with Taylor Tryon could be called friendship; but he sold. Always and every day, he sold, rising early and calling late, selling premium because the brand was not greatly wanted, selling service and reliability and supply. But, most of all, selling premium. Every year his catalogue of premiums was expanded, to give the dealer a wider choice of more attractive articles.

The competition of Bull Durham permitted no spectacular success. He came to recognize very quickly that his dream of O.K. Durham becoming the dominant factor in smoking tobacco was totally unrealizable. His presence was scarcely noticed in the market; he was only one of dozens of small brands scrambling for the crumbs of acceptance left by the Bull. He was getting his share of the crumbs; he would never get more than crumbs.

He lay awake nights thinking about the Bull of Durham. He came to hate the sight of that symbol, sprouting on barns and fences and store windows wherever he traveled. They seemed to multiply like rabbits, proliferating in his sight even as he watched. That original joke of his, about the Bull's unwilling necessity of mixing tobacco with his natural product because of the extraordinary demand, became a standard of the trade, repeated over and over again until it became a part of folklore; but it, no more than any of his other activities, intense and planned though they were, served to diminish the Bull.

His success was modest, but visible to all. Within two years he had put the factory on a reasonably efficient basis, rearranging the flow of work, reducing slightly the number of hands necessary for the quantity of production, effecting economies in the purchasing and processing of the leaf. He was not satisfied with his progress in the factory; he had a feeling that machines were more economical, more reliable, than the swarms of human beings necessary to perform the intricate tasks of bagging and tagging and labeling the tobacco, in making the bags themselves, in all the myriad tasks that served to convert the raw leaf into usable form. But the machines did not exist; those that were used required considerable human attention.

Even so, he could make more smoking tobacco than he could sell; there was little incentive to increase production as long as Bull Durham dominated the market. He tried multiplying salesmen beyond himself and Taylor Tryon, but within the immediate territory the increased sales did not warrant the added expense. He tried sending salesmen farther and farther afield, often making the initial trip himself to open a territory. Everywhere the same great wall of the Bull existed. Expansion brought, inevitably, added expense and little profit.

He had reached an impasse. Whatever good could be accomplished within the limitations of the situation, he had accomplished. He was now locked into the situation.

He considered going over to Bull Durham. But the Bull had

no need of Oren Knox; he would be a small cog over there, where here he was the kingpin of the whole Fuller Factory structure. He had still no title, but his authority was as great as that of Mr. Fuller.

Oren himself was prospering. He had increased his earnings and now they were commensurate with, or maybe a little better than, his profits as a pinhooker. Mr. Fuller, of course, was fattening himself upon Oren's efforts. He had built a new house, banked more money, found himself a larger factor in the affairs of the community.

Oren, for the moment, saw no way out. After the first two years, he devoted himself to maintaining his position, doing it more and more automatically, more and more disengaged mentally if not physically. He knew that sometime, somehow, he must break out, as he had broken out of pinhooking.

Oren Knox knew the value of patience. He was not particularly frustrated by the hiatus in which he found himself, for he had ample scope in which to exert his talents. He owned a certain confidence in his own destiny that allowed him to wait. To move without being able to forecast the effects of his move would be the action of a desperate man. Moving in on Fuller Tobacco, he had overcalculated to a considerable extent. He had been right in the direction, wrong in the extent of the possibilities.

He correctly calculated that he was now in the position to make the next move, once its direction had opened itself to him. He was willing to wait until the moment had come. Come it must, for he was Oren Knox.

Mr. Fuller, during the time of Oren Knox, remained his usual placid, uncompetitive self. He allowed Oren extraordinary freedom, once the truth of his actions had asserted themselves. Mr. Fuller was content to prosper, since the efforts were not called forth from himself.

Mr. Fuller, like so many patterns of the world, remained a puzzle to Oren. He could not fathom such a man. Mr. Fuller instinctively opposed each adjustment effected by Oren in the fortunes of the Fuller Tobacco Factory; he did not oppose so strenuously as to frustrate Oren's design. His opposition stemmed more from inertia than from conviction itself. Twice Oren demanded an adjustment in his compensation; twice, after a struggle—which both of them knew in advance was futile—Mr. Fuller granted the adjustment.

Their relationship remained much as it had been at the beginning. It was confined to the factory, the office. Oren had never been inside the old house, nor, once it was built, the new house. Mr. Fuller moved in the society of Manchester, he was a factor in the political and financial community that centered about the courthouse and the banks. All that part of the Fuller position was closed to Oren.

Oren, in effect, was a hired hand who worked in the fields and slept in the barn. Trusted, compensated, even appreciated; but not taken with the family to church, not allowed in the kitchen, much less the parlor, his Christmas present handed out the back door to him standing on the steps.

Oren understood the relationship. He knew that no other would ever occur to Mr. Fuller. He also understood that Mr. Fuller trusted him, even liked him, and admired his talents, though reluctant to accept the changes Oren's talents forced upon the factory and upon himself; while, at the same time, accepting, like a king accepting his divine right, the fruits of those changes as a God-given right accruing from his ownership of the means of production.

For five years, Oren labored thus in this vineyard of his own choosing, shaping both the vineyard and himself toward the future. By dint of diligent effort he conquered his country speech patterns until all drawl and accent had been eliminated. His voice was a tool like everything else that lay ready to his grasp. He learned to talk like the businessmen and salesmen who were his constant associates; he did not forget how to drop back into the old rhythms and phrases when occasion called. He studied books on etiquette and social usage, though he had had, as yet, no opportunity to utilize the new knowledge.

Five years of shaping for the future, in which the nation also shaped itself. The country recovered from the panic of 1873; men talked of Boss Tweed's conviction, escape to Cuba and Spain, of his return and death; they were impassioned over the Tilden-Hayes presidential election and the Molly Maguires; they heard the news of the Little Big Horn and the death of Wild Bill Hickok, they talked of the great inventions of the telephone and the five-and-ten-cent store; some few people knew about Henry George and his single tax. At the end of the time, Oren came to the next step.

On the night before his twenty-first birthday, Oren Knox woke with words ringing in his mind. He lay still in his bed, looking up into the darkness, feeling the words as well as hearing them.

Don't keep on fighting the Bull; go around him.

That was all. No explanation how to accomplish the command. No instructions of how and where to begin.

The next morning he entered Mr. Fuller's office.

"Mr. Fuller," he said. "I'm twenty-one years old today."

"Well now, you don't say," Mr. Fuller said. He rose, extending his hand. "My congratulations, Oren. My heartiest congratulations."

"I've been working for you for five years now," Oren said. "You can't say I haven't done good for you."

"Yes," Mr. Fuller said with satisfaction. "I will have to grant that."

"During those five years I have never set foot in your house," Oren said.

"An oversight, my boy," Mr. Fuller said. "Strictly an oversight. We must have you to dinner one of these nights."

"How about tonight?" Oren said unblinkingly. "To celebrate my twenty-first birthday."

With scarcely a pause, Mr. Fuller said, "That's a splendid idea, Oren. Splendid. I will consult my daughter and the cook . . ."

"What time shall I come?" Oren said. "I suppose you dine late?"

"At eight," Mr. Fuller said.

"I will be there," Oren said. "Thank you, Mr. Fuller, for your kind invitation. I will be looking forward to it."

He left the office. To his surprise, his palms were damp again. Once out of sight of Mr. Fuller, he dried them angrily on his handkerchief.

VISTA: II

Amos: The Wayward Heart

TEMPLE'S STORE was located at Temple's Crossroads, twelve miles toward the Kentucky line from Jamestown, Tennessee. Ten more miles along the turnpike brought one to the state line itself. It was a region of gently rolling hills, known as the Black Patch, that lapped over the state line into Kentucky. The region was joined together by the kind of tobacco it grew, neither Burley nor Bright, but Dark Fired Tobacco. Dark Fired Tobacco, very close to the original Oronoko brought to North America from Bermuda or Cuba by John Rolfe, had broad, heavy leaves, green and strong. They were gummy to the touch. It went into snuff, natural chewing tobacco, and for export.

The people of the Black Patch were a special breed of people, as their tobacco was a special breed of tobacco. They were among the first to go beyond the Watauga settlement in the mountains that later became, temporarily, the Free State of Franklin. They had followed Daniel Boone down the Wilderness Road to Cumberland Gap, then turned northwest to the Bluegrass region of Kentucky. From the Bluegrass, where so many found the land preempted by grants and settlements, they had seeped steadily south and west into the Black Patch. They were a stiff-necked people, seeking autonomy beyond the Bluegrass in a country of their own. They found there the liberty of mind and of action that they sought and so, like their tobacco, they had remained close to what they had always been.

Temple's Store at Temple's Crossroads was an honest, matter-of-fact building behind its cheating front. The false front was high and square above the porch roof, concealing the roof line. The narrow boards that made up its pretence were painted with one coat of outside white; the balance of the building had never known the touch of a brush. Two windows in the high front admitted light into the big second-story room where extra stocks of merchandise were stored and where Amos had arranged his living quarters. Standing at the window, he could look down onto the bare surface of the hitching yard and, beyond, far down the two roads going north to Hopkinsville, Kentucky and east to Jamestown.

The front of the store was spanned by a deep porch, the floor boards scarred by feet and idle jack knives. Scarred wooden benches braced against the wall.

The store itself, behind the false front, had grown with the years. It rambled straight away in two or three additions, with sheds built along each side to hold grain sacks and large farm tools. If drinking was done at Temple's Store, it was performed surreptitiously in the subsidiary sheds.

A wide double door, flanked by heavily barred windows, led into the main store. By day, except in winter, the doors were swung open, the heavy window shutters pulled back and hooked to the sides of the building. The door jambs were mightily scarred and whittled. Drummers pulled down each other's signs and put up their own; sheriffs, auctioneers, and United States Marshals tacked their notices to them. Announcements of all-day singings with dinner-on-the-ground, brush-arbor revivals, and auction barn advertisements knew their seasons. There was also a discreet sign proclaiming that this building was a United States Post Office.

Inside the store, a potbellied stove in its sandbox dominated the geometrical center of the room. Next to the door, on the right hand, was the United States Post Office with its official oak partition, tied to the ceiling by bars made in the local blacksmith shop. Beyond the post office, long, homemade sectional counters extended all the way to the side-room door. Behind the counters were tilting bins to hold flour, rice, coffee, dried peas and other such items of luxury or necessity. There were also rows of heavy drawers with finger pulls in which to store all sorts of small merchandise.

Across the aisle was the glass showcase that was Mr. Temple's pride and joy. It was filled with fancy merchandise; ribbons, buttons, needles, collar buttons, self-tied four-in-hand ties, dollar watches and bottles of perfume, thimbles and corset stays. There were also showcases filled with an array of shirtwaists, paper collars, ladies' hats, trousers, stockings, herb tonics, talcum powder, black rubber nursing nipples and bottles of morphine.

The rear half of the store was crammed with hardware and heavy barrels of molasses, lard, salt, coffee, vinegar, coal oil and rice. There was no whiskey barrel because Mr. Temple, a temperance man, held principle above profits.

In one corner was a greasy counter bearing the mechanical cheese cutter and twenty-four-pound boxes of crackers. There were also bottles of pepper sauce, catsup and vinegar. Behind the counter were stacked the small cans of sardines, cove oysters and link sausage.

Both walls were lined with shelves. On the dry-goods side were bolts of cloth and oilcloth. There was a place for an assortment of schoolbooks, canned goods, medicine, spices, snuff and chewing tobacco and various cleansing agents. On top of one counter was the J. P. Coats cabinet, a walnut case filled with thread and trinkets. From the ceiling, all over the store, hung clusters of plow points, cedar water buckets, buggy shafts, wagon spokes, coils of rope and tobacco knives.

Temple's Store was Amos' new world, complete in itself, completing him. He had worked without pay for the first six months. Mr. Temple had been generous with him; indeed, Mr. Temple was a generous man. He was tall, with white hair and sharp blue eyes. His mustache, white also, drooped so luxuriantly that he drank his coffee from a special mustache cup with his name on it. He had a small paunch, unusual in that country where most men worked at hard physical labor of one kind or another. Temple's Store was already three generations old.

At the end of six months, Amos knew the stock better than Mr. Temple himself. It was no mean feat to carry constantly in his mind an inventory of the store, as well as the location of each item. The store was crammed with all the necessities and luxuries of living. The day he prevented Mr. Temple from ordering a new supply of chamberpots, telling him they had thirty in stock already, Mr. Temple put him on salary—one dollar a week.

"Pick you out some decent clothes, too," Mr. Temple said. "Any clerk of mine ought not to be wearing brogans and jeans britches."

Now, after two years, Amos was making three dollars a week. He wore a striped shirt with a white paper collar, a black alpaca coat, and sateen cuff protectors on his arms. He kept a pencil perched behind one ear, for much of the business was done on credit. From early morning to late at night he tended store, receiving the scribbled notes sent in by farmers too busy to come in person. He knew everyone in the trade area and the line of credit Mr. Temple allowed each; often he halved the order for flour or dried peas. But he always filled to the full the orders for coffee and tobacco. A man needed his vices.

Upstairs he had arranged one end of the big room for himself. He had built a bed out of scrap lumber in one corner and filled it with a cornshuck mattress. He had salvaged a battered dresser for his clothing. He had hung cheap outing cloth across the width of the room on a wire to enclose his private space. He ate his meals at Mr. Temple's house across the way.

He had a home, a job, a new and satisfying world of his own. He had almost forgotten that this was to have been only the first step in a lifetime of walking. He was content here—for Amos Haines was in love.

Perhaps the discontent would have remained, pushing him onward, if it had not been for the love that, filling his heart, had emptied it of all else. She was Virginia Temple, the oldest daughter of his employer.

Mr. Temple had fathered only daughters. Virginia Temple was nineteen, a year older than Amos, and she had never seen Amos, though he ate at their table three times a day. The first time Amos had seen her he had fallen helplessly in love. Whenever she appeared in the store for a spool of thread, a bit of ribbon, he waited on her tongue-tied, his hands and feet clumsy. He could feel the heat of his blood flushing through his face. She was kind, always kind; but he remained only her father's clerk, invisible to her eyes.

She was a pure marvel. She was tall, willowy, with a gay and laughing face. Her hair was the color of flame, her skin creamy white, without the hint of a freckle. When she crossed the road to the store to perform an errand, the sounds of the store hushed as the loafers and customers watched her progress with an intent regard. She greeted them all with equal pleasure, laughing, tossing her head so that the flame of hair flowed about her as though it must burn. They answered her in solemn, mumbled tones. The silence would reign until she had recrossed the road, even the men old beyond the hope of love watching her with intent mental lust until she had disappeared from sight. Even then it was a time before the normal beat of life could resume.

Amos loved deeply, hopelessly, irrevocably. He was her father's clerk, while red-wheeled runabouts behind spanking mares jingled all the way from Jamestown. Dozens of times he watched her mount gracefully into the seductive contraption and spin away, her laughter floating behind like a filmy gay kerchief.

There was one suitor, especially, whom Amos hated with a black heart. Roscoe Barnes was the son of a prominent leaf-dealer in Jamestown. His runabout was the most expensive of all, with the reddest wheels and the shiniest black body. His black mare with the four white feet was the most spirited. The mare seemed to skim disdainfully over the earth, drawing the light buggy behind her. Roscoe dressed with a natty air no other man in the county could achieve, with spats and cane and a derby hat.

Roscoe Barnes, to Amos, took Virginia's hand with a terrible familiarity when he steadied her into the runabout. He touched her hand as though he knew her whole body. Amos knew that, with Virginia, such a knowledge was impossible for any man. But Roscoe acted the knowledge anyhow, with a smirk on his face for everyone to see. Once, to his horror, Amos had seen Roscoe slip his arm around Virginia's tiny waist and lean to brush his lips against her cheek. Amos had clenched his fists, prepared to rescue her. But Virginia had laughed, turning her face away and tapping Roscoe with her folded fan.

Amos wondered how she could bear such a man. He wondered how her father could allow her to be seen with a rake such as Roscoe Barnes was known to be. His red-wheeled buggy flashed from girl to girl all over the county. More than once he had been waylaid by the boys of a particular community in an attempt to beat him up. The bright mare and his ready whip had always rescued him.

Amos was becalmed in this world of merchandise and love. He was valued here, counted on, treated almost as a son. He was contented; he wanted nothing more than that one day Virginia might see him, marry him, and that, after Mr. Temple had passed on in the inevitability of time, they might continue Temple's Store into a fourth generation.

It was a good way. He would hurt no one. He would not save the world from pain, either; but that could not be helped. His wayward heart had led him willy-nilly down this easy path. One day, he knew, Virginia must see him. Seeing him, she must also see his great love. Seeing love, she must love in return.

It was simple. He need only wait. He could wait if need be for the rest of his life.

Chapter Five

PROMPTLY at eight o'clock Oren presented himself at Mr. Fuller's place of residence. It was a big, new, two-story house, painted dark red with a white trim, the roof a dark green. It rested on a spacious corner lot, as yet looking coarse and unnatural in the raw new landscaping.

Oren was past the point of nervousness. He had committed himself so deeply to the event that he was able to negotiate the moment of entrance without difficulty. He placed his hat in the center of the square foyer table and followed the maid into the parlor where he was left alone for a time to contemplate the state of his soul.

The parlor was crammed with furniture. There were two rockers in the Morris style and an adjustable Morris chair with a padded sliding footrest. In addition there was another upright Morris chair, neither rocker nor adjustable; a parlor lamp; a parlor stove; two intricately carved tables; and over-all a scattering of cushions and whatnots filling every available space and surface. In one corner was an upright piano.

It was hot in the box-like room. Oren could feel himself sweating under the armpits. His purgatory was, however, short-lived;

the door opened and Mr. Fuller entered. He was wearing a black suit with piping on the edge of the vest. Oren had never seen him dressed so elegantly.

"Oren," Mr. Fuller said. They shook hands as though they had not taken leave of each other at the factory some two hours ago. "I am pleased to welcome you to my house, Oren."

"I am pleased to be here," Oren said in suitable tones.

Mr. Fuller turned. "May I present my daughter Trenholm," he said.

The girl entering the parlor was pleasingly plump, with an extraordinarily fair skin. Her hair was a soft ash blonde. She looked like a robust china doll, with a certain china-blankness in her features. Except for her eyes; they were a blaze of blue fire in her otherwise featureless face. They were wide apart, tilted exotically, and so intensely blue it was as painful to look directly into them as directly into the sun.

She was wearing a plum-colored dress that did its best to destroy the fine quality of her skin. The dress had a basque waist that came to a vee over the hips, accented by an elaborate bow. There was another bow just beneath her bosom, one indicating her knees, another just above the ankles. Whatever she wore beneath the dress rustled as she moved forward to greet Oren.

Oren took her hand. "I am pleased to meet you, Miss Trenholm," he murmured.

"Welcome to our home," she said. Her voice was as soft as her body. "Father has spoken so much about you, Mr. Knox."

Her hand was soft, too, rather small in the grasp of his own. He relinquished it without haste or regret.

"Shall we eat?" Mr. Fuller said, turning with ponderous slowness to lead the way.

Oren touched her elbow as they walked behind her father. He could feel the heat of her body warmth through the slight contact. He wondered if she was conscious of the grasp of his hand. She did not seem to be.

In the dining room, Mr. Fuller took his accustomed place at the head of the table, while Oren and Trenholm were ranged on each side of him. Trenholm picked up a small silver bell and tinkled it as a signal to the kitchen. Oren watched her remove her napkin from the ring, and did likewise.

The dinner was as dull and desultory as the conversation. Oren watched Trenholm for guidance in handling the elaborate service. Foster Fuller ate as stolidly as though he were alone. Trenholm kept her eyes on her plate throughout the meal, not once looking across at Oren. Oren studied her when he could, wondering what she was thinking. So far as he could tell, her thoughts were entirely on the progress of the meal, her small hand reaching forth at appropriate intervals to sound the silver bell, speaking once in a quiet voice to the serving maid.

Oren owned no small talk. As the next best bet, he addressed himself to Mr. Fuller on the subject of the day's problems at the factory. Mr. Fuller gave him little encouragement, only grunting in response. Trenholm made two remarks during the dinner, one on the present weather and one on tomorrow's prospect. When Mr. Fuller rose, to proceed once more into the parlor, Oren followed him with alacrity.

There they were served coffee and Mr. Fuller offered Oren a cigar, which he declined. They drank their coffee while Mr. Fuller smoked his cigar. Trenholm then appeared once more at the doorway to the parlor. The two men rose as she entered.

Trenholm went to the piano. She played in a tinkly, breathless style; her voice was thin and green. She favored them with three selections, then paused, her hands in her lap, without looking around.

"Thank you, Miss Trenholm," Oren said at last. "That was lovely."

It was, apparently, the signal she had been awaiting. She rose, saying, "Thank you, Mr. Knox." She came to them, while Oren and Mr. Fuller rose once more. She presented her hand, which Oren took into his own. "Goodnight, Mr. Knox," she said in her soft voice. "I hope you will come again."

"I shall look forward to it," Oren said. "It has been a delightful evening."

She exited, leaving the two men alone. Mr. Fuller looked at Oren thoughtfully, almost expectantly. He did not resume his seat in the adjustable Morris chair.

"Goodnight, Mr. Fuller," Oren said then and they shook hands again like strangers.

Mr. Fuller conducted him to the foyer, where Oren retrieved his hat. By ten-thirty o'clock he was once again in his own room at Mrs. Thompson's boardinghouse.

It did not matter. Oren had already made up his mind before he had presented himself to the Fuller household. With characteristic thoroughness, he had done everything except obtain a preview glimpse of Trenholm herself. He had learned that she was eighteen, an only child, and that her mother had been dead since she was twelve years old. She had attended a local academy for young girls until she was sixteen. She had no visible beaux and, seemingly, no friends of the same sex, though she called on, and was called on by, several young ladies who had attended the same academy. Her only outside activity, so far as he could determine, was her twice-weekly attendance at a local riding-school where she kept her own horse. Wearing a plum-colored riding habit, she rode rather well, mostly in the exercise ring but occasionally going out along one of the bridle paths.

The next morning Oren visited Mr. Fuller's office once again.

"Mr. Fuller," he said. "I want to thank you for that nice dinner last night."

"All right, my boy, all right," Mr. Fuller said with a wave of his hand. "Enjoyed it myself, as a matter of fact."

"Mr. Fuller, I would like to have your permission to call on your daughter," Oren said.

Mr. Fuller reared back in his chair. "Hadn't you better be getting her permission, instead of mine?" he said. "That's the modern way."

"I wouldn't presume to speak to her without your permission, sir," Oren said. "Do I have it?"

Mr. Fuller stared at him thoughtfully. Oren waited, without the least nervousness, while Mr. Fuller appraised him all over again.

"Oren, Miss Trenholm made one remark after you left last night," Mr. Fuller said. "She said, 'Your Mr. Knox is dull, Father.' "

The statement did not trouble Oren. "I think I might change her mind about that," he said stolidly.

"What have you got in mind?" Mr. Fuller said. "Are your intentions honorable, as they say?"

"If they weren't, I don't think I'd be talking to you, Mr. Fuller," Oren said. "I'd be talking to the young lady in question."

"She's not enchanted by you," Mr. Fuller said.

"I'll take that risk, sir."

Mr. Fuller waved his hand. "Go ahead, for all of me. See if you can talk her into it. Just don't let it take your mind off your work."

"No sir," Oren said. "I won't."

The following Saturday night, Oren was admitted to the Fuller house for the second time. Bearing a box of candy, he was ushered into the parlor. This time Mr. Fuller kept himself absent, Trenholm entering the parlor alone. The parlor door was open, the Negro cook perched solemnly on a straight chair in the foyer. Oren presented the box of candy as he and Trenholm sat in facing chairs. Oren had planned small talk this time, as carefully as he would have laid out an approach to an unknown tobacconist. But he found himself running dry rather sooner than he had expected. Trenholm sat unsmiling, her hands folded in her lap, helping him not at all. He wondered why she had consented to his call, returning her acceptance by the same messenger that had delivered his request for an interview.

At last he said, "Would you play some more of that lovely music?"

He ventured to stand beside the piano and turn the pages. The leavetaking was quite as formal. Deliberately, he did not ask for a repeat performance, nor did he dispatch his messenger until Wednesday of the following week. It was, again, accepted.

He passed every Saturday night for three months in that same stuffy parlor. Their conversations advanced little, though Oren heard more music than he had heard in all the rest of his life put together.

In spite of the stiffness, the formality, he learned Trenholm. He found in her a great passivity, like that of her father. The blankness behind her china features was actually a blankness. She remained quite comfortable in the midst of their recurrent silences. He had wondered, often, what her mind moved on during these times. So far as he could discover, it moved on nothing at all. She was quite capable of continuing the calls until they became as rigid a habit as her twice-weekly trip to the stables.

He was pleased by her passivity. There was only inertia to overcome. He was accustomed to directing people who had no direction of their own. A positive resistance could have defeated him.

He had a definite plan. He did not know whether or not he liked Trenholm, much less loved her. The thought of love had not entered his practical mind. He would have been abhorred at the prospect of committing himself to such a personal and worthless gambit. He intended to marry Trenholm. In time she would inherit the factory, and thus the factory would be his. In the interim, as Foster Fuller's son-in-law, he could proceed as if the factory were his already, because of the inert passivity of Foster Fuller himself. She was the true daughter of her father.

It bothered him, at times, that this passive, shallow girl stood in his way. Not deliberately; only by the fact of her existence. She was like a great boulder blocking the solitary trail up a mountain. He must give the boulder a momentum, and control the direction of the induced force.

After three months, he spoke to Mr. Fuller on a more serious theme.

"Mr. Fuller," he said. "I want your permission to ask Miss Trenholm to marry me."

"Well, well, Oren," Mr. Fuller said. "So you're actually making progress. Has she accepted you?"

"I haven't spoken to her yet," Oren said. "First I need your permission."

"Why?"

"I would not marry Miss Trenholm against your better judgment," Oren said. "I want your blessing upon us."

"I don't think she will give you the answer you want."

"I'll take that risk, sir."

"Go ahead, then. Ask her, for all of me."

That Saturday night, he did just that. He knew he should kneel, to fulfill her expectation. But he stood straight before her, as aware of the silent chaperone in the foyer as of Trenholm. He spoke.

"Miss Trenholm, I want to tell you that I honor and respect you beyond any woman on this earth. I have given you the love of my heart, which I have not given to any other woman in my lifetime. After sober consideration of the gravity of my words, I wish to request the honor of your hand in marriage."

He spoke the words, memorized from an etiquette book, in the proper way. She sat with her head bowed, her hands folded in her lap.

She did not look up. "Mr. Knox," she said. "I am aware of the weight of your meaning. I am touched by the honor and the respect you have displayed toward me this evening. I realize that in offering me your heart and your hand you have placed at my feet the greatest gift at your disposal. However, with deepest regret, I must decline your proposal of marriage."

He knew she had memorized her response, as he had memorized his proposal. He waited for her to look up. She did not do so.

"Do I have your permission to depart?" he said then.

"Yes," she said. "You have my permission."

He felt a sense of relief as he left the house. He had fulfilled the expected, painful though its constraint had been. With his obeisance to the traditional, he had now liberated Oren Knox; he could now, in this as in everything else, be himself.

He had confidence in his ultimate success, for he had confidence in Oren Knox. To the man he had created out of that fourteen-year-old boy, all things were possible; he stood in the center of a universe whose universal laws lay to hand like the levers of an intricate mechanism. He had studied that mechanism with the absorbed devotion of the fanatic. He looked always ahead, into the unknown, never into the past. Today's accomplishment meant little; there was always tomorrow.

On the tomorrow he descended once again upon Foster Fuller.

"Mr. Fuller," he said. "She turned me down."

"I was afraid of that," Mr. Fuller said.

Oren watched Mr. Fuller's face, wondering how he really felt about this matter of Oren Knox marrying his daughter. There was only a blankness, an interested expression that hid whatever feeling existed. Oren suspected that nothing existed behind the blankness. He did not understand passivity, neither in Mr. Fuller nor in Trenholm. How could one not care whether something happened or not? Well, here was another mountain to be moved.

"I reckon I've got myself into a sort of a box," he said in an apologetic voice, deliberately dropping back into the country rhythm of speech.

"What do you mean?"

"I can't go on working for you, Mr. Fuller. Here I put in all this time and now I got to let it go and start all over again somewhere else."

"Don't let Trenholm's decision disturb our relationship, Oren," Mr. Fuller said. "I don't hold anything against you, boy. You acted very honorably indeed."

Oren shook his head. "I wouldn't feel right," he said.

"You're not the kind of man to be bothered by something like this," Mr. Fuller said.

Oren detected a faint note of urgency in Mr. Fuller's voice. The mountain was beginning to shift just the minutest fraction toward concern and involvement.

"I would be in a false position," Oren said.

"How do you mean?"

"Well, Mr. Fuller, I had plans. I had it all laid out in my mind. I guess you'd call it brassy on my part, but ever since I went to work for you, I sort of figured like I was the son you never did have. I felt like I was working for myself, as well as for you. I know I didn't have any right to feel that way. But, right or not, I did."

Mr. Fuller looked up, a startled expression on his face. Oren plowed on.

"You can work out something mighty pretty in your own mind," he said. "After I saw Miss Trenholm, it was just as plain . . . us married, and me and you going on here at the factory, and me really your son, or at least son-in-law. Why, there ain't nothing we couldn't do. Now—I got to begin all over again."

"Are you going to start your own factory?"

The words blurted out of Mr. Fuller, revealing an involuntary fear. Oren, who knew he could not even consider such a thing, slowed his process to take in this unexpected revealment.

"I had thought on it," he said. "But just this morning I spoke to Mr. Howard."

Mr. Howard was the owner of the Two Hearts brand of smoking tobacco. His factory, smaller than the Fuller operation, was only a few blocks away.

"Mr. Howard has two sons of his own," Mr. Fuller said.

"Yes sir. John, the oldest, don't care for the tobacco trade. That I know. The other one . . ." He shrugged. "A man has to do the best he can."

"I knew all this courting was going to cause trouble the minute it started," Mr. Fuller said in a grumbling voice.

"I'm sorry, sir," Oren said with dignity. "I reckon a man can't help where his heart goes. The minute I laid eyes on Miss Trenholm I knew . . ."

"Those plans of yours," Mr. Fuller said.

"I had it all worked out," Oren said. "I had us a way figured to get out from under the shadow of old Bull Durham. As your son-in-law, and knowing I had your confidence to that extent, I was going to . . ." He stopped.

Mr. Fuller waited. Then he said, "Well? You were going to do what?"

"I reckon I better not go into details," Oren said slowly.

"Why not?"

"You can't ask me to, sir. After all, I won't be working for you. The ideas in my head are the only capital I possess. You can't ask me to give you all I've got to take into my new situation."

Mr. Fuller, with a peevish motion, pushed himself away from his desk.

"I'll talk to Trenholm," he said. "I don't want to lose you, boy. You know that."

"Yes sir," Oren said with dignity. "You and I, at least, have always understood each other."

"I'm not promising anything," Mr. Fuller said. "I'll talk to her, that's all. Will you give me the chance to do that?"

"Yes sir," Oren said.

"After all," Mr. Fuller said angrily. "She couldn't ask for a better man. I don't see them flocking around for her to choose from so high and mighty, either."

Oren never knew what passed between Mr. Fuller and his daughter. On the following two weeks he devoted himself diligently to his work. In the second week he was out of town. When he returned, Mr. Fuller met him at the station.

"Oren, she won't tell you to come back," he said. "But if you ask to call on her, I think she might consent to see you."

That Saturday night Oren, as of old, passed two hours in the Fuller parlor, turning the leaves of the music as she played and sang.

There was a stiffness beneath her politeness and her eyes did not seek his face once during the call. But the Negro cook no longer conducted her chaperonage from the hall. Oren was satisfied. When he left he took her hand, pressing it between his own.

"Next Saturday?" he said.

"Yes," she said with downcast eyes.

For three months more he pursued the even tenor of his courtship. He was punctilious, constant, considerate. He kept Mr. Fuller informed on progress and lack of progress; he fretted aloud almost daily that she would not have him, by this means courting the father more assiduously than the daughter. He made

Mr. Fuller a party to all his doubts and hesitations, allowing Mr. Fuller to bolster his confidence in the outcome.

Finally, one day, he told Mr. Fuller, "I can't stand it any longer, Mr. Fuller. Tonight I'm going to pop the question. I've got to know one way or the other. If she will have me, fine and good. If not . . ."

"Have you given her enough time?" Mr. Fuller said anxiously.

"I've given her all the time I can. If she won't say yes now, she never will. I've just got to know, that's all."

That night, in the parlor, he said simply, "Miss Trenholm, will you marry me?"

"Yes, Mr. Knox," she said. "I will marry you."

He took her hand into both his own. He leaned to kiss her. She turned her head and his lips only brushed her cheek. And so the marriage was made.

The wedding took place in July, in the Methodist church. It was a most satisfying wedding in all respects. The business community of Manchester was gratified at this aspect of continuity and common sense; everyone knew what Oren Knox meant to the Fuller Tobacco Factory and what the Fuller Tobacco Factory meant to Oren Knox. It was a formal alliance foreordained from the beginning of time; it was thus honored by substantial and tasteless wedding presents from all those approving of such things.

Mr. Taylor Tryon stood as best man for Mr. Oren Knox. The bridesmaids had been contemporaries of the bride at the local Academy for Females. The bride was suitably pale and beautiful as she stood beside her bridegroom. They were seen off from the reception with raw jokes and rice and when they found themselves on the train to New York, where they intended to spend their honeymoon, they had absolutely nothing to say to each other. Oren was glad that he had chosen to travel by parlor car rather than in a stateroom.

New York overwhelmed Trenholm with its noise and bustle. Oren busied himself with the baggage and with transportation.

Upon the recommendation of Taylor Tryon, he had chosen a modest, inconspicuous hotel. Out of a sense of delicacy, because he knew that he and his bride were strangers still, he had engaged adjoining rooms. He ushered Trenholm to her room.

"Rest well," he told her. "I will see you at dinner."

They dined in the hotel dining room. They had a table in a corner. Oren was appalled by the menu prices but he did not show it. He even ordered wine with the meal and they talked like strangers about the trip, about the strangeness of the great city. After the meal they could think of nothing to do but return to their rooms. Oren left her again at her door.

He had never owned a pair of pajamas or a bathrobe. He shaved, took a bath, and donned these new acquisitions. The pajamas were neatly striped Madras cloth, with pearl buttons and frog button loops. He had splurged on the lounging robe. It had cost seven dollars and fifty cents. Navy blue with gray stripes, it was double-breasted, with a rope-like belt ending in heavy knotted tassels. There was a rather Grecian border around the bottom of the robe, and the edges, pockets and collar were finished with silk piping. He wore bath slippers to match.

He knocked tentatively at the connecting door. No answer. He was suddenly afraid to enter the room. He could not recall being afraid; not for a long time anyway, not since he had become Oren Knox. He wiped his hands carefully on his pajamas inside the new robe and readjusted the robe. He knocked again. No answer.

He had never known a woman. He had never looked at a woman. Now, in the next room, a woman, his wife, Trenholm Fuller . . . no, Trenholm Knox . . . awaited his pleasure.

His pleasure. That thought steadied him. She was his wife. She could not deny him. His pleasure was her duty. He had never thought of it in just this way. The power of Oren Knox reigned here, as it reigned throughout his universe.

He knew quite well how he had acquired her as his wife. He had frightened Mr. Fuller with the prospect, not only of his departure from the factory, but, as well, of his competition in the tobacco trade. He did not know—he would never know—what

Mr. Fuller had said to his daughter. Whatever it had been, it had sufficed to overcome her inertia, even if there had been, in her placidity, none of the resistance he had at first expected to encounter. He had acquired Trenholm Knox with the same single-minded methodicalness he had used in setting himself up as a pinhooker and installing himself as the key man in the Fuller Tobacco Factory. She belonged to him, as did all his other possessions.

He put his hand on the knob, turned it. The door was not locked.

He entered. The room was dark. Through one window the lights of New York shone, giving a faint luminosity. He paused, adjusting his eyes, looking toward the bed. She would be waiting in the bed to serve his pleasure. I will be easy with her, he thought generously. After the first time it will be all right.

There was, even, a movement of warmth within him. It surprised him. He was grateful, not so much for her presence in this nuptial bedroom but rather for her acquiescence in furthering his plans. I will let her wait, even, if she wants to, he told himself. I will give her time to adjust. After all, I'm no stallion rearing for a mare.

"Trenholm," he said.

The bed was empty. Its emptiness jarred on him. Had she left the room, abandoned the marriage? She couldn't have done that. Why, she could never return to Manchester, she would be . . .

She came from her bathroom. She was wearing a white robe. It floated about her in the semi-darkness as she walked forward, to pause by the foot of the bed.

"Yes?" she said.

"May I come in?" he said, already advancing a few feet into the room. He hoped his nervousness did not show in his voice. He was, after all, a man . . . a man about to know his first woman.

"Yes," she said.

She came out of her pause at the foot of the bed, walked alongside the bed, her white gown floating ethereally about her. She turned back the spread and got into the bed, pulling the covers over her. He could not see her face in the distant-lighted darkness.

He advanced to the side of the bed. He let his weight down on the edge. The springs creaked, startling him.

"Trenholm, my dear," he said.

The words sounded strange in his mouth. She did not answer. He wanted to touch her hand, establish between them a fleshly communication. But he could not.

"Had you rather wait?" he said. "We don't have to hurry. Tomorrow night . . ."

"No," she said.

He detected a harshness in her voice. She wants to get it over with, he thought. She's frightened, because she's a woman and a woman's first time . . .

He rose to untie the sash of his robe.

"Mr. Knox," she said. "There's something you must know."

Her voice was harsher still, tauter. It went on without giving him time to speak.

"You are not the first," she said.

The words startled him into utter immobility. He stared down at her lying in the bed, the covers pulled up over the rounded form of her body.

"What?" he said stupidly.

"You're not the first," she said. "I made you not the first. Do you understand? I deliberately gave the first use of your new possession to another man."

He still could not react. "Why?" he said.

She did not move. She did not look at him across the darkness. The harshness had gone out of her voice; incredibly, it had resumed its usual placid, rather sweet tone.

"Because you didn't marry me for love of me," she said. "You married me for the factory."

"Who?" he said. The single word was an agonized sound in his throat.

"The stableboy at the riding stables," she said, in her sweet, penetrating voice that he could not shut out of his ears. "It was just last week, Mr. Knox."

"But why?" he said. "Why did you have to do such a thing?"

"Just once, Mr. Knox, I wanted to keep you from receiving value for value given," she said. "For once, I wanted to see you beaten in a trade. Because it *is* just a trade with you, Mr. Knox. You took Trenholm Fuller for the Fuller factory. It's a business deal."

Her voice ran out of the sudden rush of words. There was silence. He stood beside the bed, looking down at her. The incipient tenderness was withdrawn, the momentary warmth. He had felt generous toward her, anxious for her welfare. He had, for God's sake, even trembled with desire. Absently, he reknotted the tasseled ends of the belt.

"I did receive value for value given," he said. "I've got the factory, haven't I? That's all I ever wanted. You were only the liability I had to take on, like the mortgage on a piece of property. No, Trenholm—you didn't beat me in a trade. You only removed the liability."

He left the room. In his own room, he took off the new, expensive robe, folded it carefully into the seat of a chair, and went to bed. He was up at daylight, for on his honeymoon trip he had planned also to inspect the cigarette factories of New York.

No one knew it yet, aside from Oren himself, but, now that he was successfully a member of the Fuller family, he intended to begin the manufacture of cigarettes in Manchester, North Carolina.

VISTA: III

Amos: The Stubborn Heart

Amos was alone in the store when she came to him. Mr. Temple had gone to Jamestown early in the morning before the rain had started. Since midmorning the sky had wept steadily upon the earth and in the absence of customers Amos had devoted himself to catching up the ledgers and tidying the store. He had not even bothered to cross the road in the steady downpour for the noon meal.

He was surprised, therefore, when he heard her light footstep on the porch. He recognized in the thumping of his heart the sound of her walking and so he was prepared for her appearance in the doorway. She entered, lowering the still-open umbrella and shaking her head, holding it to one side, to free the raindrops caught in her flamelike hair.

In all the five years he had worked for her father, sleeping in the upstairs room of the store building and eating three meals a day with the family, he had never been alone with Virginia. Amos had thought her perfect at eighteen and nineteen and twenty. Each year seemed to bring her more greatly to her beauty and now, at twenty-two, she was in the perfect flower of herself.

Her younger sisters had already married; she seemed content

to laugh and flirt away her life, whirling away in the red-wheeled runabouts belonging to Roscoe Barnes and the other young men of the county. She had not yet seen Amos with the sight of her eyes; yet for all this length of time Amos had been becalmed in the Sargasso Sea of love for her bright beauty.

He could not remember when last he had thought about his original intention to use Temple's Store only as a way-stop along the road of higher ambition. He had not made a conscious decision in favor of Virginia Temple, of clerking in Temple's Store. He had simply known that it was impossible to go away from her. He did not have the audacity to bring himself to her attention; he could only believe, with all the depth of his love, that if he had the capacity to wait long enough the flame burning within him would light an equal flame of love within her.

"Why, Miss Virginia, what are you doing out in this rain?" Amos said.

He hoped his voice did not show his agitation. If so, she did not seem to notice. She placed the open umbrella carefully on the floor by the front door.

"I thought I might have a letter," she said.

Amos shook his head. "No mail for you, Miss Virginia," he said. "You know I would have brought it to you."

It was his self-imposed, onerous task, to bring her the love letters posted by her young blades.

She frowned prettily, tossing her head. "Shucks," she said. "I thought sure I'd have a letter today." She rid herself of the frown, as though indeed the prospective letter were a matter of small importance, and smiled brilliantly.

"I really wanted some candy, anyway."

He moved behind the showcase where the horehound drops and peppermint sticks were displayed. "What kind did you have in mind?"

"Oh, let me pick it out," she said.

She came behind the counter. They were close together in the narrow space and he could smell the faint perfume of her body as she leaned against him to peer into the case. His body suffused with unease, he waited stiffly for her decision.

She smiled at him, her voice appealing. "Should I have the peppermint?"

"The peppermint's good," Amos said, his voice feeling harsh and unused in his throat.

She put her hand on his arm in appreciation of his masterful decision. "I'll have the peppermint."

Her touch burned through the thin cloth of his sleeve. He snatched away his arm, afraid of betraying himself. She laughed a silver laugh and leaned to choose two peppermint sticks from the showcase. She put one into her mouth and, against his protest, prettily insisted that he take the other.

"I'm not supposed to eat the candy," he protested.

She laughed conspiratorially. "Who'll ever know?" she said. "We're alone here. And nobody will come on a rainy day like this."

She teased the stick of candy into his mouth. The peppermint taste was hot and sweet. He stood stiffly while she leaned against the showcase, sucking on her share of the candy and looking at him thoughtfully. She was a tall girl but she was not as tall as he, so she had to look up into his face. He wondered what she was thinking. She had never acted this way before to Amos. It was as though Amos were one of her beaux.

The thought made Amos exceedingly uncomfortable. He wanted to step away but the necessary effort seemed unduly conspicuous. He simply did not know what to do. He was mustering his courage to move when her voice shattered the resolution.

"Amos, did you ever kiss a girl?"

He blushed. "No . . . no. I never did kiss . . ."

"Would you like to kiss me?" she said demurely.

"Why . . . Miss Virginia . . ."

"Oh, shut up. And stop calling me Miss Virginia." She tilted her face. "Kiss me, Amos."

Tentatively, he leaned forward. Only their lips touched, sticky with the peppermint candy. Her arms, unexpectedly strong, went around his waist, pulling him against her. Her body was incredibly soft, warm, under the long dress. The kiss changed, mingled inextricably of peppermint and desire.

She took her mouth away. "My, you're strong," she said in a helpless, admiring voice. "You make a girl want to . . ."

Boldly, she took his hand, turned its palm, pressed it against her breast.

"Miss Virginia . . ." he said. "Somebody might come in. Somebody . . ."

He snatched his hand away. It was not his desire to touch her. He wanted to tell her about love, make the great declaration of his passion as it should be made. He had often thought about it, at night in his lonely quarters upstairs. He had worked out in his mind the exact words, her exact response. This was . . . this was something else.

"Virginia," he said. "There's something I want to . . ." She was not listening. She glanced toward the door. When she turned her eyes again to him they gleamed with a wantonness.

"Come on," she said.

She took his hand, leading him from behind the counter. He followed helplessly into the side room. She paused, glancing about. Still holding his hand, she went to the sacks of stock feed. Turning and looking up into his face, in two swift movements she bared herself from her waist to her knees.

"Lift me," she said.

He put his arms under her armpits, lifted her onto the low barricade of sacks. He stepped back. He could not look at her. He could not look away. The rain drummed steadily against the roof, dripped about the low eaves.

"Come on," she said impatiently. "Take down your pants, Amos."

There was a slight smile on her face as he obeyed. He could not fathom the expression. The desire she had shown in the kiss had vanished, as though it had never been. In its place was a determined wantonness he could not understand. His mind whirled. This that was happening between them was inexplicable. She was Virginia Temple, his beloved. She had led him by the hand into the side room, had . . .

"Come on," she said again, her voice edged with impatience at his stupid slowness.

He walked into her. She leaned back on her elbows on the sacks and now her lower lip was caught between her teeth. In his mouth was still the taste of peppermint. At first there was only the sensation; then there came into his mind the determination to alter the expression, composed of equal parts of contempt and self-satisfaction, on her face. Standing in the vee of her legs, he began the task of making her aware of him as a man, not just her father's clerk.

After a while, her mouth opened and she made a sound. She leaned toward him, gripping his shoulders with both hands. She was no longer merely receiving him. She was participating.

The peppermint taste lingered, the rain steadily fell. They were panting, joined together, abandoned into sensation. He was in control now, dominating her responses, and he revenged himself upon her for the initiative of her wantonness. When at last he came to the end, Amos collapsed over her, still submerged in her flesh.

After a time, her hands pushed him away. She slid down from the sacks and adjusted her clothing. With one hand she pushed at her hair.

"I knew you were strong, Amos," she said in a shaky voice. "But you . . ."

She laughed, pushing back her hair with both hands now, turned away as though suddenly shy.

He looked at her half-hidden face. "Why did you do that, Virginia?" he said quietly, out of the new strength he had found in the act.

She looked at him, quickly, giving him only a glimpse of her face. She was still turned away.

"I reckon we'll have to get married now, Amos," she said after a slight pause. "After you do a girl like that . . ."

He had yearned to hear the words for years. Now they dropped into a great listening silence.

"Why do you say that?" he said.

She came close, then, leaned against him, one arm around his waist. "My Amos," she said. "You love me, don't you, Amos? Haven't you loved me for a long time?"

"Yes," he said. "I have loved you."

"I reckon I just found out I loved you." She squeezed his waist with her arm. "We'll be married, Amos, and then we'll be together all the time." She shivered, standing huddled against him, a little girl in need of protection.

"You never saw me before today," he said. "Yet you come to me in the rain and . . ."

"I was a foolish girl," she said. "Wasn't I a foolish girl, not to know all the time that you were just waiting for me to come to my senses?"

He put his hands on her shoulders, holding her away from him. "I wasn't the first," he said.

She hid her face behind her flaming hair. "You shouldn't say things like that to a girl," she said. She smiled, moving her body against him. "Do you want to again, Amos? It's still raining."

A cold certainty moved in his mind. It surprised him, both by its coldness and by its sureness. Looking into her eyes, he read the truth as plain as if it had been written in large print.

"Virginia, you're knocked up, aren't you? And Roscoe won't marry you."

She tossed her head in quick anger. "What are you talking about? I may be *now,* after you . . ."

"You're carrying his child," Amos said. "He turned you down. So you decided you could play a little rainy-day game with me and then I would fall over myself for a chance to marry you."

"You *want* to marry me, don't you?" she said. Her voice showed, now, nakedly, the tinge of desperation that had underlain her every move and word since she had entered the store.

"I've loved you since I first set eyes on you," he said. "You knew it all the time, too. So you picked on me to take the fatherhood for another man's child." Fury rose suddenly in him. "You thought I was an idiot. You thought you could walk in here and make me drop my britches and I would be so grateful . . ."

He pushed her away, against the sacks.

She rose up. "Roscoe Barnes never had what you've just

had," she said, her voice crying out indignantly. "What makes you think I'm fixing to have a baby? That's just an idea you've got in your head. Just because I let *you* . . ."

The denial came too late. He knew the truth as well as if she had admitted it. His face showed his knowledge and the open knowledge stopped her protest.

"You've got to marry me, Amos," she cried out. She put her hands over her face, weeping. "I don't know what I'll do if you . . ."

He looked at her, seeing her hard and clear. In his memory were all her laughing departures in all the red-wheeled runabouts, the flirt of her body, the tap of her fan. And, along the lonely roads, her body and the bodies of the men clinging hotly together. Until nature had trapped her in the trap of her own making. Only then had she turned to him, setting that same trap for his flesh. He turned away.

He had reached the door before her voice stopped him. He turned. She was standing in the middle of the room. Her hands were clenched at her sides. Her face was paper-white beneath the flaming hair.

"Are you going to marry me, Amos?" she said.

"I'm going to make a doctor," he said. He used the words. They did not encompass his meaning. The true meaning was the outrage, the insult and, most of all, the disillusionment. He could not find the words for these.

"I'll tell Papa it was you," she said wildly. "He'll take a shotgun and make you marry me. Papa will believe me. Just you wait and see. You'll have to marry me, whether you want to or not."

In the mist of his hurt, her own desperate hurting touched him in spite of himself.

"Tell Mr. Temple I'm responsible, if it'll help any," Amos said, out of that kindliness that could not bear any hurt of the world. "I won't be here anyway."

"You're like every other man," she said bitterly. "I didn't notice you turning me down. You took what I had to offer. Then you could afford to turn noble."

"Yes," he said sadly. "I am like every other man; and that's not much. You think I don't know that? But it's all I've got, so I have to do the best I can with it, not the worst."

She collapsed suddenly in the middle of the floor. He looked down at her, realizing with that stubborn fixed heart of his that this was the last gambit to bring him to her side. He looked, and turned away, and left the world of Temple's Store, of Virginia Temple, the world of his wayward heart.

It was still raining as he went down the road to Jamestown, carrying in one hand all the possessions he had gathered so far in his pilgrimage.

Chapter Six

OREN KNOX cut his honeymoon short by several days. He was anxious to return to Manchester for a number of reasons; not least important was the fact that he had not as yet set foot in the factory in his new capacity as son-in-law to the founder. There were other reasons, too. He had spent every day in New York in visiting cigarette factories, leaving Trenholm to her own devices while he talked with men knowledgeable in the trade, while he inspected to the extent he was allowed to inspect, while he formulated his plans to go around the Bull.

He treated Trenholm with a grave consideration. Each night they dined in the hotel dining room and once he took her to a noted restaurant. She was delighted; he was bored.

The crucial matter did not arise again; each night Oren bade her farewell at the door to her room, retiring to his own quarters. Not once did he contemplate rapping at the connecting door. He had put that phase of the marriage behind him as definitively as he had discarded the idea of a successful competition against the Bull in his own pasture. When he handed Trenholm down from the train at Manchester, to be greeted by Mr. Fuller, one could not have guessed that they were not man and wife.

It had been decided that it would be foolish for Oren to establish another household, leaving Mr. Fuller alone in the big new house. So they went directly home, Trenholm entering the front door in the same condition as when she had gone away. But Oren was different; where before he had been a caller, his hat in his hand and a box of candy under his arm, he was now a member of the family. He held the door for Trenholm and Mr. Fuller to enter. There was a slight contretemps. Trenholm's bedroom had been prepared for both of them with the substitution of a big double bed.

Oren had to make a delicate statement of conditions. "Trenholm and I have decided to occupy separate rooms," he told Mr. Fuller. "I often work late at night, and the light disturbs her."

"Oh, you won't be working late any more," Mr. Fuller said jovially. "You're a married man now."

"I've still got a factory to run," Oren said seriously. "I've still got the Bull to beat. It takes the midnight oil, Mr. Fuller. Now I'm living in the same house with you, you'll find out how much."

It was arranged for Oren to have a room across the hall. That first night, Oren entered her room with Trenholm. She stopped just inside the door, as though fearful he intended to press his marital rights now that they were home and she could not protest too actively.

"I must have a talk with you," he said in a reassuring voice.

"What is there to talk about?"

"Us," he said. "What else?"

She turned away. "There's nothing to say. I know about you. You know about me."

"That's what I want to get straight," he said patiently. "Sure, I married you because of the factory. I know that. You know that. I was fond of you—but the factory was the main reason. I don't try to deny it. I don't know why you married me."

She turned on him. "Do you want to know why?" she said. "Because Father kept on and kept on after me. Every night he said in a voice of doom, 'Well, Oren is going to leave. He's all that's keeping us going, Trenholm. Oren is so disappointed in love he has to leave if you won't have him in marriage. I don't know what we'll do without Oren.' "

"You still didn't have to do it."

"Do you think he'd have let me marry anybody else? Even if there had been someone else? I'm eighteen already."

Oren watched her. "We can call it off," he said. "There *is* such a thing as a divorce."

"Divorce!" she said. "Do you think I intend to go through a scandal like that?"

"I was prepared to be a good husband to you, Trenholm," he said.

"Mr. Knox," she said. "I was not prepared to be a good wife to you."

"I don't see that the situation is so bad, Trenholm. After all, to the eyes of the world, you're a married woman now. You can take your place in the society of Manchester. No one will know the truth but you and me. I will be able to work out my plans for the factory. We know that the factory will go on, now, as it should go on."

"But what about . . . will you want . . ."

"Just put that thought out of your mind, Trenholm," he said quickly.

She paused, regarding him. "Mr. Knox," she said. "You are a strange man."

"Then it's all right . . . the arrangement, I mean, and . . ."

"If you are satisfied, I am satisfied. You have your factory. I have . . . I am a respectable married woman."

"You will have from me all the honor and respect due you, Trenholm," he said. "I promise you that. I will never by word or deed betray your position as my wife."

"I make the same promise, Mr. Knox."

Oren held out his hand. She took it. They shook hands like two businessmen sealing a bargain that both believe to their advantage.

"I will go now," Oren said. "I must talk to your father. Good night, Trenholm."

"Good night, Mr. Knox."

Downstairs, he found Mr. Fuller on the front porch. "Is Taylor Tryon in town?" he said. "We must have a talk, all three of us. Tonight."

"Yes, I believe so," Mr. Fuller said. "He was going to Atlanta, but I don't believe he intended to leave until the morning train."

"Let's send someone around to fetch him," Oren said. "I learned a lot in New York, Mr. Fuller. And it's the sort of thing we can put to use."

Within thirty minutes Taylor Tryon had arrived and the two men were watching Oren expectantly. Oren knew inside himself the curious tension that came in moments like this. It had never been enough to go alone; he had needed always to carry other men with him. It was both stimulating and frustrating.

"Let's go inside," he said.

He led the two men into the overcrowded parlor. He put his hand into his pocket and drew out a paper packet, concealed by his fingers until he placed it on the table between them.

"Gentlemen," he said. "Let me show you our future."

He withdrew his hand. He watched their eyes fall on the elegant little package of cigarettes.

Taylor Tryon looked up at Oren. "Cigarettes?" he said.

"Cigarettes," Oren said firmly. "That's how I spent my spare time in New York, in Bedrossian Brothers factory, mostly, but in all the factories where I could swing a visit."

Taylor Tryon laughed. "I think marriage has gone to his head, Mr. Fuller," he said. "We're smoking-tobacco men."

"And the Bull is starving us to death," Oren said. "Every time we find some grass, he runs us right out of the pasture. My mind is made up, gentlemen. Cigarettes are the coming thing."

"Why, nobody smokes cigarettes but foreigners and New York dudes," Mr. Fuller said. He shook his head. "I think you've made your first mistake, Oren. Why, we don't even know how to *make* cigarettes. I say stick to what we know."

"I know how to make them," Oren said. "What do you think I went to New York for?"

"Well now," Tryon drawled humorously. "I thought you went up there on a honeymoon. I'd've sworn a wife got on the train with you."

Oren did not favor him with a glance. "Mr. Fuller," he said. "I want your go-ahead. Right now. Tonight. There's no time to waste."

"I can't see it, Oren," Mr. Fuller said. "Why, where are you going to get all that Turkish tobacco? It'd cost you a fortune. Here we are, sitting right in the middle of the biggest tobacco-growing country in the world, and you're aiming to import tobacco to make cigarettes with."

"We won't make them with Turkish. We'll use good old North Carolina bright leaf . . . just like our smoking tobacco. We'll mix in a little Turkish to give it the aroma that cigarette smokers want. We'll start off high on Turkish and then taper off. Folks will like the bright leaf when they get used to it."

"Now, how do you expect to roll bright leaf into a cigarette?" Taylor Tryon said. "You've got the granulated smoking tobacco. You try to roll that into a cigarette, and what have you got? It doesn't even *look* like a cigarette!"

"I saw a cutter in New York that does the job," Oren said. "The Pease Rotary Cutter. It doesn't cut the tobacco into little bits, it shreds the leaf so you've got a long cut. Here, let me show you."

He opened the pack of Jockey Club cigarettes, took one out. He broke open the paper and poured the tobacco into the palm of his hand.

"See that? That's your Pease cutter for you." He let them study the tobacco. "You think there isn't bright leaf in that cigarette? You just bet your boots there is. Bedrossian Brothers has been using bright leaf in their cigarettes for some time."

"Who are these Bedrossian Brothers?" Tryon said.

"They're a couple of Armenians who have a factory in New York. They make a whole line of brand cigarettes . . . Jockey

Club, Turkish Elegantes, Neapolitan. They're nice people, even if they are foreigners. They let me see everything."

"Did they know you were planning to manufacture cigarettes?" Tryon said dryly.

Oren looked at him. "Well, no. They got the idea I was interested in opening up a wholesale commission house in Richmond to sell cigarettes throughout the South." He turned to Mr. Fuller. "Well, Father," he said. "What about it?"

It was the first time he had used the familial expression. It startled Mr. Fuller.

"I don't know," he said uncertainly. "It's all so new and strange. We're doing pretty well as we are. Maybe we ought to wait a while. If other people begin to make a success with cigarettes, we can go into it in a small way, maybe, later on. It's pretty risky, the way you're thinking of doing it, Oren."

"If we're going into cigarettes, now's the time to do it," Oren said urgently. "In Richmond, Lathrop and Winter are already making and selling Dominion Straight Cut and Brights. We don't want to wait until they dominate cigarettes like Bull Durham dominates smoking tobacco." He turned to Taylor Tryon. "If I make 'em, can you sell 'em?"

Taylor Tryon took his cigar out of his mouth, looked at it, clamped it between his teeth. "I can try," he said dubiously. "I don't know many people who smoke cigarettes . . . like Mr. Fuller said, it's mostly foreigners and New York dudes. We don't have many of that breed of cat in our territory."

"Gentlemen," Oren said. His voice was solemn and direct. "Our biggest job will be to create the demand for cigarettes. You've seen how smoking tobacco has cut into the plug tobacco business. Cigarettes will cut into both. We've got to make it so, whether it'll come true naturally or not. Why? Because it's a new area. It's as simple as that. We can't expand in smoking tobacco because of Bull Durham. If we went into plug, we'd meet entrenched competition that's just as strong as the Bull is in smoking tobacco. Cigars we can't think about because we don't have the leaf for cigars. That leaves cigarettes." He leaned over the table. He picked up the Jockey Club pack in one hand, held it out to the two men. "Here is our future, gentlemen. If cigarettes remain the property of foreigners and New York dudes, we might as well have stayed in hardware and pinhooking. If we can make cigarettes as American as apple pie—then we will have made our fortunes."

"But *how* are you going to make them?" Mr. Fuller said. "Nobody around here knows how to roll cigarettes, Oren. Do *you* know how? Even if you do, can you teach enough people . . ."

"Next week," Oren said. "A man named Alex Michael will get off the train in Manchester. He's a Russian Jew and he's the best cigarette roller I saw up there. He's a man with sense and some education, so I hired him to recruit rollers and bring them south. He'll have fourteen skilled rollers with him."

"Michael?" Tryon said.

"I reckon he chopped off about two-thirds of his name," Oren said impatiently. "So folks could pronounce it."

"You're bringing Russian Jews to Manchester?" Mr. Fuller said in a worried voice. "Importing foreigners when our own people . . ."

"I need expert rollers," Oren said. "Our own people can't do the job. Alex Michael and his friends can. They'll be here next week and we have to be ready for them. I'll clear space in the factory for the Pease Rotary cutter and for the rolling tables. I'll have to arrange for packaging, and invent some brand names. Guess we could use O.K. Durham right on, but we'll need a couple more. Taylor, I want you to get ready to sell cigarettes. You can start by stopping the use of cigars yourself."

"Quit smoking cigars?" Tryon said.

"You can't expect to walk into a tobacco shop and sell cigarettes while you're puffing on a Havana," Oren said.

"What are your plans for selling?"

Oren frowned. "We'll talk about that later. Production first. Get 'em made, we'll have to sell them. I'll tell you one thing—I aim to advertise like Bull Durham does. Everywhere you look, you'll see our cigarettes displayed. We'll work out a campaign."

"All the advertising in the world won't make the commission

merchants and jobbers stock quantities of cigarettes," Tryon said.

"We're going straight to the retailer and the consumer," Oren said. "We've got to start on rock bottom, Taylor. Make the consumer want them and the retailer will stock them. Make the retailer stock them and the commission man will want a piece of the business." He frowned. "Maybe by then we won't need the thieves at all. That's something I'd like to see happen."

Taylor Tryon looked from Oren to Mr. Fuller, back again. "So it's cigarettes, I guess," he said.

"Oren seems to have his mind made up," Mr. Fuller said. He laughed. "Besides, what would he do with his fifteen Jews if we didn't agree?"

"Yeah," Taylor said. "What *would* you have done, Oren? Paid their fare back to New York—or charged them for their Southern holiday trip?"

Oren looked at his father-in-law, at his star salesman. "I was going to rent me a building and go into business for myself," he said, slowly. "That's how much I believe in the cigarette."

More conversation ensued, but the matter was decided. Taylor Tryon left, for he had to catch an early-morning train. After he was gone, Mr. Fuller and Oren strolled out on the porch for another breath of fresh air.

"Would you have really left my employ, son?" Mr. Fuller said.

"Yes," Oren said.

"Why?"

"Because cigarettes are our only chance. How many ways of using tobacco are there? Five—using snuff, chewing plug, smoking a pipe or a cigar, or smoking a cigarette. The Indians in olden times invented all the ways of using tobacco there is. Bull Durham has got smoking tobacco sewed up, and we'd meet established competition just as bad in snuff and plug. It takes the Havana leaf to make a good cigar. Cigarettes are still marginal—and that gives us our chance. We can take the risk that other manufacturers, established in a profitable line, can't afford to take. It's our only chance."

He stopped, looking out across the sleeping town.

"Mr. Fuller," he said. "I aim to take the cigarette and build me a kingdom. The way Bull Durham is in smoking tobacco ain't gonna hold no candle to the way Oren Knox will be in cigarettes. I wanted to do it with the Fuller factory. But if I had to do it alone, I was prepared to cut my own way."

Mr. Fuller did not answer. They stood silent for a time in the darkness.

"Father," Oren said then. "I'm asking one thing more. I've been a salaried man for five years. I want a piece of the business. I want the sign on the front of that factory to read FULLER AND KNOX."

"All right," Mr. Fuller said. "I reckon you are entitled to it. It's all in the family, anyway."

"We'll still make the smoking tobacco, of course," Oren said. "But let's make the name read FULLER AND KNOX CIGARETTE COMPANY."

"I'll see to it," Mr. Fuller said. "The lawyer will draw up the papers tomorrow. In the meantime, you see to the new sign."

"Good night, Father," Oren said.

"Good night, son."

Oren went upstairs. When he entered his room he did not pause even for a moment to glance at the closed door to his wife's bedroom across the hall.

The top floor of the Fuller and Knox Cigarette Factory was in bedlam. On the two lower floors, the accustomed manufacture of smoking tobacco continued at its usual pace. On this floor, fourteen highly-paid handrollers stood by while Oren Knox and their compatriot production foreman labored to get them to work. For two days they had been idle while men swarmed through the room, installing the new Pease cutting machine and the tables for the rollers.

Today, at least, the Pease rotary cutter was in operation. It had already shredded an ample supply of tobacco. But the carpenters were still installing the long tables where the handrollers would work. They had been installed once but the production foreman, on his first visit to the factory, had disapproved the arrangement and they had been torn out. The production foreman, his vest open, his sleeves pushed up to his elbows, worked alongside Oren to complete the preparations.

When Alex Michael had led his troupe of cigarette rollers off the train in Manchester, it was difficult to tell who was more aghast; the city of Manchester or the handrollers themselves. They had clustered close together in the strangeness of the city, clutching the handles of their suitcases as though fearful someone would steal them. The sounds of their voices were exceedingly foreign.

They wore dark clothing, some wore heavy beards, and their black hats were wide. They were short, swarthy men, who looked even shorter and swarthier under the weight and blackness of their hats.

The stationmaster, watching them, said to his porter, "I reckon you better go tell Oren Knox his Jews have done got here. Tell him he better hurry up or somebody might steal 'em from him—that is, if anybody else in this town got any use for a foreign Jew."

"Who is them strange folks, anyhow?" the porter said. "They look mighty odd to me."

"Come to think of it, we probably look pretty odd to them," the stationmaster said. "I reckon it's all what you're used to. Go on now. If a train come through here going North, I reckon they'd pile on it before you could stop 'em, and Oren Knox would be out another way of making a dollar."

There was no need to fetch Oren. He entered the train station, hurrying directly to the alien cluster of men. The world of Manchester watched as he shook Alex Michael's hand.

Alex Michael was not a young man—neither was he old. He wore a black suit, with a vest, made out of a heavy woolen material. His shirt had blue stripes and a white collar and there was an opal stickpin showing above the vee of his vest. Unlike the others, he was bareheaded, his hair laid straight across the top of his head from the part. His nose was broad, strong, with a deep ridge of flesh running from the flanges diagonally past the corners of his mouth. His hands were slender, nimble, stained with tobacco. His ears were high on his head and his eyebrows were heavy, black, straight across the brow-ridge.

"Well, I see you made it," Oren said, pumping his hand again. "We're nearly ready for you. I think you all can go to work tomorrow."

"Yes sir," Alex Michael said. "We are here." He glanced around at his men. "Some of us are wishing we had not come."

To the ears of Manchester, his voice was guttural-sounding, with strange inflections. Oren tilted his head and leaned forward to catch his meaning more clearly. It was not that Alex spoke bad English; indeed, his English was better than that habitually spoken in Manchester; but the accents and emphases were misplaced. Even the rhythm was different.

One of the men, pressing urgently forward behind Alex, said something.

"What did he say?" Oren said. The words had been English, but they had been completely unintelligible to his ears.

"He asked if there was a men's room," Alex said.

"Tell him we'll be at your boardinghouse in ten minutes," Oren said. "Tell 'em to come on."

He led them out of the station. They walked down the main street, passing through the principal business block. Heads turned to watch. Alex marched beside Oren, his eyes unflinching as he gazed on this strange Southern town to which his destiny had now fetched him. Behind him straggled the fourteen men whom he had persuaded to accompany him to the South.

Alex Michael had been born in Kovno, Russia. His family, driven from Russia by one of the countless pogroms, had fled to England while he was still a boy. He had been apprenticed to the cigarette trade in London. When he had reached manhood, he had himself emigrated to America.

His America was like London; indeed, rather like Kovno itself. As in all his life before, he heard more spoken Russian than he did English. Where he lived, where he worked, where he went for a drink after work, he was surrounded by Russian-Jewish talk and thought and laughter. Their minds leaned back to the old time, the old country.

Alex felt that this was wrong. Here was America, a new place and a new time for a new people. He attended night school, studying assiduously in his spare time. He put the old world of London and that more shadowy world of Kovno behind him. When a man named Oren Knox asked him to come to a place called Manchester, North Carolina to aid in the installation of a cigarette factory, he had felt that this door had been unlocked with the key of all his study and yearning.

Now he was afraid. But there was the familiar work. He jumped into the work as he had jumped into the opportunity. For a double reason; he knew that, the longer his fourteen men had leisure to speak fearfully among themselves about the strangeness of this place and these people, the better the chance they would desert homeward into their known world. He was a Christopher Columbus yearning for the sight of land in order to quell mutiny in the ranks.

"All right," Oren said. "Think that'll satisfy you?"

Alex surveyed the room. "Yes," he said. "Now we will begin."

He motioned to his fourteen men. They filed into place, taking off their coats. Each sat on his stool, putting his hands on the work surface before him. Alex nodded to Oren.

"Now we are in business," he said.

Oren turned. "All right, boys, start moving the tobacco to the tables," he said. "Let's go now. Look sharp!"

In a few minutes, with no fanfare, the cigarette factory was in operation. The expert rollers, fifteen in number counting Alex, began operations by fitting the cigarette paper into the small trench, the length of a cigarette, that was grooved into the table and putting a pinch of shredded tobacco on the paper. The other hand, gloved with a strip of felt over the palm, swept over the trench, catching up the protruding edge of the paper and whirling the cigarette into shape in one deft motion. The other hand reached synchronously for the paste that sealed the paper tube.

There was a number at each place, with a numbered can that

held three pounds of tobacco, sufficient for a thousand cigarettes. The roller had to show a thousand finished cigarettes for each can of shredded leaf; the count was strictly kept in order to control costs and wages, since they were on piecework. Each roller could average four per minute, with the exception of Alex Michael, who occasionally would leave his place to expedite the work, to run a random count on his own, and for general supervision of the quality of the output. Fifteen men rolling approximately twenty-four hundred cigarettes a day gave the Fuller and Knox Cigarette Factory a weekly production of fourteen thousand, four hundred cigarettes, or fourteen hundred packs of tens.

Oren watched the operation for a time before retiring to his office, the figures busy as acrobats in his head. The weekly production of cigarettes was worth three hundred and seventy-eight dollars at wholesale. The rolling cost worked out at forty-eight cents a thousand, or one hundred and three dollars and sixty-eight cents. Say all other costs worked out at about thirty-two cents a thousand—he knew that was close—that would be seventy dollars per weekly production. So he would show about two hundred dollars a week clear profit. Multiply that by fifty-two weeks and you got ten thousand, four hundred dollars. Of course, that was a rough estimate . . . but not too rough.

He contemplated the figures with satisfaction. That was with only fifteen rollers. It figured out at six hundred ninety-three dollars and thirty-three cents profit per hand per year. Say you built up to two hundred rollers, yet held your profit per hand to a minimum of five hundred dollars. He contemplated the figure with awe. One hundred thousand profit a year.

If he could sell the cigarettes. Looked at from the production end, fourteen hundred packs of tens was nothing. Looked at from the sales end, it seemed an enormous number to move weekly. It would take some doing, all right.

If necessary, he would curtail daily production to a thousand cigarettes a man while he opened up the market. Frowning, he went over his figures once again. There was one thing sure; the cost of rolling was the outstanding figure. Forty-eight cents a thousand. That would have to come down. There was nothing he could do about it for the present; he had to have the expert rollers. Without them there would be no cigarette production at all. But it would be worthwhile to keep his eye on that item.

If only someone could perfect a practical cigarette machine. It was being tried, he knew, by innumerable inventors. That was all right for impractical visionaries; he would begin to think in that direction when he saw one of them actually turning out cigarettes.

One thing he could do, as soon as the rollers had settled down to their production. He had already discussed with Alex Michael the plan to hire a local girl to match each imported roller. They would set them up side by side so each roller could teach each girl. When they were taught, they would be moved to another floor and a new batch of fifteen apprentice girls brought in. Alex didn't like the idea—there was nothing stupid about Alex Michael—but he understood, too, that, as they expanded production, Oren couldn't rely on a steady importation of rollers from New York. There had been trouble in finding the original fifteen willing to leave their accustomed surroundings for this barbaric southland.

Oren rose from his desk, walking toward the cigarette floor. On the way he met Taylor Tryon, returned from his drumming trip.

"How's it going?" Taylor said.

"Come up and see," Oren said. "We finally got into production."

They went up together. Oren opened the door onto the cigarette floor. No one looked up at their entrance. The flow of work was beginning to run smoothly now, the white cylinders piling up beside the rollers. They were quiet men, withdrawn, hunched over their work, busy in the intricate patterns of making, as though their hands were disembodied from their minds.

Alex Michael looked over at Oren and nodded. He too was rolling now, lifting his head occasionally to survey the working area, rising occasionally to attend to his foreman-duties.

"Well," Taylor Tryon said. "Now I have seen the elephant."

Oren led him to the packaging table. He picked up one of the flimsy paper packs and handed it to Taylor.

"What do you think of it?" he said.

Taylor Tryon looked down at the gaudy label. "O.K. DURHAM CIGARETTES," it said. The shy girl still peeped around the leg of the K.

"Don't you need an oriental brand name?" Taylor said. "Most cigarettes . . ."

"We'll make an oriental brand later on," Oren said. "If we have to. We want to sell an American brand, Taylor. We've got to make the cigarette as American as corn whiskey." He took the pack from Taylor, broke it open. "Here," he said. "Try one. It's mostly bright leaf. Just a little Turkish mixed in. After we get folks to smoking it, we'll cut down on the Turkish and step up the bright leaf. Before they know it, they'll be smoking bright leaf and liking it, claiming it's the best cigarette in the world."

Taylor Tryon struck a match, lit it. He drew on the cigarette, blew the smoke out through his nose. He coughed.

"It tastes like hell after a good cigar," he said. "It'll be hard to switch your cigar man, Oren."

"Smoke 'em for a week, a cigar will be too strong for you," Oren said. "Here—take the pack. That's your smoke from now on. O.K. Durham Cigarettes."

"You really mean that about giving up cigars?"

Oren tucked the pack into Taylor Tryon's coat pocket. "That's your fortune, there in your hand," he said. "You're not going to let a little habit stand in your way, are you?"

Taylor Tryon drew on the cigarette again. "I guess you *could* get used to it," he said. "Awful dry, though, in comparison to . . ."

"Smoke O.K.," Oren said. "Sell O.K. Then you'll be O.K. And we've got a lot of 'em to sell, Mr. Tryon. Right at fifteen thousand cigarettes a week . . . fourteen hundred boxes. Think we can do it?"

"I can sell anything," Taylor said belligerently.

"All right," Oren said. "Let's get at it. Those fellows there . . ." He waved his hand at the rollers. "Those fellows there are breathing down our necks right now."

Chapter Seven

OREN found himself on the road once again, drumming the South for his new product. He had expected the network of jobbers and dealers he had built up behind O.K. Durham Smoking Tobacco to be of great value to the new venture. But on Taylor Tryon's first swing around the territory, only two of the regular dealers would take on the cigarettes. Oren intensified the premium approach, giving the dealers more reason than ever before to buy and stock the Fuller and Knox product, but even that did not help much.

From Atlanta, he wired Manchester to cut production to fifteen hundred cigarettes a week per roller. He knew he was giving Alex a difficult task, for the rollers were like the tobacco-growers—they felt a compulsive necessity to operate at the total limit of production. It did not matter, to them, that the cigarettes were piling up in the warehouse.

After he had sent the message, he walked down Peachtree to call on a new tobacco shop that had just opened. At the corner of Peachtree and Marietta Streets, a blank space on the side of a drugstore caught his glance. He measured it with his eye. Some ten by fourteen feet, looking right down Peachtree, where all Atlanta moved at one time or another. Instead of continuing on to make his call, he entered the drugstore and asked for the proprietor.

"That's Dr. Albert," he was told. "Back there."

He went to the prescription counter. "Dr. Albert?" he said. "My name is Oren Knox. I'd like to talk to you for a minute, if I may."

They shook hands through the high opening behind which Dr. Albert plied his esoteric trade.

"That space on the side of your building," Oren said. "Got any plans for it?"

"What did you have in mind?"

"I am introducing our new cigarette, O.K. Durhams, to the Atlanta public," Oren said. "I thought a poster-picture of my brand would be of considerable help in acquainting them with . . ."

"I hadn't really planned anything," Dr. Albert said. "To tell you the truth, it never crossed my mind to use that space for advertising. I've got my store name up out front and . . ."

"It's just going to waste," Oren said. "I hate to see anything wasted, Dr. Albert. Now, how much would you charge me to display my brand there?"

Dr. Albert wiped his hands on his white coat. "I'd hardly know how to set a price on it."

"Do you smoke, Dr. Albert? Here, let me give you a package of O.K. Durham Cigarettes. Light one up and try it."

Dr. Albert took the cigarettes gingerly. "I'm a pipe man myself," he said.

"I'll tell you something about pipes," Oren said. "Pipes are going right out. All the people in New York and London and Paris are turning away from pipes. They are considered very low in polite society. The smoke offends the ladies, and besides there's all that gurgling and lighting and relighting. If you're a married man, Dr. Albert, you know what I'm talking about, because I'll bet you a red cent your wife . . ."

He saw he had scored a mark.

"All the best people are turning to cigarettes," he said. "Cigarettes don't offend the ladies like pipes do. Why, they've been known to sneak a puff or two themselves on occasion, when they're sure no one will see. Your wife would be a grateful woman, Dr. Albert, and when you wait on trade . . . here, try one. See how you like it."

He held the match for Dr. Albert. Dr. Albert puffed cautiously, coughed, manfully tried again.

"Sorta dry, ain't they?" he said. "They've got a harsh . . ."

"Dry?" Oren said in astonishment. "Harsh? That's mildness you're tasting there, Dr. Albert. You just don't recognize it because you're so used to that strong pipe tobacco. You smoke O.K. Durhams for a week, then try a pipe, and you'll see what I mean. O.K. Durhams are made of the best bright leaf, blended with Turkish. Once you're used to it, it's the smoothest, mildest smoke you've ever had in your mouth."

Dr. Albert experimented with the cigarette. "I'd feel rather silly smoking these things," he said. "Now, pipe and cigar, that's a man's smoke. But cigarettes . . ." He shook his head.

"You're going to see more and more men smoking cigarettes," Oren said. "Why? Because they're clean and neat. They're the coming thing, Dr. Albert. First they'll be taken up by the men who are the leaders of taste and fashion. When you see a man smoking a cigarette, you'll think, 'Now there's a man who's right up with the times.' Why, when your customers come in here and see you smoking an O.K. Durham cigarette, they'll say to themselves, 'He keeps up. Nothing old-fashioned or old-fogeyish about Dr. Albert. I'll bet he keeps up with the drug trade the same way he does with the style.' "

Dr. Albert attacked the cigarette again, rather doggedly this time. He was pleased with himself.

"Now, that space on the side of your building," Oren said. "I don't know the money value of that space myself. But here's what I'll do. I'll furnish you with a hundred packages of O.K. Durham cigarettes per year for every year you let me use that space. That'll be two packs a week for your personal use; enough for any man's desires. Of course, I'd appreciate it if you'd stock my cigarette for your customers, too, and let them see you smoking them. A community leader like you, that's a good man to have on your side."

"Well now," Dr. Albert said. "I guess that's a square deal." He laughed modestly. "After all, it wouldn't look right to advertise your cigarette on my drugstore wall and me inside puffing on my dirty old pipe. But I don't know about stocking cigarettes. I never have before."

"Why, with the town's largest advertisement on your wall, you'll have lots of calls," Oren said. "Your customers will be disappointed if you can't supply the demand."

"Put me down for five hundred, then," the druggist said reluctantly.

Oren left the drugstore in a fair state of excitement. This was what was needed—advertising. Burned into his brain was the image of thousands and tens of thousands of Bull Durham signs scattered over the countryside, nailed to fence posts and to the silvery-gray sides of country stores, painted on the sides of barns. Everywhere you turned, there was the Bull. O.K. Durham Cigarettes needed the same thing. They had to be drummed into the consciousness of the nation.

He paused to look at the space he had acquired, visualizing the label blown up to ten by fourteen feet. He could visualize it, all right. But, somehow, it was not satisfactory. It would only be the giant letters, O and K, and even at that size the coy beauty hiding behind the K would not be an eye-puller. A close look at the label was always good for a laugh. It wouldn't do for a giant display. Too subtle.

He went on down the street, thinking furiously. He could not allow this opportunity to go to waste. He paused, deep in thought, before the window of Phillips and Crews. In the window was a life-size lithograph of Madame Rena, the French actress who was the current sensation of Atlanta. She gazed out at him seductively, her soft curves voluptuous through the flimsy gown she wore. Her hips and breasts swelled alarmingly, her waist tiny, a hint of a trim ankle peeping out to snare the unwary.

An immediate thought flashed in Oren's mind. Without pausing for another look at the voluptuous sight, he hurried on to the Kimball House. He collared the desk clerk.

"Is Madame Rena staying here?" he asked.

The desk clerk watched him warily. "I'm not supposed to give out that information," he said.

"Then she *is* here. Will you send her up a note?"

"I . . ." the clerk said.

"I insist," Oren said fiercely. "I'll have it ready for you in two seconds."

He sat down at a writing desk in a corner of the lobby and pulled paper and pen in front of him. He thought deeply before he took pen in hand:

DEAR MADAME RENA:

I write to ask if I may use one of your life-size lithographs, to have the same duplicated in oil on canvas with the inscription below: "Atlanta's Favorites"? Also extended in the right hand a package of O.K. Durham Cigarettes? Yours truly,

OREN KNOX, *salesman*

He sealed the envelope, handed it with a dollar to the desk clerk. "See that this gets to her right away," he said.

He sat in the lobby, waiting. His suspense did not long endure. The bellboy paused before him, extending a note. He tipped him, took the small envelope. It exuded a faint fragrance. He was interested only in the words.

I will be pleased to receive Mr. Oren Knox, salesman, in my suite.

MADAME RENA
Atlanta's Favorite

He grinned at the last words under her name. He followed the bellboy to the second floor where, left alone, he tapped on the door. It was opened by a Negro maid.

"Madame Rena?" Oren said. "Oren Knox, at her service."

"Come in, Mr. Knox," the maid said. "Madame Rena will be with you in a moment."

Oren entered the sumptuous suite. He sat down gingerly on a plush sofa, looking about. He had never stayed in a hotel room as luxurious as this one. He rose as Madame Rena entered. She came forward regally, holding out her hand.

"Mr. Knox," she said in a thrilling voice. "What is this silly idea that you have about me?"

She was not as tall as she looked on the life-size poster he had seen. She was elegant in a flowing dress, low-cut over her massive bosom. There was a heady indication of the perfume he had sniffed on her letter paper. Her voice was throaty, thrillingly foreign. He took her hand, not knowing what to do with it. He could not shake it and he would have felt an utter ass if he had kissed it, as she seemed to expect. He compromised by holding it firmly until she took it away.

"It's not a silly idea, Madame Rena," he said. "You *are* Atlanta's favorite, you know."

"But to show myself with a packet of cigarettes?"

"Have you seen our cigarettes?" He took a package out of his pocket, held them out. "Here's the brand, Madame Rena. O.K. Durham."

She took the package, looked at it closely. Her eyes shifted to his face. "Why, you naughty man!" she said in a delighted voice, seeing immediately the semi-nude woman hiding behind the K. Her eyes swept over his face. "You don't look like the kind of man who owns that kind of imagination, Mr. Knox."

He shrugged his shoulders. "It sells cigarettes," he said.

"And this . . ." her hand indicated the letters. "It says Oren Knox. It is your own cigarette?"

"Yes," Oren said modestly. "We have an O.K. Durham brand of smoking tobacco, also. But the cigarette is the most important item. In a year or two, with your help, it can be the biggest-selling cigarette in the country. And everywhere that O.K. Durham Cigarettes go, Madame Rena will go also, if you give me your permission."

Madame Rena, frowning, sat down on the sofa in one voluptuous, complicated movement. She motioned Oren to a seat beside her. She opened the package and took out one of the cigarettes, holding it elegantly between two fingers.

"A light, please," she said in an imperious voice.

Oren fumbled in his pockets for a match. He struck it, held it carefully. She drew lightly, then more deeply. He watched her, horror-struck. He had never seen a woman smoke a cigarette. She drew the smoke deeply into her lungs, breathed it out.

"A good cigarette," she said. "It is not Turkish, but it is good. I have smoked always Turkish Elegantes."

"That's good old North Carolina bright leaf," Oren said. "The best cigarette tobacco in the whole world. Got a touch of the Turkish, though."

He was fascinated by her practiced smoking. Why, he thought to himself, I hadn't even thought about women smoking cigarettes. I've just worried about getting the men to smoke them. Women—there's a brand-new market no one has ever thought of. Lots of women use snuff. A few smoke a pipe. Why not cigarettes as well?

He toyed with the idea of a lithograph showing Madame Rena actually smoking an O.K. Durham cigarette. His mind backed away. That was too daring. It would raise a storm of protest that would sweep both Oren Knox and Madame Rena off the map.

She finished the cigarette, rose, swayed across the room to dispose of the stub, and returned to the seat beside him. She put a hand on his arm.

"Tell me about yourself, Mr. Knox."

Her closeness was overpowering. The warmth of her palm seemed to burn through his coat sleeve.

"I've been a tobacco man all my life," he said. "I reckon I always will be." He tried to laugh. "I was buying and selling tobacco when I was fourteen years old."

"And you yourself thought of the little creature hiding behind the letter K?"

"Sure," Oren said.

She watched him speculatively. "You look like a dull little

man, Mr. Knox," she said. "You are not dull at all." She gestured widely with her other hand. "You have a . . . I do not know the words for it . . . you have a furnace burning in you." Her tone changed abruptly. "Are you married, Mr. Knox?"

"Yes," Oren said.

She watched him shrewdly. "But not happily," she said.

He shrugged. "Are marriages supposed to be happy?" he said. "About the lithograph, Madame Rena . . ."

She unexpectedly put one hand on the side of his face. He wanted to jerk away but he did not dare move.

"You are a lonely man," she said. Her voice was throatier. It carried a feeling that had not been present before. "You are as lonely as a French actress in a strange Southern town."

She took her hand away, rose, and moved with her voluptuous sway across the width of the room. She paused, looking out of the window, one hand holding the heavy drape.

"I must have time to decide," she said, without turning. "I will see you after the performance tonight. I will then give my decision."

He rose, holding his hat in his hand. "Shall I . . . ?"

She turned, then, looking at him across the width of the room. "Will you have a small supper with me?" she said. "Here? After the theatre? A bottle of champagne, a cold chicken . . ."

"I shall be honored," Oren said.

"You will see me perform tonight," she said. "Yes. You must. Then you will come backstage and we will have our little midnight supper. By then I shall have decided."

Though his heart was not in it, Oren made calls for the rest of the afternoon. His mind was filled with Madame Rena, as his nostrils were filled with the scent of her perfume. She was a strange woman. He wondered if she had shown him anything of herself or whether it had all been stage projection. There, toward the end, she had seemed to be real.

That night, for the first time in his life, he bought a ticket to a play. He sat in the audience and watched her voluptuous sweeps across the stage. He did not follow the play, but kept his attention on her voice, her movements. It was a love farce, and the audience loved Madame Rena's performance. Toward the end she had a song; during it she came down to the footlights and sang directly to the audience. There were many curtain calls.

Oren pushed his way out of the crowd and went down the alley to the stage entrance. The doorman let him in when he gave his name, so Madame Rena must have prepared his way.

Her dressing room was crowded. She sat before her big mirror in a peignoir with a feather collar, leaning into the mirror to remove the stage make-up. People swirled, talking, in the room. Oren, wedged against the door, was unable to make his presence known.

The people seemed unusually loud and demonstrative. Oren saw that several were smoking cigarettes. The air was gray with the smoke.

Finished at last with the mirror, Madame Rena disappeared behind a dressing screen. When she emerged she was wearing a green velvet gown similar to the one she had worn this afternoon in the hotel suite.

"Where is my tobacco man?" she cried, her thrilling voice rising over the conversations.

The noise subsided. Madame Rena, seeing Oren near the door, crossed to him and slipped her arm through his. The dressing-room crowd stared at him curiously. Oren was embarrassed. Madame Rena blew a kiss to her admirers, then whispered to Oren, "Let's get away from these people. I am so tired of them."

Oren had had the foresight to have a hansom cab standing by. He handed her up into the seat and settled himself beside her. She turned warmly to him.

"Did you like the performance?" she said eagerly.

"It was wonderful," he said.

"Do you think it is a good play? Everyone thinks the play is just right for me."

"To tell you the truth, I didn't pay much attention to the play," he said. "I reckon just about any play would be right for you."

"Ah, you are the gallant man," she murmured in a delighted voice.

"That's not being gallant," he said. "That's just the honest truth, Madame Rena."

At the hotel they alighted and Oren paid the driver. They moved through the lobby to the accompaniment of turning heads. Oren was unaccustomed to the glare of publicity. He was both flattered and flabbergasted.

Once safe in her suite, she took a cigarette from the package of O.K. Durhams lying on the table where Oren had left them. Oren lighted it for her. She blew smoke toward the ceiling.

"The theatre is so exciting," she said. "It is difficult for one to stop. You know? . . . you want to go on and on. I always sleep badly after a good performance."

"I can imagine," Oren said.

"Ah, the hotel has been of good service," she said. She went to the table, flicked away the covering cloth. Supper was laid out for them, along with a bottle of champagne cooling in an ice bucket alongside. "I am ravenous. I am also always hungry, afterward."

Oren opened the champagne, clumsily because he had never before performed the elegant task. Madame Rena was already eating the cold chicken greedily. She ate without talking through the whole meal, until at last she leaned back with a sigh.

"You are a good companion," she observed. "You know when to be silent."

He smiled at her. "I am content to watch you," he said.

"And all the time you are not wondering about my permission to use the picture?"

"Of course. I figure you'll get around to that."

She leaned to pat his hand. "You are a lovely person," she said. "So dull on the outside. But on the inside . . . all flame. I should like to be a woman whom you loved."

He looked down at the white tablecloth. "I have never loved a woman," he said.

"But when you do . . ."

"I don't reckon I'll ever be in love," he said. "I don't seem to be turned that way."

She smiled at him mischievously. "You do not wish to speak to me of love? You do not have a great declaration to make? . . . how in the moment of meeting I have smitten you and you will die without the grace of my favors?"

"I reckon every man you meet tells you things like that," Oren said. "So, even if I felt that way, I'd figure it wouldn't do me any good."

"You merely want to know about your cigarettes?"

His senses were still overwhelmed by her. But he had not forgotten that empty space on the drugstore wall.

"Will you grant your permission?"

She looked at him thoughtfully. "If I give you permission, everywhere your cigarettes are known, I will be known," she said in a shrewd, practical voice. "If your cigarette becomes the most famous, I will be the most famous woman. Is that not so?"

"I believe so."

She rose from the table, disappeared into her bedroom. In a few minutes she returned and handed him a sheet of paper. He looked down at it.

My Dear Mr. Knox:

I certainly will allow you to use my picture to advertise your cigarettes.

Madame Rena

"I will suggest something," she said. "Make a small picture and place one in each packet of cigarettes."

"Yes," he said. "That's a good idea. We will make a lot of poses, number them 'Number 1 of 10" and so on, so people will keep buying the cigarettes to get the full set." He rose, folding his napkin and putting it on the table. "I thank you with the deepest sincerity," he said. "This means a great deal to me, Madame Rena."

She smiled. "Now that business is out of the way, we can talk as friends," she said. "I do not sleep until the sun is up, Mr. Knox. Stay with me and be my friend."

She lifted the champagne bottle and filled his glass. Oren drank from the glass.

"I was hoping I could," he said.

They moved the champagne bucket and the two glasses to the low table before the sofa. They drank and talked for some time, while Madame Rena smoked two more of the cigarettes. It was a pleasant time.

"How long have you been in this country?" Oren asked during the last glass of champagne.

She straightened, looking at him. "All my life," she said. She smiled at his start of surprise. "Yes," she said. "I am not French. Not French French, anyway. I am from Thibodeaux, Louisiana."

"But why . . . ?"

"The great American public thinks foreignness has a greater appeal," she said. "They cannot fall in love with an American actress. But a French actress . . . ooh la la!"

"Well, I'll be damned," Oren said. "But how do you know I won't spread it all around and ruin your deception?"

"Because you are my friend," she said. "I will tell you. There were twelve brothers and sisters in my family. With twelve of us, there was not much to eat. When I was fourteen, I ran away with a circus man because I wanted to go to New Orleans. He intended to make me a snake lady. But I . . . I desired New Orleans."

"At fourteen I was buying and selling tobacco," Oren said.

"At fourteen I was selling myself," she said, quite as simply. "At sixteen I had enough money for the passage to France. I went to France. There I put the selling behind me and I acted. Then I came back to this country and, voilà! I am a great success."

He looked at her with new eyes. "You're a tough little lady," he said.

"You are a tough little man."

She lifted her champagne glass, touched his. There was the

tiny ringing clash of glass against good glass. She drank down the last of her portion.

"Will you make love to me?" she said.

Oren sat still. "Yes," he said then. "I want to, very much."

She smiled mischievously. "Would you have asked me to make love?"

"I don't think I'd have dared," he said with a laugh.

She put her hand on his. "I thought so," she said. "That is why I was so brazen." She rose. "Come," she said. "Let us make love together. For a little time, neither of us will be lonely."

Within two days Oren Knox had mounted the lithograph of Madame Rena in the empty space. The following day, when he visited the drugstore to view his accomplishment once again, Dr. Albert called him inside.

"I've had a dozen calls for your cigarettes already," he said. "I'll order five thousand to start with."

Oren multiplied the poster in smaller sizes and began posting them in store windows all over town. Before the week was out, he had taken orders for thirty thousand cigarettes and had wired Alex to step up production to the limit.

On Friday, he paid his last call on Madame Rena. "I'm leaving town," he told her. He smiled. "Got to let the rest of the country get acquainted with Madame Rena and O.K. Durham Cigarettes."

"Tomorrow I go also," she said. She smiled, sadly, holding out her hand. "Goodbye, Oren."

He took her hand. He held it for a moment. Then he raised it to his lips, for the first time kissing her hand like a gallant gentleman.

"Goodbye," he said.

It had ended between Oren Knox and Madame Rena; for these three days they had loved without once speaking of love. But Madame Rena of the lithographs and O.K. Durham Cigarettes would travel a long road together. She was the first woman Oren Knox had ever known.

The rest of his trip was an unalloyed triumph. From Atlanta

he went to Birmingham, Chattanooga, Nashville, Memphis and Louisville. He plastered every town with Madame Rena's picture, holding out the package of O.K. Durham Cigarettes, with the legend beneath, "Louisville's Favorite," "Chattanooga's Favorite," changing the legend for each city. He placed smaller posters in the tobacconists' windows and in each place he sold enormous quantities of the cigarette.

He stepped off the train in Manchester late one night, tired with the traveling, glad to get home. Taylor Tryon met him at the station. From the expression on his face, Oren knew something was wrong. Visions of disaster flashed through his mind; the factory had burned, the rollers had quit in a body to return to New York, the . . .

"What's the matter?" he said.

Taylor Tryon's voice was grave. "Mr. Fuller died in his sleep early tonight," he said.

"Dead!" Oren said. "Why, he was a healthy man."

"He came down with the cramp colic day before yesterday," Taylor said. "After the doctor saw how serious it was, we tried to get in touch with you. But we couldn't find you."

"Trenholm?" Oren said quickly.

"She's bearing up," Taylor said, his voice still grave with the intonations of death. "She is waiting for you."

Taylor had a buggy waiting. Oren put his sample case and bag into the back and climbed up on the seat beside Taylor. They passed through the deserted center of town, the horse's hoofs loud in the after-midnight stillness. At the house, Oren got down. He looked at the house for a moment. All the lamps were lighted, blazing forth their message of death's vigil here in the town's darkness.

Oren entered the front door. He saw the casket through the open door of the parlor, saw three men sitting out their night watch.

"Gentlemen," he said.

They nodded, gravely. Oren went up the stairs to the second floor. He hesitated, his hand on the knob of the door, then he lifted the hand to knock instead of opening it without announcement.

"Come in," her voice said.

He opened the door. She had risen from her chair. Her hands were clenched at her sides, her face was pale.

"Trenholm," he said.

"It's all yours now," she said. "All yours, isn't it? Just like you wanted."

He looked into her eyes. She did not need him. Beneath that placid inertia, she was all steel and strength.

"Yes," he said. "It is all mine."

He turned, walked through the door, closed it gently. He went down the stairs and entered the parlor. Approaching the casket, he stood for a still moment, contemplating the face of Foster Fuller. He had been close to Mr. Fuller; yet there had been no closeness at all. Mr. Fuller had never understood. He had used Oren Knox as one uses electricity, without any comprehension of the nature of the natural forces involved.

After his moment of contemplation, Oren left the parlor. Taylor was waiting on the porch.

"Is Mrs. Knox all right?" he asked awkwardly.

"Yes," Oren said. "She is bearing up."

"It's a shame, him dying like that," Taylor said. "A man in the strength of his life. That's cramp colic for you. It comes on you unbewares and in just a few hours you're gone. It's a shame, all the same."

Oren looked at him. "He was unhappy with the way we're going," he said. "He would have become more and more unhappy as time went on. He wanted to own a small factory, do a small, comfortable business."

"And you, Oren," Taylor said. "What do you want? Do you know yet?"

Oren clenched his hands into fists at his sides. It was dark, so Taylor could not see.

"Yes," he said. "I know." He thought of Madame Rena, the lush scent of her body, of how she had come from Thibodeaux,

Louisiana, at the age of fourteen. He thought of the lithographs plastered all over several towns, of the cigarettes waiting in drugstores and hotel lobbies and tobacco shops. "I know, all right," he said. "I want to make and sell every cigarette that's smoked in the United States of America. I don't just want to be top dog. I want to be all there is."

He began telling Taylor Tryon about Madame Rena's permission to use her picture in the advertising, how successful it had been. They stood on the porch for a long time, in the quiet night, planning the full exploitation of the opportunity that fortune had handed them.

Chapter Eight

On a spring day in 1884, Oren Knox alighted from a train at a way stop in Virginia. He dusted his coat with his hands and looked about him. The station was only a small wooden building alongside the tracks, a watering tower, and a dirt road crossing the tracks and winding away into the distance. There was one man inside the station. Oren approached, rapped his knuckles on the wooden window ledge to get his attention.

"Tell me," he said. "Where does Mr. Charles Whitfield live around here?"

"About three mile up yonder," the stationmaster said, jerking his thumb to the west. "Just follow the road, it'll take you there. You'll see a white house setting up on a hill."

"Got any transportation?"

The stationmaster shook his head. "Sent my buggy to town to have a wheel shrunk," he said. "Won't be back till tomorrow, I don't reckon."

Oren sighed, hefted the bag. "I reckon I'll hoof it, then," he said. "You can always depend on shank's old mare."

The stationmaster slapped his thigh. "Yes sir," he said. "You can always depend on shank's old mare. Want to leave your grip here? Be safe enough."

"Thank you, sir," Oren said.

He handed it through the open door. The stationmaster stowed the bag under the counter. "Be right there when you get back," he said. "Gonna try to make the next train?" He consulted his watch. "Be through here in about three hours and a half, going south."

"I'll try," Oren said. "I'm not sure."

He set out down the road.

Oren Knox, in these five years since the death of his father-in-law—after which event he had assumed full command of Fuller and Knox Cigarette Company—had made enormous progress toward his stated goal. Now he had arrived at another impasse. That was the reason he was walking on this April morning up a lonely Virginia road in the spring sunshine.

Some of his plans had worked out; some had not. He had used his imported rollers to train local girls in the art of making cigarettes. He had not, as yet, been able to get rid of the high-priced imported labor; indeed, it had been necessary to send Alex Michael again and again to recruit new members of his faith, until now he had one hundred and twenty-five Jewish rollers and forty-five girl rollers. He worked them on separate floors, paying the male rollers forty-eight cents a thousand while he paid the girls forty cents a thousand. He had not been able to lower the female wage rate as much below the male wage rate as he had wished, because he had early discovered that the art required reasonably intelligent workers. It had been necessary to keep the piecework rate up in order to attract the quality of girl who would be good at the job.

He now had a weekly production of over two million cigarettes; he had sales of over two million. Madame Rena had given them the start. Oren had spent a lot of money promoting Madame Rena's endorsement of O.K. Durham Cigarettes. However, to meet the competition, he had found it necessary to begin manufacturing five other brands. These brands were promoted in various ways, by inserting cards of sports figures, other actresses, naughty pictures, lithographs of historical scenes, flags of all nations—just about everything they could think of that would induce the consumer to purchase one more package of cigarettes.

He had four competitors, of whom Lathrop and Winter in Richmond, with Dominion Straight Cut and Brights cigarettes, was the strongest. Workman Tobacco Company of New York and Richmond, Barth and Company of Rochester, New York and Oxford, North Carolina, and Coffey and Company of New York, were each carving their own slice of the market. It was necessary to run at full tilt just to remain in the same place. Every year the advertising expenditures rose, every year the premiums increased in fanciness; while production increased only slowly, at the expense of tremendous added cost. Oren could find no way around the costs of hand manufacture. He was a captive of his laborers. If he cut the piecework rates, the imported labor would return en masse to New York. They were not too happy in Manchester, anyway. They had built a small temple by assessing each worker a thousand cigarettes a week; the first week it had been open, with a rabbi imported for the occasion from New York, the building had been vandalized. Oren himself, for goodwill, had paid for the repairs. Still they had no resident rabbi, but had to rely on bringing one in occasionally from a larger town. The workers lived in an enclave of their own, in the midst of a latent hostility that occasionally emerged in overt acts. Oren had separated the girl rollers to another floor not solely for the purpose of concealing the differential in wages; there was often scandalous talk in the town about the Jewish rollers teaching the native white southern women how to roll cigarettes. There were not yet enough trained native rollers to permit Oren to dispense with the imported labor.

With Taylor on the road and Alex in the factory, Oren could divide his time efficiently wherever the need lay, from buying the leaf to selling the cigarettes. He even had a good accountant in the office to run that end of it; one day, walking through the factory, he had noticed one of the girl rollers, on her lunch hour, studying a book while she ate her sandwich.

He stopped before her. "What are you reading?"

She looked up, her face flushing with embarrassment. Her voice failed her, so, as a child would do, she held up the book.

"Principles of Accounting," Oren said. "Why are you reading that?"

She found her voice. "I'm studying at night," she said. "I won't bring the book to work any more, sir. I promise." She was greatly frightened.

"What's your name?"

"Helen Fowlkes."

"Tell the foreman you are relieved here. Come to the office."

"Don't fire me, Mr. Knox. I need . . ."

"I'm not firing you. I'm moving you into the office."

She was a gawky, skinny girl, awkward in her movements. She had a nondescript face, nondescript hair and a nervous habit of holding her hand before her mouth. It came both from fear and from her awareness that her upper teeth were too prominent. She was an excellent accountant, intensely conscientious, and within six months she was in full trust of the factory ledgers.

Taylor Tryon gave the second impetus to their progress. Taylor, reconciling himself to smoking cigarettes, had become a master salesman of the new product. He allowed himself only three cigars a day; one after each meal. He was rarely in Manchester, but stayed continuously on the road. He remained a bachelor, flamboyant in his sales talks, easily recognizable by casual acquaintances because of his red hair and elaborately brocaded vests.

In 1883, when the internal revenue tax was lowered from a dollar and seventy-five cents to fifty cents a pound, Taylor came riding in all the way from New Orleans to bear his message to Oren.

"What are you going to do about the tax cut?" he asked Oren half an hour after he had descended from the train.

They were in the office that had once belonged to Foster Fuller. It was Oren's office now and he sat behind the desk, looking at Taylor.

"What are you doing here?" he said. "I thought you were in Memphis."

"New Orleans," Taylor said. "What are you going to do about the tax cut when it takes effect May 1st?"

Oren frowned. "I'd like to absorb it into profits," he said. "I'm afraid we won't be able to get away with that. If there wasn't so much competition in this trade, we could quietly absorb it and two weeks later nobody would be the wiser. But you know somebody would break the line . . . probably that damn Lathrop and Winter in Richmond. So I guess we'll have to let the dealers have a little bit of it."

"Listen, Oren," Taylor said. "This is no time to be stingy." He was still standing. He leaned over the desk. "Lathrop and Winter, all the rest, are thinking along the same lines you are . . . how much of the tax cut can they keep for themselves? That's all they're interested in." He straightened. "I think we ought to pass it along. Not just to the dealer. To the consumer."

"Are you out of your mind?" Oren said. "You know what our costs are. We need that added profit."

"You'll get twice, three times, the profit," Taylor said intensely. "Listen to me now, Oren. Give the dealer some of it. Give the consumer some of it. *Don't keep a penny of it for Oren Knox*. And let 'em know about it. Put out a circular to the trade that you are *dividing* the profits among the dealers and the consumers. Cut your wholesale rate; and cut your retail rate."

He paused. He was breathing hard.

"Listen, Oren, I've been on the road a long time. I know what I'm talking about. You cut that price to five cents for ten, ten cents for twenty, and you'll double your users. They'll flock to our brands. This is better than all the premiums and half-nekkid actresses and flags of all nations you can dream up."

Oren stared at him thoughtfully. "By God, you might be right, at that," he said. "It's a bold move. The Good Lord knows we need a bold move right now."

"Oren, if it doesn't work I'll . . . I'll give up my three cigars a day. I'll even give up my commission on the sales."

Oren pulled a piece of paper in front of him. "Let's lay it right on the line," he said. "Let's try something like this. *The Fuller and Knox Cigarette Company announces the reduction of their prices* THE FULL AMOUNT OF THE INTERNAL REVENUE TAX REDUCTION, *while the majority of the other manufacturers have reduced prices on a small portion of that reduction. We state quite frankly that we are ambitious for a very large cigarette business and to obtain such are* DIVIDING OUR PROFITS *among the dealers and consumers. The object of this action is to push and extend the sale of* O.K. DURHAM *Cigarettes. Our prices* WILL BE CUT IN HALF; *five cents for ten cigarettes, ten cents for twenty*. He paused for a moment. "Let's make them move on it right now, before the tax cut goes into effect. How's this, Taylor? *Orders will be received* AT ONCE *at the new rate, provided that the dealers will agree to accept three-fourths of the goods after May 1st.* THIS PROCEDURE GIVES YOU A TWENTY-FIVE CENT BONUS."

"That'll do it," Taylor said. "That'll do it or I'll eat my straw katy."

The gambit was successful. Orders flooded in. The factory was swamped with the demand for production. Alex made another trip to New York to recruit workers and the training of the local talent was intensified. It had brought the new expansion that Fuller and Knox now enjoyed; and it had been a major coup against their competitors. Oren gave Taylor Tryon a ten per cent interest out of Trenholm's share of the factory. It served two purposes; legally it reduced Trenholm's share to forty per cent, the equal of Oren's, and it ensured that Taylor would not be seduced by a competitor. Taylor and Oren were fast friends; but in business Oren did not depend on friendship—or even marriage.

This was how matters stood on that spring day in 1884 when Oren Knox walked up the dirt road in the Virginia sunshine. It was an impasse. They could sell as many cigarettes as they could make. They had strong competition, but they owned their share of the market. Oren doggedly continued to try to raise production without raising costs. It was impossible. A ceiling had been reached. Increased production, on the old basis, brought an enormous increase in costs. It would mean building a new factory to supplement the old one, for with the continued production of smoking tobacco and the enormous increase in hands needed to increase the production of cigarettes, they would be crowded out of the old space.

Oren needed to double his production. If he doubled his production, Helen Fowlkes would have to buy a bottle of red ink. Fuller and Knox could no longer operate at a profit.

Worse still, Oren had made little progress toward his stated goal of manufacturing every cigarette consumed in the United States. The competition had almost kept pace with his own progress; as the market expanded, Oren's share expanded more than commensurately. He had gained on them; but not enough. He had made it his business to know the history of each man who was his competitor. They would listen to reason only when he had the power to back the reason.

He smarted still under the first approach he had made to Willard Lathrop of Lathrop and Winter. He had paid a visit to the Lathrop and Winter office. He had been ushered into the office of the junior member of the firm.

Mr. Lathrop rose, holding out his hand. "I am delighted to meet you at last, Mr. Knox," he said.

"Pleased to meet you, too," Oren said.

Mr. Lathrop was a portly man, with a red, beaming face. He sat down, patting his massive stomach. "Now what can I do for you?"

"Mr. Lathrop, I think we've fought each other long enough. Me and you, between us, are doing about sixty per cent of the cigarette business in the country. But we're fighting for it like a cat and a dog going at it. That don't seem right to me."

"How are you planning to remedy that situation?"

"Merger," Oren said bluntly. "Put our strength together instead of fighting each other. Why, with Lathrop and Winter merged into Fuller and Knox we could dominate . . ."

He stopped. Mr. Lathrop was laughing. Both hands holding his great stomach, he threw back his head, laughing uproariously. His small hands groped ineffectively to control the explosion.

He laughed until he ran out of breath. Oren sat still, watching. While he watched, he hated the man. Mr. Lathrop paused, panting for breath.

He wiped his eyes. "Well, they say a good laugh a day is better than the doctor," he said. "I'm grateful to you, Mr. Knox. I don't know when I've had a better one."

"Is that your answer, Mr. Lathrop?" Oren said stiffly.

"Knox, you couldn't buy out Lathrop and Winter to save your neck. You don't have that kind of money. You couldn't even *borrow* that kind of money."

He laughed again, holding his stomach. Oren did not wait for the end of the new spasm. He rose. He was full of hate for the jolly, contemptuous man across the desk. No one had laughed at Oren Knox since he was eight years old, when he had tried to buy his father's rifle for ten cents.

He had the words in his mouth. *Mr. Lathrop, you'll see the day you'll be glad to merge with Oren Knox. You'll laugh when you sign the papers.* But Oren was not a man to make idle threats. Now, on this day and in this place, it would be only a threat. Without speaking, he left the office.

It had rankled. It would continue to rankle until the day of signing came. At the moment, he could still not see it on the horizon of the future.

He saw the white house on the hill. He turned in at the narrow road. He paused at the edge of the yard while three fox-hounds bulged out at him from under the house. They surrounded him, yapping, their bodies tense, their heads outstretched. A young man appeared on the verandah.

"Begone!" he said. "Begone, I say!"

The dogs obeyed, relaxing, wagging their tails, circling Oren as he entered the yard.

"Mr. Charles Whitfield?" he said.

He thought the young man must be the son of the man he had come to see. But the young man said, "Yes, I'm Charles Whitfield."

"I'm Oren Knox," Oren said. "I've come to see your cigarette machine."

Charles Whitfield came down the steps to shake Oren's hand. "Pleased to meet you, Mr. Knox."

Charles Whitfield was tall, fair. He did not appear to be more than twenty years old. His hair was light blonde and he was as pink-cheeked as a child. He had the look of a fresh-faced English schoolboy, his nose thin, sharp, his lips delicate, his eyes a bland blue. He wore a wisp of a mustache on his upper lip, so light in color it was almost invisible.

"I heard that Lathrop and Winter are giving one of your machines a trial," Oren said.

"If you can call it that," Whitfield said. "They installed it, tried it for a week. Now it's just sitting there."

A bitter tone lay in his voice. Oren looked at him curiously. "Did they pay you for it?"

"I'm not selling the machines," Whitfield said. "I'm leasing them on a royalty basis."

"A lot of people have tried to invent a cigarette machine," Oren said. "I've looked at half-a-dozen models myself in the last two years. Does yours work?"

He had walked from the country railroad station with considerable hope in his breast. But, hearing the results of the Lathrop and Winter test, his confidence was ebbing. It seemed as though the problem of a cigarette machine was insoluble.

Oren knew by now that machine-rolled cigarettes were the only possible salvation for the cigarette business. Everyone in the business was interested in a practical machine; some of the companies had offered large cash awards for a winning design.

"It's a sound approach," Whitfield said in a dogged voice. "There's nothing wrong with the basic idea of my machine. It's a tough proposition, Mr. Knox. The process of rolling a cigarette, when you break it down step by step, is very complex."

"You don't have to tell me that," Oren said.

"Up to this point in history, only the human hand has had the flexibility, the ingenuity, to perform that act," Charles Whitfield said. "But it *can* be done by a machine, Mr. Knox. Do you know what that means?"

They were walking around the big house, through a side yard to a building erected under a shade tree. It was a long, low building, made of rough lumber. There were big windows on both sides, a wide double door set in the front.

"It costs you eighty cents a thousand to manufacture hand-rolled cigarettes. That includes about fifty cents a thousand for the labor alone. The Whitfield machine can reduce your manufacturing costs to thirty cents a thousand."

"Thirty cents?" Oren said.

"Thirty cents," Whitfield said firmly. "Now, we are leasing the Whitfield machine on a royalty basis. You *know* your costs for making won't run more than thirty cents a thousand. Now, you add your raw material, about three and a half pounds of tobacco at twenty-five cents per pound, your revenue tax of fifty cents, the expense of packaging and shipping—and your over-all cost, exclusive of overhead, of producing a thousand cigarettes works out at about one dollar and eighty-five cents." He paused, looking shrewdly at Oren. "You sell that thousand cigarettes wholesale for four dollars a thousand, less ten per cent discount, and it leaves you a margin of one dollar and seventy-five cents a thousand for overhead and advertising. You're a man who likes to advertise, Mr. Knox. You'll have plenty of room to indulge in it."

Oren studied Charles Whitfield with increased respect. He laughed. "Whether your machine works or not, you've got your figures down pat," he said.

"I've spent hours figuring on it," Whitfield said. He looked as fierce as his bland, friendly face would permit. "My machine will do the job, Mr. Knox. I've been working on it since I was seventeen years old. My father kept telling me to raise tobacco and not worry about the making end. But I knew I could do it."

"If it'll do all that you say," Oren asked bluntly, "why won't Lathrop and Winter use your machine?"

Whitfield was fumbling in his pocket for his key to unlock the big padlock on the double doors.

"There are still some things that aren't quite right," he said. "It clogs, and then it takes a while to clean it. After all, we're still in the experimental stage." He unlocked the padlock. "That's not the real reason they won't use the machine, though. They're afraid of the public prejudice against machine-made cigarettes. They're afraid to really test the market with them. Right there is the whole truth of the matter."

He swung the door open and they entered. There were long tables on each side of the room, cluttered with tools and parts. In the middle of the floor stood an awkward-looking contraption, all belts and wheels and pulleys.

"Here it is," Charles Whitfield said with quiet satisfaction in his voice. "The Whitfield Cigarette Machine."

Oren approached the elaborate mechanism. It was incomprehensible to him. It seemed a jumble of parts unrelated to each other. It was big, awkward, too complicated. He thought of the rollers sitting at their desks, their deft hands whirling the white cylinders into shape.

"It doesn't *look* like it'd do anything in particular," he said dubiously. "I've seen perpetual-motion machines that made better sense."

Whitfield laughed. "That's everybody's reaction at first. You ought to have seen my father's face when I showed him my first model. He's a believer now, though."

"Explain it to me."

"There are three fundamental parts. Here's the feed, that apportions the tobacco uniformly. This is the forming tube, where the cigarette is shaped into a continuous roll, and here's the knife for cutting the roll into cigarettes of equal length.

"The feed device consists of an endless traveling belt, with a roller distending the other end of the belt. See how it works? The tobacco feeds onto this receiving-roll right here. Next there's a feed-roller with a roughened surface, a roller covered with card-cloth, and a stripping roller. They transfer, card, and distribute the tobacco with a spreading action onto the traveling belt. I got the idea for the feeding mechanism from a device on the carding machines of a woolen mill that belongs to my uncle.

"Now here's the forming tube. The cigarette paper passes through a tapering tube. These spiral grooves form the cigarette paper around the tobacco, then it passes through the pasting mechanism to seal the cigarette.

"Next we have the problem of cutting the cigarettes into uniform lengths. Here's the holding tube, the knife, and the mechanism to revolve the knife around its own axis. I had a problem devising a driving mechanism for actuating the knife with a more rapid movement during the moment of cutting than during the rest of its stroke. I solved it, but when I tried to patent it I found somebody else had invented a device so similar I couldn't get a patent. That's when I had to make my father believe in the machine. He bought the patent for me."

"How many will it make in a day's time?" Oren asked. He had only half-understood the explanation. He was not a mechanically-minded man.

Charles Whitfield paused, impressively. "Two hundred cigarettes a minute," he said. "It can turn out daily as many cigarettes as fifty handrollers."

Oren Knox pursed his lips in a soundless whistle. "It don't sound believable," he said.

"It's the truth," Whitfield said. "I will guarantee it. Two hundred cigarettes a minute."

"How many minutes a day?" Oren said.

Whitfield nodded. "That's the problem right now," he said. "There's time loss to be figured. Naturally. It's a new machine. It hasn't been adequately tested under actual working conditions."

"What's the trouble you run into?"

"The basic principles are right," Whitfield said. "It's only a matter of adjustment; getting the feeder, the former, and the cutter to run in an accurate synchronization. If your feeder outspeeds your former, you have tobacco clogging the machine. If the cutter gets out of whack, you get mangling of your continuous cigarette, or uneven lengths. It's small things, Mr. Knox. When they pile up on each other, the machine must be stopped and adjusted."

"If you can't make the parts cooperate with each other, you don't have a successful machine."

"It needs to work under actual factory conditions," Whitfield said in an intense voice. "Work day after day, turning out cigarettes. It's ninety per cent perfect now. Give me three months work on it under factory conditions and I'll have it ninety-eight per cent perfect. Then you will have a valuable machine."

"I'd like to see one in operation."

"I don't have power here," Whitfield said. "There's one installed at my uncle's woolen mill, using the power that operates the looms. We can go over there if you want to. It's about five miles."

"Let's do that," Oren said. "I'd like to talk to you about the machine, how you plan to manufacture and everything."

"My father formed a joint-stock company with my uncle, myself, and a banker who lives in town," Whitfield said. "We don't plan to manufacture ourselves. I've constructed by hand the machines that have been made so far; three of them, one here, one at the woolen mill, one at Lathrop and Winter. I have two more nearly completed. We will arrange manufacture and then license the machines on a royalty basis. My father is negotiating with a French firm to manufacture the machine."

"Is your father here?"

"I think he's at the woolen mill. You'll have an opportunity to talk to him if you want to." Charles Whitfield, leading Oren out of the workshop, paused to lock the door behind them. "Listen, Mr. Knox," he said earnestly. "You give the Whitfield machine a try and I'll come down there and live with it in your factory. I'll work night and day to make it work properly for you. That's all it needs. I'll stay with it until you're satisfied. I'll take full responsibility for its operation until it can be handled by an employee of yours and I won't charge you anything extra."

Oren looked at him. "You believe in this machine like I believe in cigarettes, don't you?" he said.

"Yes sir. I do."

"Let's go see it operate."

They made the five-mile trip in Charles Whitfield's runabout buggy, behind a spanking mare. Oren tried idle conversation, for he had not yet made up his mind about the machine. Charles Whitfield contained no idle conversation; he could talk only about his machine. Oren was both amused and impressed.

At the woolen mill, Oren was introduced to the father and the uncle. They were twin brothers, both tall, lean; older versions of Charles himself. The father had a beautiful sweeping mustache, straw-colored, and a goatee. He wore a wide gray hat, vaguely Confederate, that made him look like a planter of the old school. The uncle wore a business suit and was clean-shaven. The father was named Herman, the uncle Sherman.

"My boy been bending your ear about his machine?" Herman Whitfield said.

"I reckon he has, at that," Oren said, smiling. "He's a believer, all right."

"All he's ever wanted to do is tinker," the father said proudly. "No more interested in raising tobacco than a rattlesnake. By the time he was ten years old he could tell you more about the operation of this woolen mill than any man that works here. He's made a believer out of us, too—not to mention the local banker."

"Mr. Knox wants to see the machine in operation," Charles said.

They went in a group into an empty room of the woolen mill. The grotesque machine, an exact copy of the one Oren had seen before, crouched in the center of the room. It was hooked up by a belt to an overhead drive shaft. The hopper was already loaded with tobacco.

They watched while Charles went about the intricate business of starting the machine. He tinkered interminably before he threw the power lever. The machine groaned into life, the sundry parts shuttling back and forth, shifting in mysterious, purposive patterns. Oren watched, fascinated, as the machine began spitting cigarettes into the receiving basket.

The parts shuttled, the tobacco sifted onto the traveling belts. He leaned closer to watch the paper curving itself as if by magic about the tobacco. The knife whirled on its axis, cutting the continuous cigarette into lengths. The finished cigarettes flowed from the machine in a continuous stream. He could believe, with no effort at all, that it was producing two hundred cigarettes a minute.

Suddenly, in his mind, the phalanxes of hand-rollers stooped over their individual desks became a scene out of the Middle Ages. It was so incredibly slow, so out-of-date. From this moment on, he would take no pride in surveying the rolling floors of his factory. He would see only the laborious hand-shaping, as mankind has slowly shaped things since the dawn of history. He had seen other machines, built on varying principles. None had been as immediately convincing as the Whitfield.

His mind saw, instead, a new scene to replace the actuality of his factory. The same factory floor contained a row of the Whitfield machines, each tended by assiduous helpers, each spitting a continuous stream of the white cylinders. Each machine the equal of fifty handrollers. Thirty cents a thousand. And each machine quiescent; without loneliness, without religious problems, never alien no matter where they might be.

He straightened. There was an ominous sound from the machine. The forming tube jammed with too much tobacco. The continuous roll tore, spilling tobacco wastefully on the floor. Charles Whitfield jumped to throw off the power before the machine could damage itself.

He was crestfallen. "That's what happens," he said. His voice was almost desperate. "It's just a matter of tinkering and adjusting. Maybe work out some way of regulating the various speeds from one source. But it works, Mr. Knox. It works. And I'm designing an attachment that will print your brand name on each and every cigarette—automatically, as the cigarette is made."

Oren's face did not change. He could not let it show his conviction, for there was still a bargain to be struck. He believed in the machine. Even the breakdown did not alter his opinion. He intended to have the Whitfield Cigarette Machine in his factory—and soon.

He had learned long since that there was more to business than work and the infinite taking of pains. Not that work and minute attention to detail were not important. But they could take one only so far. Inevitably came the time of the giant step. If a man refused the giant step, the future closed against him forever. Oren had taken three giant steps already; staying in town when he was fourteen to become a pinhooker; asking for the job with Foster Fuller; going into cigarette production in the first place. His progress to this point in time and space demanded another. It might be the right one, it might be wrong. One could never know. He was not afraid. There was within him a mighty conviction in the rightness of his own instinct.

"You say you're asking thirty cents a thousand royalty," he said, looking not at the boy but at his father. "I've got a proposition for you. Give me exclusive licensing rights to your machine and I'll give you thirty-five cents a thousand on a long-term agreement—say twenty years."

It was the boy who answered. "No sir, Mr. Knox," he said. "I didn't invent my cigarette machine for the benefit of one man. We decided about that when we set up the joint-stock company to handle the machine. It will be available to all upon proper payment of royalty."

"Son, I don't think you know what competition is like in the cigarette business," Oren said. "Suppose I take one or two of your machines. I go to all the risk and trouble and expense of installing them and helping you to perfect their operation. As soon as they're in economical operation, my competition comes along and signs a licensing agreement with you. They'll be in exactly the same position as me—with none of the risk and the expense involved."

"Lathrop and Winter have already installed one of the machines," Herman Whitfield, the boy's father, said.

"So Charles told me," Oren said. "He also told me they're not using it, because they're not sure whether or not the public will accept a machine-made cigarette." He dusted his hands, began moving toward the door. "Gentlemen, I'm willing to put my faith behind your machine. I don't think the public cares how a cigarette is made, as long as it's a good cigarette. But I can't do it on that basis. If I take the risk of becoming the first manufacturer to rely on machine production, I must also enjoy the benefits of that risk."

They walked together into the factory yard. The uncle bade them farewell. The three men got into the buggy and began the return trip to the Whitfield house. They were crowded together in the light runabout. After a while Charles got out and walked alongside. His long legs kept pace easily.

During the trip, Oren and Herman Whitfield talked inconclusively about installing the machine in the Fuller and Knox factory. At the house once more, Oren took his watch from his vest pocket.

"Be time for my train pretty soon," he observed. "I'd better start moving in that direction."

"I'll take you down in the buggy," Charles said.

Oren looked at him. "You want a chance to make that machine work?" he said. "You know a lot of people are working on this problem. Before too long, somebody is going to come up with the machine to do the job. If you get started first, you're a wealthy man; if somebody else gets in ahead of you, you've wasted your daddy's money and your time since you were seventeen years old."

"Yes sir, I do know that," Charles said earnestly. "Give me a month or two under factory conditions and I will guarantee . . . I'll live with that machine, Mr. Knox, I'll . . ."

"Here's what I'll do, then," Oren said. "You know the chance I'll be taking. I will sign an agreement with you that I will pay you twenty-four cents a thousand royalty. You will guarantee in writing that you will not permit anyone else to license your machine for less than thirty cents a thousand. You will further guarantee that throughout the life of your patent you will grant me a royalty agreement on any number of machines at least six cents a thousand less than the lowest figure you have allowed anyone else."

"Why should you have such an advantage over the other cigarette manufacturers?" Mr. Whitfield said bluntly.

Oren looked at him. "Because I'm first. Because I'm taking the chance."

"Lathrop and Winters was first."

"Their machine is just sitting there. They've abandoned it. They're waiting to see if you come through . . . *then* they will begin using it. Meantime, it's not costing them one red cent because they're not making any cigarettes on it." He paused. "I will guarantee that every effort will be made to keep your machine in operation. I can't guarantee I'll make cigarettes on it, of course, until we know it will make cigarettes. But I'll guarantee to try."

"If the other manufacturers knew you had such an advantage, we couldn't place another machine," Mr. Whitfield said.

"No need for them to know," Oren said. "*I* certainly won't tell them. You're a fool if you should."

"Father . . ." Charles said.

"I'll go even farther than that," Oren said. "I won't take just one machine. I'll take every machine you have ready and available. According to Charles, that's three machines. I'll install all three, with Charles' help. If we have those working, then I'll take the other two he's got in work as soon as they're finished.

Mr. Whitfield looked thoughtful. "At maximum production, that's one hundred and twenty thousand cigarettes a day per machine . . . three hundred and sixty thousand daily for the three machines."

"Over two million a week," Oren said. "That's what we're talking about, all right."

"Can you *sell* that many cigarettes?"

"Don't worry about selling them. You just worry about making them. Selling is my job."

"Father," Charles Whitfield said. "Take his offer."

"We said thirty cents a thousand royalty and that we'd stick to it for all comers," Mr. Whitfield said.

"Take it, Father," Charles said. "Don't you see? If we don't take his offer, somebody with a machine will."

Mr. Whitfield wavered. "I'll have to talk to our other partner," he said. "He would have to be in on such a decision. After all, he put up a lot of money . . ."

Oren consulted his watch. "Gentlemen, I have a train to catch," he said. "I thought you had the power of decision. If you don't have, I've wasted my time and yours."

"Take it, Father," Charles said in a desperate, pleading tone.

Mr. Whitfield turned away for a moment, staring sightlessly across the distance of his landholdings. Oren and Charles watched him, momentarily one in their anticipation.

Mr. Whitfield returned to them. "All right," he said. "We will take it."

Oren let out an imperceptible sigh. He was committed. It was always good to be committed. These were the great moments for which he lived.

Mr. Whitfield had had standard royalty agreements printed. They went inside the house and, in the parlor, Oren went carefully over the wording. They made the requisite changes.

"Make that Fuller and Knox Cigarette Company or their successors," Oren added. "I might change the name of the company, you know, and we want that to be clear."

They called in the Negro cook and the yardman to witness the instrument, Oren signing for Fuller and Knox, Mr. Whitfield signing as president of the joint-stock company.

They arrived at the station as the train was sounding its whistle in the distance.

"Well, I see you made your train," the stationmaster said, handing Oren his suitcase through the ticket-office door.

"Yes," Oren said. "I made it."

Chapter Nine

OREN moved with secretive speed to install the cigarette-making machines. Charles Whitfield came down to Manchester to supervise the installation of overhead shafts to bring the power from the steam engine, a newer and larger one that had been installed in the basement to accommodate the added machinery. A small steam engine had sufficed to run the cutters and threshers. They brought the machines in on a midnight freight and hauled them to the factory through the sleeping streets of Manchester with pieces of canvas thrown over them to conceal their function.

The next morning, when the handrollers came to work, they clustered about their rolling desks, their voices as low and ominous as a disturbed hive of bees. They had been aware, of course, of the extraordinary activity; only now had they discovered the purpose. Oren, standing by the machines as Charles Whitfield labored to bring them into production, beckoned to Alex Michael.

"Get them to work, Alex," he said. "Don't let them stand around and watch."

"But what is all this?" Alex said, gesturing with one hand toward the awkward-looking contraptions.

Oren watched his face. "They're cigarette-rolling machines," he said. "We're giving them a trial."

Alex glanced dubiously toward his legion of imported hand-rollers. "I don't know whether I can quiet them down or not," he said. "There have been rumors among them that this was happening. Now the rumors are confirmed."

He turned his back on Oren, walked slowly toward his men. Oren watched him merge with the group, saw them flow toward him. For a moment quiet fell, and Oren knew that Alex was telling them the truth of the situation.

Oren had not anticipated this. It had never crossed his intent mind that the handrollers might cause difficulties. There were one hundred and twenty-five of them, not counting the girls on the other floor. He stood tensely, watching.

They made a collective sound, lower, more charged and ominous than before. Alex raised his arms, gesturing, but their sound, their movement, swept over his ineffectual protest. With the coordination of a single animal, rather than the anarchy of one hundred and twenty-five individual human minds, they began moving toward the machines. Alex backed before them, holding out his arms, talking, gesturing, to no avail. There was an ugly stain of fear and hatred in the atmosphere.

"Charles," Oren said in a quick voice.

Charles stuck his head out from under one of the machines.

There was grease smeared on his face. One hand held a heavy wrench.

"My God!" he said, his voice breathing the words.

He scrambled from under the machine, still holding the wrench. He stood beside Oren. His face was so pale he looked like a dead man.

"You've got to stop them," he said, his voice whispering the words. "They're going to destroy my machines, Mr. Knox. You've got to."

Before Oren had time to reply, the men were upon them.

The mob flowed around them as Charles struck once, twice, with the wrench in his hand. His defense had no effect. They were intent upon destruction. Human flesh and blood could not forestall their desire to destroy.

Oren screamed. It was a wordless, curdling screech that echoed in the long room, bouncing off the walls into their ears in palpitations too rapid to register.

They milled, startled by the ragged sound. It cut into their anger like a knife, destroying for a crucial moment their intensity of focus upon the machines.

"Men," Oren said, now that he had their attention. "You cannot destroy these cigarette machines."

They screamed back at him. It was collective, anguished, overpowering. The sound swept them once again into group anger. Oren lifted his arms, his voice going quickly on.

"Do you think these machines are going to replace you?" he said. "Do you really think the machine-rolled cigarette can ever replace your work?"

They were paused now, listening. His words instilled an uncertainty that made them amenable to talk. Alex came panting to Oren's side. The three men faced the phalanx of protest.

Oren took one step forward. He swept a scornful hand toward the machines. "Do you really believe such a thing?" he said. "Did you expect me to fire the lot of you the minute these machines were working?" He paused, watching them. "Why, I think you did believe it!"

They answered him, not singly but together. It was as though Oren were talking to a single man, instead of one hundred and twenty-five.

"I'll tell you here and now," Oren said. "These machines are not replacements for your work. No sir! I need all the production I can get. We'll still have more demand for your output than you can possibly supply." He lifted his arms. "Why, these machines will just take the pressure off of you. You know how we have to drive so hard to try to build production. The machines will make a cheap cigarette for the cheap trade. They'll keep us from having to cheapen our handrolled cigarettes in order to make more of them." He paused. "I'll promise you one thing, men. One simple promise. As long as there's an O.K. Durham cigarette on the market, it'll be a handrolled cigarette."

The anger was ebbing. They nodded, murmuring at each other. Oren watched their faces, dark and bearded, alien still after their years in the town, and he saw that he had won. He drove the victory home.

"Why, no man of taste and discrimination would smoke anything but a handrolled cigarette," he said in a scornful voice. "You know that. I know that. The machines will manufacture a cheap cigarette for those folks who can't tell the difference anyway. We'll go right on making the best handrolled cigarettes in the world—and you will do the handrolling. Now, get back to your benches and get to work."

They ebbed away, shuffling their feet, ashamed now of their violent anger. Oren watched them.

"Go on, Alex," he said. "Get them settled down."

Alex looked into his eyes. "This is the truth, Mr. Knox?"

Oren returned the look. He wavered for a moment. Then he said, "Alex, you're an intelligent man. It is the truth for the foreseeable future—because we need both kinds of production. But you know as well as I do that if these machines are successful, handrolling will soon be a thing of the past."

"What about my people? Do you expect me to go among them, knowing these things?"

"Do you owe your loyalty to the factory or to your people?" Oren said sharply. "You're my production foreman, you know. You're not a roller."

"I owe it to both," Alex said simply. "You cannot ask me to deceive these men, Mr. Knox. I have brought them here . . ."

Oren put his hand on his arm. "Don't worry about it, Alex," he said. "When the time comes, I will ease the way. Now, that's a promise to you, man to man. We'll slack off gradually on the handrolling, letting a few go at a time instead of dumping them on the street. We will retrain those we can to handle the machines. We'll make the change as painless as possible."

Alex continued to watch his face. "I know you are a hard

man, Mr. Knox," he said. "Why should you do such a thing, for the benefit of other men?"

"Because it's to my benefit," Oren said. "Do you think I want them wrecking my factory? Do you think I want them stirring up dissension here in town?"

Alex watched him a moment longer. Then, without a word, he turned away. He went to his men, moved among them, settling them down to work.

"Don't worry about the machines," he kept telling them. "Just do your job, that's all. Just do your job."

Charles had disappeared under the first machine. Oren stood watching as he labored delicately with the mechanism. After a while, Alex returned to his side.

"Will they really work?" he said.

Oren nodded. "They've got to work," he said. "The principle is there . . . it's just a matter of getting practical use out of it. Little troubles keep cropping up."

"A machine to roll cigarettes," Alex said. "I did not believe such a thing could be possible."

He approached the machine, examined it closely. Oren watched him trace out the various mechanisms. He squatted beside the machine for some minutes to watch Charles.

Charles turned his head. "Hand me that wrench there, will you?" he said briefly.

Alex found the wrench, passed it. As Charles took it, he smeared grease on the side of Alex's hand. Alex looked at the grease, slowly, took a piece of waste and wiped it away.

"If you . . ." he said in a hesitant voice, after five more minutes of watching. "If you pulled this up to here." He pointed with one finger.

Charles paused, cocking one eye toward him. "You know anything about cigarette machines?" he said.

Alex was abashed. "No," he said. "It only seemed to me that . . ."

Charles studied the adjustment. He loosened a bolt, shifted the slide with a couple of quick taps, tightened the bolt.

"It won't work up there," he said. "You can't bring it that far . . ." He stopped. "Yes. Yes, it might . . ."

He began working furiously. There was no more conversation until he came out from under the machine, wiping his hands on his thighs.

"By golly, I think that'll work," he said. "Now, that takes care of that little problem. But what are we going to do about that feed roller? See how it . . ."

He was pointing, showing Alex the problem with the feed roller. Alex stooped, peering into the machine. Oren came close.

"You like that machine, Alex?" he said.

Alex glanced at him. "It is . . . fascinating," he said. "To do the work of a human hand . . ."

"You want to help Charles out?"

Alex rubbed his hands together. "But I am not a mechanic," he said. "I am only a cigarette roller. Besides, my job is there."

"Those men can work along without you," Oren said. "Make one of them your assistant. Then you can stay here and help Charles get these machines into working order."

"If Mr. Charles needs me . . ." Alex said, his voice still hesitant. Yet Oren could tell that it was eager, also.

"What about it, Charles?" Oren said. "Think he could be of any help?"

"I need somebody, all right," Charles said. "He took one look at the machine and he knew what it was all about." He straightened, looking at Alex. "What's your name, anyway?"

"Alex Michael," Alex said. "And you are Charles . . ."

"Whitfield," Charles said. "He's got a mechanical sense, Mr. Knox. Why, he showed me something there I've needed to see for a month and I never had."

"I am not a mechanic," Alex said again. "I am only a roller."

"You stay here and help Charles out," Oren said. "We've got to get these machines into production."

Oren went away. When he returned, two hours later, Alex had his coat and vest and shirt off, working bare-chested under the machine. There was grease up to his elbows and a happy expression on his face. He grinned up at Oren.

"It is a thing," he said. "It is really a thing, Mr. Knox."

"Think it'll make cigarettes?" Oren said.

"Yes," Alex said positively. "It will make cigarettes like a dog making puppies."

"O.K., Alex, let's put the power to her," Charles said. "Ready?"

"Ready," Alex said.

The hopper was loaded with tobacco. The machine made a sound within itself as it began to move. The belts came into motion, the wheels turned. The sounds were ratchety sounds, of slipping and sliding, of turning gears and moving belts. The first cigarette fell out of the machine. Alex picked it up, feeling it with practiced fingers.

"Too loose," he called over the sound of machinery.

Charles stopped the machine. Oren looked toward the hand-rollers. They were watching, stopped momentarily in the practice of their art. Charles and Alex, descending on the machine in concert, worked furiously for ten minutes.

"Try it again," Alex said.

The machine started once more. The first cigarette emerged. Alex took it, rolling it between his fingers.

"It is good," he called. "Let it roll."

The machine began spitting cigarettes. It ran for fifteen minutes, the white cylinders piling up with incredible facility, before the continuous cigarette tore, dumping tobacco on the floor underneath. Charles stopped the machine and the two men bowed over it, high priests in their ritual.

Oren left them. He was satisfied. The production was in good hands. The selling was in his. They were also good hands. On this day, Oren was very content.

It was three months before a full day's production with all three machines was achieved. Several times they got a full day from one machine, or even two out of the three. But it seemed impossible to get them all operating at one hundred per cent of capacity.

It was a time of intense concentration for everyone. Alex and Charles practically lived with the machines. They had the job not only of making the machines reliable but of training men to run them once they were. After the first few days chosen operators were standing by to be instructed by Alex and Charles. Alex had virtually abandoned his role as production foreman of the handrollers. He was, by now, as committed to the machine as Charles Whitfield himself. He had descended from a family of handrollers, for that had been his father's trade in Mother Russia. The tradition did not matter now. He had not only become an American; he had acquired the American faith in machinery and mass production.

There was a great deal to do. Oren did not want to release the machine-made cigarette until he could be assured of quantity production. There was also the task of designing a new trademark and a sales campaign to go along with it. He chose the name Manchester, after the town, for the leading brand. The cheap brand, he decided, would be named Machine.

"It's going to be hard to switch folks to machine-made cigarettes," he told Taylor Tryon. "We might as well take the bull by the horns and brag about it. Make people think they're *better* than the handrolled variety."

He decided to put a replica of the Whitfield cigarette machine on the cheap cigarette, along with the legend, *Untouched by Human Hands.* After further thought, he decided on the same legend for the Manchester brand.

"That'll be our line," he told Taylor. "Untouched by human hands. Talk about spit, Taylor. You can imply that handrolled cigarettes are sealed by the mouth-spit of the rollers."

At first he considered putting the Manchester cathedral on the label, but decided against it.

"Let's just use a pretty woman," he said. "Use that best picture of Madame Rena."

"But how does that tie in with Manchester?" Taylor asked.

"A picture of a pretty woman doesn't have to tie in with anything," Oren said. The memory of Madame Rena smoking O.K. Durham cigarettes in her sumptuous suite in Atlanta flitted across his memory. "You know, Taylor, we use pictures of women to sell cigarettes to men. One of these days we'll be selling cigarettes to women, too."

"That'll be the day," Taylor said, a wrinkle of disgust crossing his face.

"There's a whole unexploited market," Oren said. "Half of our population, if not more." He looked thoughtful. "I wish I could think of some way to open it up."

"It'll never happen," Taylor declared. "Why, you know the kind of woman who does smoke a cigarette occasionally. Do you think our mothers and sisters and wives will ever . . ."

"One of the greatest ladies I ever met in my life smoked cigarettes," Oren said.

At the expression on his face, Taylor shut up.

"What I wish is, we could get a better package," Oren said. "These damn paper wrappers are too cheap; you can crush your cigarettes in them. The box that the Egyptian brands use is too expensive for our mass production."

This particular problem was solved by Alex Michael. He came to Oren one day, excitement gleaming in his eyes.

"Mr. Knox," he said. "We need a better package for our cigarettes."

"You're not telling me a thing," Oren said. "Have you got one?"

"I think I have," Alex said. "Not only that. One that can be made by machinery."

"Tell me about it."

Alex showed him two pieces of flimsy pasteboard. "You start with this," he said. "Now look. This one is folded like this, forming the cover. It will carry your label." His hands manipulated the cardboard rapidly. "The other makes the box itself to hold the cigarettes. Now. The cover slides over the box. Like this." He demonstrated.

Oren studied the package with interest. "Just like a bureau drawer," he said. "How much will it cost to make? I've thought about boxes before—but they're so damned expensive."

"I think Charles and I can design machinery to stamp and cut both pieces," Alex said, suppressed excitement in his voice. "I thought about it one night and the next day I talked to Charles."

"By God, we'll patent that," Oren said. "Along with the machinery to make it. You and Charles go ahead on it." He frowned. "I'll have to make an arrangement with Charles if he's going to work on it. He's not an employee, like you." He looked at Alex. "It's your idea, not his?"

"Yes," Alex said.

"All right. You work it out yourself. We'll patent it in the name of the factory. I'll see you get your reward. Hell, you're due a reward anyway, for what you've done with the machines. Of course, you know you're the production foreman on the machines now, just like you used to be on the handrolling operations."

"That is all I want," Alex said quietly. "But Charles . . . he already knows about the slide-and-shell box."

"Let him advise you. But make it clear that it's a Fuller and Knox patent, not a Whitfield patent."

The box was designed, handmade at first while Alex and Charles were designing the machinery to stamp and cut the components automatically. By the time the cigarette machines were in full production, they were making the boxes with machinery, also. There was some trouble about securing the patent, because similar boxes were beginning to come on the market. But, with the patent on the cutting and stamping machinery, they succeeded in securing the exclusive patent to that particular type of box.

One afternoon, near quitting time, Alex and Charles appeared in the doorway of Oren's office. Oren looked up from a column of figures he had just added.

"Yes?" he said.

"All three machines have been going all day long," Charles said. "Not a breakdown. Not a clog-up."

"I want to see that," Oren said.

They went to the making floor. Oren paused, watching. The three machines were tended by male operators. The work flow was smooth, uninterrupted. A crew of girls was handpacking the finished cigarettes in the slide-and-shell boxes; Negro boys were packing the filled boxes into cartons and wheeling them away.

"That, gentlemen, is a sight to behold," Oren said. "You are to be congratulated."

"One of these days it'll all be automatic," Charles said. "There will be machinery to pack the cigarettes in the boxes, the boxes into cartons, and a moving belt to carry away the cartons to the shipping room. But this is the beginning, Mr. Knox."

"Yes," Oren said. "The beginning." He looked at the two men. "Tonight we will have dinner at my house. It is time for our conference about how we will exploit the opportunity we've worked up for ourselves. Taylor will be there, too."

Trenholm presided over the dinner table. They were all wearing their best clothes. It was the first time Charles and Alex had been invited to the Knox home. Trenholm was gracious with Alex, with Charles, with Taylor. During the meal they talked about the factory but only when they had retired to the parlor and Oren had passed around cigars did he broach the real subject of the meeting.

"I have been thinking, while you all have been working," he said. "You have the results of the work. Here is the result of my thinking."

He turned his head, looking at Charles. "Mr. Whitfield, I would like to make you a partner in our operation. If you will assign your patent rights to Fuller and Knox, you can come in with us."

Charles shook his head. "No," he said. "It's a generous offer, Mr. Knox. But I don't want my machine to be limited to one factory in the industry. I want it to be used by everyone who makes cigarettes."

"In time we will be the cigarette industry," Oren said. "I'm offering you a place on the ground floor, Charles."

Charles smiled. "When you're the whole industry, you will have exclusive use of the machines," he said. "Not until then."

Oren studied him. Then he rose. Charles rose, also, to take the hand that Oren extended.

"We won't fuss about it now," Oren said. "What are your present plans?"

"Alex can handle the three machines here," Charles said. "I'm going home to make more machines. If Alex runs into trouble, telegraph me. I'll come a-running."

"When will you have another machine ready?"

Charles frowned. "I don't know. A few weeks."

"I want that machine," Oren said.

"Are you expanding already?" Taylor said. "When we haven't sold the first cigarette yet?"

Oren turned his head. "I'm going to New York," he said. "We must open up a national distribution. I think the best way is for me to go up there, install one machine to start with, and manufacture on the spot." He looked at Charles Whitfield again. "You let me know when that machine is ready. Will you install it for me in New York?"

"Sure," Charles said. "Anywhere you say."

Oren led Charles to the front door. "Good night, Charles," he said. "I appreciate all you've done. Let me know about the new machine."

He returned to the parlor, sat down. "I wanted him to come in with us," he said. "But he's stubborn. One of these days, though, I intend to have *exclusive* use of the Whitfield machine."

He paused before going on. "Here's the plan of organization," he said. "First, I want you to know what my purpose is. I intend to run our competitors out of business or into a merger with us. All four of them. If anybody else starts manufacturing cigarettes, in quantity at least, we'll add them to the list."

"What about Bedrossian, those others in New York?" Taylor said.

"Don't worry about the specialty makers. Our competitors are Lathrop & Winter, Workman Tobacco Company, Barth and Company, and Coffey and Company."

"Lathrop & Winter, at least, hate your guts," Taylor said.

"They're businessmen," Oren said. "When they see the handwriting on the wall, they'll come to taw. Alex, you are the factory manager. You will be in complete charge, from buying the leaf to shipping the finished product. Your prime responsibility will be the machines, of course. But I have a suggestion or two for you."

"Yes sir?" Alex said.

"Train female operators for the machines," Oren said. "They'll be better at it in the long run, and cheaper, too. Find a promising man and train him, like Charles trained you, in the mechanics, so you won't be tied down to the machines all the time. Your responsibilities will be much larger than before, because I won't be here."

He turned to Taylor. "It's your job to sell these cigarettes. While you're selling them, I want you to build a sales organization that can stand on its own feet. Because you're going traveling."

"Traveling?" Taylor said.

"Furrin travel," Oren said, grinning at him. "The world is your backyard, son. Just as soon as you can, I aim for you to be selling Manchester and Machine cigarettes in Europe. Why, they must be a raft of folks over there who're paying a nickel apiece for those Russian and Turkish cigarettes. They ought to welcome a better cigarette at such a lower price."

Taylor drew a deep breath. "Well, you sure socked me with that one."

"I want a sales organization that can stand on its own two feet," Oren said. "With you in Europe and me in New York, it'll have to. I can supervise it to some extent, but not day to day."

He paused, watching the two men. "Gentlemen, do you understand what I'm saying? More than anything else, right now we need good men. Don't be afraid to delegate authority. If they live up to it, fine. If they don't, fire them out of your way before they become deadwood. I've found me two good men already, named Alex Michael and Taylor Tryon. We need more. There's nothing more important to us at this point. Alex, think about the time when you'll be supervising our Manchester factory, our

New York factory, as well as the six factories that belong to our competitors. You'd better think about eight good factory men. I want men who've worked with us before, not men who've worked for our competitors. We want their loyalty to us, not to them.

"Taylor, take this thought into your mind for a minute. We'll have machine production in eight factories. What kind of sales organization will you need to sell that many cigarettes? Find me men, Taylor. You can't do it all by yourself."

"Do you really think you can organize the entire cigarette trade?" Taylor said.

"I'll do it or go broke trying," Oren said. "Rockefeller has done it in oil. Carnegie has done it in steel. They talk about the Oil Trust now. They talk about the Steel Trust. Before too long they'll be talking about the Tobacco Trust. That will be us."

"How long will it take?"

"Seven years," Oren said without hesitation. "Give us three years to get started; build our production, find our men, gather our capital. By 1887 we'll be in position to start the war. By 1891 we'll have them driven to the wall and ready to talk terms."

"How?"

"Advertise, advertise. Premium them to death. Flood the dealers with chairs and clocks, whatever will make 'em take Manchester and Machine cigarettes. Just like we've been doing with O.K. Durhams—except on a grander scale. Premiums for the consumer. Put numbered pictures in each package. Get the kids to collecting them. Nothing new. Just more money spent on it, more energy, more thought. It's worked, up to now. Think how it'll work with our margin of profit on our machine production."

Oren rose. "Here in this room stand three men," he said in a quiet voice. "We hold the cigarette industry at our mercy. All we have to do is reach out and grab it. Alex on the producing, you on the selling, me in the middle, helping where I can and working out the over-all strategy. Are you with me, gentlemen?"

Taylor grinned. "I'm gonna be rich yet, ain't I?" he said.

"We'll all be rich," Oren said. "More than that. We'll be men of power in the world."

They shook hands, solemnly, as at a wedding or a funeral. Three men; the elegantly-dressed, hearty salesman, the strange, dark alien who had found the love of machinery in this new land where fate had brought him, the stumpy man with the nondescript face and the cold blue eyes.

After they had departed, Oren locked the front door and ascended the stairs to the second floor. He knocked on Trenholm's door.

"May I come in?" he called.

"Come in, Mr. Knox."

Oren turned the knob, entered. Trenholm was sitting up in bed, a bed jacket over her shoulders. One light was on, beside the bed. A book lay across her lap.

"Yes, Mr. Knox?" she said.

"That was a fine dinner you served my guests tonight," Oren said.

"Thank you, Mr. Knox," Trenholm said. "That Alex Michael is a strange little man, isn't he?"

"He's a Jew," Oren said heavily. "They're not like us. He's a man to have around, though. He knows them cigarette machines as good as Charles Whitfield by now."

Trenholm took off her reading glasses. "I believe he is the first Jew we have ever had in the house," she said. "I wondered if he would eat anything. They say . . ."

"I guess he's had to quit worrying about kosher since he come south," Oren said. "What I come to tell you, I'm going to New York."

"A business trip?"

"I will be there for some time. I intend to establish a factory in that city. It may be a year or more before I'm home permanently, except for a day or two at a time."

"Why are you telling me your plans, Mr. Knox?"

"I thought you might want to go, too."

"But what would I do in New York? I know no one there. I have my friends here, my clubs. I have social obligations that I can't leave. No, Mr. Knox. I do not wish to go to New York."

Oren watched her. It was a strange marriage. He had to admit that fact to himself. There had never been a cross word between them since that first night. They were polite, even friendly at times, but always distant. She lived her own life, she ran the house efficiently, she met his rare demands for hospitality among his business associates with uncomplaining attention.

He put his hand on the door knob. Then he turned back. "Trenholm," he said. "Do you want a child? I could give you a child and then you would have . . ."

"Why, Mr. Knox!" she said in a scandalized voice.

"I reckon not," Oren said. "I'm sorry I brought it up, Trenholm. Well, I'll be off to New York as soon as I can manage it."

"Let me know in time to pack for you," Trenholm said. "Be sure your shirts are clean, and all." Oren stepped through the door. "Is the business going well, Mr. Knox?"

"Yes," Oren said. "Very well."

"Good night, Mr. Knox."

"Good night."

Chapter Ten

THE train wound its slow way through Virginia. Oren, ordinarily, would have been alert for the condition of the crops along the right-of-way, for the number of Fuller and Knox Cigarette Company, Inc. brand-name advertising signs he could see from his window, for the general air of easy times or money-tightness as evidenced by the dress and demeanor of the people. He was prone to count the number of cigarette smokers he could see within a given hour, comparing it to last week's or last month's or last year's count.

Though these things were of constant interest, today far more important matters occupied his mind; two important questions that had come to assume an over-riding importance in his life.

Oren Knox was twenty-nine years old. During his three years in New York, he had become heavier both in body and in face. Clean-shaven always, the cold blue eyes remained his most dominant feature. His jaw was heavier now, as was his body. He did not have a paunch, but it was easy to see that within ten years he would have. He wore more expensive clothing, of better material. His coat was cut in the Prince Albert style and there was a discreet piping along the edge of the vest. His derby hat rested on the seat beside him. His solid-black shoes were made of supple kangaroo leather. He looked exactly what he was; a solid, conservative, successful businessman, with no nonsense about him.

There was, indeed, no nonsense; behind the façade reposed the mind of a pirate, keen and rapacious, honed to a fighting edge. Yet, within the pirate-mind, there inexplicably dwelled a soft yearning; as random as cancer, he felt, and just as dangerous. Little wonder that he could not pursue his usual travel-games.

Oren Knox was returning home for good. For some time he had considered returning his base of operations to Manchester. The New York factory was operating on a profitable basis—had, indeed, been profitable since its first year. There were now four Whitfield machines in the loft on Rivington Street. He had built an excellent sales organization that could, at a moment's notice, be transferred over to Taylor Tryon. The factory already had its production manager, capable and trustworthy, on whom Alex Michael could keep an occasional eye after Oren's departure.

Only last week the signal had come. Even before then he had found within himself a yearning to go home. He had sternly suppressed it as personal indulgence. He was afraid of the wish. He did not understand its cause, its meaning. It was a feeling he had never expected to encounter within his soul. But, after being given the signal, he had known that unconsciously, because of the fear, he had been postponing his inevitable return. Oren Knox was a man without fear, though in tense moments his hands sweated in the palm and he would feel an almost irresistible impulse to rub them against his thighs. In this he was truly afraid—of his wife.

New York had been a new horizon, a great adventure. On his first day he ate breakfast from a high stool at the Astor House. It was good to eat his meal in such surroundings. Over his second cup of coffee he scanned his newspaper, finding ominous news of tight money in Wall Street. It was to be a long time before he again ate such a meal in such surroundings.

On that first day he had leased a small loft on Rivington Street, had rented a three-dollar-a-week furnished room in which to live. While his first machine was being installed he had started calling on the retail and wholesale trade, selling the output of the Manchester factory until he could begin production in the Rivington Street loft.

He had never experienced the joy of starting his own factory from scratch. He had, perforce, built on the substructure of the old Fuller Tobacco Factory, adapting himself to the exigencies of Mr. Fuller, of the factory itself. Here he was beginning from nothing. New York absorbed him as it had absorbed millions more like him, unheedful of his presence, his ambitions, his needs.

His day was eighteen hours long. He spent the working hours, at first, watching the machines as they spewed forth cigarettes. He inspected the product at irregular intervals, by this means keeping the work force on its toes. After factory hours he visited tobacco shops, talking incessantly with proprietors and customers. On the dark side of midnight he would be awake in his three-dollar-a-week room, planning new posters and advertisements.

His first business connection was with G. Houghtaling and Company, the largest billboard and sign-posting concern in the country. His second and third business connections were with Ward and Company and Goldman, Sachs. After the Rivington Street factory had reached full production, he negotiated small loans, in the form of thirty or sixty-day notes. He did not need the money, for the firm's bank account was substantial. He carried a small calendar in his pocket, the due dates circled as heavily as they were circled in his mind. He paid each note promptly two or three days in advance. The day a well-groomed gentleman from Goldman, Sachs dropped into his office to take him to lunch and inquire tactfully concerning his financial needs, Oren felt an exceeding gratification.

His second year in New York, Oren purchased for cash Lichenstein Brothers' works at 38th Street and First Avenue. He made a quick trip home to reshape the enlarged organization into a corporation, with a capitalization of two hundred and fifty thousand dollars. The new stock was closely held among Oren,

Trenholm, Taylor Tryon and Alex Michael. He gave a few shares to Helen Fowlkes and was surprised when she burst into tears. Oren himself retained sixty-five per cent.

The other cigarette factories were beginning by now to feel his presence. He doubted seriously that Willard Lathrop was doing much laughing when he thought of Oren Knox. They had dozed for some time, secure in their conviction that handrolled cigarettes were superior to machine-made. Belatedly they had started installing cigarette machines, preparing to fight Oren on his own grounds.

They had fought hard. Oren steadily increased the money poured into advertising and premiums. Taylor Tryon opened up the Midwest, then departed for Europe. His trip was a spectacular success. He remained abroad for a year, leaving a small but excellent organization behind to carry on the missionary work. Oren's opponents spent money, too, reckless of profits, knowing that they were steadily going down under the intensified assault from Fuller and Knox.

Oren was never worried about the outcome. His competition had started too late, too reluctantly, with too little conviction, and they would never catch up. He had a six-cents-a-thousand advantage on the machine royalties, though two other makes of machines came into the arena. He exploited his advantage to the full. He continued to install more Whitfield machines, steadily cutting back on the handrolled production until the O.K. Durham cigarette had become a specialty item. He had four Whitfield machines in the New York factory and fifteen in Manchester, giving him a production of one and a half million cigarettes per day at home and four hundred thousand daily in New York.

Last week, at last, the signal had come. He had learned a few days before, from one of Tryon's salesmen, that Workman Tobacco Company had abruptly closed its Baltimore plant. He was, therefore, not overwhelmed with surprise when Mr. Thomas Workman handed in his card one day at the Rivington Street office, requesting an interview with Mr. Oren Knox.

Oren still lived in his cheap furnished room. He had not yet eaten another breakfast at the Astor House. But in the Rivington Street factory he had fixed up a fine office, with a new roll-top desk and a thick carpet. He met Mr. Workman at the door, shook his hand, and led him to a comfortable chair.

"What can I do for you, Mr. Workman?" he said.

He had never met the man. He had, indeed, met only Willard Lathrop among his rivals. Oren knew the principal men in each of the four companies met at least once a year for an annual banquet. They called it the Cigarette Manufacturers' Association. In his own mind, since he had first heard of it, Oren had called it the How-The-Hell-Can-We-Stop-Oren-Knox Association.

Mr. Workman was a tall man, lean, elegantly dressed. His face was thin and pale, almost English except for a luxuriant mustache that swept exuberantly across his upper lip. He carried a silver-headed cane and even on entering Oren Knox's office—an action, Oren was sure, Mr. Workman would have sworn he would never perform in his lifetime—there was about him an air of grace and certitude. Mr. Workman sat down, folded his hands over the top of his stick. He regarded Oren with bland, seemingly untroubled eyes. Watching him, Oren was acutely conscious that he, Oren Knox, had once been a barefoot boy in a farm yard, he had once worn a ten-dollar suit of clothes.

"I think it's rather what we can do for each other," Mr. Workman said.

One would have thought that this was Workman's own office, that Oren had asked for the interview.

"What you got in mind?" Oren said bluntly. "I heard about you having to close your factory in Baltimore."

He saw the flicker in Mr. Workman's eyes. He recognized it. Fear. This elegant, well-dressed man was afraid. Oren leaned back in his chair.

"So there's no point in trying to hide the fact that you're in trouble," he said.

Mr. Workman looked down at his hands folded on top of the cane. "It's been a tough fight," he said. "I think it's time we began to think about bringing it to an end." He took a deep breath, looking up at Oren once again. "I want to discuss with you the possibility of a merger of our two firms," he said. "You know what we can bring to such a merger. Our Merlin brand was at one time the most popular cigarette in the country, leading even Lathrop and Winter's Dominion Straight Cut. Our Daisy Chain is a good second-line cigarette."

Oren had to admire the man. He wondered how many sleepless nights of staring at impossible alternatives had contributed to the making of that little speech.

He did not allow his impression to show on his face. "Mr. Workman," he said. "I am not interested in merging with Workman Tobacco."

Astonishment, bewilderment, showed in Mr. Workman's face. "But I thought . . ." he said. "This war we've been carrying on . . ."

Oren tented his fingers. "Have you discussed the situation with your friends in the Cigarette Manufacturers' Association?" he inquired delicately.

"Yes," Mr. Workman said. "We have had several meetings in the past month."

Oren peered at him shrewdly. "They didn't give you much comfort, did they?" he said.

"They have their own troubles," Mr. Workman said.

Oren chuckled. "Yeah. I reckon they do. They got the same trouble you got, Mr. Workman. A disease named Oren Knox."

Mr. Workman rose. "If you're not interested, there's no point . . ." he said with dignity.

"Sit down, Mr. Workman, sit down," Oren said. "I didn't say I wasn't interested in forming a combination."

Mr. Workman sank slowly into his chair.

Oren thought for a moment. "Here's the situation as I see it," he said. "What is required is a combination. Putting our businesses together wouldn't alter a thing. We're all spending too much money on premiums and advertising. I can spend that kind of money and still make a profit. You cannot. Not one of the Big Four can. If you and I should merge, the war would go on with the other three. That is why I am not interested in whatever proposition you might be inclined to offer, Mr. Workman."

"Together we would be stronger," Mr. Workman said. "You would have two well-established brands, Merlin and Daisy Chain, to add to . . ."

Oren waved his hand. "Your organization is weak, or you wouldn't be here," he said. "I have to consider the fact that you might weaken my organization, instead of mine strengthening yours." He shook his head. "No. I'm sorry, Mr. Workman. I can't see it."

He read the despair in the man's eyes. He went on quickly.

"I would suggest that you talk to your friends," he said. "Show them the advantages of combination. Point out the great things that are being done in oil and sugar and steel. Those are the men who are pointing the way we should follow, Mr. Workman. In combination, the five of us would control the cigarette industry. We would all make a great deal of money. Tell them they can have Oren Knox working *for* them instead of against them."

"You would, of course, head up the combination," Mr. Workman said, a trace of bitterness in his voice.

"Naturally. I'm the best man."

"You're not the biggest company. In fact, you . . ."

"I will be the biggest. You might also point out to your friends the alternatives. It's either combine or get out of the business. That is the proposition you yourself are facing at this point. Their time will come, too." He paused, studying Mr. Workman. "I am an ambitious man, Mr. Workman. But I am not greedy. I don't want to drive my competitors into bankruptcy. I just want them to get to the point of reason. The sooner you can bring them to it, the better it will be for everyone concerned."

He rose, held out his hand.

"That is what I have to tell you, Mr. Workman. Combination. Bring the other three companies with you and, instead of being a concern on the edge of bankruptcy, you will have a respectable and profitable portion of a combination."

Mr. Workman rose, also. He did not take the proffered hand. "I don't think you know how those men hate you, Mr. Knox," he said.

"I'm not exactly in love with them myself," Oren said in an unperturbed voice. "But you can't let hate stand in the way of business, can you?"

It was the first break in the ranks of his enemies and he could no longer delay his return. Once the decision to go home had been made, he was disconcerted by the eagerness that had built itself unawares within his soul.

The truth was, Oren Knox wanted a son.

The New York years, in spite of his absorbed busyness, had been lonely years. He had, it is true, returned to Manchester on several occasions for a day or two at a time. He had slept at the house. But he had seen Trenholm only on arrival and departure.

Oren, though he had been alone all his life, had never known loneliness. He was astonished to discover the emotion within himself. Trenholm had been always a stranger, since their wedding night and before. Eight years married, their relationship, strange though it was, long since had settled into a pattern as real and enduring as a true marriage. Trenholm counted on Oren for status in the community, sufficient money on which to run the house and buy her clothes, a future wealth. He counted on Trenholm to preserve the fiction of their marriage before the world, to maintain the home, to entertain his business friends when occasion demanded. She was as much an asset as if she had been entered on Helen Fowlkes' books at the factory.

The relationship contented the needs of both. There was no bitterness in Oren—not any longer—for the message she had brought on their wedding night. He considered it as he would have considered being worsted in a business deal. She had denied him an asset that was his by right, as a businessman might have got away with a damaged inventory. At least, he was sure that he felt this way about it.

Now, inexplicably, he had an intense desire to alter this viable relationship, established over their eight years together. Oren had never thought of himself as a man who needed sons. He built for himself alone, for wealth and power and prestige, out of a hunger he had known all his life.

This new demand for continuity had crept upon him unawares during the lonely New York years. At random times he had felt a momentary lethargy that was as alien to him as anything could possibly be. On an occasional morning he rose to face a day that did not seem worthwhile at the expense of effort it would call forth. These moments were never long, for with characteristic energy he bustled them into submission by summoning the ever-present dream of the tobacco trust of which he would be the head and symbol.

He began actively worrying when, one day, the thought crept into his mind that even if the combination should be achieved it would not be worth the effort he would have expended to bring it about.

That day he had called on a man in his office.

"Mr. Knox, I want you to meet my son," the man had said. "I've told him about you and he's anxious to make your acquaintance."

Oren shook the boy's hand. He was handsome, clean-cut, with a becoming modesty at meeting such a great man as Oren Knox.

The father put his hand on the son's shoulder. "Thomas will succeed me in this business when the time comes," he said proudly. "He's working during the summer to learn how a brokerage firm does business."

"Why, you've got a right to be proud of him, then," Oren had said.

On the street once again, Oren could not banish the memory of the handsome, clever boy. There's a man who's got a world of time to look forward to, he thought. The world don't come to an end with him, because his son . . .

He stopped dead still. He had found the missing element in his own great plans. They came up against a dead end; that curtain behind which all men vanish from view, leaving only their works to mark their passage. Unless he should own an heir.

Oren Knox needed a son. To work for one's own ambition was, in his book, a great thing. It would be greater still to know that a Knox would carry on the design. A king needed a dynasty; a dynasty called for a fruitful flow of heirs.

From that moment the need grew within him until it rivaled the hunger for power, for the one complemented the other. He came to realize that his offer to Trenholm to provide her with a child to occupy her time during his long absence had come from his own unconscious wish, rather than from a desire to accommodate Trenholm. Something within him had known the future need.

Now, on his way home to accomplish his need, he was afraid. He must break the established pattern of their lives, run the risk of destroying everything in the effort to begin a new pattern. The risk and the opportunity overrode even the risks and opportunities inherent in achieving the combination of the cigarette interests into a tobacco trust. The two were linked together into the most daring hazard of his life. If he failed to establish an inner hegemony to match the outer empire, neither would be of consequence. Or vice versa; he must have it all or whatever part was successful would be without meaning.

It was dark when the train arrived in Manchester. He descended, to be met by Taylor Tryon and Alex Michael. He shook their hands, looking about involuntarily for Trenholm, though she never came to the station to greet him.

"I have the new campaign all laid out," Taylor said. "If you can look at it tonight we can start first thing in the morning."

"There is trouble with the handrollers," Alex said. "They are talking about quitting in a body and returning to New York. We need to discuss what you will say to them tomorrow, Mr. Knox. They must hear something from your own lips."

"Not tonight," Oren said. "I'm going home now. I'll see both of you early in the morning at the factory."

He departed alone in the factory buggy, leaving the two men staring after him.

Before his house, he alighted from the buggy and took the two suitcases the driver handed down to him. He had gone away with one suitcase, had returned with two. But he had gained much more, learned much more, during the three years he had spent in New York. He stood on the brick walk, looking at his house. The Fuller house. The thought came unbidden to his mind; *One day soon I will build my own house, instead of living in a house built by another man.*

He hefted the two bags, went slowly up the walk. The front door was locked. He put down the bags, took his key chain from his pocket, unlocked the door. The foyer was dark. Setting the bags down inside the foyer, in the darkness he knocked over a hatrack. A gleam of light showed on the stair-well wall as a door was opened upstairs.

"Is that you, Mr. Knox?" Trenholm's voice said.

"Yes," he said. "It's me."

He did not bother to turn on a downstairs light because the stair well was lighted indirectly from above. He lifted the bags and went up the steps to the second floor. Trenholm was standing in her bedroom doorway.

"Welcome home, Mr. Knox," she said.

"Thank you, Trenholm," he said gravely.

She was much the same as when he had married her eight years ago; a trifle plumper, but with the same bland face, creamy-skinned, and the same marvelous eyes. She was wearing a floor-length dressing-gown, plum-colored. He remembered that she was now twenty-six. He wondered suddenly if she enjoyed her life as much as she seemed to do. Once there had been a fear in his mind that, given their unusual marital arrangement, she might return to her stableboy. But since her marriage she had given up horseback riding, remarking that, to her mind, it did not become a married woman.

"Have you had dinner?" she asked.

"I ate on the train."

He had bought a sandwich and a pop from the train butcher, with a candy bar for dessert. He never ate in the dining car if he could avoid it. In spite of his light repast, he was not hungry.

"Did your business go well in New York?" she asked.

"Very well," he said. "I can leave it to run itself, now, with just an occasional trip to see to things."

"Then you are home for good."

"Yes," he said. "I am home for good."

There did not seem to be anything more to say. She closed her door, leaving him standing alone in the hall. He opened his own door and took the suitcases into his room. Meticulously he took out his clothing, hung up the suits and arranged the shirts and collars and underwear in the drawers.

When he was finished, he left the room, bearing the gift he had bought in New York, and paused to knock on Trenholm's door. "Trenholm," he said through the wooden panel. "There is something I wish to discuss with you. I will be in the parlor."

He went on downstairs, entered the parlor. It remained as it had been during his courting days, crowded with furniture, overstuffed with pillows, littered with whatnots. A piece of music lay open on the piano. The small room still seemed to hold the stale fragrance of Foster Fuller's after-dinner cigar.

It was some time before she came. While he waited, Oren moved restlessly about the room, touching each heavy piece of furniture, looking at each decoration, as though he were viewing them for the first time. When Trenholm entered, he saw that she had prepared herself as though for a new day. She wore a dress with a ruffing of lace on the high neckline, the white lace cascading down her bosom. She had not bothered to put up her hair, at least, and it floated about her face, making her seem nineteen again. He was surprised that he should be so pleased at this sign of their eight-years formal intimacy.

"I brought you a box of candy from New York," he said, extending it.

She took the box. "Thank you, Mr. Knox," she said.

It was the first time he had brought her a gift from his traveling.

"Open it," he urged. "It's the best candy you can find in New York."

"What did you wish to speak to me about?" she said.

The candy, no more than the ritual candy of courtship, had had no effect. She stood facing him, her hands clasped over the gaudy candy box, her eyes fixed on his face. She was wary, waiting. He turned away, not knowing how to begin. He wandered momentarily about the room. He had manipulated men—his business life consisted so much in persuasion and manipulation—but he had no words to begin with this woman, his wife.

"Trenholm," he said at last. "We have been married eight years. It has, all in all, been a good span of time for both of us—because we have respected each other, we have each done our duty to the other. We have built something. So don't think I'm not pleased with you, Trenholm. No man could ask a wife to do more, under the circumstances of our marriage, than you have done." He paused. Still he did not look at her. He stood facing the wall, staring at a chromo of Niagara Falls.

"There is one duty you have not performed," he said. "There is one duty I have not performed."

A small pause filled the room with its emptiness. Trenholm did not move. Her face remained placid, her lovely eyes watched Oren's back. He had run out of words. He could advance no farther.

"Mr. Knox," she said in a calm voice. "Are you telling me that you have found a woman in New York, whom you intend to make your wife in my place?"

He turned, startled. "A woman!" he said. "What are you talking about?" He paused then, seeing her tenseness. "You know I'm no womanizer," he said. "I never have been, I never will be. Just put that thought right out of your head."

"There was that actress in Atlanta," she said. "The one you used in all the advertising."

He was surprised. "How did you know about her?" he said.

Trenholm did not answer. She stood erect before him, her hands clasping the candy box. Oren was desperate. The conversation had taken a direction he had not anticipated. All the way home in the train he had thought of what he would say, what she must answer; each time he had rehearsed it the conversation had trended exactly to the desired conclusion. Trenholm was refusing to fulfill her role, had instead turned into the channel of her own fears.

"Madame Rena was a lovely woman," he said with dignity. "My relationship with her was purely in a business way. I needed her consent for the advertising. I admired her and respected her, Trenholm. Nothing more."

"Then why do you wish a divorce?" she said.

"I don't want a divorce! I want a son!"

Forced to abandon his careful approach, he blurted the words reckless of their unplanned impact.

It was her turn to be startled. Her face paled, then blushed. She turned away to sink heavily upon a sofa.

"Oh. I see," she said.

He came to stand over her. "I have a right to demand it," he said, doggedly. "That is a husband's right, even if I have waited eight years to exercise it. No wife can deny that demand. But I want your consent, Trenholm. I want you to perform your duty willingly, without begrudging me the act or the consequence."

For the first time, her voice trembled. "You are asking me to . . ."

"I need a son, Trenholm," he said. His voice cried out with the words. "You know what I am doing in the world. You can't ask a man not to want a son to leave it all to, when the time comes." He sank down on the sofa beside her. He wanted to touch her arm. He did not dare. "A man needs more than his own life to look to," he said. "Your own drive will carry you only so far. Then you come to think about the generations. I'm a man who likes power, Trenholm. I intend to have it. But power comes to a stop when you have no future. No man without sons has a future, because the future is more than one lifetime."

She did not answer. He rose, pausing in the middle of the room.

"You know the Oren Knox that first set foot in this parlor," he said quietly. "You know the kind of man I am now. Within the span of three years, I will hold the cigarette industry in the palm of my hand. In five more years I'll have the chewing-tobacco trade, and along with it the snuff and the smoking tobacco. Then I will move out into the world." He turned to her in an intense, controlled movement. "I will be The Tobacco Man. I will control the entire tobacco trade, from the growing of the leaf to the consumption of the final product. That is the man you are married to, Trenholm. I will have power beyond measure, wealth beyond counting. Can you ask a man like that to live his life without a son, to die without someone to leave it all to? You might as well ask a king to destroy his own crown."

He stopped. He could only wait on her now. He felt powerless, as he had never been powerless. For a wild moment he hated her for holding within her secret strength a dominance over him no man had ever held. With a single negative word she could erect a wall to his ambition, beyond which he could never go, no matter how far he might travel in his lifetime.

She looked up. "What will you do if I do not perform this duty?" she asked. "Will you force me?"

For a fixed moment, the will to force her flared within him. Then he shook his head. "No," he said in a calmer voice. "You must be willing. You must not only bear the child, you must raise him." His voice tightened, became harsher. "You are only the vessel, Trenholm. You are the best vessel. But if a vessel won't hold water, you find another one to replace it."

She bowed her head under the harsh words. He thought she was beaten. He had not wished to bring that last irrevocable statement to the fore. But her strength was beyond his understanding. She lifted her head.

"You can come home, demanding your right, when you know how I feel about you?" she said. "When you know that in my soul I have never forgiven you for the manner in which we married? The factory was before me. It is before me still, it will always be before me. Bearing your son will not change that. Yet you can come home, demanding your husband's right?"

Oren's breathing was hard in his chest. "I am not asking for love," he said. "There has never been love between us, Trenholm. Respect. Understanding. A feeling for our mutual duty. All I am asking is that you be a vessel for my seed."

Her face did not change in its freshly acquired calmness. "Then, when I have produced your son, it will be over?"

"Of course," he said. "I am not an idle man, Trenholm."

Her lips tightened. She looked directly into his face. "I will do it," she said. "On one condition."

"The condition?"

"I have never had an allowance of my own. I have had only the money you have paid into the household account at the bank. I want my own allowance, to dispose of as I please."

"Name it. It's yours."

It was like the moment of getting down to brass tacks on a business deal. The agreement was hammered out, only the compensation left to be arranged. Looking down at her, he thought, I'm glad I had Foster Fuller to start with, not Trenholm Fuller.

She named the figure.

"Five hundred dollars a month!" he cried out. "Why, that's more than I've ever drawn from the business myself . . ." He stopped. "All right," he said. "Five hundred dollars a month."

"For life," she said. "Whether or not I succeed in producing a son."

"For life."

"I want it in writing."

"There should be no writing between man and wife, except the marriage certificate. You can be sure . . ."

"In writing," she said.

He did not pause to protest further. He went to the desk where she tended to her household affairs, opened it, secured a piece of her stationery. Without sitting down he leaned over the desk and swiftly penned the agreement. He signed his name, brought it to her. She read it carefully, folded it neatly, tucked it under the cuff of her sleeve. She rose, walked to the parlor door.

"Let me know when you are ready to begin," he said.

Without turning, she said, "There's no point in putting it off, is there? We might as well begin tonight."

He remained motionless in the parlor until her door closed

upstairs. Then, abruptly, he swung his arms, striking his hands together. By God, he thought. There's a woman to birth a son of mine.

Stirred by the exultant, admiring thought, he made a turn about the room. He felt virile, his body crammed with power as his mind was crammed. A worthy vessel awaited.

He delayed an inexplicable time before he ascended the stairs. He went first to his own room, undressed, and donned his bathrobe. It was the same robe he had bought eight years ago for his wedding night. He was naked under the robe and he was intensely aware all over his body of the soft harshness of the fabric against his flesh.

He did not pause to knock, but opened the door. The room was pitch-dark, the curtains drawn at the windows.

"Trenholm," he said.

"Come in, Mr. Knox," she said out of the darkness.

Guided by her voice, he groped toward the bed. And within the darkness he found her warm flesh, the vessel of all his needs.

Chapter Eleven

OREN left for the factory before breakfast, not wanting, as yet, to face Trenholm. Long after he had returned to his own room he had lain awake, realizing just how shaken he had been by the events of darkness.

He arrived at the factory in time to see the hands come to work. They flowed into the factory from every direction; bevies of handsome young girls, laughing and chattering among themselves but sobering as they passed through the portals; Negro men and Negro boys, as well as a few white men and boys; Alex striding alone in his black suit. The Russian Jews arrived in a body, their faces glum and suspicious, as alien still as the day the first group had descended from the train into the town.

Oren, with Alex, embarked upon a tour of the factory. The word of his presence had seeped through the work force. As he moved among them, studying the operations, they assiduously avoided his attention, bending themselves to the machines. He took his time in surveying his domain. He had not been here for a long time, except for cursory visits to the office, and he felt it necessary to assert his presence.

Oren paused before reaching the handrolling floor. "Now what's the trouble with your people?" he asked Alex.

"They are dissatisfied with the quota you sent down from New York," Alex said. "They can't make a living, rolling one thousand cigarettes a day each. That's two dollars and eighty-eight cents a week. It's not a living wage, Mr. Knox. Besides, they have too much time on their hands. They can roll their thousand in about half a day's work. They spend the time talking their grievances. You can't leave a working man's hands idle, Mr. Knox, without expecting mischief."

"Damn it, man, we don't need any more handrolled cigarettes than that," Oren said. "You know how things are going. Within a year or two, at the most, the handrolled cigarette will be a thing of the past. Have you taken as many as you can off the handrolling and put them to work somewhere else?"

"A few," Alex said glumly. "They resist learning a new skill, Mr. Knox. They're handrollers. They want to stay handrollers. They despise the machine-made cigarette, as well as the machinery that makes it. I've got some of the younger men dispersed through the factory. But most of them . . . the older ones, especially . . ." He shook his head.

Oren was irritated beyond measure by the problem. Usually he was capable of taking infinite pains with even the smallest details of the business. This morning, he was uncertain within himself. Instead of remaining in the factory, his mind, in spite of himself, kept drifting back to last night.

"I'm afraid I can't stir up much comfort for them," he said in an angry voice. "All I can give them is the hard facts. It's a dying trade. There's nothing we can do about that. They've just got to face the situation, that's all."

"You told them once that as long as there's an O.K. Durham cigarette, it will be handrolled," Alex said, stubbornness creeping into his voice.

Oren looked at him. "I said, for the foreseeable future," he said. "We've just about run out of stock on that particular item, Mr. Michael."

"You must tell them something," Alex said. "It's not only agitation among themselves; a man from Coffey and Company in New York has been in town, talking to them. He's telling them

Coffey and Company need experienced handrollers—they're willing to pay to get them and give them a full day's work, to boot."

Oren's face cleared. "Why, that's the best solution all the way around," he said. "Let them go back to New York. Then Coffey and Company can worry about their welfare. I tell you, Alex, we don't need them. So don't you do a thing to discourage that particular line of thought."

"Will you speak to them?" Alex said.

"Of course. Now I know exactly what to say."

They went together to the handrolling floor. As they entered through the double doors, the men paused in their desultory work, expectant. This was the quietest floor in the factory, though the original Whitfield machines were still installed and working at the other end of the room. There were fewer of the rollers now and they had yielded much floor space to the demands of the machines.

Oren held up his hand for silence. "Men," he said. "Mr. Michael has asked me to say a few words about the situation here in the Fuller and Knox factory. I have been aware for some time that you are dissatisfied with your working conditions. So I have come from New York to give you an understanding of the position we have come to."

He paused, looking into their faces. They watched him, silent, still. One man completed the rolling of a cigarette, gummed it, laid it aside.

"I'm not going to feed you a lot of guff," Oren said. "I think you are entitled to the truth." He took a breath, watching their faces. "The truth is, within a year Fuller and Knox will not be making a handrolled cigarette. It is no longer economical to do so. What remains of the handrolled business will be left to the specialty manufacturers."

They stirred, looking at each other. Oren was acutely aware of the danger. When the first machines had been installed, he had only narrowly averted their destruction. You couldn't take a man's livelihood away from him with impunity.

"Mr. Michael will begin, this week, a program to end the

handrolling operation," he said, his voice showing a calmness he did not feel. "You will be reassigned as machine operators, or in other jobs. If you do not wish to become a machine operator, I can only suggest that you begin looking elsewhere for employment. For a time, we will continue the handrolling as a charitable gesture, limiting each man to one thousand cigarettes a day. But I know not a man among you wants charity—he wants a job."

He waited a full minute for the reaction that did not come. They sat at their tables, quiescent under his words, the despair gone deeper into their faces.

"That is all I have to say," Oren said. He turned on his heel and left the room.

He stopped outside, listening for the sounds of their revolt. There was only stillness. Alex came through the double doors.

"They accepted it," he said. "They did not become angry."

"They knew they had to accept it," Oren said. "They knew the truth of it. They just hadn't faced it yet."

"They will not stay," Alex said. "They will listen to the Coffey man, now."

Oren nodded. "That's what I want them to do."

The doors opened. The men came through in a body. They marched silently, massed in their black clothing, their bearded faces grim and still. They were wearing their hats and coats.

Oren and Alex moved out of their path as the men marched by. They were not moving in step, but their minds were geared to a common impulse. Oren and Alex fell in behind them, following warily. The men did not seem to be aware of their presence.

The close-grouped mass descended the stairs, marched across the factory yard, and went out at the gate. Oren paused on the steps.

"Well," he said. "That was quick."

"They were on the edge of it before you came," Alex said. "Your words convinced them there was nothing else to do."

They returned to the rolling floor. The tables were deserted. Only five of the men had remained behind.

"Do you want jobs here?" Oren asked.

They were younger men. They sat quietly in their shirt sleeves and vests. They nodded their heads.

"Take care of it," Oren said to Alex. "And get these tables cleared out of here. We need this space for the new machines."

"What about the girls downstairs?" Alex said.

"We will begin the same process with them," Oren said. "Put them on a quota of a thousand cigarettes. The girls won't give us any trouble. They don't care whether they tend a machine or roll a cigarette. Fire the worst ones right now, let them go home to their families."

He left Alex, returning to the office. Helen Fowlkes was there, prepared to show him the books.

"How are you, Helen?" Oren said. He took off his Prince Albert coat, his derby hat, and hung them up. He sat down behind his desk.

"I'm fine, Mr. Knox," she said in her still-bashful voice. Except where her precise figures were concerned, she remained as uncertain of herself as a schoolgirl.

"Well, are we broke yet?" Oren asked.

Helen smiled shyly. "Not yet," she said. "I don't think we ever will be."

Oren chuckled. "Let me see the books," he said.

He pored over the figures. His mind was restless, skittering away into random thoughts. The memory of Trenholm kept intruding. He shook his head, thinking. A man oughtn't to bring his wife to work with him. He ought to be able to leave her in bed at home. His flesh fevered at the thought. Abruptly, he pushed away the books.

"I'll see to these later," he said.

Helen retired hastily from the office. He knew he had hurt her tender feelings. He could not help it. Oren could not concern himself with her. He had more important matters on his mind.

All right, he told himself, now that he was alone. Let's look at it.

He looked at it. He could not believe it, any more than he

had believed while it was actually happening. He had expected Trenholm to be cold, still, quiescent only. He had not demanded ardor from her, only acceptance.

She did not appear to be a woman to contain ardor. She was too placid, too deep within her own self, to participate in the act of love. Within the darkness she had become a lovely, warm stranger. There had been, at first, a totally feminine reluctance, a slow yielding. But, once yielding, she had yielded all the way.

Oren's only previous experience had been with Madame Rena. She had been gay, shameless, uninhibited and experienced. Her virtuosity had taken Oren's breath away. His own stolid concentration on the business at hand had been to her a sheer delight. With Madame Rena, the act of sex had been a glittering toy, to be played with and tossed away without further thought once the interest of novelty had flagged.

His wife—had been different. Last night had been a dark, sullen surge from deep within them both, wordless, caressless. It had been a velvet time. Oren, torn loose from the moorings of himself, had tossed on a dark and tropic sea, had been drowned time and again under the velvet waves. Yet at the end, while Oren was still trembling from the experience, her unchanged voice had said, "Good night, Mr. Knox."

He could not understand how her voice could retain still its cool placidity. He had been shaken out of himself. Surely she, too, had felt the same impact. The cool tones of her voice had spoken differently.

Sitting at his office desk, he faced the fact of last night. A new dimension had been added to Trenholm. He was like the man who had set out for India, had discovered instead a new world. Here was an entire continent to explore.

Oren was not a man to deny the facts. Sex alone could not open to him such a world. Love had been present, too, under cover of the darkness.

Love. He examined that word. Oren Knox had considered love a deed for weaklings. It was an excuse men used to turn away from the main business of their lives, dallying instead in the comfortable boudoir of womankind. He had loved no one—

not his father, not his mother, not his brothers. He had known duty toward them, respect. His aunt and uncle, who had taken him to raise, had aroused in him no feeling. Yet—here was love. He took that fact, studied it, turned it. Oren Knox was in love with his wife, Trenholm.

Her voice, at the end, had put him off. That same voice; cool, deliberate, bland as cream. She *could* not have remained unstirred by something that had stirred Oren Knox so deeply that he had come to a new knowledge of himself.

I must see her, he thought. I must look into her eyes. Then I will know the truth.

He was afraid of the thought. He rose, reaching for his hat. He was not a man to delay because of fear. He was certain that her eyes must reflect the darkness of their love.

Taylor entered the door. "I want to talk to you about the new campaign," he said. "Were you leaving?"

"No," Oren said, sinking into his chair. "No. What's on your mind?"

"I need some guidelines to go by," Taylor said. "How much money on advertising can we expect to spend this year?"

Oren frowned. "Last year we spent just a little under four hundred thousand dollars," he said. He leaned back in his chair. "It's beginning to pay off, too."

"We can continue the same level of expenditure," Taylor said. He sat down in the chair. "I want to talk to you about the new line of cigarette cards, too . . ."

"I think we ought to raise it," Oren said. "Let's go to six hundred thousand this year, and plan on eight for next. By 1890 we can go to a cool million and if that don't bring them to heel I don't know what will. Not a one of them can or will match it."

"My God," Taylor said. "Are you planning on making a living—or just making cigarettes?"

"Have you figured out our cost per thousand on that basis?" Oren said.

"Well, not exactly. But it seems an awful lot of money."

"I have. We have a production right at two million cigarettes a day. Figure we operate at full production an average of three hundred days out of the year. That's six hundred million cigarettes a year. Spend six hundred thousand dollars advertising six hundred million cigarettes a year, what have you got? One dollar per thousand. We figure it costs roughly a dollar and seventy-five cents a thousand to make the cigarettes."

"You're spending more on advertising than you're taking as a profit."

"Profits are the least of my worries at this point," Oren said. "We'll run at a loss if we have to. Of course, that dollar a thousand is on the high side—that's why we've got to step up production, keep our cost per thousand down as much as possible. Once we form the combination, we'll have profits running out of our ears. Given control of the market, we'll raise prices, cut premiums to the bone, and ease back on the advertising. Then just watch the money roll in. Make it six hundred thousand, Taylor. By the end of the year I'll guarantee to raise production enough to cut the outlay to seventy-five cents a thousand."

"Can we do it without borrowing money?"

"I think so. I've just closed out the handrolled cigarette division. That will be a considerable savings, besides giving us room for more machines."

"That brings us to another point," Taylor said. "Kimball is selling a cheap cigarette called Captains at twenty cigarettes for a dollar seventy-five a thousand and tens at a dollar eighty-five. We need to get our Machines down to, or under, that price—or start a new brand to compete."

Oren thought for a moment. "We don't want to cheapen the Machine brand," he said. "We've got those new Whitfields coming in next week. Let's install them to manufacture O.K. Durhams as a cheap line of goods. It'll have carry-over from the handrolled line we've been making. It's a well-established brand name, so we won't have to go to the expense of establishing a new brand."

"But O.K. Durhams were your first brand. They've got your own name on the package."

Oren grinned. "I don't mind going cheap to meet the competition. Now, get out a circular to the trade. Tell them we don't believe in cheap cigarettes. But if they *want* a cheap cigarette to sell, to meet the competition we will offer them an established brand, O.K. Durhams, at the same price of one seventy-five and one eighty-five, F.O.B. Manchester, for cash. Tell them that a cigarette this cheap can't satisfy their customers—but they're better than anything the other manufacturers can run against Fuller and Knox."

"Can we make a profit?" Taylor said. "Or will it be a losing proposition? In other words, should we push it at all or will we lose money on every thousand we sell?"

"You keep worrying about profits," Oren said. "We'll make a profit. We'll manufacture the cigarette out of shorts and sweepings. We'll even borrow a little manure from old Bull Durham if we have to. Got anything else on your mind?"

"We need some new premiums. We need some more cigarette card ideas, too."

"I think I can leave that to you."

"Those damn cigarette cards," Taylor said, grumbling. "Sometimes I wish they hadn't caught on like they have. We, or our competitors, have used everything going. Baseball players, actresses, singers, flags of all nations, American heroes, fictional characters. It's getting hard to think of something new."

"How about money?" Oren said. "Nobody's used money."

"What do you mean?"

Oren took his 1858 dime from his pocket, turned it over in his hand. It was getting smooth from constant wear.

"Everybody, just about, carries his lucky piece," he said. "Everybody likes the feel of old money. What about a series illustrating American coinage since the revolution? There's been lots of changes and if somebody set out to get him a complete set he'd have to buy a lot of cigarettes."

"That's the best idea I've heard all day," Taylor said. "I've been racking my brains."

Oren leaned back in his chair. He was enjoying the session. This was the sort of thing he had been born to do; not maundering in his mind like a lovesick calf about a woman. He jerked away from the thought.

"What would you think if I told you that Thomas Workman paid a call on me before I left New York?" he said.

Taylor jerked upright. "I'd say we're beginning to make a dent," he said. "Did he want to sell you his Baltimore plant?"

Oren grinned. "He wanted to come in with us, lock stock and brand name." He leaned forward. "We're beginning to hurt them, Taylor. Now's the time to bear down."

"We take in Workman and Company, we . . ."

Oren shook his head. "We're not negotiating with Workman."

"But . . ."

"I want all of them sitting around one table when we talk combination," Oren said. "Workman, Lathrop, Coffey, Barth, and Old Man Winter."

"Can't you eat them one at a time?"

"There's going to be some hollering done when we form the tobacco trust," Oren said. "Might as well get it all over with at one and the same time, so as to get the hollering done with, too. Let folks see it coming, we might have a lot of opposition building up on us. No. I sent Workman to work on the other three. Workman's got to do it, to save his own neck. He can talk to them, where I can't . . . not at this stage of the game."

"It'll be a pleasure to quit fighting those other cigarette drummers. It's rough as a cob out in the field, Oren. You don't know how rough it can get."

"That's one thing I meant to talk to you about, Taylor. We're getting mighty close to make or break. The next year or two will tell the difference. I want you to get your people to knowing we're in the middle of a war."

"What do you mean?"

"I want every man to enlist in the battle. When he sees an opposition advertising sign, tear it down. When he walks into a tobacco shop and sees a display of Dominion Straight Cuts, or Merlins, or any brand made by our competitors, I don't want him to leave that store until that display has been taken down and one of our own built in its place."

"They already do that. Some of them."

"I want all of them to do it. Tell them not to pay any attention to the store-owner's objections. Just go right ahead and do it. We can always cut off his supply of our cigarettes. We can give him a hard time on discounts and premiums."

"It can get expensive. They'll do the same thing to us. You can't expect to gouge a man's eye without him gouging back."

"Let 'em try. If one of their men looks good at gouging, we'll hire him away. Pretty soon, we'll have all the good drummers, and they'll have the duds, who think they're on the road just to sell cigarettes. I think you'd better have a meeting of your men, as soon as possible, to lay out your battle plans."

"It'll have to be a series of meetings. I can't get them all . . ."

"Call them into Manchester. All of them at once. I'll talk to them myself."

"You know how much that'll cost?"

"We've never had a regular sales convention. Bring 'em in for two days, fill 'em full of liquor and fighting spirit, and send 'em out again. It'll be worth it." Oren rose. "I'm going home," he said. "If you need me, I'll be there."

He walked out abruptly, leaving Taylor puzzled. Oren had never been known to leave business before anyone else.

Oren walked home in order to give himself time to think. The decision to see Trenholm without waiting another hour had grown within him, during the talk with Taylor, until it had reached a pressure he could no longer suppress. He had enjoyed the familiar pleasures of business today. At the same time he had found it difficult—impossible—to keep his mind on the problems and opportunities that confronted him at this juncture of time. In spite of himself his thoughts had flitted away time and again to Trenholm, to last night, to a wondering observation of the emotion moving inside his own soul.

Manchester had prospered since he had been a fourteen-year-old pinhooker in the streets about the tobacco warehouses. Tobacco was the growth; not a little of it Fuller and Knox Cigarette Company itself. People greeted him with a combination of awe and respect as he passed on the street and often they turned to look after him. He had never given much thought to his position in the town, though he had known it was solid and respectable. They'd be mighty surprised if they knew the kind of thoughts I'm thinking, he told himself. Just about as surprised as me myself.

He paused, before crossing the street, to observe his house on the opposite corner. It had been newly painted last year; he supposed Trenholm had taken care of that. The garden was prospering now; it had been nearly bare when he had first visited here. The house had settled out of its newness, had become a part of its background. It looked exactly as it should; the home of a prosperous businessman, solid and stolid and highly respectable. It was bigger than necessary for the number of its occupants, too rich in furniture and decorations. But not ostentatious.

It was built by my father-in-law, Oren thought, crossing the street and going up the path to the front door.

He opened the door. He had rarely been in the house in the daytime, except on Sundays. The runner in the foyer was up for cleaning and a maid, on her hands and knees, was going over the floor, while another dusted the furniture. Trenholm was standing on the staircase, wearing a house dress, her head tied up in a kerchief.

"Why, Mr. Knox, what are you doing home?" she said.

"I . . . I wanted to talk to you," he said.

She looked down, frowning, at the maids, then beckoned toward the upstairs.

"After you finish here, I want the parlor cleaned and dusted," she told the maids. "And I mean dusted, Matilda. Pick up things and dust *under* them. Do you understand? Do it right the first time and you won't have to go over it again."

"Yes'm, Miz Trenholm," Matilda said.

Oren threaded his way through the foyer and mounted the

stairs. Trenholm had preceded him to her bedroom. Oren entered, approaching her.

"My dear," he said.

He put his hands on her forearms. She was as tall as he as he leaned to kiss her. She turned her cheek so that his lips brushed her flesh with only a fleeting contact.

"What did you want?" she said.

Oren stepped back, nonplused. "I . . ." he said. He turned away. Then, determinedly, he turned back. "I wanted to tell you," he said. "I'm going to build you a new house, Trenholm. We can plan it together, just where we want to build, what kind of house, how many rooms and everything."

"I don't want . . ."

Oren pushed on. "We'll furnish it new inside out. We'll pick out new furniture and new drapes and new kitchen equipment. It can be exactly the kind of house you've always wanted, Trenholm. When we move in it'll be new from the foundations to the last whatnot on the shelf."

"There's nothing wrong with this house that my father built."

"But it's not *our* house. I want you to have exactly the house you would wish to have. Down to the smallest detail. That's the least I can do for my wife."

"If you gave me another house, I would want it exactly the same as this one," she said. "So it would be foolish."

"But this house was built by your father." He knew he was defeated. Yet he could not keep himself from trying to convince her further.

"What's wrong with that?" she said indifferently. "Did you intend to take lunch at home, Mr. Knox?"

"It's not time to think about lunch yet," Oren said. He approached her again. "My dear, last night . . ."

She turned away. "I do not wish to discuss last night," she said. "It is indecent to talk about such things in the light of day."

"Indecent? When I held you in my arms, when I loved you . . ."

Her face was flushing, he could not tell whether with anger or embarrassment.

"Yes," he said rapidly. "That's what I'm trying to tell you, Trenholm. I found out something last night. I found out I was in love with you. Ain't that ridiculous . . . married eight years and not even know . . ."

She had regained her composure. "Mr. Knox," she said. "The maids will hear you."

He lowered his voice. "Couldn't you call me Oren? Just once? Because . . ."

"I think a wife should grant her husband the respect due him," she said primly. "My mother called my father Mr. Fuller all her life."

"I don't want you to respect me. I want you to love me."

He was into it now. He had dragged out the feeling into words so that he himself could no longer deny it. He was trembling inside like a schoolboy. His hands were hot, moist, and his heart thumped in his chest. He had all the symptoms; he suffered the great disease of mankind.

She turned to look at him. Her voice was calm, as always, her face was placid. "You expect a lot for your five hundred dollars a month," she said.

"That doesn't have anything to do with it," he cried. "Don't you hear what I'm telling you, Trenholm? I'm eaten alive with love for you. I can't think, I can't work, for thinking about you, about last night, about how . . ."

She held her hand against the words. "Mr. Knox," she said.

"All right," he said. He calmed himself. He approached her and put his arms around her waist, pulling her resistant body against him. He held his hand against her cheek, preventing her impulse to turn away. "You must believe me, Trenholm. I love you. There's nothing I wouldn't do for you. I know we got off on the wrong foot, those eight years ago. But that's all past and done."

She stood quietly within his embrace. "Do you really expect me to believe you?" she said. "If you had to make a choice today between me and the factory, which would go first? Tell me that."

"The factory," Oren said without hesitation.

"You are lying, Mr. Knox. I don't know what you think you are up to. We both know why you married me in the first place. We both know why you desire a son. Let us not begin deceiving ourselves, Mr. Knox. Let's keep things straight and clear."

She put her hand against his chest, disengaging herself. She stood free, touching her kerchiefed head with one hand to assure herself her hair was in place, smoothed her dress with the other. Enchanted, he watched her dedicated, self-absorbed movements.

"Trenholm," he said, his voice trembling.

"You have discovered lust, Mr. Knox," she said in a factual voice. "You have mistaken it for love. Once you get your son, you will return to your usual rational demeanor."

"You are wrong, Trenholm," he said. His voice was quiet. "One day you will have to recognize the love I hold for you. I guess I've loved you for a long time and I just didn't know it because I'm not acquainted with love. But I'm a man to look a fact in the face. And this is a fact as real as any factory in the world."

"You are lusting for your wife, Mr. Knox," she said. "That is the fact of the matter."

"What's wrong with that? You've got lust, too. In the dark, you . . ."

"Mr. Knox," she said warningly.

"All right," he said. "You're a lady, and a lady doesn't discuss such things. Not in the daylight, anyway." He paused, watching her. "Tonight?" he said. "When the lights are out, will there be love? Will I come to your room . . . ?"

"You will exercise your privilege until its purpose has been accomplished," she said primly.

He watched her. "God, you're a hard woman," he said in a fatal voice. "I guess I couldn't love any other kind."

"Did you wish to take lunch at home?" she said. "I will tell the cook . . ."

"Do you want me to?"

"Today is cleaning day," she said. "You would be rather in the way, Mr. Knox. However, if you . . ."

"I'll go back to the factory," he said. "I don't want to be in the way."

"But you will be home for dinner?"

"Yes," he said, watching her. "I will be home for dinner. And after." She was ready to dismiss him, he saw. He cast about in his mind. "There's something else I wanted to tell you," he said. "Why don't we have a tray with some coffee brought up?"

"I have no time for coffee today," she said. "What did you wish to tell me?"

All day he had known the urge to tell her of the future he saw before them. This was not the right atmosphere in which to broach the matter. But he could establish no better.

She stood quietly, listening while he talked about Thomas Workman, about the future combination, how it would be achieved, how long it would take, the form he would impose upon the Tobacco Trust. There was no response in her, only an acceptance, and at last, in the face of her silence, he ran out of words.

"That's how it'll be," he said. "It's a great thing, Trenholm. I'll be the Rockefeller of tobacco. What he's done in oil, what Carnegie's done in steel, I will do in tobacco."

"Why are you telling me all this?" she said.

"Why?" he said, taken aback. "Because you're my wife, Trenholm."

"I've been your wife for eight years."

"But I . . . I'm doing it all for you, Trenholm."

"If you had never laid eyes on me, you'd be doing the same thing," she said indifferently. "It's not for me, Mr. Knox. I'm just a small part of the plan. I've known that from the beginning."

"You were," he said. "But not any longer. You are . . ."

"My only purpose is to bear your son," she said.

"Don't you want to be the mother of my son?"

"Not particularly," she said. "I am fulfilling our bargain. That is all."

Recognizing defeat, he went away. There was no penetrating the endless defenses she had erected against him. But there was also a flaming certainty that one day she would recognize Oren Knox. When he had achieved the Tobacco Trust, she would know that he was a great man. Knowing him, she must love him with the same passion he felt for her.

That night, when he entered her darkened room, they came together without words. In the darkness, he found the different Trenholm he had known last night, for which he had groped so ineffectually in the light of day. Afterward, as he lay by her side, his arm over her body, holding her close, he found within himself a mighty overriding wish—that he might not give her a son to bear, that this warm, dark loving might go on forever.

VISTA: IV

Amos: The Homecoming Heart

THE town had not changed. When he got off the train in Jamestown it was as though he were walking into his own past. He paused, looking up and down the street that ran by the railroad station. The tobacco warehouses were down that way, where they had always been. There was the hardware store, the dry goods store. Dr. Allgood's shingle still hung above the stairway that led to the second floor above the bank. He looked at the sign. Dr. Allgood was the first and only person he wanted to see.

Amos had changed. He was thirty years old and the time of his passage was marked in his face plain to see. He had always been dark, with black hair, and even at sixteen there had been lines in his face. Now the lines were deeper, the mouth more grave, than when he had gone away nine years ago.

He was entitled to put the word Doctor in front of his name. In one hand he carried the suitcase that contained his worldly getting, in the other the shiny new black bag he had been given as the outstanding member of his graduating class. He wore a rusty black suit with a professional-length coat that went almost to his knees. He had bought the suit secondhand in Louisville with most of the money remaining in his pocket. He had put it on for the first time this morning in the fitting room of the store.

He walked down the street toward the bank and mounted the stairs to Dr. Allgood's office. The door was closed. He tapped on it. No answer. He opened the door, looked inside. The office was empty. He entered and sat waiting for Dr. Allgood's return.

Two hours passed before his vigil was rewarded. He was patient, sitting in a wicker chair with his long legs thrust out in front of him. He was tired from the train trip. He did not sleep, neither did he think, but merely waited, as he had learned so well to do.

When the door opened he stood up. "Dr. Allgood," he said. "I'm Amos Haines. Dr. Amos Haines."

Dr. Allgood was an old man now, his shoulders stooped with the permanent weariness a country doctor is heir to. He was the doctor who had come to the birth of Amos' youngest sister. Dr. Allgood looked at him without recognition, noting only his professional appurtenances, the knee-length coat and the shiny new doctor's bag.

"What can I do for you, Dr. Haines?" he said.

"Well sir," Amos said. "I want you to teach me some medicine."

Dr. Allgood looked surprised. "You're a doctor, aren't you?" he said. "Don't they teach medicine any more in the medical colleges?"

"They don't teach enough of it," Amos said. "Not in the school I went to, anyhow. Dr. Allgood, I'm the son of Art Haines. He lives out there in the country at Temple's Crossroads."

"I know Art Haines," Dr. Allgood said. "He still owes me some hog meat since the time his wife was took down with her last child. Art never did know how close he came to losing her that time." He shook Amos' hand. "Well now. So you've gone and made a doctor."

"Yes sir," Amos said. "At least I've started. I was counting on you to teach me the rest of it."

"Come on in here and let me sit down," Dr. Allgood said. "These country roads are hard on an old man."

He led the way into the inner office. The room was dusty, as though little used. The furnishings, the equipment, were old-fashioned. He sat behind his desk, motioned Amos to a straight chair beside it.

"Now, tell me what's on your mind," he said.

"Dr. Allgood, I decided a long time ago I meant to make a doctor," Amos said. "I didn't have any money to do it with. I went on up to Kansas City anyway, to try and find me a medical school. I found one all right; but, to tell you the truth, it ain't much. I got a license to cut and poke, but they didn't teach much about where and when to do it."

"What was your school?"

"The Hodkins Medical Institute of Kansas City."

Dr. Allgood nodded. "They'll just about mail you your diploma, you pay them enough money," he said. "How come you to go there?"

"It was the only medical school I could afford," Amos said.

"It took you nine years? They'll give you a diploma in three that's just as good."

"I didn't have any money," Amos said patiently. "I had to work. Besides, I needed to get whatever they had to offer. Some courses I took twice. They had a little lab there and once in a while we got a free cadaver from the city. I cut on those free cadavers every chance I got. It took me nine years. Whatever was there, though, I got."

"Why did you come to me?"

"You tended to my mother once," Amos said. "That's where I got the notion about being a doctor in the first place. I figure you know a lot of medicine they don't teach in any school. I tried to get into a hospital but I couldn't find one that'd have me." He looked up at Dr. Allgood. "So you either teach me, or I start in cutting and poking in the midst of my ignorance."

Dr. Allgood grunted. "At least you know you're ignorant," he said. He paused in thought. "Amos, I'm an old man. I don't have much practice left, because I just can't get over the roads any more. You can see, I don't even keep an office nurse. I'm about ninety percent retired."

"I'm not asking for money," Amos said. "I'll find me a night job to pay my keep. Or I'll find me a day job and go with you at night. Whichever you like. I need me some medical knowledge, Dr. Allgood."

Dr. Allgood watched him. "Any man would rather be a town doctor than a country doctor. Do you plan to practice your skills on the country folks until you're good enough for a town practice?"

Amos looked at him, surprised. "But I aim to be a country doctor," he said. "That's what I had in mind."

"Why?"

"Why? Well . . ." Amos stumbled around in his mind. "The folks out there in the country need it the most. It's mighty little doctoring they get anyhow. You know Papa nearly let my mother die, having Vivian, before he even called you." His voice took on body and dignity. "I figure to go where the need is," he said.

"If you start out to be a country doctor, you'll be one the rest of your life."

Amos nodded. "That's what I want to be," he said.

Dr. Allgood smiled. "You don't know what a shock it was to me when I realized you were Art Haines' boy. Have you been in touch with your family?"

"Not for a long time."

"Your mother is dead, son," Dr. Allgood said. "Did you know that?"

"Yes sir. My father sent me a postcard. I couldn't come home."

"Art is still alive. He gets meaner and more no'count the older he gets." He watched Amos' face. "Your younger brother Ed is sharecropping, just like his daddy before. Art lives with him. Your sisters are all married and got a passel of young'uns." He paused. "Except that one I helped into the world, what was her name, Vivian? She's living here in town. Got three young'uns that don't know their daddy's name."

Amos listened to the history of his family. Whatever he felt did not show on his face.

"Your other brother cut a man in a fight and got sent to the penitentiary," Dr. Allgood said. "He ought to be out any year now."

"John always had a temper."

"Can you come back into the country of your family and be a doctor?" Dr. Allgood said. "You know the healing art still has a lot of witch-doctoring to it. Folks have to believe that magic walks in a doctor's shoes. I don't know but what the magic doesn't do more good than the medical knowledge."

"I stepped away from my family a long time ago," Amos said slowly. "No man likes to leave his own behind. But it was the only way I knew to go and do what I had to do. I had to put them away from me." He stopped, thinking. "I didn't belong to them, anyway," he said.

"Son, you get you some medical knowledge, I think you'll be a right good doctor. I can't help you out, though. I'm an old man. My medical knowledge is years out of date. Besides, my practice hardly exists any more." He paused. "I'll give you a letter that might help you get into a hospital somewhere."

"Dr. Allgood, I'm thirty years old. It took me nine years to come this far. I've been to the hospitals. I begged and pleaded to even be allowed to work as an orderly, or a male nurse. A letter won't do me any good." He looked down at his hands. They were big hands, square, with thick fingers. The ends of the fingers were spatulate.

"If I don't get my hands on some human pain, I'll go crazy," he said. "I put in the first half of my life just trying to get to the starting place. I've got to start now." He looked gravely at Dr. Allgood. "I'm putting the responsibility onto you, Dr. Allgood. It's yours, because you put me on the road I've traveled up to here, even if you didn't know it at the time. You either teach me to practice medicine, or you'll carry on your soul the people I'll kill trying to learn."

Dr. Allgood made a grimace. "And I was thinking you might be too tenderhearted to be a good doctor," he said. "You've learned the lesson well, I must say."

"It's just come to the place of got-to," Amos said. "A man

comes to that place a few times in his life. He either faces it or he turns away."

A boy hurried into the office. There was mud on his face and his voice was trembling.

"Dr. Allgood," he said. "You got to come."

"What's the matter, son?" Dr. Allgood said, his voice calming the fear in the boy.

"My daddy," the boy said. He gulped for air. "Mama says come. My daddy got drug by a horse. He . . ."

Dr. Allgood rose. "How far is it?" he said.

"About five miles. I rode here as fast . . ."

Dr. Allgood picked up his bag and followed the boy to the door. "Is he hurt bad?"

"Real bad," the boy said, his voice trembling. "The horse drug him and he couldn't get his foot out of the stirrup and we couldn't catch the horse." He stopped. Tears were streaking his dirty face.

Dr. Allgood turned to Amos. "Well," he said impatiently. "Come on!"

Amos reached to pick up his shiny new doctor's bag and rose to follow him.

Chapter Twelve

IN THE following weeks, the world was strange to Oren Knox. He lived two lives, so utterly different he wondered how they could be encompassed within the soul of one man. His daytime world remained the same; the fixed plan to create the tobacco trust, the day-to-day steps to achieve that end. He rose early and worked late; he bent, it seemed, as he had done always, the sum total of his thought and energy to the goal. He spent hours in conference with his lieutenants, in secretive planning, in seeing that his plans were carried out in the field. He devoted his attention to the home factory, supervising the installation of the new machines, taking the old machines out of line long enough to install the new attachment that printed the brand name on each individual cigarette. He returned to the auction houses and personally bought tobacco. When Taylor Tryon brought in the sales force for the convention, he devoted full attention to preparing them for the intensified battle. To his associates, after the aberrations of his first day or two at home, Oren Knox seemed quite himself.

In the night-time hours, a different Oren Knox lived in a different world. This Oren Knox was flamingly in love, totally concentrated on winning Trenholm. In the dark hours he courted her assiduously. He gave her each day of his life as a gift from the heart, telling into the silence of her indifference the smallest detail of his deeds, his intentions, as they had developed in the hours since he had last seen her.

He was fatuous in love. He gave her the first month's payment wrapped in tissue paper and tied with a dainty ribbon. He hoped it would make her laugh. She did not laugh; instead she meticulously counted the money. He brought her candy and flowers; when he found it necessary to make a quick trip to the New York factory he took Trenholm with him. They stayed at a plush hotel; every night they dined in an expensive restaurant and went to an entertainment. For her sake he bought a suit of formal clothes, a top hat, and a cane. He sat patiently in fashionable shops while she made her decisions. He wished to pay for the clothes but she would not allow it; she spent her own money. At last he persuaded her, reluctantly, to accept an advance on future months, that she might buy everything she desired.

He had not believed he could be such a man-in-love. Love had welled up irresistibly, coming from some depth he had never suspected. It was as though, inside the Oren Knox he had created, had dwelt another Oren Knox as neglected as Cinderella. The hidden man, upon the first opportunity, had exploited the weakness of Oren's desire for a son to grow overnight into an equal partner.

He had been unable to know love because that part of Oren Knox had remained hidden during those eight years. Not recognizing the hidden man, he had failed to recognize love. The conscious part of himself had maneuvered the marriage, for his own conscious purposes. The unconscious part had silently conspired, without Oren's knowledge, toward the same end.

Oren had always known that there was more to Oren Knox than to most men. He had, somehow, an access to himself that other men did not enjoy. He had considered it as applying only to business. This total self had given Oren Knox a purpose beyond other men, an intense concentration other men could not achieve. Where others dallied in forgetfulness, Oren Knox never did. Take Taylor Tryon, for example; Taylor was an excellent salesman. He was intelligent, industrious, devoted. But he liked good food, a good cigar, a lovely woman. A bachelor still, he devoted quite as much thought and effort to these ephemeral goals as to that of being the best cigarette salesman in the world.

Oren had never expected to be concerned with ordinary living. The facts of daily living existed only to be tolerated. He shaved and bathed and fed himself simply because it was necessary. He shook hands, spoke greetings and farewells, because convention demanded it. These formalities of life seemed often ridiculous to him. Two men, coming together in a battle for survival, would shake hands, dine together, tell each other jokes. A man, in the midst of a business deal that would make him or break him for life, would wander his eye and his mind momentarily after an attractive woman who chanced to stroll by. Oren believed that most men would happily abandon the success of the deal for an immediate and total possession of the strolling woman. At least, in their own minds, they did so abandon themselves, if only for a second.

Oren-in-love had come to a new appreciation of money and leisure. Time and money were not only instruments of ambition; they could also be used in the flattery and conquest of a woman's heart. Eating a meal was more than a necessary evil; it could be used for companionship in a quiet moment that drew two people closer than they had been before.

Oren believed every day, with a lover's optimism, that each night must bring Trenholm to a recognition of his love. Recognition was the stumbling point; once admitting his love, she could then confess to her own. He believed with deephearted sincerity that, in spite of all, Trenholm loved him. Bitterness alone could not have carried her through their eight years, no more than calculation could have sustained Oren Knox. He even understood why she should be so bitter. He shuddered within himself when he involuntarily remembered how he had coldly courted Mr. Fuller, playing upon his fears, in order to bring an indirect pressure to bear upon Trenholm. Despite all, there must have been more in Trenholm than mere acquiescence—for Trenholm had within her soul a best-quality steel that Taylor Tryon had never had the fortune to sell during his hardware-drummer days.

Aside from all else were the times of darkness. Each day, as inexorable as the advance of the sun, excitement built within him as the moment drew nearer. Each night he entered into the darkness of her waiting, his limbs trembling, his heart thudding in his chest. When he touched her flesh his breath would lock in his lungs until he was strangled with love and desire.

Always in darkness, until the darkness became a part of love; he did not need eyes. There was seeing, as well as feeling, in his flesh. He could indeed, in the darkness, discern a truer Trenholm than ever daylight showed him. She was the Trenholm he wanted her to be, the steel sheathed in softness, her breath quite as explosive as his own, her passion as overwhelming.

There was only the one barrier—a barrier he could never break. When he spoke of love she congealed into the daytime Trenholm, turning away into her bitterness, leaving him as abruptly alone as if she had departed the bed. At last he ceased to speak love, though often he had to choke the passionate words in his throat. If he could not speak it, he could show it; so each night in darkness he demonstrated the great passion he felt for her, not only in lust but in tenderness, in gentleness, in every way he could think of. Eventually his persistent presentation of himself must break the barrier.

He came gradually to see as little of the daylight Trenholm as he ever had. He could not bear the contrast between the two women. With Trenholm-in-the-dark he had a chance. The other Trenholm remained, as always, inaccessible.

The end came with shattering abruptness. Upon a night, entering eagerly into the darkness that contained her, her voice reached out to stop him.

"Mr. Knox," she said.

He paused, for she never spoke in this moment of their coming together. "Yes?" he said.

"Mr. Knox," she said. "I am in a family way."

The announcement desolated him. It had been days, weeks,

since he had thought about the original purpose to which he had persuaded her. He had shut it out of his mind in order to deny its possibility. *I like things the way they are,* he cried out within himself. *I don't care whether I ever have a son or not.*

It was intolerable that he should lose that little he had gained. Not her love, not her recognition of his love, but only the darkness in which love could be exercised. Faced with the impossibility of more, he would have settled for that which he already possessed.

He could find no answer. He groped his way to the bed, spread his hands to find her.

"Don't touch me!" she said sharply.

In the speaking of the words, he found her. She flung herself away. For a moment there was a brief fierce wrestling in the darkness, until he held her pinned to the bed. Their breaths panted into each other's faces.

"Do you intend to force me?" she said, gasping the words.

He rose away from her, a great reluctance in his soul. He stood upright. His body was trembling.

"No," he said. "I will never force you, Trenholm. But . . ."

"I have fulfilled my bargain," she said. "Can you ask more of me?"

"Trenholm," he said. "I thought . . ."

"You thought that, once accustomed, I would have to keep on willy-nilly," she said, her voice, her daytime voice, calm and factual as always. "I have fulfilled my bargain, Mr. Knox. I am bearing your child."

"What if it's not a boy?" he said, his mind running quickly to his last hope.

"Then you may return to my bed. But not before we know. Goodnight, Mr. Knox."

The anger that rose in him defeated itself by its very ferocity. If he had touched her, he would have hurt her. He could not bear the thought. He made himself walk to the door. The doorknob was as cold as ice in the palm of his hand. He turned, to cast his last hope across the darkness that bridged between them.

"Trenholm, I love you," he said. "I love you with all my heart and soul. You are the love of my life."

He waited until he knew there would be no answer. He fumbled the door open and left the room.

Late at night, in anger and despair, he came once again to challenge the barrier. He would force her. He would make her do his will, tonight and tomorrow night and every night until the barrier should be destroyed once and forever.

The door was locked. He could have broken it down. He did not do so; he retired again to his own room.

The time of darkness was ended. They resumed the old way of life, in which they were polite, respectful, distant. Oren did not try again to enter her room. In that moment of discovering that she had risen from her bed to lock the door against his fatal return, something had died within him. It was not the love he had felt for her; it was, perhaps, his confidence that such a deep, true love must and would prevail.

Trenholm devoted herself to preparing for the child. She knitted continuously, except when her hands were not busy with other tasks, shaping bootees and sacques and wrappers. She had assumed the role of mother, apparently, upon the instant of impregnation.

Oren, pinning his last hope upon the birth of a daughter, threw himself with renewed ferocity into the battle against his business rivals. The long empty nights were an agony, so he slept less than ever in his life. His usual sleeping time had been five hours. Now he cut it to three or four. He could not sleep anyway; he might as well be up and doing.

He began traveling once again. He toured the territory to check on the sales operations. The result was immediately apparent. Once again they were straining the capacity of the factory, and new machines were ordered from Whitfield.

For the first time, he paid a call on each of his four rivals, talking the advantages of combination. He brought facts and figures with him. He was unsuccessful, except with Thomas Workman. Workman was ready, indeed eager, to have the plan consummated. But, at least, the other three listened and they did not laugh. He returned to New York for two or three months at a time, spending most of his effort renewing and enlarging his access to the Wall Street houses he would one day need.

In April, when the baby would be born, he returned home. Trenholm, plump and placid with the smug knowledge of achievement of every pregnant woman, greeted him in her usual way.

"Are you all right?" Oren asked her.

"Of course," she said.

"When will it be?"

"Any time now."

"You must put a bell at your bedside," he said. "There must be someone in the house at all times."

The birth began at midnight. For a week Oren had kept the Negro yardman standing by day and night. Roused by the sound of Trenholm's bell, he dispatched the yardman for the doctor. He waited in Trenholm's room. She lay in the bed, her face pale. Once every five minutes, as regular as clockwork, her body clenched into a knot of pain and she put her lower lip between her teeth as she endured it.

Oren stood over her. There were no words. There was nothing to say. He looked down at her body, covered by the bedclothes against his sight. He had never seen her whole, he had seen her only in darkness. Even in childbirth she covered herself against his sight. When the doctor came, he left the room gratefully. He waited in the parlor through the remainder of the night. She was still in labor when daylight came. He finished his breakfast, mounted the stairs. The doctor, in shirt sleeves and vest, met him at the door of Trenholm's room.

"It will be a while yet," he said. "She's having a hard time, Mr. Knox."

"Is she all right?"

"She's fine. It's just that she waited so long to have the first one." The doctor smiled. "The next one will be easy."

Oren put on his hat and coat and went to the factory. He worked all morning with Helen Fowlkes on the books. At eleven o'clock the yardman appeared in the doorway.

"The doctor say come."

Oren rose, put on his hat, and went home. When he entered the house he was greeted by a practical nurse in a white uniform. She had a plain, broad face, efficient hands.

"Go right on upstairs, Mr. Knox," she said cheerfully.

Oren mounted the stairs. The doctor was meticulously washing his hands in a pan of hot water, the maid holding a fresh pitcher in readiness.

The doctor jerked his head toward the bed. "It's all over, Mr. Knox," he said.

"Is she all right?"

"She's fine," the doctor said. He finished drying his hands, rolled down his sleeves, slipped on his coat. "I'll be back this afternoon," he said. "Goodbye, Mr. Knox."

"Goodbye," Oren said. "Thank you, doctor."

They left the room. Oren approached the bed, looking down into Trenholm's face. It was pale, fatigued. She seemed to be asleep. A featureless bundle nestled against her side. He leaned over, trying to see the baby's face. Her eyes opened.

"Are you all right?" he asked.

"Yes," she said peacefully. "I'm fine. Just tired, that's all." She closed her eyes again.

"It seemed to take a long time," he said.

He ached with tenderness. He had never seen Trenholm beaten down like this. Her face seemed thinner than before, as her body under the coverlet was thinner.

She opened her eyes. "Do you want to see the baby?"

Painfully she shifted in the bed. Carefully, she unfolded the blanket. He stared down into the squeezed tiny face, purple and red. The sensuous mouth worked spasmodically in sleep.

"Is . . . ?" he said.

"A boy," she said. "Just like you wanted."

His last hope was gone. He looked, not at her, but at the sentient bundle that was flesh of his flesh, blood of his blood. He hated the nameless bundle as he would have hated a man who had taken away his tobacco kingdom.

"I want to name him Fuller Knox," she said.

"Name him whatever you like," he said, going toward the door.

"That's a fine boy you got there, Mr. Knox," the practical nurse said as he passed her on the stairs. "It's always nice to get a boy the first time. The boy ought to be the oldest."

He returned to the factory. He had only that, now; the original dream. Perhaps, in time, he would recover the feeling for a son who would continue him after his death. He could not yet do so; he was once again shut within himself.

There were six men in the room. Their names were: Willard Lathrop and John Winter, of Lathrop and Winter; Thomas Workman of Workman Tobacco Company; Edward Barth of Barth and Company; Franklin Coffey of Coffey and Company; and Oren Knox of Fuller and Knox Cigarette Company, Inc. There was one woman; her name was Helen Fowlkes.

The room was in the Manchester Hotel of Manchester, North Carolina. The other five, each well aware of the mounting rumors and speculations that reached beyond the tobacco trade into the area of public concern, had come secretively, by various routes, to this meeting. They had registered under false names at the hotel.

Oren looked about him with satisfaction. He had labored for many years to bring these men around one table. It had often seemed impossible of accomplishment. But he had never flagged.

Mr. Winter, as the oldest man in the room, had the honor of presiding at the head of the table. He was thin, tall, aristocratic, and he had not shaken Oren's hand when he had entered the room. He had been the last holdout. Beside him sat his partner, Willard Lathrop. He was as fat as ever, but he was not jovial. He looked gloomily at his thick hands lying on the polished surface. There was a diamond ring on the little finger, that caught and focused light into shiftings of brilliance.

Oren turned his head to look at Thomas Workman. Mr. Workman had aged since their first meeting in New York; there were lines of anxiety in his face. His dapperness had frayed under the pressures of these last years.

Edward Barth sat directly across from Oren. He was a burly man. He smoked great black cigars, his head continually wreathed in the fragrant smoke. He spilled the ashes on his vest, flicked them away with an absent hand. He stared into Oren's face with intent regard. Franklin Coffey had a tight face, a drab suit, a clipped New York accent. His lips were thick, laid together like two slabs of meat.

These other men knew each other well; some of them were friends, though they were rivals. Oren was the stranger in their midst. But it was Oren who had brought them together. They sat around the table silently, waiting to begin. Oren waited on the old man at the head of the table. Outside, it was a fair day, and the people of the nation called The United States of America moved in a world that did not know of this meeting. They talked about it though, among themselves and in public speeches, crying out against the remote possibility. Inside the room, cigar smoke curled thickly from Edward Barth's cigar.

John Winter laid his hand flat on the table top. "We have come to hear what this man has to say," he said in his thin, precise voice, as cold as ice water. "Let us listen to him."

Oren Knox rose. "Gentlemen, I am happy to welcome you to Manchester, North Carolina," he said. He looked up and down the table. "It is a meeting I have long desired."

They stared back at him. Their faces were hostile, except for Thomas Workman's. He was merely anxious. The hostility did not disturb Oren.

"Miss Fowlkes, here, will make a record of the salient points as we speak," he said. "There will not be a formal record of the meeting. Some of us may wish to say things that should not enter any formal record and it is my belief that we should be free to open our minds without fear or favor. Each of you may inspect her notes after the meeting. Is that satisfactory to all?"

He waited. They did not indicate their assent, neither did they register their disapproval. Oren went on.

"Gentlemen, in this room is represented the manufacture and sale of over two billion cigarettes per year. That is, for all practical purposes, the total American cigarette production. Of that total, I myself, in the person of Fuller and Knox Cigarette Company, represent nine hundred and forty million cigarettes. The rest of you all together aggregate one billion, sixty million."

There was no response in their faces. But they were listening —precisely because of the figures he had mentioned so casually.

"Last year Fuller and Knox did a business of between four million and four million five hundred thousand. Our net profit was a cool four hundred thousand dollars."

Their faces did move, then. These were figures that were secret outside the higher echelons of the firm. A man simply did not reveal to his rivals the extent of his penetration into the market. Oren watched them look at each other, not in surmise but in confirmation.

"I don't know too much about anybody else's business affairs," he said. "But, at a rough guess, I'd say that's about equal to the total combined profits of your four concerns." He paused, looking about him with satisfaction. "I think I have earned the right to call this meeting."

The silence continued after the fall of his words. Oren waited, watching their faces. He was determined upon an acknowledgement of his position. The pause stretched intolerably; until, at last, Mr. Winter spoke.

"We are here," he said. "We are listening."

"I will reveal one more figure to you," Oren said. "Last year, Fuller and Knox spent no less than eight hundred thousand dollars on advertising and promotion."

He heard the collective catch of their breaths. He smiled.

"That's right—eight hundred thousand. Double our profits." He leaned forward. "That figure right there, gentlemen, is the reason why one magic word dwells in my mind like a dream of paradise. *Combination.* That is the word, gentlemen. That word is our lost paradise, where a man don't have to spend two dollars of promotion to make one dollar of profit."

He had them now. He felt the power of conviction flow as smoothly in his mind as a dream. He held these powerful men in the strength of his concept.

"We are the most backward industry in the nation. Competition is a thing of the past. We're like a pack of wolves, eating each other instead of chasing the game. The new mode is combination. The greatest man in this country today is John D. Rockefeller. Why? Because he has formed the greatest combination of them all.

"Why is competition wrong? Because it keeps us weak. John D. Rockefeller is the most powerful man in the United States; more powerful than the President, the Congress, than the people of the United States themselves. Through combination." He smiled. "Well, I'm not saying we can be as powerful in combination as John D. Rockefeller. But, if we can muster sense enough to put our strength together, we can make a dollar.

"You want to know who our real enemy is? The plug-tobacco people. Yes sir. I'll bet not a one of you has thought of that. Why? Because they've got the allegiance of more consumers than we have. It's our job to switch people to cigarettes. Putting our forces together, we can accomplish that task. Putting our forces together, we can take over the plug-tobacco industry and even if people keep on chewing tobacco instead of smoking it, they'll be ours right on."

Their faces were startled with the sudden expansion of the proposition. He stood erect, smiling at them.

"I will guarantee you one thing," he said. "Consent to the combination of our forces and within ten years we will *be* the tobacco industry in the United States. And, after the United States, the world. John D. Rockefeller is doing it in oil. We can do it in tobacco."

Edward Barth looked skeptical. "Do you really believe such a thing can be done?"

Oren looked straight across at him. "I believe *I* can do it," he said. "If I can get you folks on my side instead of fighting me behind my back."

They watched his face. Each man in this room bore scars from his competition with Oren Knox. They knew him thoroughly as few others did; as an enemy. He felt the strength of their knowledge working on his side. They were enemy; they had come into his camp to parley. A man is known by the enemies he keeps, he thought. Not by friends, not by those he loves. Because an enemy defines a man in all his strength and in all his weakness. A man wouldn't know he was alive without his enemies. The thought was like a breath of pure oxygen to his lungs.

He briskened his voice. "Here's the proposition," he said. "I could stand here all day trying to convince you. If you aren't convinced by now, the figures won't mean a thing. So I'm through talking. I'm laying my cards on the table, face up, for you to see. If you say No, I will walk out of this room. If you say Yes, we will call in the lawyers and take off our coats and get to work."

He consulted a scrap of paper on which he had scribbled figures, though they were written in his mind like words on stone.

"I propose a new corporation, to be called the Allied Tobacco Corporation. I propose that the Allied Tobacco Corporation secure a charter to cure leaf tobacco and to buy, manufacture, and sell tobacco in all its forms, to establish factories, agencies and depots for the sale and distribution thereof, and to transfer and cause the same to be transferred as an article of commerce, and to do all things incidental to the business of trading and manufacturing." He paused, a slight grin on his face. "We don't want to come up hamstrung by the terms of our incorporation.

"I propose that the Allied Tobacco Corporation be capitalized at twenty-five million dollars—three hundred thousand shares of common stock at fifty dollars each and one hundred thousand shares of eight percent noncumulative preferred stock at one hundred dollars each. The fifteen million dollars of common stock will be exchanged for the plants, chattels, brands, good will, etc. of the five constituent companies, the percentage of stock allotted to each firm to be based on its live or active assets. The ten million dollars of eight percent preferred stock will be offered solely to the tobacco trade."

"Wait a minute," Franklin Coffey said in his hard New York voice. "I doubt that our combined assets will equal the value of the common stock, much less the preferred-stock issue you're including."

Oren's voice was calm. "I estimate our combined tangible assets, counted as inventory, at five million dollars."

"Now, let me understand you," Coffey said. "For our estimated assets of five million, we will divide common stock worth fifteen million, plus ten million in cash generated by the sale of the preferred."

"Less the eight percent guaranteed dividend on the preferred," Oren said. "On every share of the preferred, the company will be obligated for eight dollars in dividends. That is eight hundred thousand dollars a year before any dividends can accrue to our common."

"That's a lot of water," Coffey said flatly.

"A lot of water? You don't know what the hell you're talking about!" Oren's voice exploded indignantly in the room. "You run some figures on our combined profits, once we work together instead of fighting each other. The profits will support that capitalization, gentlemen. I will personally guarantee it." He paused, looking from one face to the next. "I have studied these figures for many months," he said. "I will stake my life on them."

"Perhaps it would be better to forget the preferred issue and capitalize at fifteen million," Thomas Workman said in a tentative, anxious voice. "Begin cautiously . . ."

"We need the cash flow from the preferred issue," Oren said. "There's no cheaper way of getting ten million in cash so quickly. At the same time, the control will remain in our hands. Any time we are in the position to do so, we can dispose of the preferred stock."

"I think you're being optimistic about the total combined assets," Willard Lathrop said. "I don't think it'll add up to five million dollars."

"Of course, we can't know exactly until the lawyers and accountants have done their work," Oren said. "In the event the total assets do not quite reach five million, the company will accept individual notes to make up the deficit. I don't intend to freeze anyone out in the cold on this proposition. I want every man in this room to make money. Lots of money."

He looked at the old man at the head of the table. He knew his most determined opposition rested there. Mr. Winter's face was tight, withdrawn, noncommittal. He glanced at the other men.

"I suppose *you* will be the president of the new company?" Edward Barth said.

"Yes," Oren Knox said simply.

"You would not consider anyone else being president? I think as a gesture of good faith . . ."

"There is no other man in this room as well qualified as Oren Knox," Oren said bluntly.

"How can you make that statement?" Willard Lathrop said, temper showing in his voice. "That is the most arrogant . . ."

"If any man here has a plan laid out to put the Allied Tobacco Company into position within two years to tackle the plug-tobacco companies, I would like to hear it," Oren said calmly.

"Do you really believe you can take on the plug-tobacco people and beat them?" Edward Barth said. "Why, put us all together, we're nothing compared to them."

"I was David to your Goliath," Oren said. "I have laid you low with a river rock, haven't I? You give me some rocks to throw, I don't mind being David to any man's Goliath." He kept his eyes on Edward Barth. "This time, at least, you'll be holding my coat instead of standing out there in a shower of stones." He went on before the others could speak again. "I will be president. The principals of each constituent company will make up the board of directors. I hope Mr. Barth and Mr. Coffey will be vice-presidents, and that Mr. Workman will accept the position of secretary, while Mr. Lathrop will be treasurer. I think Mr. Winter can contribute more to the company in a general advisory capacity, rather than being tied down to a specific job. We would want to use his wisdom and knowledge in many areas."

Unconsciously, they turned to Mr. Winter at the head of the

table. Even Oren waited on him. Here consent abided; the other men, Oren sensed, would follow his lead.

Mr. Winter sat still for a moment, returning their look.

"Do you really believe that you can get away with this combination?" he said at last. "There is already discontent in the trade, just at the thought of it. You will create more enemies, Mr. Knox, than even your undoubted talents can handle." He paused, looking at them one by one. "They will rise up and destroy us, gentlemen. They will rise up and destroy us."

Oren waited until the words had died away. When he spoke, his voice was quiet, even.

"Enemies do not frighten me, Mr. Winter. I am a man who thrives on enemies."

"When every man's hand is turned against you, you will be destroyed. We will be destroyed also, if we associate ourselves with you. There is much agitation against the cigarette already, as all of you know. Add to that the agitation of frightened men, gazing at the colossus you will have created, and your combination will not stand against it."

"The climate of opinion is favorable to combination," Oren said. "John D. Rockefeller is a great man. So is Carnegie, and . . ."

"The climate will change," Mr. Winter said. "Oil and steel do not touch directly upon the people, as tobacco does. They touch them, but not in a day-to-day, immediate way. You will be bringing combination under their very noses, Mr. Knox. It will stink to high heaven in their nostrils."

Oren, still on his feet, thought rapidly. This was an opposition on unexpected grounds.

"I have thought about that problem," he said, stalling for time. He grasped at the concept with the eager fingers of his mind. It eluded him. Then—he had it. The myriad nation rose up as a colossus, the greatest combination of them all, moving ponderously, but moving, along a path it understood but dimly. Ponderous. Slow.

"I have considered these matters," he said. "We all know how slow a nation is. Why, it takes a couple of years to make up its mind who to pick for the next president. Say you're right—I won't oppose you on that. But we will have a minimum of twenty years before the reaction comes." He paused, looking triumphantly from one to the other. "Give us twenty years, there'll be no cutting us down. Why, they could cut us into little pieces, each little piece would be mightier than all of us put together are now."

He warmed to the theme. "We know that'll never happen, anyway. The business of this nation is *business*. The almighty dollar, they call it. The dollar *is* almighty. They might give us a hard time, with taxes and tariffs and all that—but you and I will never see the day when the government of this nation will be turned to the task of making our great enterprises into many small enterprises. I don't think you'll ever have to fear such an eventuality."

The other four men nodded in agreement.

"If it could ever happen, the tobacco trust you are contemplating would bring it about," Mr. Winter said. He rose from his seat. "However, this is all speculation. No one will know this side of twenty years whether I am right or Mr. Knox is right. I am basing my decision on more immediate matters." He paused. His voice was slow, fateful. "I am a man of business. I am also a gentleman. The very essence of a gentleman consists of the things he will not do. I will not . . ."

Oren knew, as though he had heard the words in advance, that Mr. Winter was announcing against the combination. If he should be permitted to speak his mind, the other men would follow like sheep.

"Mr. Winter," he interposed roughly. "I think there is one more thing you should know."

His rudeness stopped the old man. He drew back his head, looking down his nose at Oren. "Yes, Mr. Knox?" he said coldly.

"I have one more card I haven't shown you folks," Oren said. "I promised to show them all." He could sense the unlistening granite of the old man. He turned to the others.

"We all know that the Whitfield machine is the best cigarette machine in the world," he said. "We're all using the Whitfields, under license from the Whitfield Tobacco Machine Company. Lathrop and Winter own outright the patents on the Allison and the Emery machines. But, after thorough tests, Lathrop and Winter scrapped them in favor of using the Whitfields on a royalty basis."

They were already sensing the trend of his words.

"When I first committed Fuller and Knox to the Whitfield machine, at a time when no one else was using it, I tried to persuade Charles Whitfield to grant me exclusive use of his machine. He would not agree to my proposition at the time.

"However, a few weeks ago, I succeeded in reaching an agreement with the Whitfield Company. For exclusive use and control of the Whitfield machine, I guaranteed him a royalty of two hundred and fifty thousand dollars a year. In return, the Whitfield company has obligated itself to see to it that not a single Whitfield machine remains in a competing factory after March 1st of next year, 1891."

Their breaths were caught in their lungs. They stared aghast into his calm face.

"Furthermore," Oren said. "The contract can be cancelled immediately if, in any twelve consecutive months, as many as one hundred million cigarettes should be manufactured by any rival company, or upon any machine not controlled by the Whitfield Machine Company."

The words stunned them. It was a full minute before any one of them could speak. Edward Barth recovered first.

"Charles Whitfield always said . . ."

"Charles Whitfield once told me that, when I was the whole cigarette industry, he would grant me exclusive rights," Oren said. "I showed him the figures I have been talking about in this room. He became convinced that within a few years, combination or not, Oren Knox will be the cigarette industry. Or so near that the difference won't matter." He stopped. "That agreement with the Whitfield Cigarette Machine Company is one of the . . . intangible . . . assets Fuller and Knox will bring to the proposed combination."

Mr. Winter took two steps, paused. "Mr. Lathrop," he said

to his rotund partner. "I am withdrawing from active participation in the affairs of Lathrop and Winter."

Mr. Lathrop's face turned white. "Mr. Winter," he said, beginning to rise.

"I am an old man, Mr. Lathrop," Mr. Winter said. "I have contemplated retirement from active management, as you know, for some time. I am old, and perhaps too rigid in my thinking for this new day that is upon us." His gaze swept Oren Knox briefly. "I do not wish to restrain you, by my presence, from any decision you may feel it necessary to take." He drew himself up, put his hat on his head, brushed at his graceful mustache with one hand. "You have my power of attorney to act as you see fit in behalf of my share of the company." His eyes swept the room once more. He bowed his head slightly to each in turn, except for Oren. "Good day, gentlemen."

He left the room.

A silence followed his departure. The men looked at each other. They looked at Willard Lathrop as he sank heavily into his chair. Then they looked at Oren.

Oren stared back for a moment.

"Gentlemen," he said. "I think we might as well call in the lawyers."

It was late in the afternoon when Oren Knox arrived at home. The moment he opened the front door, Fuller ran against him tumultuously.

"You didn't come, Papa," he said. He grasped Oren's legs convulsively, tears bursting out of him. "You didn't come."

Oren looked down at his two-year-old son. He reached down, grasped the boy by the upper arms, set him away from himself.

"What are you talking about, I didn't come?" he said.

He looked up, to see Trenholm standing on the stairs.

"Today was his birthday," Trenholm said. "Last week you promised you'd come home for his birthday party."

The boy was again tight against his legs. Oren set him away.

"I couldn't," he said. "I had all the men in the cigarette industry . . ." He stopped. "I forgot about it," he said.

Wails broke afresh from Fuller. "You promised," he said. "You promised, Papa."

"Sometimes you can't keep your promises," Oren said. He was still looking at Trenholm. "Today we agreed on the combination, Trenholm. We are organizing the Allied Tobacco Company, according to my plan. I have succeeded in forming the Tobacco Trust."

"He cried all through the party," Trenholm said. "He couldn't understand why you didn't come."

Again Oren set the boy away. He turned, abruptly, and left the house. He stopped on the porch. Until now he had not let himself feel the full impact of his accomplishment. He let out a deep breath. The Allied Tobacco Company; President, Oren Knox.

That was not all. He had learned a great truth from the old man named John Winter. He had sensed the truth all his life; he had never known it with the cold, hard factuality he now possessed.

Inside and out they were hostile. They all hated Oren Knox; as John Winter hated him, as Trenholm hated him. It was a lifting thought, larger still than the combination he had sought for so many years. Oren Knox was a great man indeed, for the whole world was his enemy. He was, at last, the giant he had always felt himself destined to become.

He stood on his front porch, the knowledge as fresh and vital in his mind as the air in his lungs. Out there, the enemy lay in wait. He was eager to pursue the fight.

Book Two: Counterforce

Chapter Thirteen

In the middle of the afternoon, on a summer day in 1904, Dr. Amos drove his buggy along a country road. The mare was tired; she plodded with her head down. Dr. Amos sat in the buggy, his head nodding, letting the mare choose her own gait. He had been called at two last night and because it had been a difficult birth he was only now getting toward home. He felt frazzled, dirty; his underwear stuck to him with limp irritation. He remembered how the sweat had run down his face as he had worked with the forceps.

He was not as tall as he had been in his youth. His shoulders, even when he stood erect, were rounded. He walked with his head thrust forward, in a dogged gait remarkably like the gait of his mare. So often his only rest came while returning from one call, traveling to answer another. He shifted in his seat, thinking about the doctors who were buying automobiles because, they said, they could cover the ground so much more rapidly. How did they expect to get their rest? You couldn't turn an automobile loose to find its own way home.

Tobacco grew on each side of the road. It stood tall, the green leaves lustrous and gummy in the sun. Here and yonder people worked in the fields. With tobacco, people were always in the fields, from first setting to last cutting. People stooped and sweated under the hot sun, their backs bowed beneath the weight of this year's work, last year's, the year's before . . .

He snapped upright, jerking the mare to a halt. He cursed to himself with a fluent eloquence. The mare pricked up her ears at the stream of language. Dr. Amos leaned out of the buggy, looking ahead. He slapped the reins on the mare's back, starting her at a brisk pace. He continued a hundred yards down the road before turning her in a wide space.

The mare knew immediately he intended to return the way they had come. She did not like the prospect. She yielded reluctantly and, once headed away from town, her ears were dispirited, her gait slower than before.

They returned two miles, the mare registering her disapproval every step of the way. He stopped near where some people were working in the tobacco, got down, and led the mare under a shade tree. He took a weight out of the buggy and tied the line to the bit ring. Stepping long-legged over the rail fence, he threaded his way carefully through the plants toward the laborers. The smell of the tobacco came up nostalgically into his nostrils and involuntarily he remembered his own days of working the tobacco, the stickiness of the gum on his hands from the broad leaves and from the myriad tobacco worms.

Jacob Whitehead straightened as he approached. "Why, Dr. Amos," he said. He grinned through his scraggly teeth. "Come to help us with the worming? God knows we got a plenty."

"Didn't I tell you Sarah wasn't to work in the fields?" Dr. Amos said angrily. "Back in the spring I told you that, as plain as two and two."

They were all straightened now, watching. Sarah, Jacob's wife, stood with her hand pressed into the small of her back. She was frail, pallid, with sunken cheeks where she had lost her teeth two years ago. Dr. Amos looked at her, thinking, She looks seventy years old. She's not over forty.

Jake Whitehead grinned apologetically. "Well, I tell you, Dr. Amos," he said. "We're right short-handed this season. My oldest boy took foot in hand and left between the dark and the daylight. My young'un ain't got the sense to worm tobacco. So I told Sarah, 'Sarah, I know the doctor told you to set in the shade and take it easy. Them's fine words to hear from your doctor man. But Sarah, God knows the worm is taking my tobacco. You can lay awake at night and hear them chewing!' Sarah said, 'I reckon God meant me to worm tobacco, because I done wormed tobacco all my life. I reckon one more season of worming ain't gonna kill me.' Sarah's a good wife, Dr. Amos. Where her man goes, she's got to go, too. When her man worms tobacco, she worms . . ."

"I told you if you put her in the field, you would bury her before first snow," Dr. Amos said brutally. "You aim to bury her, Jake?"

"Well, now, Dr. Amos, she's been holding up right well. And I can't just let the worm take my tobacco."

"You might as well let the worm have it as raise it for the Trust at four cents a pound," Dr. Amos said. "You work real hard, you might be able to come out deeper in the hole than last year."

Jake slapped his knee. "I'God, that's right, Dr. Amos. You said it that time. The more you raise, the deeper you go in the hole. I'm a tobacco-raising fool, Dr. Amos. I'd be content to go to hell when I die iffen they'd just give me a nice patch of tobacco to tend. There ain't but one thing to do, Dr. Amos. When tobacco goes down to five, I got to raise more. If it goes down to four, then I got to fill me another barn. When . . ."

Dr. Amos wasn't listening. He approached Sarah, putting his hand on her shoulder. He could feel the bone sharp under his hand. He looked down into her face with the certain knowledge he could not communicate to these people. He heard the sounds in his memory as clearly as if at this moment he held a stethoscope to her breast: those muddy, irregular rhythms that meant a tired heart, ready to quit under any moment of stress. Last spring it had stopped, then had started. One day it would quit again, and there would be an end.

He looked at the three strapping boys and the girl. He looked at the father and husband, the grinning Jake Whitehead. He looked at the idiot boy, a three-year-old mind in a thirteen-year-old body, sitting on a quilt at the end of the tobacco rows. Each had taken a part of the woman Sarah. He wondered which among them had subtracted the heart.

He said gently, "How do you feel, Sarah?"

"I feel pretty good, Dr. Amos," she said. "I get a dizzy spell once in a while but . . . ." She glanced at her husband. "We got so much tobacco, I just felt like I . . ."

"You go on to the house," Dr. Amos said. "Don't let me see you in this field again. You hear? You set down in the rocking chair and you stay there. Maybe one of these days I'll even let you start rocking."

She looked at her husband. She did not move. Dr. Amos turned to Whitehead.

"Jake," he said. "Tell her to go on."

Jake looked stubborn. "God knows I got a mess of worms," he said. "God knows I'm short-handed. My oldest boy up and gone . . ."

"Tell her to go on," Dr. Amos said.

"Go on, Sarah," Jake said. "Like the doctor tells you."

Sarah went on.

Dr. Amos called after her. "Don't you be stirring around cooking supper, either. You let the girl do that."

After she was out of earshot, he turned to Jake. "Jake, I know you've got a crop to raise," he said. "You feel like you've got to raise it, even if you won't get back half what you put into it when it's in the hogshead. But there comes a setting-down time in everybody's life. Sarah has come to hers. You've got to quit thinking about her as a hand, Jake. Why, when I drove by here a while ago and saw her working in the field, I could have wrung your neck."

"What am I gonna do about these worms?" Jake said sullenly. "They're taking the leaf. I ain't never seen the worms so bad. And then there's suckering and . . ."

Dr. Amos had already started toward his buggy. He paused.

"Go see Babe White," he said. "Tell him I said to let you have his drove of turkeys for a week. Those turkeys will clean the worms out of here quicker and better than ever the human hand."

Jake brightened. "Yes sir, Dr. Amos," he said. He chuckled. "Why, I'll be setting in the shade right alongside Sarah, watching them turkeys do my work."

Dr. Amos returned to the road, put the curb weight into the buggy, climbed in. He headed the briskened mare toward town. He did not drowse. He remembered too sharply that he had traveled a mile or more beyond the sight of Sarah in the fields before his attention had been nudged.

He made one more stop before Jamestown. It was a Negro shack under a large oak tree, set back from the road. This family, too, was working in the tobacco field near the house. Dr. Amos got down and walked out to them.

"Why, Dr. Amos," Charlie Blake said, a wide grin on his face. "I'm so glad to see you."

"How's your boy doing, Charlie?" Dr. Amos said.

"He's doing fine, Dr. Amos. Just fine. Says he aims to be working come Monday morning."

"Let me look at him."

They walked together down the tobacco rows until they came out into the yard. The yard was bare, clean-swept this morning but with fresh chicken-droppings here and there. The house was very old, built half of logs, leaning in on itself under the oak tree. It contained only two rooms, with a dogtrot between and a porch in front. On the porch a grown boy sat in a rocking chair, a quilt, ragged but clean, drawn around his body though it was a hot day.

Dr. Amos stepped up on the porch. "How you feeling, boy?" he said.

The boy smiled up at him. "I aim to be on my feet come Monday morning," he said.

"You take your time," Dr. Amos said. "Charlie, make him take his time, now."

"Yes sir, I aim to do that," Charlie said. "He's a fool to have to be setting in that chair in the first place. He be a double fool to start walking around too quick."

"Mr. Wilson come by this morning," the boy said. "Wanted to know why I wan't in the field. He said Papa come on to sharecrop with five hands and when you come on to sharecrop with five hands, he expects to see five hands in the tobacco."

"Don't you worry about Mr. Wilson," Dr. Amos said. "You worry about not getting on your feet too quick. Here. Let me look at it."

He laid aside the quilt. The boy wore no shirt. Working quickly, because he knew it was going to hurt, Dr. Amos removed the bandages to get at the wound. He kept talking while he worked.

"You know you're a big man in town now, Will?" he said. "That's all they've talked about this week. Even the white folks." He glanced up to see the pleased smile on the boy's face. "I wouldn't recommend you try to better your record, though."

"He's a fool," the father said. "That's what I told him when they brought him home. A plain, blamed fool."

Dr. Amos looked at the cut, examining particularly for inflammation and pus. The wound looked good, the stitches holding it neatly closed, showing only as a puckered, angry welt across the width of his stomach. Dr. Amos shook his head.

The boy had lost an argument about a girl. Dr. Amos hadn't seen the argument, but he had heard enough about it. For fifteen minutes the two boys had fought with razors while a crowd had gathered. He had even heard that the sheriff had watched also, making no attempt to stop the fight. They had circled each other and circled each other, the bright razors gleaming in the sun, while the crowd had waited to see one Negro kill another.

It had almost happened. At last Will had made a rush, slashing his enemy on the shoulder but receiving the quick slash that had emptied his guts out of his body. It had been clean and quick and deadly. His enemy had stepped back to watch the boy, lying on the ground and staring down at his insides spilling out of his body.

No one had come to help him. Bemused by the imminence of death, they had watched him gather his guts into his hands and then followed as, holding his hands pressed against his stomach, he had walked all the way across town to Dr. Amos' office.

Dr. Amos remembered how the boy had entered, had sat in a chair to wait because Dr. Amos had been busy with a patient. His nurse had paid no attention to the boy. When Dr. Amos was free, the boy had risen again and, holding himself in, walked into the inner office.

"Can you help me, Dr. Amos?" he said. Then he had fainted.

He had lost a lot of blood, though fortunately the intestines had not been punctured. Dr. Amos could do nothing but clean the wound as best he could and sew the boy up again. He had not expected Will to live. Yet here he sat on his front porch and the wound looked clean and healing.

"How he doing, Dr. Amos?" Charlie said anxiously.

"It looks good," Dr. Amos said. "Now, I want you to watch him carefully. The first sign of pus or tenderness, you let me know. There's bound to be dirt in there; I couldn't get it all out without puncturing his intestines. It looks as if it's coming along fine, though. We've just got to be careful about infection. So you watch it."

"We'll watch it," Charlie said. "But is he going to be all right?"

Dr. Amos looked thoughtfully at the boy. "Anybody who's done what he did deserves to live," he said. "I don't reckon you could kill him with a shotgun. I hate to say it, boy—but you've got a lot of guts."

Dr. Amos and Charlie laughed. The boy laughed, too, but stopped immediately, pain passing over his face like the shadow of a cloud.

"It hurts to laugh," he said apologetically.

Dr. Amos was bandaging again. "You might even live long enough to get some sense," he said. "Though that may take a while."

He finished the bandaging, closed his bag. "I'll stop in the next time I'm by," he said. "But you come get me if it starts to bother him. And don't feed him anything but soup. We don't want to put any strain on those stitches."

"Yes sir," Charlie said. He hesitated. "You need some sweet taters, Dr. Amos? I got some of the nicest sweet taters you ever . . ."

"Why, yes," Dr. Amos said. "I don't like anything better than a good sweet potato. Now, you just give me what you can spare."

Dr. Amos returned to the buggy and waited while Charlie Blake brought a sack of sweet potatoes from the barn. Dr. Amos stowed it into the buggy.

"Take care, now," he said, climbing in. "Mind what I said."

"Dr. Amos, I don't rightly know when I'll be able to pay you," Charlie said. "I got me a good crop of tobacco. But if them prices are like last year, it's gonna cost me to raise it."

"Don't worry about it, Charlie," Dr. Amos said. "Everybody's in the same fix. It just don't pay to raise four-cent tobacco and that's what everybody in the Black Patch is having to do." He looked down at Charlie. "You won't believe it, but Mr. Wilson is hurting nigh as bad as you are."

Charlie shook his head. "I don't know what po' folks is gonna do," he said. "It look like tobacco ain't no living no more."

"It's the Trust," Dr. Amos said. "They just keep on squeezing, that's all."

"They just about got all the blood out of this-here turnip," Charlie said. "Looks like they aim to get the turnip, too."

"I don't know what they think they're up to," Dr. Amos said. "Don't nobody know, Charlie. Bigger men than you or me don't have any idea what to do about it."

Charlie stepped away from the buggy wheel and Dr. Amos departed toward town. The boy on the porch lifted his hand in farewell. Dr. Amos looked down at the sack of sweet potatoes at his feet. He knew that Charlie could ill afford the gesture; he knew also that Charlie had needed to make it. He sighed. There were others, far more able, who seldom felt the necessity.

Dr. Amos had had three years under Dr. Allgood, the last year making all outside calls alone while Dr. Allgood remained behind. Dr. Allgood had come to the office until the day of his death, however; older each day, whiter, those moments more frequent when he retired into the inner sanctum to roll up his sleeve and inject the morphine that alleviated the pain of his disease.

Dr. Amos could remember that scrawny arm, the fist clenched, the dead-whiteness of the skin. Dr. Allgood would never allow Dr. Amos to make the injection for him. Afterward, his lined face would relax, slowly but inevitably, and for a time his pain would be bearable.

"Dr. Allgood," Dr. Amos had said once. "You know your tolerance is building. You're taking more and more all the time."

Dr. Allgood had nodded, soberly. "I don't think I'll outlast it," he said.

At first Dr. Amos had been accepted hesitantly; by the time Dr. Allgood had died the patients were coming to him rather than to the old doctor. Of the three doctors in Jamestown, Dr. Amos served virtually all the country needs. By then, within his soul, Dr. Amos had felt himself truly a doctor. At Dr. Allgood's side he had seen all the illnesses and accidents that human flesh knows. At night he had sat late, reading under Dr. Allgood's instructions. It had been a medical education far more real than that he had obtained in nine years in Kansas City.

What was more important, the people of the county had accepted Dr. Amos. Dr. Allgood had rightly anticipated the effect of the Haines family upon Dr. Amos' reputation; one could scarcely imagine that a son of old Art could have made himself a doctor. There was, too, that old scandal of Temple's Crossroads to overcome. Dr. Amos overcame it, except in the immediate vicinity of Temple's Crossroads itself—he was never called there.

It had been generally rumored that he had got Virginia Temple into trouble. They still talked about how Mr. Temple had ridden after the fleeing clerk with his pistol in his pocket, but had failed to catch him. Since his return, Dr. Amos had not met

Mr. Temple face-to-face. Even in the old days, Mr. Temple had seldom come to town.

The whisper had never touched Roscoe Barnes. Indeed, Virginia's entire era of red-wheeled buggies and high-stepping mares had been forgotten. People remembered only her beauty, her smile, her red hair; how she had disappeared from their ken, never to be heard of again. If the family had news of her, they never spoke of it to others. Roscoe Barnes had married suitably and now lived in Jamestown, the heir of his father, a prosperous dealer in tobacco leaf, his voice still loud and laughing in the clusters of men. Dr. Amos saw him occasionally in the streets and each time, as in the old days, a dart of hate stuck in his heart for an hour afterward.

Actually, Dr. Amos remembered the whole episode far more vividly than did anyone else except Mr. Temple. After all, Virginia Temple was neither the first nor the last girl to get into trouble in this way. There was a flurry of revival, of course, when Dr. Amos had returned, but it had died down as people had found newer matters to talk about.

Dr. Amos did not forget. Once, driven by the guilt he had known all these years, not of responsibility but because he had refused her dire need, he had called on one of her sisters who lived in Jamestown.

The sister had kept him standing on the porch. "I'm afraid I can't help you," she said in a cold, high voice. "I don't know where Virginia might be."

"I thought you might hear from her," Dr. Amos said.

"I'm afraid I can't help you."

Defeated, he had turned away. Once in the yard, he had paused, saying, "If you could only tell me that she is all right . . ."

"I can't tell you that," the sister had said. "Even if I knew myself, I wouldn't."

He had turned away from so much that was painful to look upon. There was his family; his mother especially. There was Old Man Temple, Virginia herself. Despite all, or perhaps because of all, he had accomplished what he had set out to accomplish. Every mile of country road, every wound healed or illness treated, was payment on an account that reached over as many seasons of time as those debits in the Temple store ledgers he had once mastered so assiduously. Like those sharecroppers and tenant farmers, he wondered if ever a good year would come when he would be paid out in full.

Dr. Amos prospered in his practice. He continued to live as simply as a student. After Dr. Allgood's death he had arranged a tiny apartment behind the office. He ate most of his meals in a restaurant down the street. He had tried eating at a local boardinghouse, on a regular basis, but he had missed too many meals because of his irregular hours.

He had long since become a familiar figure in the streets of Jamestown, along the country roads. Tall and dark, forever weary as good doctors are always weary, since disease and accident inevitably outrun the endurance of any one man, no matter how dedicated, he plodded his rounds, his shoulders stooped under the rusty black coat that reached almost to his knees. People watched in awe as he entered the house of illness. He sat down, opened his bag; was instantly focused into a total absorption. His hands were both strong and gentle. The weariness seemed to slide from his shoulders, even the age that built perceptibly in him year by year. At such moments he seemed young again, even eager. His voice, disembodied from his concentration upon the medical problem, would speak, often in jest or admonishment. He seemed to come back into the ordinary world from some bourne no one else could know. He would become once more the familiar man, aging, weary, exasperated.

He delivered babies, bound wounds, eased the pains of dying. More than once he operated on a kitchen table, his instruments beside him in a steaming dishpan, a father or a mother holding a lamp high away from the fumes of the combustible anesthesia. He walked away from houses of death and from houses of life, he left behind weeping or joy or, worst of all, an anxious uncertainty. Yet each day of practice diminished only infinitesimally, if at all, the debit balance of the ledger in his soul. Yet, in a strange, discontented way, he was content. It was the bargain he had made.

He had now reached the outskirts of town. People spoke as he passed. He nodded in reply. He alighted from the buggy before the livery stable and surrendered the reins to the Negro boy who ran out to meet him.

"Rub her down good and give her some corn," Dr. Amos said.

"Yes sir, Dr. Amos," the Negro boy said, busily taking the tired mare out of her harness.

"How's that nigger boy you sewed up, Dr. Amos?" one of the men spoke out of a group lounging along the lot fence.

"He's going to live," Dr. Amos said. "I just took a look at him. Looks might' nigh as peart as you do."

"I'll be damned," another man said. "I'd a never thought it. I taken one look and I said to myself, 'There's one dead nigger.' And him toting them guts all the way across town."

Dr. Amos shifted his bag. "He was lucky," he said. "If the intestines had been punctured . . . if it had been anything but a clean cut with a razor."

"Now *there's* your reason for razor-fighting," the first man said. "If you get cut it's as clean as if the doctor here had done it for you. No dirty old jagged knife cuts for me. I'll take a razor any time."

"You remember that story about the two boys fighting with razors? One takes a swipe at the other and the other one yells, 'You missed.' The first one smiles and says, 'Just wait till you try to shake yo' head.' "

Dr. Amos laughed with them and said good-day, going on toward his office. It was only a block away. He climbed the stairs, and opened the door, saw the group of men sitting and standing about the room. He paused.

"What's the matter?" he said.

Walter Wingo thrust himself forward. "We've been waiting for you, Dr. Amos. We'd just about given you out."

"I had a hard delivery," Dr. Amos said. He was alert. It was seldom so many people gathered at once in his office. Whatever was wrong must be wrong indeed. He looked at the men. They were, like Walter Wingo, prosperous, or once-prosperous, planters of tobacco. They were the men who rented to tenant farmers and sharecroppers, as well as growing their own crops. "What's up?"

"Nobody knows the people of this county like you do," Walter Wingo said. "We need your advice, Dr. Amos. We need to know what we can do about this tobacco situation."

Dr. Amos put down his bag slowly. "So it's come to that," he said.

"It's come to that," Walter Wingo said grimly.

Dr. Amos looked from one man to the other. Walter Wingo was the biggest man in the group, both financially and physically. He had a large farm ten miles from town, a brick house that could easily have been called a plantation house if it had only had a white column or two. He was six feet tall, with bulky shoulders and a big, meaty face. His hair was still black, but his beaver beard was interlaced with startling slashes of silver. He wore a high collar and a four-in-hand tie, but his trousers legs were stuffed carelessly into knee-high riding boots.

The other men were, in varying degrees, his compeers. Dressed in differing combinations of city style and country clothing, they owned gold watch chains and good tobacco land. One or two, like Walter Wingo, owned reprocessing plants in Jamestown.

"Here's the fact of the matter," Walter Wingo said. "We're up against something that's a lot bigger than any of us. It may even be bigger than all of us put together. That's to be found out. I think we've got to find out—this year."

"What do you think, Dr. Amos?" Lewis Carnett said anxiously. "You know the folks better than anybody else."

"I've ridden this country night and day for fifteen years," Dr. Amos said. "I've seen bad times and good times." He shook his head. "I've never seen times as bad as they are now. Seems like, since the war, folks get dragged down a little bit more with every year that comes."

"It's not the crops, it's the Trust," Mr. Wingo said angrily. "A bad crop year a man can weather, one way or the other. But the Trust—why, if it's a good year, they cut the price because there's so much tobacco. If it's a bad year, they cut it because of the quality. Come hell or high water, they cut the price." He snorted. "They keep on, we're going to be paying old O.K. Knox for the privilege of putting a sprout of tobacco into the ground."

"You hear about that house O.K. Knox is building hisself over there in North Carolina?" Tom Meacham said. "They say he's putting millions of dollars into it. They say it's gonna be the showplace of the nation."

"I figure I've built a room or two of that mansion my own self," Mr. Wingo said.

"It's hard to figure a man like that," Mr. Carnett said. "Way I heard it, he's common as mud—come offen one of them North Carolina farms just like anybody else. Nobody even *heard* of the Knoxes till he come along."

"I reckon he's like some of us," Dr. Amos said dryly. "He's still scratching to get out of the tobacco patch."

"He's scratching too hard and too deep to suit me," Mr. Wingo said, his voice growling.

"You still haven't told me what you've got in mind," Dr. Amos said.

Walter Wingo looked at the other men. He cleared his throat. "Well now. We've been talking amongst ourselves. Last year the Trust divided the tobacco country into districts. They made an agreement with the Italian Regie people and the other foreign buyers so there ain't but one buyer per district. That buyer comes and gives you a price and that's it, take it or leave it." He grinned fiercely. "Me, I was lucky. I got me two buyers. You know the turnpike runs right through my place. I got one buyer east of the turnpike and I got another buyer west of it. But here's the funny part. Those two buyers offered exactly the same price. One was a Trust man and the other was a Regie man, buying for the Italian Government. But somehow or other they happened to light on the same figure, just like flies on a piece of meat."

He cleared his throat again. "So we've been figuring amongst ourselves. We have decided that if the Trust aims to use one buyer per district, keeping everybody else out, we ought to make it easy for them. We ought to put all the tobacco in the Black Patch into one big bunch. Then the Trust can come to one place and buy all the tobacco they need."

"What if they refuse?" Dr. Amos said.

"They've got to have tobacco," Mr. Wingo said. "They can't make a dime without the tobacco to make it on. If they refuse to buy from us, then we hold on to it until they're ready to buy."

"The Trust doesn't have to eat," Dr. Amos said. "People do. How long do you figure to hold out? A year? Two years? You've got mortgages. You've got tenants and sharecroppers to worry about. You've got money borrowed at the bank to make your crop on."

"We've *got* to hold out," Mr. Wingo said. He gripped his fists. "I'd rather starve myself than let the Trust do it."

"How do you figure to bunch everybody's tobacco like that?"

"We form a Dark Tobacco Growers' Protective Association," Walter Wingo said rapidly. "Every man agrees to put his entire crop into the Association pool. If we can, we'll pay him a little on it. We'll store it for him until the tobacco is sold. The Association will charge him a fair commission for selling his tobacco. We won't sell piecemeal—we'll put a price on the whole crop and we'll set down and wait till the Trust comes to taw."

"What are you going to do about the folks who won't have anything to do with the Association?" Dr. Amos said.

"There won't be many of those," Mr. Wingo said confidently. "A man would be a fool not to see the advantage of the Association. They'll come in, all right, once we get it started."

"What price are you thinking about?"

"Six cents this year," Walter Wingo said. His voice mingled with other voices bursting from the men, ranging from five cents up to ten. "Six cents," Walter said firmly. "This year. Next year —well, we'll see."

They paused, looking expectantly at Dr. Amos.

"What do you think?" Mr. Wingo said at last.

Dr. Amos thought of today's ride through the countryside. Slowly, he nodded his head. "I don't know whether your Association is the answer or not," he said. "But the people are ready for something. They're getting mighty desperate." He raised his head. "You know what you're getting into? Once you put your hand to the plow, there'll be no turning back. You show fight to O.K. Knox, he'll do his best to break you. He's broken some big men in his time."

"What else is there to do?" Mr. Wingo demanded.

Dr. Amos nodded. "Yes. What else is there to do?" He looked from one to the other. "But you all better start big right from the beginning. You'd better have a majority of the growers this year, and just about all of them by next."

"We aim to hold a big rally," Mr. Wingo said eagerly. "Get in folks from all around, tell them about it, and sign them up."

"There's one other thing," Dr. Amos said. "You'd do good to keep politics out of it. You want everybody, Democrat or Republican or Free Silver or Prohibitionist. You let folks start dividing on political lines, your Association will be a failure."

"No candidates, no politicking," Mr. Wingo said. "We've already talked about that."

Dr. Amos smiled. "I wish you good luck," he said. "I'll do what I can to help."

There was a silence following his words. The men looked at Mr. Wingo. Mr. Wingo cleared his throat.

"Well now, we had another little matter in mind," he said. He cleared his throat again. "We want you to head up the Association."

Dr. Amos was startled. "Me?" he said. He smiled. "Why I don't own a leaf of tobacco. I . . ."

"That's exactly why you're the man," Mr. Wingo declared. "Everybody knows you, from the big owner to the least sharecropper. Everybody respects you. Everybody knows that you'll do the best for all concerned. They'll put the confidence in you they couldn't bring themselves to put in any other man. You let a lawyer be the head, they'll figure he's using the Association to build his power up to where he can run for office. You let a big landowner head it up, they'll figure on him using it for his personal benefit. You're the man, Dr. Amos. You're the key to the success of the Association."

"I'm a doctor," Dr. Amos said. "My business is healing people's illnesses."

"Isn't this an illness?" Walter Wingo said. "The whole countryside is sick, Dr. Amos. It's got the Trust fever."

"I don't have the time," Dr. Amos said. "You know my practice. Why, I don't sleep now more than . . ."

He stopped, seeing in their faces the effect of his denial. He thought again of today's ride, and yesterday's, and the day before. Most of all, he thought of tomorrow's ride, and next week's, moving among the people, easing their suffering, knowing all the while how much of their trouble came simply from worry, from lack of food and the proper medicines they couldn't even think about buying.

"I haven't thought about it," he said, then, slowly. "Give me some time to think about it. Then I'll give you my answer."

Chapter Fourteen

DR. AMOS, standing at his office window, watched the people come into town. The movement had started with first light; now nearly noon, it continued unabated. They came in buggies and wagons, on horseback and afoot. There were men riding alone, men with their entire families. The center of town was knotted with their mass, and the belated ones hastened to join the turmoil. Babies squalled, women chattered, men laughed and shouted. Down the street there was the flurry of a fist fight and someone, somewhere, let off his pistol in sheer exuberance.

Yet it was an essentially somber massing. Their faces bore the same look as when, only a few years ago, they had gathered to sign up for the Cuban war; on the surface the exuberance of men gathering for a hunt, underlying the exuberance a sober realization of commitment. Men talked among themselves, shifting from group to group. They were of all classes, from the raggedest sharecropper to the most prosperous planter. There was even a cluster of Negroes, though Negroes seldom turned out when the white people did.

Dr. Amos saw that the people of the town were watching, with a curious air of reserve, the incoming country people. The professional men leaned in the open windows of the second and third stories of the buildings. The merchants stood shirt-sleeved in their store entrances. The stores were empty, though the streets were full. Today was not a buying day.

Dr. Amos was impressed by the outpouring. September, they should have been busy in their crops. The call to the rally had overridden all other concerns.

Some of those passing beneath his window looked up and waved. He did not wave back, but stood watching soberly. Perhaps no other man in the county could know quite so well as he the deeper meaning of today. These were a people of individual action, each man turning instinctively inward to seek the answer to his own needs. Yet they were here meeting together in the common good.

Dr. Amos had not made his decision. Mr. Wingo, the others, had pressed him to announce his adherence before the big rally, hoping it would bring in the reluctant, the doubtful. Dr. Amos had resisted the pressure. He did not yet know his own mind; there was no doubt that the Association was a good idea, but it was so far from his picture of himself in the world that he hesitated to follow his sympathies.

He turned away from the window, surveying his cluttered office. He had shaped a way for himself; he had paid dearly for the privilege of following his chosen path. His life had been a succession of abandonments; first his family, then Virginia Temple, then his own ease and comfort.

He remembered the day his father Art Haines had visited the office. Dr. Amos had been in Jamestown for nearly a year by then, immersed in his practice. He had not seen his father, his brothers and sisters.

The door had opened, Art Haines had entered. "Well, son," he had said, standing there, looking about the office. "So you've gone and made a doctor."

Dr. Amos had been shocked by his appearance. Art Haines was an old man. He had lost his teeth, his cheeks caved in over his gums. He had not shaved for two days, his white scrag of beard nearly an inch long. His mouth was browned with tobacco juice.

"Hello, Papa," Dr. Amos had said. "Come in and sit down."

Art Haines rolled his chew of natural twist in his mouth. He pursed his lips and spat on the floor.

"Didn't come in to set down," he said. "Come in to see if you still looked like a Haines." He peered at Dr. Amos. "Why, if a man didn't know any different, he'd swear you *were* a Haines."

Dr. Amos saw that his father was drunk. It did not show, except in the heightened flush of his face or if one listened closely to the voice. Art Haines spat again.

"Don't spit on the floor," Dr. Amos said sharply.

"Gitting too good for your old daddy?" Art said in an insinuating voice. He approached Dr. Amos. "Of course, no Haines ain't never wore no fine alpacker coat like that there you got on your shoulders. So I reckon you ain't no Haines after all."

"Papa, I think you'd better go," Dr. Amos said. He picked up his bag. "I have a call . . ."

"Now, don't rush your old daddy off in the heat of the day," Art said in a complaining voice. He stood close to Dr. Amos, peering up at him. "*Are* you a Haines, son? Are you?"

"Of course I'm a Haines."

Art Haines shook his head. "I reckon not," he said mournfully. "There ain't a Haines in the world wouldn't come to his own mammy's funeral. There ain't a Haines in the world but wouldn't come to see his own daddy, not to mention his brothern and his sistern."

"Papa," Dr. Amos said. He stopped himself. "What do you want, Papa?"

Art Haines shook his head. "A man figures to ride off and leave his trouble behind him. Ride off from home and you ain't a Haines no more. Ride off from Temple's Store and you ain't knocked up no pretty little redheaded gal. But son, I'll tell you one thing. You ain't never gonna ride far enough nor fast enough to keep from being a Haines right on."

"What do you want, Papa?" Dr. Amos said. "I have no time for talk."

"No time. No time," Art said, mimicking his voice. He

peered at Dr. Amos shrewdly. "If you're in a generous mood, I might take a dollar or two. I need me a pint to see me on my way home."

"I won't give you money for drinking," Dr. Amos said.

"I didn't figure you would. I just wanted to hear you say the words." Art Haines drew himself up, started for the door. He stopped. "Son, I'm a tobacco man. Been a tobacco man all my life. All I know is raising the weed. I never worked an acre of land that I could name my own, but I been a tobacco man right on. Now I'm old, and my joints ache in the morning from all the days I've spent stooping. I figure I'm entitled to a pint of rotgut now and agin."

"Papa," Dr. Amos said, moving toward him.

Art Haines waved him away. "I ain't asking you," he said. "I just come to see whether you was still a Haines or not." He went to the door. He paused, working his mouth. He spat into the middle of the floor. "Don't look back, son. Don't never look back. They might be gaining on you."

Dr. Amos seemed in these days to spend more and more time looking backward. Perhaps it was only the penalty of celibate middle age that he could remember so vividly how Virginia Temple had crossed the road that day in the rain, that he could recall every word of the conversation that had ensued. But why should he remember equally well the day he had sat on the porch, his youngest sister a-borning, the very feel of the air tainted with the cries of pain? There were cries of pain enough in his own daily life on which to concentrate his mind.

Like a surgeon, he had cut away so much of his life, that the remainder might exist in all purity and simplicity. He lived without woman or wife or family. His living quarters were sparse and clean, his clothes few, his wants simple. He was Doctor, nothing but Doctor; he had given fully of himself.

Now—they wanted more.

Down the street, where the temporary wooden platform had been erected, a brass band had begun to play. The sound skirled brightly, picking up the tempo of the day. The people in the street began to move more purposefully toward the bright sound.

More than a thousand must have passed under his window this morning. God knows how many had entered down other streets beyond the sight of his eyes. Their sound, muted under the brass, reached up to his second-floor window.

The door opened. He turned, to see Roscoe Barnes.

"Dr. Amos?" Roscoe said. "Got a minute?"

Roscoe in middle age looked much like the young Roscoe who had called so frequently in his red-wheeled buggy for Virginia Temple, to whirl her away laughing into unimagined rendezvous. He was heavier, his face permanently reddened by the constant drinking of bourbon whiskey. Broken patches of veins stood on the point of each cheek. His eyes were white-rimmed, rather bulging, as though he suffered from high blood pressure.

His voice was gusty, outgoing, calling to Dr. Amos as though he were a long-time friend. Muscular and stocky, he wore a business suit today, though usually he fancied riding breeches and boots, an open-collared shirt, and a riding crop which he carried like a wand of power.

"Of course," Dr. Amos said. "Though I was just leaving."

He had hated Roscoe Barnes for so long that the hate had become as much a part of his life as the black bag he carried constantly in one hand. He knew it was purely jealousy. For years his mind had been inflamed by the thought of Virginia in the embrace of those thick, muscled arms, of her kisses lavished on the meaty, high-colored face. The jealousy had now faded from the immediate vividness; the residue remained.

Roscoe Barnes had returned discreetly to town a year after Virginia Temple had disappeared from local knowledge. Now he owned the leaf factory he had inherited from his father. He also had warehouse interests, and acted as a buyer for distant, smaller concerns.

Roscoe crossed to the window, looked out into the street. "They sure are flocking in," he said. "Did you ever see such a sight in your life?"

"No," Dr. Amos said. "I doubt if we ever will again, either."

Roscoe put his hands on the window sill, bracing himself on the strength of his arms. "The fools," he said. "They think they can gang up on the Trust." He watched for a moment, then turned to look at Dr. Amos. "Dr. Amos, I've heard the rumor you might be in on the Association that Walter Wingo and the others are planning."

"I've talked to them about their plans," Dr. Amos said noncommittally.

Roscoe exploded a harsh laugh. "Surely you don't think it can be done," he said.

Dr. Amos shook his head. "Something's got to be done." He paused, watching Roscoe. "You've been hurt too, Mr. Barnes. Your leaf factory is just existing on the crumbs left after the Trust gets through. The independent dealers, the landowners, the sharecroppers are all in the same boat."

"I haven't been doing a tenth of the business we used to do," Roscoe said. He spoke the words in a hearty, self-assured voice, as though he were announcing a triumph. "But I've got more sense than to think I can buck the Trust." He paused, watching Dr. Amos. "I don't believe the people ought to be encouraged into thinking that they can."

"What do you suggest we do?"

"Do? Do nothing. That's the ticket, Dr. Amos. You get the Trust all stirred up, ain't no telling what old O.K. Knox will put his mind to. You leave him alone, he'll leave you alone."

"I've never seen the country so poor," Dr. Amos said. "People can't see where the winter's bread is coming from, Mr. Barnes. Every year the Trust squeezes just a little harder. You'd think they'd let up after a while. You'd think they'd recognize that people have to eat if they're going to raise tobacco at all. But the Trust is soulless."

His voice was becoming agitated. He took a turn about the room.

"I can't figure a man like O.K. Knox. They say he came right off a tobacco farm. How can a man like that squeeze the tobacco planter the way he's doing? If he was one of those New York financiers, maybe I could understand it. But he's had the smell of tobacco in his nostrils. He's stooped to plant and he's stooped to worm."

"He's forgot all that," Roscoe said indifferently. "Besides, the Trust isn't one man. It's more than O.K. Knox. It's a living, breathing thing, running on its own steam. It's a juggernaut, Dr. Amos, and if any man gets in its way, that man's going to be run down."

Dr. Amos shook his head. "No," he said. "I don't care what the law says about a corporation being an entity and all that. It's still run by men, and it's the men who are responsible. Our enemies are men, Mr. Barnes. Men of flesh and blood and bones just like we are."

"So you *are* a part of the Association," Roscoe said.

"I didn't say that," Dr. Amos said sharply.

"If I were you, I'd think a long time before I put myself against the Trust," Mr. Barnes said. "It's power you'll be fooling with. You figure you can stand up to O.K. Knox? Why, it'd be like an amateur going into the prize ring against James J. Jeffries. You let your little old Association bring itself to O.K. Knox's attention, he'll swat you in the same absent-minded way he'd swat a fly. What kind of power do you think you can bring against the power that man has at his disposal?"

Dr. Amos took thought before he attempted to answer the question. O.K. Knox was a distant, fabulous figure, moving grandly in the great mysterious world of finance. He was a figure of newspaper fame, announced as departing for Europe on great ocean liners, or returning from Europe, always tight-lipped, uncommunicative, upon the conclusion of mysterious transactions. Yet this remote figure had brought the flood of humanity up the street under Dr. Amos' windows this morning. O.K. Knox, in one way or another, touched every life that Dr. Amos knew.

O.K. Knox was a much-cursed man. Dr. Amos had heard many men lay the shape of their tongue against him in imaginative and creative terms. Yet he continued to move, serene and indestructible, above the human scene. He was untouchable; his great riches, his immense power, brought him unscathed through court trial after court trial. He had been indicted both civilly and criminally; the Trust lawyers, indeed, were constantly employed in one court case after another. None of it touched Oren Knox; he continued on his inevitable way, toward whatever obscure goal he sought.

"What power?" Dr. Amos said slowly. "Why, the power of the people. That's the sovereign power, you know. It may be slow, and difficult to bring to bear; but when the people decide that an evil exists, that evil will disappear. The Trust is a force; the force of the people is a counterforce."

"You get this counterforce all stirred up, what will you do with it?"

"Once it has conquered that which brought it forth, it will wither away," Dr. Amos said sharply. "We will know exactly what we are doing. Our aims will be limited. Once achieved, we will know they have been achieved." He stared at Roscoe Barnes. "The Association is being formed by men of morals and stature. It will exist only to oppose the evil of the Trust."

"I read in the paper the other day that the Trust controls eighty per cent of the cigarette production, seventy-five per cent of the smoking tobacco, and eighty per cent of the chewing tobacco. The only way you're going to oppose power like that is to control one hundred per cent of tobacco production in the entire Black Patch. Now, just how do you aim to make every single man, without exception, put his tobacco into the Association? You know how independent these country folks can be."

"We will reason with them," Dr. Amos said.

Roscoe's frankly skeptical look made Dr. Amos furious. The black hate boiled up to add itself to the fury.

"It's easy to be cynical!" he cried. "It's the easiest thing in the world to stand off and predict disaster. But what did a cynical man ever contribute to this world? You've got to believe, Mr. Barnes. I've always believed in people; that's why I became a doctor in the first place."

"You'd better stick to your doctoring," Roscoe said. There was a faintly superior smile on his face. He was pleased at having succeeded in arousing Dr. Amos' temper. "You catch a man flat on his back, he might let you do him some good. On his two feet, he'll fight you like a wildcat."

Dr. Amos gestured toward the window. "Does that look like they're fighting it?" he said, more calmly now.

A burst of brass welled through from the street. Roscoe's face clouded.

"They're flocking in, all right," he said, his voice grudging the words. He studied Dr. Amos again. "So you are going to lead them, after all."

"I am going to help," Dr. Amos said, correcting the position but not the commitment.

He was surprised at himself. He had not realized, as yet, that his mind was made up. The announced decision settled itself in him, calming the turmoil of his mind. *All right,* he told himself. *So even the doctoring isn't enough any more. It's not just physical ills, it's the body politic that I must aid in healing.*

He was watching Roscoe Barnes now, studying his face. "What about you?" he said. "You'll have to choose sides, too. The Trust is hurting you, too, as an independent leaf dealer. If you try to stand in the middle between the Trust and the Association, you'll catch it from both sides. So what are *you* going to do?"

Roscoe smiled, faintly. There was no laughter behind the expression. He turned toward the door, halted, turned back.

"Do?" he echoed. "I've already done it." He watched Dr. Amos' face. "I've joined the Trust. In fact, I'm the local representative now for the Allied Tobacco Corporation."

"But why? These people are your folks, too . . ."

"I believe in staying with a winner," Roscoe said lightly. "I'll put my money on the champion every time." He laughed. There was pleasure in the laughter this time, sheer enjoyment of the expression on Dr. Amos' face. "Nobody's ever beaten old O.K. Knox as yet," he said. "He's a pretty good fighter to put your money on."

Dr. Amos was beginning to be angry again. "You might at least have told me," he said in a cold, withdrawn voice.

"Then you wouldn't have talked as freely," Roscoe said candidly. He paused, his hand on the door. "Let me tell you something else, Dr. Amos. I've made it my business to speak to a lot of men in this town the last few days. I've sounded out every man of importance—the newspaper editor, the banker, the mayor, the store owners—on this whole question of the Association. This is a Trust town, Dr. Amos; Jamestown is one hundred per cent for the Trust."

"I don't believe it," Dr. Amos said flatly.

"You will find out it is true. For one simple reason, Dr. Amos. Jamestown needs the Trust; the Trust doesn't need Jamestown. If the Trust pulled out of here, this town would dry up and blow away. You think the banker doesn't know that? And how much advertising does the Trust give the newspaper? Think about it, Dr. Amos. You're in enemy territory, right now."

A knock sounded on the door as Barnes began to open it. Roscoe continued with the movement, to reveal Walter Wingo, with Lewis Carnett and Thomas Meacham.

"The speaking has started, Dr. Amos," Walter said. "Will you speak to them, too?"

"Yes," Dr. Amos said. He started to join the men, hesitated, thinking he was forgetting something. Then he realized that he was looking for his doctor's bag. He never left the office without the bag in his hand and his body was feeling the absence of the familiar weight. Exasperated at his absent-mindedness, he went on to join the Association men.

"Coming to the rally, Mr. Barnes?" Mr. Wingo said. "Be glad to have you."

"I reckon not," Roscoe Barnes said, "Good day, gentlemen," He went on past them down the stairs.

"Is he one of your patients?" Walter asked Dr. Amos.

"No," Dr. Amos said shortly. "And not likely to be."

They went on down the stairs. The streets were deserted now, except for the storekeepers standing in their doorways staring toward the distant sounds of the rally. Dr. Amos, as he passed along the street, looked into the town faces. He could see their hostility, overlaying a faint fear. They are afraid of the tobacco men, he thought suddenly. They've never been afraid before—but then, they've never seen them massed into one purpose.

His face settled into grim lines, he strode on, hurrying the men with him. In the distance they could hear an orator's voice. As they came nearer, they could make out the peaks of the sentences as the voice rose and fell.

A platform of rough lumber had been constructed in front of the courthouse. The tobacco men were massed about three sides of the platform, spilling out into the street. They stood quietly in the hot sun, crowded together, their faces lifted toward the speaker. Their jaws moved on chaws of natural twist. Occasionally one or another of them would jerk his head in emphasis or approval at the words of the speaker and expectorate vigorously on the ground.

It was a silent throng. Their faces were hard, tight; at first sight one would have thought them hostile to the man yonder on the platform. But it was his words that were angering them. This was not a time for cheering.

Dr. Amos paused near the platform. He was surprised at the fieriness of the man speaking. Dr. Amos had known John Thomas all his life; he owned a small farm miles from town, which he worked with the aid of his eight growing boys. John Thomas was a little man, scarcely five and a half feet tall. With his bulky neck shaping into his round head, he looked like a miniature wrestler. Though small, he was muscular. He had on occasion displayed political tendencies, running for and winning several times the post of constable, running for and losing several times a place on the road commission.

"How did John Thomas get to be one of your speakers?" Dr. Amos asked Mr. Wingo.

Wingo grinned. "He demanded the right to lead off," he said. "He brought me thirteen signed pledges to join the Association. I figured he couldn't do no harm, and it might help. Show the folks the little planter is important to the Association."

Dr. Amos grunted, turning his attention to the speaker.

John Thomas had worn his best suit for the occasion. The

coat was now blotched with perspiration, spreading from his armpits across his back and across his chest. He had pulled his bow tie loose and his hair was standing straight up on his head.

"I want to tell you," he shouted. "The Trust has turned hawg, so we've got to turn butcher. We've got to pick up our butcher knives and let that hawg's blood run red from its throat. We got to hang the Trust up by the heels and skin the hide offen it. And we're the folks who can do it, I tell you that. We are the folks who can do it."

He paused. He thrust the flat of his hand across his forehead, flung the sweat from his palm. The drops of sweat glistened like rain.

"Our forefathers come into this country fighting the Injuns. Our granddaddies fought the land itself. They taken the trees off the land and they bridled that land and they tamed that land till you could grow the best tobacco in the whole wide world on it. They built houses on that land and they throwed fences about what they owned and they dared any man to set foot on it withouten their sayso. And they had the guts to back up their words.

"Then our daddies had to choose up sides and fight amongst themselves for a while. Some went to the South and some went to the North and they laid in the mountains and in the canebrakes and they fought the bitterest war in the memory of man for what they believed. That's the kind of folks we've got around here—they'll fight for what they believe. And when it was all over they picked up their guns and they patched up their wounds and they walked home to find that they had another kind of fight all over again on their hands.

"They found the country tore up by the war. They found their womenfolk making do with acorn coffee and sweet taters, they found that the sassafras and the huckleberry was a-taking their hardwon fields in their absence. And so they fought some more.

"Now we got a different kind of enemy. The Trust is the sneak thief who comes around in the dark of the night and takes the food out of the mouths of babes. They'll steal up and rob a man's tobacco barn. They'll smile at a man with one hand while they pick his pocket with the other. There ain't nothing more lowdown on God's green earth than a sneak thief.

"I want to tell you something. A man has got to look into his children's faces every day. Now, I know what I'm talking about. I got eight growing boys at home. This very morning my good woman put eight bowls of grits in front of them boys for breakfast. She put one bowl of grits in front of me. I watched them boys eat them grits that was all they had for breakfast and I saw them get up from that table with a hungry look still in their eye. I turned around and I looked at my good woman. I tell you, that woman was like to cry. Then I seen that she didn't have a bowl of grits. 'Eat you some breakfast,' I told her.

" 'I just don't want any,' she said. She was lying, my friends. That good woman was lying out of the goodness of her heart. She had put all of the grits into those nine bowls for me and the boys and she had shared her portion amongst us. I got up from that table and I put my arms around that woman. That was all I could do. I couldn't put any food into her belly, I could only put comfort into her heart.

"Now folks, I'm a man who made a good tobacco crop last year. I've got a good tobacco crop in the fields this year. But I'm standing here right now and I don't know how I'm going to make the winter.

"There's something wrong when a good tobacco crop won't feed a man's family. If it comes hail or storm or tobacco worm, if our barn burns up while we're curing, a man can understand that. He can count it bad luck and look to next year. But what can a man look to when it's somebody setting yonder in New York town and coldbloodedly squeezing every nickel he can out of every tobacco planter in the Black Patch? That somebody's gonna be there next year and the year after that and the year after that—unless we do something about it."

He wiped his forehead again, flung his sweat from him. His voice rose into a shout. "I say unto you, we got a war on our hands. It's a mean kind of war—but there ain't no other kind. We got to enlist in this-here war. Every man within the sound of my voice has got a duty and a responsibility to put his name down today. It takes an army to fight a war. The Trust is big. It's so big that sometimes you can't tell whether it's O.K. Knox or the President of the United States who's running this country. But it ain't as big as an army of the people, I can tell you that.

"Put your name down. Enlist, like your daddy enlisted in the War Between the States and like your granddaddy enlisted in the war agin the Injuns. When you get home, go to your neighbor and make him put his name down, too. It's going to take every dadblamed one of us."

He paused. He lowered his voice. "I say this unto you, men. If you don't put your name down on the list, I want you to go home and look into your children's faces. I want you to line them up and look at them—and then I want you to try to tell them why you didn't join the Association. Just try it! Just try it!"

He stopped. He stood belligerently, his hands on his hips. He jerked his head, lifting one fist high over his head.

"Fight the Trust!" he shouted. "Kill the Trust. Here's a great choosing day come upon us. You're either for us or against us. You're either an Association man or a Trust man. There's no in-between. I don't believe there's a man here today who can deny it."

He stopped, abruptly, and without waiting for applause walked to the back of the platform, jumped down to the ground, and disappeared into the crowd.

The crowd, startled by his abrupt ending, was slow to respond. The sound of their approval, once started, kept growing. Dr. Amos saw that John Thomas had truly moved them with his fieriness.

"Let's go," Walter Wingo said. "He's got 'em warm now."

They pushed their way to the platform. The applause grew as they climbed upon it, punctuated by shouts and rebel yells. Walter Wingo held out his hands.

"You've heard what we need to do," he shouted. "Now here's how we're gonna do it."

He launched into a description of the Association, reading the articles of incorporation from a handwritten sheet he took from his coat pocket.

"Article One: This Association shall be known as the Dark Tobacco District Growers' Protective Association of Kentucky and Tennessee. Article Two: The object of the Association shall be to assist each member in grading and selling his tobacco. Article Three: The government of the Association shall be vested in . . ."

Their attention began to wander. Walter Wingo droned doggedly through their shifting restlessness, pausing occasionally to say, "Now folks, I want you to listen to this. This is important to each and every one of you."

Children were beginning to cry and play and fight. The men were clustering into groups once more, talking among themselves. Dr. Amos seated himself among the other leaders in the row of chairs at the back of the platform.

"Article Seven," Walter Wingo said. "This Association being organized and officered alone for the protection of the tobacco planter, each member of the Association, becoming a member, obligates himself and binds himself to obey all legal and reasonable rules and regulations made by the board of directors. Each member realizes that without a united effort and willing obedience to the action of the board of directors no good can be accomplished. Each member of this Association also obligates himself to use his influence and strong endeavor with those tobacco planters who are not members of this Association, to become members. It is understood that no member of this Association is to receive a salary for services rendered, but realizing it may become necessary to employ expert salesmen or handlers of tobacco, in disposing of same, each member of this Association agrees and binds himself that his crop of tobacco shall bear a reasonable and pro rata part, when sold, of such expense as the board of directors deems necessary to an advantageous sale of the whole crop of the tobacco district."

He paused, shaking his head, looking at the inattentive crowd. He lifted his voice.

"Are you in accord with the foregoing?"

They shouted their accord, beginning to look lively now that the boring speech had ended.

Walter Wingo shook his head again, glancing at Dr. Amos. "So be it," he said. He lifted his arms. "Now I want to introduce to you a man you all know. I don't mind telling you that this man is my nomination for president of the Dark Tobacco District Growers' Protective Association of Kentucky and Tennessee. Dr. Amos Haines!"

Dr. Amos rose, came forward into the teeth of their approval. He stood quietly, looking down into their faces as they whooped and hollered. There was not a man in the crowd who did not know Dr. Amos Haines, few who did not think well of him. Dr. Amos felt a sudden sense of dislocation. This man, standing here in the public view, seemed to be someone other than the man Dr. Amos Haines had always been. A doctor is a private man, dealing privately with pain and disease, not someone who stands in the hot sun on a platform receiving the plaudits of the throng before he has had a chance to speak. This was indeed a new road on which he was setting his foot.

He felt an almost irresistible impulse to deny the step. He was not the man for such public doings. Why, even John Thomas was better at this sort of thing than he was.

He had to quiet them. He could not let them go on and on until they had worked themselves into an hysteria. He lifted his arms, as he had seen Walter Wingo do.

The crowd hushed with uncanny immediacy. Dr. Amos, when he spoke, talked in tones almost conversational. In the deep silence his words carried clearly to the back of the crowd.

"Mr. John Thomas has given you the feeling behind the Association," he said. "Mr. Walter Wingo has given you the reason. I don't know what else there is for me to say."

He paused. They waited. He could feel the sweat on his forehead. He removed it with his hand, looked at his damp palm absent-mindedly.

"I don't own a foot of land or a stalk of tobacco," he said. "So I was puzzled when Mr. Wingo and the others came to me and asked me to join the Association. Not only join it, but head it up. I told them I didn't think I should."

A shout of protest welled up, to be hushed almost immediately.

"But I'm a part of you and you're a part of me. I grew up with mud between my toes and the scent of growing tobacco in my nostrils, just like you did. I reckon a man can't ever separate himself from his beginnings."

He stood above them on the platform, tall, somber in his black suit. He looked down into their faces, talking in the same tones he had used at bedside after bedside throughout the county.

"If you want me to be the president of your Association, I will be your president." He moved quickly to forestall the applause. "But I want to tell you the important thing. It's not who's president and who's vice-president and who's treasurer. What's important is for every tobacco planter in the Black Patch to put his tobacco into the Association. This is a testing time. The test is whether men of good will can put their minds and their intentions together, of their own free will, to make a strength greater than themselves. If we can do that, the Association will succeed. If we cannot, the Association will fail and we will be subject to the revenge of the Tobacco Trust.

"So I ask you to do one thing for the Association. If you have a neighbor who is not joining the Association, go to that man and reason with him. Tell him that we've all got to hang together or hang separately. If you have to, get down on your knees and pray for that man to see the light of reason. Will you do that? For me? For yourselves? For the Association?"

They answered him in one mighty voice. This time Dr. Amos let the sound build, for the ring of their assurance was good to hear. There is strength here beyond counting, he told himself. There is reason and right here. It is a good thing to which I am joining myself.

For the first time, in this as in his medical practice, he felt a sense of joy. Those old dark guilts were swept into the farther recesses of his being.

He let the sound continue until it had died of its own accord. He had one further word to say. He said it without gestures, without heroics, indeed without lifting his voice beyond the level it had employed before.

"Good," he said. "Now let us begin."

VISTA: V

Oren Knox: A Man's Castle

TODAY was Oren's day of victory, the culmination of his years of triumph. Today he was going to Trenholm with the greatest gift of all in his hand.

He stepped into the carriage and told the driver to take him home. He sat back on the horsehair cushions, savoring in his mind the words he would use to tell Trenholm. She had known of his intent, of course, for some time—she did not know that it was now accomplished.

It was a time for retrospection as well as for victory. Looking over the fourteen years since he had stood triumphant over his rivals in the cigarette trade, the many days seemed foreshortened into an incredibly rapid passing of time. He had been a busy man. Until 1895, Oren had been utterly absorbed in the task of molding the merged cigarette manufacturers into an organization amenable to his will, as well as making it a profitable unity. He knew that the battle with the plug-tobacco manufacturers, when it began, would be long, bitter, and expensive. He had used every device he could think of, from rebate systems and consignment schemes in the selling of the cigarettes, to efforts to control and lower the price of the raw leaf, to manipulations of Allied Tobacco stock on the exchange. He had met opposition; from inside the tobacco trade, from the traders in the stock market, from the newspapers and legal authorities—even from the nation itself. He was harassed by lawsuits in various states; Oren himself was indicted in Texas, in Illinois and in New York. He had won the battles one by one, using the strength of the Trust within the trade, his wits in the market place, his lawyers in the courts. Yet each individual victory had brought him a greater public defeat; the public outcry grew with each successful maneuver.

Oren disliked his new-found notoriety. He did not believe in public relations; when in New York he seldom allowed himself to be trapped by the eager reporters and, on those few occasions he was forced to make a public appearance, he refused to answer any questions. "I'm minding my own business," he told the reporters. "Why don't you mind yours? I have nothing to say."

The greatest profits lay in the manipulation of Allied Tobacco on the stock exchange. In 1895, Oren had, after selling short, singlehandedly issued a notice of a passed dividend, though Allied Tobacco had from the beginning paid a handsome dividend of twelve per cent. The stock exchange committee had been greatly exercised by Oren's action, taken without consultation with his board of directors. The next week, however, the board of directors had ratified Oren's action, after an impassioned discussion of two hours, then had rushed out individually to place their own secret orders for the depressed stock. Two months later the full board of directors unanimously declared a two per cent dividend on common, two per cent on preferred, and a twenty per cent additional script dividend. The market in Allied Tobacco had zoomed from a low of sixty-seven to a new high of ninety-five.

The resultant profits had allowed Oren to launch his long-planned campaign to conquer the plug-tobacco industry. The bitter fight had lasted for four years and in the process Oren's Tobacco Trust lost over three million dollars.

His enemies were bitter far beyond the bounds of business war. Long after they should have yielded to the onslaught of his Tomahawk brand, underpriced and overadvertised with all the resources of the Tobacco Trust behind it, they continued to refuse his merger offers. In the end, he found it necessary to set up, with his own capital, an ostensible rival, Universal Tobacco Company, with a dummy board of directors headed by a young man of unimpeachable family and position in the financial world.

Universal Tobacco entered the arena against the Tobacco Trust with great fanfare. Within a year a combination of Universal with all the other great plug-tobacco firms was organized with the avowed intention of creating a Trust even greater than Oren's Allied Tobacco.

It had been a great moment when the young man had announced, at the close of the signing ceremony, "Gentlemen, I know you would like to meet my principal," and Oren had walked into the room to gaze quietly into their stricken faces.

These years had known their moments of danger also. The young man he had used as a Judas goat had organized Oren's own board of directors to demand Oren's resignation as president of the company. During the many financial manipulations stock control had been dispersed into many hands and Oren had found himself helpless, with only Taylor Tryon, now a director, head of the sales division, and the happily married and very wealthy father of seven daughters, standing at his side.

Oren had won that fight by threatening to start another tobacco company. He had then proceeded ruthlessly to consolidate his control and prevent any future challenge by reorganizing the entire Trust structure.

He set up a new corporation, World-Wide Tobacco, which was international in scope and capitalized at thirty million dollars. He intended it as his instrument for domination of the world trade in tobacco, as well as to consolidate his control. World-Wide issued four per cent fifty-year gold bonds in exchange for the common stock of Allied Tobacco and Universal Tobacco, the two arms of the Trust. With the success of this offer, ensured by the fact that Allied Tobacco paid a dividend of only six per cent, while Universal paid none at all, Oren found himself, as intended, holding all of World-Wide stock in close and friendly hands—with a substantial majority in his own—and World-Wide, in turn, owning virtually all the stock of Allied and

Universal. The only public obligation was the eight per cent gold bonds issued by World-Wide Tobacco in exchange for the common stock of the two original corporations.

The eight per cent interest on the gold bonds represented an enormous lien on the yearly earnings of the operating companies. The financial community decided unanimously and with great glee that Oren Knox had taken leave of his senses. After all, if Allied Tobacco's earnings would permit only a six per cent dividend, while Universal Tobacco paid none, how could Oren Knox possibly hope to pay such a liberal interest on the gold bonds?

They waited with anticipation for his downfall. It did not come. Oren had learned in advance, through his Washington connections, that the war taxes on tobacco were to be reduced by act of Congress. Precisely, the tax on chewing tobacco, smoking tobacco, and snuff went from twelve cents a pound to nine point six cents, on cigarettes from a dollar-fifty per thousand to a dollar and eight cents, and to fifty-four cents a thousand on the cheaper grades.

The last time there had been a tax reduction, Oren had, with great public effect, passed it on to the consumer. This time he kept it, despite great outrage on the part of the public and the retailers. Neither the public nor the retailers had anywhere else to go. As a result, within three years, after paying all fixed charges, Allied and Universal paid over to World-Wide Tobacco one hundred per cent of the initial capitalization of thirty million dollars.

It was the ammunition he needed to begin his assault upon England, the opening round in the battle for world-wide domination of the tobacco trade.

Pursuing the same tactics in England as he had in America, he won the battle in a remarkably short period of time. The English tobacco men, after fighting him for a year in their retail market, offered an agreement. In exchange for agreeing to stay out of Great Britain itself, Oren was made president, and awarded control, of a joint British-American corporation to deal in all countries that did not have a state tobacco monopoly.

Except for the public reaction, Oren Knox had won an unbroken series of victories. And he cared little for the public. Besides the big triumphs, he had known also a series of smaller satisfactions, among them the almost casual purchase for cash of his old rival, the manufacturer of Bull Durham smoking tobacco. He had gathered about him the best men in the tobacco trade to run his great enterprises, prominent among them Taylor Tryon, head of retail sales, and Alex Michael, now head of all cigarette production. Oren himself had amassed one of the greatest personal fortunes in the world.

Not least among his smaller satisfactions—perhaps, he thought with satisfaction as the carriage bore him homeward, it would come to be the largest of all—was the building of his great estate in North Carolina. He had bought the land, had imported landscape gardeners from England, and had closely supervised their work, rising at daylight each day to have several hours before he must turn his mind to business. Only later, after the garden had been achieved, did he build his house.

The carriage stopped in front of the house that Trenholm's father had built. Oren stepped down, told the driver to wait, and walked toward the front door. He smiled to himself as he walked, thinking of the expression on Trenholm's face. No—this was not one of the small satisfactions, not at all.

Inquiring of the first maid he encountered where he might find Mrs. Knox, he was informed that she was still in her bedroom. Oren mounted the stairs, reluctant to intrude upon her privacy. Trenholm always made him feel unwelcome in her own quarters. Today, however, was a different day, so he knocked on the door and waited for her signal to enter.

Trenholm was propped up in bed, reading. She spent a great deal of time in bed now, often passing several days at a time without leaving her room. Books were stacked on her bedside table, along with an assortment of pills and medicines.

"How are you, Trenholm?" Oren asked.

"I am fine, Mr. Knox. How are you?"

"Fine, fine," he said heartily.

She had always been plump, even as a girl. In the last year

she had lost weight; her face seemed strangely haggard, her skin was pale and smooth. The bones showed more apparently through her flesh, imparting an ascetic look. Her beautiful eyes alone remained brilliant, youthful.

It had been many years since Oren Knox had spoken of love. Each time he saw her, though, he realized anew how deep and true was the feeling he held for her. Yet, for more than twenty-five years, except for that brief interval during which their son had been begotten, they had lived together as strangers. They spoke politely when they met, and through the years Oren had made a habit of telling her of his victories. Somewhere inside him dwelt the unshakable idea that if he could only reach some unheralded pinnacle of success, she must accept him and his works.

Today, he had brought the great news.

"The estate is finished," he told her. "Everything is in place, down to the last hand towel. You have only to walk through the front door."

She seemed to shrink into her pillows. "I've told you—I do not intend to leave this house," she said in her most forbidding voice.

She had said so from the beginning. He had not believed her, comforting himself with the constant assurance that when the time came she would accept the great mansion. Perhaps it would be also an acceptance of Oren Knox.

He brought a chair from against the wall and sat down. "Come see it anyway," he said. "I built it for you, Trenholm, and you haven't even laid eyes on it."

"I don't intend to see it," she said sharply.

He leaned forward. "There's never been anything like it," he said. "Listen, Trenholm. There's twenty-five hundred landscaped acres, with eighteen miles of fine driveways. I've brought gardeners from England, beautiful shrubs and trees and plants from all over the world. It's landscaped in a series of plantations, each one different in design and character . . . an English formal garden, a French garden, an old-fashioned American garden, and so on." His voice was intense with the beloved description.

He had told it to her in bits and pieces, as the work had progressed. He had never before joined it all into one great whole.

"There's fifty thousand dollars worth of greenhouses and nine acres of lakes, with an artificial waterfall. There's a huge fountain right out front, pouring water night and day, and the fountain is stocked with the rarest goldfish I could find. There's a nine-hole golf course, tennis courts, bridle paths, and thoroughbred horses to ride. I remember how you used to like to ride." He paused, watching her face. "You know what I told them? I told them, 'Hang the expense—but give me my money's worth.' And they did. They did."

"I am not leaving my father's house," Trenholm said.

"That's just the grounds," Oren said. "I did the grounds first, and then I built the mansion in the middle of it. It's made out of rough stone, Trenholm, with a balustrade and a wall terrace. You enter into a large central hall, which is also a picture gallery. I've brought great paintings from Europe, all picked out by experts, to hang there. The central hall is three tiers high, lighted by a dome skylight. At one end is a music room, at the other the dining room. There's a billiard room and a library, too. I won't bother you with the details of the bedrooms and the kitchens and the staff I have waiting for you. You won't have to concern yourself with such things any more. There's a butler and a housekeeper to run things. There's a head gardener to take care of the gardens, a groundsman for the tennis courts and the golf course, and another man to manage the stables. Why, Trenholm, you'll be a queen there."

He stopped. He waited. Trenholm was silent. He continued waiting, until he saw that Trenholm did not intend to respond.

A shyness moved within him as he fetched out his last enticement. "I haven't named it yet," he said. "I wanted you to find the right name."

Trenholm shifted under the emotional weight of his words. She pulled herself up in the bed.

"Is this . . . place . . . your monument?" she said. "Is this what you plan to leave behind you?"

He was bewildered. "I intended the estate for you," he said.

"I've told you so from the beginning. I want you to live there. You can go today. I've told you—it's all waiting, down to the last hand towel. The staff is installed and everything, just waiting for you to walk through the front door."

"You have gathered one of the greatest fortunes in the world," Trenholm said. "You began with my dear father's factory and piled up millions upon millions. You have shown imagination and daring in doing so—yet this is all you can think of to do with it."

His hands were sweating in the palms. He rubbed them against his trousers legs. "Trenholm, if you will go to the mansion, I will make you a promise. I will sign it over to you, lock stock and barrel. I will promise you that I will never set foot inside the grounds." He could not look at her. "You do not have to accept me to accept my gift. It is offered freely out of my heart."

She was unmoved. "I shall not leave this house," she said. "You can spend several more millions and my answer will remain the same."

He rose. "Can you never forgive me for marrying you?" he said. "Never in this world?"

She turned her head away. "It's rather late to be talking about such things," she said. She reached for a bottle of the medicine on her bedside table with a shaking hand. "I am feeling rather faint."

He turned to go. In spite of her stated opposition, he had held onto an unreasonable hope. There was nothing further to do, nothing further to say.

Her voice stopped him at the door. "Fuller is coming home from school," she said.

He turned. "Expelled?"

She nodded. "I have not yet received the letter telling us why."

"What will we do with him now?" Oren said heavily. "This is the third school . . ."

"I thought perhaps a military academy," Trenholm said. "I will take care of it, of course."

"Of course," Oren said.

He went down the stairs and, without pausing, left the house. He, the man who had never known failure in any other phase of his life, had failed with Trenholm once again. Never the man to accept defeat, he remained determined; somehow, sooner or later, Trenholm must know, must accept, his love. If it took all his great fortune . . .

He climbed into the seat, spoke to the driver. "Take me to the mansion," he said.

"Sir," the driver said. "A telegram came for you from the New York office. They brought it from the factory."

Oren took the yellow flimsy, glanced at it. It was from the man charged with the purchase of all raw tobacco used by the Trust.

"Have been informed that Tobacco Growers' Protective Association just established in Black Patch of Kentucky and Tennessee. Urgently request meeting with you to discuss same."

A flick of irritation moved in Oren Knox as he scanned the words. Still dominated by it, he turned the wire over and wrote a reply.

"Don't bother me with such small matters. Handle it yourself. Oren Knox."

He handed up the message to the driver. "Send that off," he said. "But drop me at the estate grounds first."

Chapter Fifteen

FOR THE first time in his life, Dr. Amos felt himself a part of something larger than himself. There was a necessary good in surrendering himself to a larger imperative. It took him out of that old preoccupation with the sins of his past and, so taken, he found a joy in this new life he had never known even in the doctoring.

As before, he rode the countryside, on horseback much of the time, in preference to the buggy, for astride the mare he was not confined to the roads. As before, he talked to man after man, concerning himself most intimately with that man's life. He was no longer practicing a private mystery, but was engaged in a public association for the good of all. Instead of making his private way, he was swept along on the tide of events.

He was no longer solitary; other men, like he, were riding the country roads, stopping at farmhouse after farmhouse, talking with passion, with reason, about the necessity of joining the Association. John Thomas, that first fiery speaker at the big rally, had devoted himself wholly to the cause. Though he had his own crop to put into the barn, every night he paid far-ranging visits. He was particularly effective with the small farmers, the tenant farmers, the sharecroppers. Walter Wingo concerned himself with the more prosperous planters, those men of his own kind who understood the language he spoke.

Dr. Amos cut across all barriers. He was the only man whom the Negroes trusted. The first Negro member of the Association was Charlie Blake. Charlie was a deacon in the Negro church of his community and he brought the entire church membership into the Association. Many of the Negroes were signed up willy-nilly by the landowners for whom they sharecropped; but Dr. Amos and Charlie, between them, engendered a willingness where there might have been only a sullen acquiescence.

Lewis Carnett, Thomas Meacham, many others, devoted surprising amounts of time to the missionary work in their own communities. They organized meetings, at which Dr. Amos or Walter Wingo or John Thomas would appear to speak. Often Dr. Amos conducted an impromptu medical clinic after the pledges had been signed, thus combining his public and his private functions.

The Association made no real attempt to pledge the immediate tobacco crop. The initial rally had been held too late in the season to hope for such success. They set their sights on pledging seventy per cent of the 1905 crop, with the intention of securing an average price of eight cents a pound for the pledged crop—double the average price paid by the Trust and the Regie buyers in the three previous years.

There was much to do. The Association was spreading itself from community to community over the Black Patch. It became necessary to organize a Speakers' Bureau to meet the demands made upon the central organization by the various county and district subsidiaries. Contracts had to be negotiated with members in various towns and villages to receive the pledged tobacco when the 1905 crop should come in, to prize it into hogsheads and ship it on to storage houses in the central towns. Where they could not secure the cooperation of an erstwhile independent dealer for the use of his facilities, joint-stock companies were organized to build or lease warehouses.

A system was worked out whereby representative samples

were taken from each hogshead and sent to the Association salesroom at Jamestown, where they were put on display for the prospective buyers. At first, there were no buyers; the Trust promptly boycotted the Association salesroom.

These activities entailed meeting after meeting, with endless discussion of each succeeding phase of decision. Dr. Amos, as president of the Association, presided at most of them, sitting night after night in the meeting room above the Association salesroom in Jamestown. Often he became impatient with listening to the continual fieriness of John Thomas, the ponderous, careful movement of Walter Wingo's mind. In his impatience he could have imposed his own will upon the decisions. He did not do so. He was, for the first time in his life, involved in a group movement. He wanted the decisions to be made by the group.

The Association held tobacco from the 1904 crop, though their firm pledges were made only for the following year. It remained unsold. Otherwise, they suffered no open opposition. Dr. Amos was surprised by the lethargy evidenced by the Trust. Roscoe Barnes had, of course, succeeded in buying all the 1904 tobacco the Trust wanted at four cents a pound.

The Trust, embodied in the stocky, red-faced figure of Roscoe Barnes, moved blandly about the town. Barnes seemed unconcerned about the Association, though he laid the whip of his blunt wit against it at every opportunity. They had invited Roscoe Barnes to one of the first directors' meetings of the new year, with the intention of offering him all the 1904 tobacco available.

Roscoe Barnes came to the meeting. "Gentlemen," he said. "The Association tobacco will not sell, or if it does it will sell for less than we've been paying. You haven't got any backing, you won't be able to get an advance on your tobacco, and without money the banks will foreclose on your mortgages and the merchants will sue you for their accounts." He paused, standing at the head of the table, tapping a riding crop against his boot. "We don't need your tobacco. We've been expecting this, and we've got enough surplus to last us a year. By that time you'll be begging us to take it off your hands at any price."

He walked out of the meeting without looking back. The men seated around the long table stared at each other wordlessly.

"He'll be back," Walter Wingo said.

John Thomas bounced up in his place. "The son-of-a-bitch," he said furiously. "You'd think he didn't blow his nose in a snot-rag just like everybody else. We ought to show him; by God, we ought to show him."

Dr. Amos looked at John Thomas. "How do you intend to show him, John?"

John Thomas sat down, sputtering. He put his hands on the table in front of him. "I'll show him," he muttered. "I'll show him yet."

When the time came for the second rally, in the following September, they had reached their goal of seventy per cent of the tobacco crop pledged to the Association. The board of directors announced the rally with the taste of success strong in their minds.

Dr. Amos had considered last year's rally phenomenal. By the middle of the morning, on this September day, he realized that last year wasn't a patch on this year's achievement. The Association had behind it a solid year of organizational effort. There was twice, three times, the number of people here than there had been last year. It was necessary to use the fairgrounds on the edge of town.

It was a happier occasion. They paraded through the streets of Jamestown on foot, on mules, on blooded horses, behind prancing teams that sparkled in oiled harness and polished trappings. A brass band blared ahead of them. At the fairgrounds there were flags and bunting, banners and lemonade, hamburgers and ice cream and soda pop. Firecrackers were fired off, as though it were the Fourth of July, and when the sun went down a fireworks display was scheduled, paid for by the Association.

Last year the planters had been glum, suspicious, concerned. This year they enjoyed the feeling of victory. They knew that twenty-two counties had branch associations, with a grower-membership of seven thousand. Many growers had come from the northern and Bowling Green district counties to find out how such palpable success had been achieved by this new kind of Association.

Dr. Amos, on the platform, spoke in his quiet way. "The Association is before the world on its merits. It invites investigation. It is the champion that dares to stand against the Trust's effort to reduce the tobacco grower to menial servitude. It appeals to you to save yourselves from ruin, and if all work together it can surely be done. Obstacles have been daily thrown in our way: First, to prevent our organization; next, to belittle our efforts by ridicule; and then to prevent the sale of our tobacco. Now, we are ahead. The tobacco world expects us to win, and that we must do so upon an honest, conservative basis should be the one thought in the mind of every honest tobacco planter."

John Thomas stood sweating in the sun and harangued the crowd. "Now I want to tell you! It's the bounden duty of every farmer to stand by the Association. It's the bounden duty of every *friend* of the farmer to stand by the Association. Those businessmen and those professional men who fail to encourage the tobacco growers in their struggle for better prices are not worthy of your trade. Now I want to tell you! A man with some sense in his head buys from the man that is his friend; and he walks right on by the establishment of his enemy! I say unto you —you've got the power! I say unto you—use the power that lies in your hands.

"I want to tell you something else. There are seven thousand of us in the Association. But there isn't a community in this whole area that ain't infested by Hillbilly scum who won't join the Association. You know who they are. I know who they are. They grin like a possum when the Trust man comes around. I want to tell you! I think it's time to lean on people like that. I think it's time to let them know what you think about 'em. Wherever they walk in your community—in school, in church and store—turn your faces against them. You've got the power! I say unto you—use the power that lies in your hands!"

They cheered. Dr. Amos stood on the platform, looking out

over the sea of faces, listening to the thunder of sound welling out of their collective throats.

He turned to Walter Wingo. "Sometimes I wonder what we've started here," he said quietly.

"We need men like John Thomas," Walter said. "He does good, Dr. Amos. A lot of good."

"I guess you have to appeal to men's emotions, as well as their minds. I just wish . . ."

John Thomas came back to them, a grin on his sweaty face. "How about that?" he said happily.

"Boycott is not the policy of the Association," Mr. Wingo said. "It hasn't even been discussed in our meetings as yet."

John Thomas glanced at him sharply. "You heard how they hollered," he said. "We'd better make it Association policy, if we aim to keep out in front of the members."

In the beginning he had been a beaten little man, dragged down by the effort of trying to feed eight boys on a small tobacco acreage. Now he was cocky, self-assured, aware of the prestige he had earned within the Association through the power of his voice.

"Sometimes we got to run hard to stay out in front of 'em," he said. "We lag back, we're gonna find some new leaders taking our place. Remember, we stand on this platform by the vote of the membership—not in our own right."

He left them, going down off the platform into the waiting maw of the people. They swallowed him up, a man too small to stand out in the midst of the crowd. Standing on the platform together, Dr. Amos and Walter Wingo could follow his progress by the swirl of movement as men pressed forward to shake his hand, to slap him on the shoulders. Dr. Amos wondered if his words had been intended as a warning.

"Well," Mr. Wingo said, grunting the word. "I reckon it's time for me to get up there and tell them the dull facts of life. Not that they'll listen. They'd rather swallow fire than facts any day of the week."

"Today especially," Dr. Amos said. "They're all bunched up today."

The board of directors had known from the beginning that their vulnerability lay with the Hillbillies who had refused to join the Association. They had brought every legitimate pressure to bear. Organized teams of men called on the more important holdouts in order to reason with them. If a man's mortgage lay in hands friendly to the Association, the holder of the mortgage was asked to reason with the man. If a man's storekeeper, who kept credit ledgers on him, was friendly, he too was enlisted on the side of the Association. In this way, many were brought reluctantly to the signing of a pledge.

There remained, inevitably, the stubborn residue, who, for one or another hard-held reason, refused in spite of all persuasion and pressure to join the great majority in the Association. Here was, inevitably, the point of attack when the Trust decided to move into active opposition. It began before the new crop was in the curing barns.

Walter Wingo and John Thomas were waiting for Dr. Amos at the livery stable. Dr. Amos, returning from a medical call, stepped down from the buggy and yielded the mare to the stable boy.

"The Trust is buying tobacco," Mr. Wingo said without preamble or greeting.

"Ours?" Dr. Amos said.

John Thomas snorted a laugh. "Ours, hell," he said. "Hillbilly tobacco."

"They bought Hillbilly tobacco last year," Dr. Amos said. He stood holding his saddlebags over his arm. "We have to figure on a few people selling to the Trust. But they can't get enough tobacco that way to keep their factories going. The Regie people will need export tobacco, too."

"It's not just that," Wingo said. "They're paying eight and ten and even twelve cents a pound, for what they call 'free' tobacco."

Dr. Amos frowned. "They can get Association tobacco for eight cents. They don't even have to ride the country roads to buy it."

"They're out to break us," John Thomas said angrily. "Let

folks know they can get better than our price by staying out of the Association, how long you think we're gonna be able to hold the membership? These folks raise tobacco to sell it, not to put it up for a keepsake."

"Anyone can see what the Trust is trying to do," Dr. Amos said. "They won't get any Association tobacco by such tactics. They'll buy up the Hillbilly tobacco; then they'll have to come to us. I think we'll have the right to ask the same price for Association tobacco then. If they're willing to pay twelve cents a pound for Hillbilly tobacco . . ."

"It's something, all right, when the Association does more good for the Hillbillies than they can do for their own members," John Thomas said. "We can't let it go on, Dr. Amos. We just can't."

"The others are waiting in the meeting room now," Walter Wingo said. "Can you come?"

"I need to call by the office first. You all go on. I'll be there in half an hour."

He walked slowly away from the two men. Moving up the street alone, he felt the change that had come upon the townspeople. Where once, in his capacity as country doctor, the storekeepers had greeted him heartily, now they stood silent, their eyes following as he progressed up the street. He was popularly supposed to have created the Association out of his own single-minded effort and inspiration. In the eyes of the townspeople, he had become the focus and symbol of the dangerous power that had erupted so suddenly out of the angry massed will of the farming population. The Association was a new power structure and they, like all possessors of things, were afraid of new fountainheads, inevitably spelling change. Many of them disapproved of the Trust; but the Trust was a devil they had lived with for a long time.

Roscoe Barnes came down the street riding a Tennessee Walking horse. The beautiful horse was solid black, with long mane and tail. He moved in the classic gait of the breed, diagonal legs working almost in unison, the left forehoof touching the ground an instant earlier than the right hind. Barnes' mount had a tremendous overstride, the hind foot coming forward at least two feet beyond the right front hoofprint.

Dr. Amos, in spite of himself, stopped to watch the beautiful animal moving down the street, his head nodding in time, his ears swinging, his teeth clicking like castanets. Roscoe Barnes sat carelessly in the saddle, swinging gently with the steady, smooth gait. He saw Dr. Amos and stopped the horse with a touch of his knee.

"Well, well," he said loudly. "How's the good Association doctor?"

Dr. Amos smiled wryly. "Fine. And how is the good Trust buyer?"

Roscoe slapped his boots with his riding crop. The Walking horse pranced with the sound. "Well, to tell you the truth, I'm busy," he said. "I'm running around like a chicken with its head cut off, buying tobacco right and left. Did you want to talk to me? I saw you waiting . . ."

"I was just admiring your piece of horseflesh," Dr. Amos said.

Roscoe leaned to pat the black horse on the withers. "He's a great goer, all right," he said with satisfaction. "He'll take you all day long without turning a hair." He paused, looking down at Dr. Amos. "Of course, we don't really have anything to talk about. I'm not buying Association tobacco—not this season."

"You think there's going to be enough free tobacco to satisfy your needs?" Dr. Amos said.

Roscoe laughed. "There will be, time I get through," he said. "We're paying good prices, Dr. Amos. Mighty good prices. The kind of price the Black Patch hasn't seen in a long time."

"Sure," Dr. Amos said. "Until you get the chance to drop it to four cents a pound again. You think the grower doesn't know what you've got in mind?"

Roscoe laughed again. "I'll tell you something about your tobacco planter," he said. "He worries about one crop at a time. Give him a good price for this year's crop, he ain't going to worry his head about next year till next year comes around. That's the way to live, Doctor. One year at a time. It makes for a long, happy, and hard-working life."

"I think you may be wrong about that," Dr. Amos said quietly.

Roscoe Barnes was passing on by. Whistle blowing, a train began moving slowly across the street two blocks down. The horse bent his ears toward the sound, but remained quiet. Seeing his way blocked by the passenger train, Roscoe reined the horse close to the curb. He leaned down to Dr. Amos to make himself heard over the noise.

"You know why I bought this Walking horse?" he said, lifting his voice.

"I can't say that I do," Dr. Amos said. He was annoyed by the nearness of Roscoe's red face thrust down toward him. He moved away a step or two.

"He's named Tobacco Man," Roscoe said loudly. "When I heard the name, I knew I had to have this horse to ride. Ain't that a good name for a horse belonging to a Trust buyer? Tobacco Man."

"Just be sure he doesn't buck you off," Dr. Amos said.

Roscoe laughed. "Oh, he's gentle. Just as friendly as a red-speckled puppy, and got a gait like a rocking chair. Why, you couldn't ask for a better mount."

The short train slid across the street, disappeared. The whistle blew again. The noise was receding.

"By the way, I been meaning to ask you something," Roscoe said, his voice louder than need be, now that the train was gone. "You remember that pretty little redheaded gal lived out there at Temple's Crossroads? Remember her?"

"Yes," Dr. Amos said unwillingly. He did not want to talk to Roscoe Barnes about Virginia Temple.

"I reckon you would," Roscoe said loudly. "Ain't a man wears pants would ever lose her out of his mind. Whatever happened to her, anyway? You got any idea?"

"No," Dr. Amos said shortly. He started on.

"Why, I'd ride Tobacco Man a hundred mile just to call on

that little girl again," Roscoe shouted jovially after him. "She was a woman and a half, I tell you."

Dr. Amos felt a sudden impulse to pull him down from the beautiful horse and grind his face into the dirt of the street. He made himself go on.

"You ever see her again, you tell her old Roscoe's still thinking about her," Roscoe shouted after him.

Dr. Amos gritted his teeth. Roscoe's casual reference to Virginia had stirred within him the bile of old hatreds and old defeats. You'd think a man would get to where he didn't care, he thought. Here I am, forty-seven years old, and it comes up as fresh as yesterday at the sound of her name in Roscoe's mouth.

He mounted the stairs to his office. It was empty; in his preoccupation with the affairs of the Association, his practice had dwindled. He had, indeed, lost the few town patients he had once had.

He put down the saddlebags and sat for a moment behind his desk. He needed to settle himself before going on to the meeting.

Heading the Association was like riding a wild stallion. Seemingly tractable, there was at all times the possibility that momentarily the stallion might explode out of control. The membership was so closely knit that rumor or fact seethed through it with an amazing instantaneity. Dr. Amos had never dealt with a group before; his concern had been always with the individual man in his individual hurts and ailments. John Thomas' fieriness had, from the beginning, made Dr. Amos uneasy. On a speaker's platform the small planter lacked an essential restraint. He owned a curious oneness with a crowd; he both led them and followed them. But he followed only their emotion, not their rational thought. He took their emotion, shaping it into words, and thus he seemed to lead them. That boycott thought, for instance; he had projected it at the rally without consultation beforehand, as though he had picked it out of the ambient air. The directors, afterward, had been forced to acknowledge the idea of boycott; they had found it necessary to draw up a list of merchants friendly to the organization in order to keep them from being hurt by the thoughtless enthusiasm of the members.

Dr. Amos heaved himself out of the chair, thinking, They'll be waiting on me. He did not take his doctor's bag with him, but left it sitting in readiness beside his desk. He walked down the stairs into the street.

It seemed that, no matter what a man did, nothing could satisfy the needs crying out within him. He had found a purposeful joy in the beginning of this new road he was now traveling. He had at last been swept into something so much larger than himself that it could swallow him whole, guilt and all.

It had been a short-lived euphoria. He was now more apprehensive than joyous. He felt an ominous foreboding in the atmosphere. It lay in the quiet watchfulness of the townspeople; in the clustered talk of the Association men wherever they gathered. Often, the talk ceased abruptly upon the friendly approach of Dr. Amos or Walter Wingo, of others among the leaders. Except John Thomas. He seemed always the center of these concentrations, his passionate face thrust forward into their faces, his mouth moving in low fierce whisperings that seemed as violent, as ominous, as his public speeches.

Dr. Amos almost consciously mustered forward his doctor-toughness. They were in the midst of a battle; indeed, day by day, the situation was shaping more and more toward open warfare between the Trust and the Association. That was the thing; to keep clearly in focus the great purpose, the overriding reasons. Yet, as he mounted the stairs toward the meeting, he could not shake off the sense of foreboding that rode like a succubus in the reaches of his mind.

He opened the door. The men looked up, wearing grim faces. He paused, glancing from the directors to the tobacco planter who waited in a corner of the room. He was Marvin Rakestraw, one of the first to join the Association.

Mr. Wingo's voice was flat, hard. "Tell Dr. Amos what you've just been telling us, Mr. Rakestraw."

Mr. Rakestraw stood holding his black felt hat in his hand. He was wearing a pair of jeans britches, a gray workshirt, brogan shoes cut away across the toes in order to liberate his corns from the pressure of the leather. Dr. Amos saw that his toes were curled tightly in his agony of stubborn embarrassment.

"I told you once," he said. His voice muttered the words rapidly, like a child confessing fault. "Mr. Roscoe come around to me yesterday, offering me twelve cents a pound for my tobacco."

"That's Hillbilly prices he's offering you," Dr. Amos said. "Did you tell him that your tobacco is pledged to the Association?"

"He said I wouldn't even have to prize it and haul it to town," Mr. Rakestraw said miserably. "Said he'd send a team and a wagon after it just to save me the trouble."

Dr. Amos looked about the room, puzzled by the angry tenseness among the directors.

"He's just trying to tempt you, make you feel uneasy in the Association," he said in a kindly voice. "You know better than to pay attention to anything that Roscoe Barnes tells you."

Mr. Wingo's voice was flat, accentless. "He told Barnes he could have the tobacco."

"You can't do that," Dr. Amos said sharply. "It's pledged tobacco, Mr. Rakestraw. You can't go back on your pledge."

"The Association," Mr. Rakestraw said. He cleared his throat. "The Association don't even promise no more than eight cents a pound. And it ain't sold hardly none, at that." He lifted his eyes to Dr. Amos' face. "Dr. Amos, I didn't get but one hundred and thirty-five dollars on my tobacco last year. The rest is still stored, along with everybody else's."

John Thomas was squirming in his seat. "That's what's going on," he burst out. "That's what's starting now. They not only got the Hillbilly tobacco, they're gonna start getting Association tobacco. A man can't stand to watch the Hillbillies sell their tobacco at a higher price. I told you. I told all of you!"

Dr. Amos did not bother to look at him. "Shut up, Mr. Thomas. Let me handle this."

Mr. Thomas subsided. Dr. Amos turned to Mr. Rakestraw.

"You'll have to go to Mr. Barnes and tell him you made a

mistake. You can't just unpledge your tobacco when you take a notion. Why, if everybody did that, we wouldn't have an Association any more."

"I can't do that," Mr. Rakestraw said in an agonized voice. Behind the agony lay the hard stubbornness still.

"You must do it," Dr. Amos said. "You have no other choice. You have signed a paper making yourself and your tobacco a part of the Association. You cannot withdraw from the Association at will."

"Now you're going to hear the rest of it," Mr. Wingo said fatefully.

Mr. Rakestraw firmed his voice into a more obvious stubbornness. "Well now, I went to Lawyer King to ask him about that before I come here," he said. "Lawyer King done some lawyer work for me at one time. He told me that the Association was my agent in the disposal of my tobacco. The Association is the agent and I am the principal and so I can revoke my agreement with the Association any time I please."

He parroted the words, the sound of the lawyer showing through the sound of his own voice. He stopped, staring defiantly at Dr. Amos now, strengthened by the words he had bought from the lawyer.

Dr. Amos paused a moment, considering. "Mr. Rakestraw," he said at last. "The Association has lawyers, too, if you want to get into lawyer-talk. The Association lawyers tell us that the Association is a body corporate." He turned to Mr. Wingo. "Mr. Wingo, do you have that opinion with you?"

Mr. Wingo shuffled among his papers. "Here it is," he said. He cleared his throat, began reading in a loud, emphatic voice. " 'The planter is himself the Association, and when he signs the articles of agreement he becomes a part of the body, engaging with others to do certain acts for their mutual benefit. It stands in the same relation to its members as the state does to its citizens. A citizen of a state is himself a part of the body, and cannot revoke himself, nor do certain acts inimical to other citizens with whom he stands bound by solemn compact. If a citizen commits some offense or injury to his fellow citizens, the state retaliates with legal procedure. So it is with the Tobacco Growers' Association in dealing with refractory members.' "

"So you see," Dr. Amos said, his voice kindly once again. "The Association is not your agent. You cannot withdraw at your own free will."

The words had made an impression on Mr. Rakestraw; they had served to arouse an anger he had not shown before.

"My tobacco is in my barn," he said. "Ain't no man in the world can tell me what to do and what not to do with tobacco that's still in my own barn." He clapped his hat on his head. "Any man tries to, he's gonna catch hell on Friday."

John Thomas bounced to his feet. "Goddam you, Mr. Rakestraw, if you . . ."

"Wait a minute," Dr. Amos said. He came close to Mr. Rakestraw. "Marvin, I want you to remember that time I laid your oldest boy down on your kitchen table one stormy night and took out his appendix. I saved that boy's life, Marvin, just as sure as I'm standing here."

Mr. Rakestraw looked into his face. "Dr. Amos, I got tobacco, and I got the right to sell it at the best price I can find. I got young'uns at home that needs food in their bellies and clothes on their backs. That's all I can afford to think about. I aim to sell that-there tobacco."

Dr. Amos knew that he was defeated. He had saved the personal appeal until the last, though he had used it without reluctance. Mr. Rakestraw was a good man; he had been one of the first to pledge his tobacco. Dr. Amos turned away, his heart aching for the necessity in the man that had driven him to this stubborn confrontation.

John Thomas surged around the table. He thrust his face into Mr. Rakestraw's, his eyes bulging with anger. "I'm gonna remember you," he said, almost shouting the words. "Don't you forget it for a minute. I aim to keep you in mind."

Mr. Wingo's voice was flat and hard still. "Mr. Thomas," he said. "Idle threats will do no good. Leave the man alone."

John Thomas returned reluctantly to his seat. His lips were thin, bloodless, in his angry face.

"Mr. Rakestraw, we will have to proceed against you," Mr. Wingo continued in the same tone. "You know that, of course."

With dignity, Mr. Rakestraw nodded. "I know that."

"Good day, Mr. Rakestraw."

Mr. Rakestraw hesitated, looking from face to face in the room. His stubbornness did not soften itself. He left the room.

Dr. Amos came to the long table, took his seat. He put his big hands on the surface before him, looked at them.

"We ought to . . ." John Thomas said, sputtering. "We ought to . . ."

The others ignored him. "So now we've gotten down to it," Dr. Amos said quietly. "If we can't stop Mr. Rakestraw from selling his tobacco, the Association is busted. I knew it was coming sooner or later; I just hoped it wouldn't be a man like him." He lifted his head, trying to smile. "I hoped it would be somebody I could turn my anger against."

John Thomas stared at him with belligerent disbelief. "He's our enemy now, isn't he? Why the hell can't you . . ."

"Some of us don't have our anger as close to the surface as you have, Mr. Thomas," Dr. Amos said.

Mr. Wingo shifted in his seat. "I'll have the lawyers bring suit against him, restraining him from selling his tobacco in violation of his Association pledge," he said.

"We must rely on the courts," Dr. Amos said. "It's obvious what's happening. The Trust is making its move to break us this year."

"Are you sure the courts will uphold the Association?" another man asked.

"We can't be sure about anything," Mr. Wingo said gloomily. "Our lawyers believe they will. It's just got to be tested, that's all."

"You think the Trust won't have their own high-priced lawyers in that courtroom?" John Thomas said.

"Of course they will," Dr. Amos said. "That's the way it ought to be. When the passions of men are aroused, the issues must be decided within the impartial confines of the law." He looked about the table. "I don't think we've relied sufficiently on the law in our fight against the Trust. In the market place, they are well-nigh invulnerable. It's in the courts that we can find their weakness."

John Thomas snorted. "Yeah. About twenty years after we're all dead and gone the courts might decide something."

"What do you have in mind?" Mr. Wingo said, looking at Dr. Amos.

"We can move in two directions," Dr. Amos said slowly. "First, we take Mr. Rakestraw into court on the immediate issue of whether he can withdraw his tobacco from the Association. If we win that suit, then I think we can go to the legislatures of Kentucky and Tennessee and ask for a specific law embodying that decision. We have friends in the legislatures to press for such a law, not only prohibiting any grower from selling tobacco he has pledged to any association, but also prohibiting any buyer, under penalty, from knowingly buying tobacco that is so pledged."

"And the other direction?" Mr. Wingo said.

Dr. Amos took a deep breath. "I think we ought to go to the President of the United States," he said. "Old Rough Rider Teddy may be a Republican, but he's no friend of the Trusts. Within six months after that man shot down McKinley, he was taking out after the Northern Securities Company with his big stick. And you remember how he made the mine owners sit down at the bargaining table during the anthracite coal strike."

"But does he know anything about the tobacco situation?" Lewis Carnett asked.

"It's our job to see that he does," Dr. Amos said. "I believe he's the kind of man you can talk to. I believe if we can get to him, make him understand what's going on, he'll want to do something about it. Anything Teddy Roosevelt wants to do something about, he's liable to do it, one way or the other. The Trust has had trouble with the different states here and there. They've never had to come up against the Federal government."

"On what grounds can the Federal government move against the Trust?" Mr. Wingo asked.

"I was talking to our lawyer the other day," Dr. Amos said.

"There's the Sherman Anti-Trust Act of 1890. It's been pretty much of a dead letter until President Roosevelt took office."

"You will go, of course, as the president of the Association," Walter Wingo said.

Dr. Amos shook his head. "I think you should, Mr. Wingo. You're a tobacco planter yourself. You are personally acquainted with our senators in Washington."

"But what will I say to him?" Mr. Wingo said rather desperately.

"You'll take the Association lawyer, of course, in case they want to bring in the Attorney-General. Have the lawyer draw up a whole history of the Tobacco Trust from its beginning. Show what has happened to the people of the Black Patch as a result."

"When do you think this should be done?"

"As quickly as possible."

John Thomas had been fidgeting in his seat. He burst out of his silence. "Suppose old Teddy does decide to do something. You think any of us will still be alive time the case comes to court? How you figure the tobacco planters are gonna eat while the case inches its way along?" He stood up in his place. "No sir. We ain't got time for no such slow doings. We got to do something now." He was breathing hard. He leaned over the table, his hands placed flat on the wood surface. "Suppose you put your faith in the law and the legislature. Just suppose, for instance, that the court decides Rakestraw can sell his tobacco any way he wants to, regardless of his pledge to the Association? Are you gonna fold up and quit then? Are you gonna go out of business?"

He paused to catch his breath.

"Suppose you do get Teddy Roosevelt on your side. Suppose you get a suit. It'll take a year or two to get it tried. Then just suppose you win—the Trust appeals the suit. It takes another two or three years for the appeal to be heard. You win the appeal and then what does the Trust do? It appeals to the Supreme Court of the United States of America. Ain't no telling how many years it would take for the case to be heard before the

Supreme Court. The Association won't even exist by then. Then just suppose—just suppose, now—that somewhere along the line them smart Trust lawyers figure some way to wiggle out of it and the suit goes against you. You're not only back where you started from, you got a court decision standing against you to boot."

He straightened. He slammed one fist into the other palm. The dull smacking sound of flesh against flesh echoed in the still room.

"No sir. There ain't but one thing to do. To hell and damnation with your courts and your lawyers and your Presidents of the United States. You can't put your problems into other men's hands and expect them to tidy it all up and put you on easy street." He paused, glaring about the room. "There ain't but one thing to do. Stop them damn Hillbillies from selling their tobacco to the Trust at them high prices. You stop them damn Hillbillies from selling, our Association members won't be hankering to sell to the Trust neither."

"How are you going to stop them all?" Dr. Amos said wearily. "We have tried. God knows we've tried. We've reasoned with them. We've pleaded with them. There's a certain percentage of them that will not see reason."

John Thomas sat down. His body was taut with indignation. "So you aim to set here and do nothing whilst the Trust tolls our members away one by one," he said. "For two years in a row, now, the Association members have seen Hillbillies getting them high prices. Now they're going to Association members and offering those same prices to them. Yet you're going to set here and do nothing. You're going to talk law and legislature and the President of the United States."

"What *can* we do?" Walter Wingo said.

"There are ways," John Thomas said ominously.

"What ways?" Mr. Wingo said in an exasperated voice. "Short of scaring a man into joining the Association, whether he wants to or not . . ."

He stopped, abruptly.

A silence ensued. The Board of Directors of the Association looked at each other. The words had been spoken in open meeting. For a long time they had been in the atmosphere. Every responsible man had assiduously avoided them.

John Thomas slammed his fist against the table. "*Now* you've got it!" he exclaimed. "Now you've got it!" He leaned back, triumph showing on his face. "You take Old Man Temple out there at Temple's Crossroads. He's turned that whole community into a Hillbilly stronghold. He's lowly got it in for us. You change his mind, you'll change the mind of that whole community."

Dr. Amos rose in his place. "We are getting into an area of discussion that ought not to be in our minds, much less talked about the way we're talking." He looked from face to face around the table. "We are honorable men, engaged in honorable association," he said. "There might be what looks like easy roads. We must remember that our goal must not only be right, we must take the right road to that goal. We can win; we must win; but in the right way. We have the courts, the law, and the legislature. We have reason in the minds of men. Let's don't forget those things."

Dr. Amos felt a strength rising in him. He had been overwhelmed, at first, by John Thomas' arguments. They were the easy arguments, offering quick and violent solutions. They had swayed the meeting close to the dangerous edge of their own secret thinking. Now, having mustered reason and intelligence and moderation, he was pulling them away from that brink. John Thomas knew it, too; his face wore a sullen expression. But he remained silent when Dr. Amos paused to give him an opportunity for rebuttal.

"Mr. Thomas is right, of course, in his insistence that we must redouble our efforts to persuade the Hillbillies to come into the Association," he said slowly. "I wouldn't attempt to deny that. We must all exert ourselves in that direction. We must even . . ."

He stopped, involuntarily unable to speak the words he had intended to speak. He looked into the faces of these men, his friends. They knew of the old scandal; not once had their knowledge been spoken, not even to the extent of showing an awareness by gesture or attitude. He did not want to say the words, knowing they would understand both his reluctance and his necessity.

"Mr. Thomas mentioned Temple's Crossroads a few minutes ago," he said painfully. "Mr. Temple is not opposed to us on principle, as you well know."

"I don't care why he's opposed," John Thomas said rapidly. "I don't think that makes any difference. But he's a man of property. You take any man that owns property . . ."

Dr. Amos' voice overrode that of John Thomas. "Mr. Temple is against the Association because he hates me. It is my task to go to Mr. Temple and try to correct the situation."

He stopped talking, offering them time to say whatever they might wish to say. He looked into their faces, seeing their understanding. Only their understanding—nothing more.

Mr. Wingo nodded gravely. "Do you think you can?"

"I can try," Dr. Amos said. He raised his voice. "We will pursue all three tactics recommended here. We will go to the courts. We will go to the President. We will begin a new and more vigorous campaign among the Hillbillies." He lifted his hand, looking at John Thomas. "Open and aboveboard, however. We will threaten no man. We will reason with him. We will appeal to his sense of community and duty."

"It won't work," John Thomas said flatly. "I say . . ."

"I say the meeting is closed," Dr. Amos said sharply.

It was the first time he had overridden any director who wished to speak. He could do nothing else. He could not permit John Thomas to speak the fateful words that burned on his tongue to be spoken.

Instead, as a kind of personal substitute, he must himself confront the old man who felt himself so grievously wronged those many years ago.

Chapter Sixteen

It was a cool and sparkling morning. The mare paced briskly toward Temple's Crossroads, as though Dr. Amos were in a hurry to arrive at his destination. When he had started riding horseback most of the time, he had bought a new saddle, with saddlebags large enough to hold his professional equipment on one side. The other pocket was stuffed with Association pledges and literature. If he went out as a doctor, he took the buggy. If he went out on Association business, he rode the mare.

The new leather of the saddle creaked beneath him. The mare traveled better hitched to the buggy; her saddle pace had a jolting roughness that wearied one on a long ride. Dr. Amos thought enviously of the Tennessee Walking horse named Tobacco Man owned by Roscoe Barnes. A man could cover the countryside on a horse like that.

Dew sparkled on the tobacco leaves alongside the road. The crop stood ripe and ready to cut; indeed, much of it was already in the barns. The scent of wood smoke tanged the air, hung visibly in long flat streamers from the barns that had already been fired. Deliberately, Dr. Amos savored the cool morning, the faint smell of the mare's sweat, mingled with the smell of the new leather, the rhythmic sounds of her roofs on the hard-packed dirt of the road. It was the kind of morning in which you were glad to be alive.

Deliberately, he used the sensations to keep his mind away from lurking thoughts of his destination. He had not been inside Temple's Store since he had left on that rainy afternoon so many years ago. Occasionally he had passed the crossroads in his buggy, though he had no calls in that community. On those occasions he had driven straight through. Most times there would be men on the store porch and their heads would turn as he passed. He could imagine the old gossip warming itself in their words.

Every man, he had thought last night in the darkness before going to sleep, must have an area in his past which he cannot revisit. The thought did not help. He had lain awake for a long time, trying to think of what he would say to the old man who felt so severely wronged.

What could one say? You could not tell a man to his face that his daughter, a wanton bitch, had come across the road in the rain to offer herself with another man's child in her belly, hoping to catch Amos in the same trap that held her fast. You could not tell a man that his daughter had been a byword among the wild young men, that Roscoe Barnes had not been alone in leaving the country during that moment of crisis.

Lying in his bed last night, he had thought wryly of that old joke about sending a wire saying, "Fly. All is discovered," to each of the twenty-five most prominent men in town and how twenty-three left town before daylight and the other two shot themselves.

The thought held little comfort. Other men's deeds did not assuage his own. Yet, if he had not denied her, he would not be the man he had now become, the trusted doctor, the president of the Tobacco Growers' Association. How many lives would have been lost in that event? This hand, that had wiped the death-sweat from so many faces, had also pushed Virginia Temple away into a limbo of scandal, of bitterness. That old bitterness had engendered a hotbed of resistance to the Association, fueled by the old man. How could you separate the good from the evil when it seemed sometimes that the good generated the evil within itself?

Such a thought was contrary to all the teachings of his life. Good stood on the right hand, evil stood on the left. Like oil and water they did not mix but held themselves separated into their separate entities. Dr. Amos was a man who had hoped to choose good as his way of life. He had to admit that he did it as much out of his own need as out of an altruistic regard for others. He needed to do good as other men needed a woman or a drink of whiskey. But such motivation did not diminish the sum total of good he had created in the world.

Or did it? He brooded on the question in the darkness of the night, knowing that tomorrow he must have an armor in which to stand before the old man he had wronged. At least, the old man had felt wronged by him, and so was there a difference between feeling and reality?

He had been disturbed more than he could admit by Marvin Rakestraw's apostasy. He had known Rakestraw and his family for years. Rakestraw, a sober, hard-working man, had been one of the early stalwarts of the Association. Yet he had stood with stubbornness in his face, telling them that he must now think of his children rather than the greater good of the Association.

The trouble was, one became institutionalized. You hewed out a path down which you meant to travel. It was your own choice in the beginning; too soon you became the prisoner of your choice. Confined within the limitations of your path, you had no further choice, but must follow it out to the bitter end, even when it led farther than you had intended in the beginning. When a man set his foot to the first step, there was no telling where the path would lead.

Institutionalized, too, by the structure you had erected to carry out your purpose. The Association *must* turn its weight against the errant member. The Bible had said that; if your eye offends you, pluck it out. The institution was all; it had become its own good, its own arbiter of goodness. One was imprisoned by his creation, so that in the end there was not only no turning to the path, one was no longer even aware of the possibility of turning.

On a stormy night in Mr. Rakestraw's kitchen, he had held a scalpel in his hand while Mr. Rakestraw had raised high the coal-oil lamp. The white flesh lay bared before him. He had dripped ether into the boy's breathing until the boy had lain sensationless for the cutting. In the air was the strong sweet sickness of ether. There was always a danger with an open flame and ether in the air. But the boy would die with a burst appendix if Dr. Amos did not take the risk. There had not been the slightest trace of hesitation in his mind or in the movement of his hand. He had leaned forward and while the boy's father had watched, holding the lamp high in his steady hand, he had used the scalpel, moving it in a precise McBurney incision that opened a mouth in the flesh. Down under the ether, the boy had moaned. Dr. Amos had turned his head, looking to see if he was far enough under.

There had been a time, not so long ago, when even the dangerous ether would not have been available. Strong men would have held the boy's arms and legs, the doctor would have given him a bullet to bite on. Even then, Dr. Amos would have made that same smooth precise stroke, for otherwise the boy would die.

He had long since separated in his own mind the random pain that other men inflicted upon each other and the pain-with-a-purpose he himself inflicted out of a greater necessity. Why could he not, then, extend that clear decision into this more esoteric area where good and evil mixed themselves inextricably? Should he yield simply because the problem was more difficult, the lines more subtly drawn, the true good and the true evil harder to know?

He knew the troubled equivocation in his own mind. John Thomas was absolutely right in his facts. The Association *had* benefited the Hillbillies more than they had benefited their own members. The Hillbillies profited effortlessly by the efforts of others. Mr. Rakestraw demanded the right to feed his children at the expense of the other members. Could he not see that the Trust was not a friend, but only used him as a weapon?

Dr. Amos could even understand the anger that bubbled inside John Thomas. He himself felt the frustration that, in John Thomas, made his words blustery, violent. More importantly, John Thomas was the representative of an undercurrent of restlessness that was running like a brush fire through the membership. The other directors, unlike Dr. Amos, did not seem to sense the danger of that potentially reckless mood. The directors talked interminably, in endless meetings they plotted slow strategies.

Dr. Amos, too, was guilty of that same fault. How many of his words were motivated, not by his rational moderation but by the equivocation within his own mind? Words of right and reason should take a stronger grip on men's minds than his had yet done. He had stayed the flood, that was true—but just barely. He knew that a greater certainty within his own heart would lend a greater strength to his argument. He, too, felt a restless urgency; toward what path he did not yet know.

He had slept at last, had come awake into the fresh morning with no idea of what he should say to Mr. Temple. Drawing near to his destination on the brisk mare, he still did not know. Somehow he must reach Mr. Temple, assuage the personal bitterness that held him so strongly against the Association and all its doing. It was ironic that Mr. Temple, by his intransigence, should thus be helping Roscoe Barnes, the real object of his long-held bitterness.

Dr. Amos could not savor the irony. He could think only that the old evil he had generated was tainting this new good to which he had committed himself. It must not be permitted to happen.

He came into sight of Temple's Store. He trotted the mare up to the hitching rail. He stepped down and carefully looped the reins. Without hesitation, he walked through the bare yard and mounted the step. Several men were seated on the porch. They watched him silently, their heads turning to follow his progress. He passed into the dim coolness of the interior.

He paused just inside the door. The store had not changed. The familiar mixture of odors—leather and print goods and molasses, tobacco and coffee and flour—were so inextricably compounded into a total individuality one could not begin to sort out the components. Indeed, he might have stepped outside an hour ago, might have just returned from an errand. Except that he was forty-seven years old.

Why, she's nearly fifty, too, he thought immediately. The thought astounded him. In his mind, she was as young as the day she had come to him in the rain. Like the fabulous Helen, she had remained ageless, unchanging.

Shaking the thought out of his mind, he stepped forward. The old man behind the counter had raised his head at the entrance. He had not moved since, staring toward Dr. Amos with a fixity of regard. His head thrust forward, he stood leaning on his hands braced on the counter before him.

Dr. Amos was shocked by the age that showed in Mr. Temple's face. Why, he must be nearly eighty, he thought.

He had held that time of Temple's Crossroads still within his soul, forgetting that the years would have passed here also.

"What do you want, Amos Haines?" Mr. Temple said.

His voice, vigorous still, had not become thready, as so many men's voices do in old age.

"I came to talk to you, Mr. Temple," Dr. Amos said.

A man stood at the counter in the rear where crackers and cheese and canned oysters were bought for immediate eating. Carefully, he put down a piece of cheese and walked past Dr. Amos toward the porch. Outside, where the other men waited, there was a stillness. Dr. Amos knew their voices carried to the listening ears.

"We have nothing to talk about, Amos."

"I have come on Association business, Mr. Temple," Dr. Amos said. "I think we are both reasonable men. Regardless of what you think you may hold against me personally, there are more important matters to discuss, in this day and time, than old grudges." He paused, clearing his mind, holding onto the important thought. "I have come, Mr. Temple, to persuade you to give up your opposition to the Association."

The old man continued to stare at him. "They have sent you, have they?"

"Yes sir. They have sent me."

Mr. Temple held the stillness for an immeasurable length of time. Then he took his weight off his arms, walked around the end of the counter toward the open door. He did not move with the shuffling tentativeness of an old man but retained his vigor, his alertness.

He paused in the double doorway. "Ain't you fellers got something better to do?" he said to the men outside.

There was a mumble of words that Dr. Amos could not hear. Mr. Temple's voice in reply was high and clear.

"Don't worry your heads none. I can handle it. Go on about your business, now."

He turned in the doorway. "So they sent *you,*" he said heavily. He went behind the counter, stood where he had stood before. "They would pick you," he said.

"Mr. Temple, regardless of your opinion of me, you have no right to hold against the Association for that reason," Dr. Amos said. "I want you to forget about me. I want you to think about the Association and what it's trying to do for the tobacco planters of the Black Patch. You know what's been going on. How many years have you sat here in this store of yours and seen whole families make the winter on the rabbits and the squirrels they could trap?" He moved a step toward Mr. Temple, making his voice strong, persuasive. "Why, you're cutting off your nose to spite your own face. When the tobacco planter is prosperous, you are prosperous. When a man can't pay what he owes you, how can you stay in business? That's what the Association came into being to correct, Mr. Temple. The Association has one goal in mind; to make a man's sweat worth what it ought to be, not what O.K. Knox sitting up there in his New York office decides it should be."

"I'm not likely to forget about you, Amos Haines," Mr. Temple said. He stared at Dr. Amos. "I swore long years ago, boy, that if ever I laid eyes on you, I'd kill you. I reckon I'd've done it, too. But I've done got past that. I ain't never killed a man in my life and I don't reckon I could if my life depended on it." He stared at Amos. "There's a .38 caliber American Bulldog five-shot double-action pistol right here under this counter. It didn't even cross my mind to pick it up when I saw you walk into the store. But if you think I'm going to shake your hand and say bygones are bygones, you've got another think coming. The best thing for you to do is to turn right around and walk out that door."

Dr. Amos was exasperated. Mr. Temple had not heard a word he had spoken. Fixed in that long-past time, his mind moved along the worn grooves of old hates. Dr. Amos knew now that it was unavoidable; he must try to clear the old grudge before he could hope to speak reason.

"Mr. Temple, I can't see any sense in going back over all that's happened," he said. "I can only tell you one thing. I had nothing to do with Virginia's trouble."

"You have taken your time to deny it."

"It was another man, Mr. Temple. I will swear that on any oath you care to name. I have reason to believe it was Roscoe Barnes who put her in the family way."

"So now you're willing to blame it on Mr. Barnes. That's mighty handy, Amos, mighty handy. He just happens to be the Trust agent now."

Amos felt his frustration mounting. "That has nothing to do with it," he cried out. "That's just happenstance. It was him, I tell you, with his bright mare and his red-wheeled runabout . . ."

"It was Amos Haines. She told me so out of her own mouth."

Dr. Amos was breathing hard. "She came to me that day," he said. "She came across the road in the rain. She . . ." He hesitated, his mind fumbling over the words. "She asked me to marry her. I loved that girl, Mr. Temple. But I couldn't marry her, toting another man's child. I knew she had come to me only because she didn't have anywhere else to turn."

His voice stopped. The two men stared at each other across the counter. Dr. Amos had to go on, painful though it was. It was the only chance he had ever had in his life to explain himself.

"Maybe I was wrong. I don't know. Maybe if I'd loved her like I thought I did, it wouldn't have made any difference. I couldn't hold but one thought in my head. I'd never make a doctor—not for love, not for anything except pretending to be the father to another man's child." His voice rose. "She didn't have the right to put that onto me. She hadn't ever looked at me before, flirty as she was. She just didn't have the right."

"She said it was you."

"She told me she would say so, if I wouldn't agree to marry her. It was a lie, Mr. Temple. She was angry and hurt and desperate. Ask her now. Maybe, after all this time, she'll tell the truth. She's known the years, too, she . . ."

"I can't ask her," Mr. Temple said.

Dr. Amos paused. "Don't you know where she is?"

"Yes. I know. I know where she's been all these long years. In a graveyard in St. Louis, Missouri."

The words slid into Dr. Amos' mind like needles of ice. "Dead?" he said.

"She died giving birth," Mr. Temple said. "She didn't want to have that baby. She fought it and she fought it. But that baby of yours was stronger than she was. It killed her, getting born."

"I didn't know." Dr. Amos breathed the words into the tense atmosphere that lay between them. "I asked her sister once. She wouldn't tell me a thing."

"How could you know? You left the country. You abandoned her, knowing she'd be disgraced. All for a few minutes of . . ."

The muscles in his arms were standing out like ropes as he leaned braced on the counter. Dr. Amos knew that Mr. Temple was experiencing that old suffering all over again.

"It was not me," he said hopelessly. "She lied, Mr. Temple. It was not me."

The old man stared at him. "Don't you want to know about your child?" he said. "It was a boy. A fine healthy boy, weighing ten pounds at birth." His voice was seared with the bitterness. "You couldn't have asked for a bigger, healthier son, Amos Haines."

"He was not mine," Dr. Amos said doggedly. "You must believe that, Mr. Temple."

"You can ask from now on," Mr. Temple said. "I couldn't tell you where he is, even if I would. I gave him into an orphanage. I took him and put him into a basket and I laid him on the doorstep. I went away." He paused, his eyes watching Dr. Amos' face. "That son of yours is twenty-five years old now, Amos. He's the only son you'll ever have. And you'll never know anything about him, beyond the fact that he weighed ten pounds when he was born."

"He was not my son."

Mr. Temple sighed. "I reckon you aim to maintain that lie to your grave," he said. "Though what good it would do me to hear you admit it . . ."

"Mr. Temple, I wish there was some way I could convince you that I'm telling the truth," Dr. Amos said. "Not for me. I've borne the scandal for years and I reckon I can bear it a while longer. For the Association. You don't have the right to hold against the Association simply because of me."

"The best thing you can do is turn around and walk right out of the sight of my eyes."

"We still haven't talked about the Association," Dr. Amos said doggedly. "I'm not leaving until we've threshed that out."

The old man's face firmed. "There's nothing to talk about," he said flatly.

"The people who trade at your store respect you, Mr. Temple," Dr. Amos said. "A man like you must be careful what he says, because he's listened to. Don't you see what you're doing? You're damaging every tobacco planter in the Black Patch by your actions."

"Seems to me like, by keeping them from joining the Association, I'm doing 'em a fair amount of good," he said. "Mr. Roscoe Barnes been riding the countryside, offering the best tobacco prices I've seen in many a year."

"Yesterday," Dr. Amos said. "One of our best members announced that he was taking his tobacco out of the Association. What kind of prices do you think Roscoe Barnes will be offering after the Association has been destroyed?" He leaned across the counter. "Mr. Temple, I've been open with you. I've come to you, knowing how you hated me for what you think I did to your dead daughter. I'm asking you to think, Mr. Temple, think hard and clear what you are doing. You're an old man. Do you want to reach the time of dying, knowing the hate and bitterness you've left behind you? . . . knowing that you have helped to destroy the only organization with even a promise of helping the tobacco planter make a decent living for his family?"

A sudden fury had been growing in Mr. Temple's face during the slow, forceful speech. He leaned toward Dr. Amos until their faces were no more than a foot apart.

"Why don't you come on with what you got to say?" Mr. Temple said. "Why don't you stop pussyfooting around? You've sounded noble and righteous about my daughter. Now why don't you lay it on the line?"

Dismayed by the sudden access of fury, Dr. Amos stepped back a pace. "I'm trying to talk common sense to you," he said. "I'm pleading with you, Mr. Temple."

"Why don't you admit that *they* sent you," Mr. Temple said, his voice rising almost to a shout. "What you've got to say, be a man and say it! You're trying to soft-talk an old man with a lot of butter words. Why don't you say what you come to say and get it over with?"

"I don't know what you're talking about," Dr. Amos said, bewildered. "Of course I came on behalf of the Association . . ."

Mr. Temple's face was congested with blood. He was panting as though he had been running. He leaned over the counter, possessed by the explosion of anger.

His voice was heavy with sarcasm. "I reckon you don't know that a band of men rode through here at midnight last night and shot up my house? I reckon you didn't send them on ahead of you in the dark to get my attention, so I'd be inclined to listen to your sweet words of reason?"

Dr. Amos' voice strangled in his throat. He stared at the old man in disbelief. "But I . . ." he said. "I . . ."

He stopped, looking away. He could not face the conviction in Mr. Temple's face. He looked toward the blaze of sunlight showing through the open door, remembering the men's faces. He remembered how Mr. Temple had had to send them away.

"I . . ." he said. "I don't believe it. I can't believe it. I . . ."

They were the only words he could find in his stumbling mind. At the moment of speaking them, something inside him knew the truth. It opened a great hole in him, where conviction and certainty had dwelt.

"If you don't care to take my word, step across the road and see for yourself," Mr. Temple said. His anger had subsided. He spoke the words in a hard, flat tone. "One of those men out there counted fifty-three bullet holes in the front of my house. They shot out every window."

Involuntarily, in the flash of a moment, Dr. Amos saw the whole scene as vividly as if he had been present. The quiet cross-roads settlement, not a light showing, sleeping in the peaceful night. On the road the muffled sound of hoofbeats as the small party of men came closer. Perhaps a dog had barked a warning of the approach of strangers; but the settlement slept on, secure in the peaceful knowledge that no one could mean them harm. Perhaps the men on the horses had paused and clustered before launching the animals into the midnight charge. The sudden drum of hoofbeats as the horses raced at full gallop through the intersection, people rousing in their sleep at the unexpected sound; then the fusillade of shots, sharp and deadly in the still-ness, the hail of bullets shattering glass, thunking into wood. An instant's terror, old wartime fears aroused; but in a minute it was over, the sounds of the horses receding into the distance.

"I didn't know anything about it," Dr. Amos said. He firmed his voice. "It was no act of the Association," he said. "The Association does not, will not, lend itself to such methods of . . ."

"If you figure to scare somebody into giving up his opposition to the Association, you'd better pick a younger man," Mr. Temple said. "I'm too old to be scared into anything, Amos." His voice was calm, hard.

"It was not the Association," Dr. Amos said sharply.

"I reckon you just happened to come riding along this morning with all your talk of sweet reason," Mr. Temple said contemptuously. "Now, deliver your threat or your ultimatum, or whatever it is, and then get out of the sight of my eyes."

"I have said all that I came to say," Dr. Amos said. "I can see there is no convincing you."

He turned from the old man. He walked toward the patch of sunlight glowing in the door.

"There'll be guns waiting next time," Mr. Temple called after him. "Just remember that. It won't be all your own way from now on."

Dr. Amos did not answer. He emerged blinking into the sunlight, moved by feel down the store steps until his feet felt the earth. He was dazzled within as well as without. He could not absorb the meaning of what had happened; it had come too heavily upon him. There was only one thought in his mind; John Thomas. *John Thomas.* It had to be John Thomas.

He looked up as he neared the hitching rail. His eyes were adjusted to the sunlight and he saw the men standing clustered by the rail. His mare was not there. Dr. Amos turned his head, searching.

"Where is my mare?" he said in a commanding tone of voice.

One of the men said, "I reckon she must have slipped her reins. Last I saw of her, she was headed for town. Looked like she aimed to make a record outen the trip, too."

Dr. Amos looked from one face to another. They were closed against him. He knew the violence that lay under the surface of these countrymen of his, beneath the thin patina of smile and joke and easy courtesy. It came out often in knifings and killings, in sudden fierce fist-fights. He looked into their faces, seeing the hate behind their flat eyes. They thought—knew—that he was responsible for that sudden hail of warning bullets.

"Yes sir," the man said. "Reckon you gonna have to hoof it, Doctor." The other men laughed. "Old shank's mare."

He spat on the ground between Dr. Amos' boots. He was chewing tobacco. The brown globule shimmered, rolled in the dust, picking up a coating of the earth. The globule remained round, entire, whole.

Dr. Amos looked down between his feet. He turned away from the men. He set out down the road toward Jamestown.

VISTA: VI

Oren Knox: The Death of Love

OREN sat beside his wife's bed, knowing that it was only a matter of time before she should die. Trenholm lay quietly under the spell of the drug, her face turned away so that it was shadowed. She had lost so much weight her body scarcely made an outline beneath the bedclothes. Her face had thinned until the bones stood out prominently. Her eye sockets seemed deep as caves.

Behind Oren's back, or on the other side of the bed, a nurse made an occasional bustle of professionally cheerful activity. Oren Knox paid the nurse no mind.

For many months, Trenholm had kept more and more to her bed. Oren, becoming alarmed at last, had called her doctor for a private consultation. In his office in the old building that had once been the Fuller Tobacco factory, he heard the fatal news.

"I have known, she has known," the doctor said. "She made me swear that I would not tell you."

For three days, now, she had been so dominated by pain and drug that she had not been aware of Oren's presence in the room. While she had been conscious, he had had to wait in his own room across the hall. Only since she had sunk below the threshold had he been permitted to sit within touching distance.

Oren had wanted to take her to the best hospital and the best doctors in the world. She had denied his demand, asking only to continue in her room in the house that her father had built.

For a time, now, he had been alone with his dying wife. His eyes fixed upon her face, within his mind he dwelt upon all the long thoughts. He had loved her with a singleminded love for so many years. He remembered the dark nights, so few, when they had made love, in order to fetch him a son. His mind flinched away from the son, in Europe now, who had failed to respond to Oren's urgent cables. Fuller was the son of his flesh. He was not the son of his heart.

There were long, bitter thoughts to think, of all the years since those so-few sweet nights. So much bitter, so little sweet. Yet he would not have wished to have never loved Trenholm at all.

Her breathing was a long, even suspiration. When it stopped, he did not at first know it; he only sensed the room strangely devoid of the sound.

His body knew before his mind, physically feeling the presence of death in that absence of breathing. He leaned forward.

"Trenholm?" he said sharply. Then, on a higher, rising note, "Trenholm? Trenholm?"

He took her hand into his, the first time he had dared to touch her even in her coma. The flesh was cold. He bowed his head upon the cold flesh. Quietly, most quietly, he began to weep.

Chapter Seventeen

SPRING brought an increasing ferment to the Black Patch. Dr. Amos, sensitive to the rising tensions within the people, moved among them seemingly in his usual manner, counseling moderation and rational conduct. At the meetings of the Association he exerted his authority and prestige in favor of legal channels. Yet all the while he could feel violence simmering under the surface, held in abeyance by the Association's successes and by the cold winter settling over the earth.

The Association could tally successes. The three judges, in the case of The Dark Tobacco District Growers' Association of Kentucky and Tennessee vs. Marvin Agard Rakestraw, handed down a judgment that was a paraphrase of the lawyer's opinion read to Mr. Rakestraw by Walter Wingo. It fully confirmed the right of the Association to hold its members to their pledges. In addition, at the fall sessions, the legislatures of Kentucky and Tennessee considered identical bills forbidding any grower from selling tobacco pledged to any association, and prohibiting any buyer from knowingly buying such tobacco, under penalty of a two-hundred-and-fifty-dollar fine. The bill, in both cases, was held over for the next session—but it was a definite threat.

With these restraints, Roscoe Barnes' attempt to break the Association failed. He was forced that winter to come to the Association salesroom to fulfill his requirements. He bargained with a grim face, buying the minimum amount of tobacco and paying the minimum price. He came late to the decision, so the Association members did not receive any money on their pledged crop until the long winter was nearly over. In the end, the Association sold nearly thirty-five thousand hogsheads of tobacco at an average price of seven dollars and twelve cents per hundred pounds.

It was a price increase of only one-half cent per pound over the 1904 crop; while the Hillbillies had received from ten to twelve cents a pound. But the Trust had been forced to come to the Association to fill its needs.

When the transaction was agreed upon, Mr. Wingo looked unsmilingly across the table at Roscoe Barnes. "Mr. Barnes, I am giving you fair warning. Next year the Association price will be the highest price you have paid to any Hillbilly tobacco planter—whatever that price may be."

Roscoe Barnes rose from signing the papers. He looked sneeringly about the room. "Next year we'll be paying four cents a pound and you'll be glad to get it," he said. "I am giving you a warning. I am going to Manchester, North Carolina to consult with Oren Knox. I intend to inform him personally what has taken place here this year, how you have bribed the judges and the legislature to get what you want. If you know what's good for you, you will dissolve the Association forthwith and throw yourselves upon Oren Knox's mercy."

He strode out of the room. Mr. Wingo sighed. "Looks like next year will be make or break," he said.

They could muster no greater joy for their immediate success in forcing the Trust to buy their tobacco.

Perhaps more important, Walter Wingo's trip to Washington, once they had succeeded in arranging it, had been greatly successful. With the Association lawyer and the Kentucky and Tennessee senior senators, he had been admitted to the office of the President. For over an hour, the President and his Attorney-General had listened attentively while they had presented the facts of the Tobacco Trust, while they had detailed the poverty and misery brought to the Black Patch as a result.

When they were finished, they waited, watching President Roosevelt. He sat silently for more than a minute, his massive head thrust forward in his characteristic gesture. He rose from his place behind the cluttered desk and walked to the long windows. For another full minute he remained looking out into the sunshine of the day. When he turned, the sunlight glinted on his glasses. With a sudden energy he strode to the desk and slammed down his fist, scattering papers.

"Damn 'em!" he growled. "Bust 'em!"

The Attorney-General arose, as though he were a soldier who had received marching orders.

"I believe you have made the correct decision, Mr. President," the Attorney-General said. He paused, thoughtfully. "Tobacco is a product that goes directly into the life of every citizen. Steel or oil is abstract, because it does not touch them directly. Tobacco does. It can be a landmark decision in the Trust field, Mr. President. If we succeed in breaking the Tobacco Trust, we will have established precedents against the Oil Trust, against the Steel Trust, against . . ."

"The Tobacco Trust is powerful," the Kentucky senator said. "They have won in the state courts."

"It won't be an easy task," the Attorney-General said.

President Roosevelt grinned his indomitable grin. "It'll be a bully fight," he said with gusto.

Abruptly, he shook hands with each of them and, equally as abruptly, they found themselves escorted from the presence, the interview ended in a breathless instant. Outside the White House, Mr. Wingo blew his breath. "By God, he knows how to get rid of you when he figures he's taken in everything you know," he said.

"He's on our side," the senator from Tennessee said. "He's a big man to have on your side in a fight."

They returned to Jamestown full of enthusiasm for their reception. Since then, however, there had been no perceptible sign of action by the Justice Department. The Attorney-General had explained to them, carefully, that it would take time to prepare an anti-trust action. Still, they had expected some signal of future victory.

They needed successes to present to the restive membership. The winter was long and hard, with little money. The Association made advances on the pledged tobacco in hardship cases. There were many hardship cases, and little money. The Association tried to borrow money on its pledged tobacco from the banks. Most of the banks were on the side of the Trust.

With the legal decision upholding the irrevocability of the Association pledges, the directors of the Association voted to accept only three-year pledges, beginning with the 1906 crop. The action was accepted by the membership, though a few took the opportunity to leave the Association. Many others, seeing the increased strength of the Association, joined at last, so that the Association succeeded in increasing its membership to more than twelve thousand.

Despite these improvements in their situation, Dr. Amos was in an increasingly grim mood. There was a danger within the Association as real as the danger without. No one else seemed to realize this fact. He heightened his activities, riding from meeting to meeting, talking to individual members, doing everything he could think of to weld the Association closer to his leadership.

He had an increasingly desperate feeling that control was being removed from his direction. There was nothing he could put his finger on; trying to pin down his feeling in a concrete form was like trying to put your thumb firmly on a ball of quicksilver.

It had started the day he had returned from Temple's Crossroads to call an emergency meeting of the directors. While he told them about the raid on Temple's Crossroads, he kept his eyes fixed on John Thomas. Mr. Thomas' face remained bland, but Dr. Amos had a feeling that a certain smug mischief lurked in his eyes, like a small boy caught stealing watermelons and knowing the punishment will not be severe.

Dr. Amos finished. "What about it, Mr. Thomas?" he said bluntly.

An expression of surprise fastened itself on John Thomas' countenance. "Well, don't look at me," he exclaimed. "I don't know anything about it."

Dr. Amos was certain that John Thomas was lying.

"This is a very serious matter," he said sternly. "We cannot, must not, allow ourselves to be associated with any such doings."

John Thomas spread his hands. "Hell, it was probably a bunch of possum hunters," he said. "You know . . . a bunch of fellows, out for a night of hunting and happening to pass that way. So they decided to give Old Man Temple a shaking up, on the spur of the minute, so to speak. Hell, they'd probably been drinking."

Dr. Amos was certain of his conviction. But what could he do in the face of bland denial? He was a man accustomed to relying on the integrity of his associates. He shifted his eyes to look at the faces of Lewis Carnett, of Thomas Meacham. Slowly he surveyed the face of every man around the table.

When he came to Walter Wingo, Mr. Wingo shifted in his chair. "After all, Dr. Amos," he said defensively. "The Association can't be totally responsible for its members. I don't doubt for a minute it was Association people—but, like Mr. Thomas says, they were probably out drinking and possum-hunting and after a certain amount of whiskey it just looked like a damned good idea." He paused, then his voice went on slowly. "I don't think any responsible member of the Board of Directors would sanction such a thing without at least consulting the board first."

Dr. Amos could see that the directors wanted to believe this easy belief. "However it happened, it will hurt the Association," Dr. Amos said. "It will be laid at our door." He snatched up a blank piece of paper from the table. "I am going to issue a proclamation, making a statement that we deplore such violence perpetrated on any man, even an enemy of the Association like

Mr. Temple. I want it signed by every member of the board of directors who can sign it in good conscience. If any man cannot do so, I want to know it now."

The proclamation was duly drawn up. Dr. Amos watched John Thomas as he perused the document. Mr. Thomas signed without perceptible hesitation, looked up, smiled, and handed the pen to Mr. Carnett. Dr. Amos had to accept it; but the moment was the beginning of anger.

The winter had been quiet, but once spring had come the "possum-hunters" began to ride with increasing frequency. They came out of nowhere, they disappeared into nowhere, a small band of men on horses, their faces covered with masks, guns in their hands. The plant beds had been burned and planted and covered, the fragile tobacco plants were beginning to push up out of the earth. They would descend upon the homestead of a prominent Hillbilly. Their horses would walk in the front yard as a voice yelled, "Come on out now. Come on out."

The man presented himself at the door, his hands empty, his face white with strain. Silently, almost gently, they surrounded him on their horses, and one of them thrust a hoe into his hands. Without words, he knew his task. Surrounded by the men on horseback, he walked on trembling legs to his plant bed. The masked men watched while he labored diligently with the hoe, tearing up the tender plants. He then stood, hoe in hand, as one of the masked men rode his horse into the soft earth of the plant bed to lean down close.

"You'd have to be as ignorant as homemade sin not to know to join the Association before you take it in mind to start another bed," the masked voice said softly. The possum-hunter straightened in the saddle. "Better make up your mind in a hurry, too—otherwise you'll be bound to miss the season."

They departed in a sudden muffled clatter of hoofs, leaving the man standing alone in the midst of his ruined tobacco beds, the instrument of destruction in his hands. He would return to the fretful arms of his family.

From sundown to sunrise the possum-hunters dominated the countryside. All, Association members and Hillbillies alike, barred their doors when darkness fell. Neighbors no longer visited back and forth; there was no movement on the roads. Neighbor suspected neighbor and men, even in the daytime, kept a tight mouth. The possum-hunters rode with impunity through the little crossroads settlements, traveled back and forth on the turnpikes. No one dared to turn a hand against them.

Somewhere, one night, an unknown child heard the muffled sounds of hoofbeats. She looked up brightly into the still faces of her parents. "Daddy," she said brightly. "There goes the night riders."

The name caught on, displacing the original name of "possum-hunters." It was indeed appropriate, for they rode the night side, they were shrouded in darkness. There was no knowing which daytime men stole forth into the darkness to saddle a horse and ride masked to the meeting place. A neighbor who spoke in friendliness by day might be the very one who leaned from his horse by night to call a man out.

There was, at first, little violence. The countryside was terrified by the Night Riders and no man dared to lift a hand against them. The first physical violence occurred the night a man thrust his gun out the door, yelling defiance as he fired bird shot into the scattering horses. A torch flamed in the darkness and he was ordered to drop the gun and come out, or the house would be fired.

Trembling, he came forth. The Night Riders tied him to a tree in the front yard and whipped him. His back bleeding, he was given a shovel and led staggering to his plant bed, where he labored until daylight digging a grave in the center of the worked earth.

The grave finished, he was ordered to lie down in it. The man broke. Whimpering, he fell to his hands and knees, trying to scrabble between the horses' legs. Men dismounted, laid hands on him, flung him into the grave. He lay on his back, looking up at their forms etched against the night sky, and wept as he waited for the bullet. The bullet did not come; the dark forms disappeared, the sound of horses faded into the distance. The sun up, his wife and brother came searching for him. He screamed when the brother came down into the grave to help him climb out. They brought him home; he lay huddled in his bed, his knees drawn up to his chin, neither sleeping nor eating. Within a few days, in despair, he was sent to the state insane asylum. His mind was broken beyond repair.

The Night Riders continued to ride.

As Dr. Amos had feared, violence had descended upon them. He knew that he was blamed for the birth of the Night Riders. He could see open fear in the faces of the townspeople now, not merely curiosity. He could do nothing for the time being but continue upon his determined path. He presided at the meetings, looking into John Thomas' bland face, hearing numberless times Mr. Thomas' denial of any knowledge of the Night Riders. The Association issued proclamations decrying lawlessness and violence. People laughed half-approvingly when they read the statements in the newspapers; or they sneered at Dr. Amos' hypocrisy.

There was one fact even Dr. Amos, in his total resistance, could not escape; the Night Riders were successful where the Association had failed. Hillbillies flocked to inscribe their names on the membership roll. One darkling raid in a country community sufficed to bring the recalcitrants of that community to pledge their allegiance and their tobacco.

Dr. Amos at first thought only of publicly resigning as the President of the Association. He knew the regard in which he was held by the membership. His resignation would have repercussions difficult to measure.

He could not bring himself to do so. In his total commitment, he had destroyed his practice. Whatever he would build in his lifetime would be built within the framework of the Association. There could be no going back to the plain country doctor he had once been, riding the country roads in safety and respect, simple and good though that time had been.

The Association was his creature. Indeed, he doubted if he could successfully withdraw himself. Even Association members would continue to believe that his resignation had been a public gesture only, that secretly he was still head of the clandestine organization.

He had to do something; he was not the kind of man to acquiesce by inaction. He simply did not know what to do. The festering sore that was the Night Riders had embedded itself so deeply within the structure of the Association that the knife of his decision could not reach it without penetrating fatally the healthy flesh in which its suppuration flourished.

One night in the late spring, before he had reached a decision, Dr. Amos was called out by a thunderous knocking on his office door. He came out of his quarters behind the office and unlocked the door, yawning, for he was, now, seldom aroused at night in his capacity as a doctor.

He unlocked the door, to stare into two masked faces. He started back in surprise. One of the masked men lifted a gloved hand.

"Will you come, Dr. Amos?" he said in a muffled voice.

"Come?" Dr. Amos said sharply. "Come where?"

He was stirred, alert. Was not even the President of the Association safe from the illicit cluster that dwelt within the organization?

"We've got a boy that's hurt real bad," the muffled voice said. "You must come, Dr. Amos."

Dr. Amos calmed himself. They were calling upon him in his capacity as healer.

"You're Night Riders, aren't you?" he said. "I will have nothing to do with Riders. If you are a member of the Association—as I hope you are not—you know my position on night riding."

"The boy is likely to die," the muffled voice said. "He's a man, Dr. Amos, and you're a doctor."

Dr. Amos stared into the masked blankness of their faces. "Yes," he said slowly. "I will come."

He returned into the office to get his saddlebags, saying over his shoulder, "What happened to him?"

"He got shot."

"So they've started shooting back," Dr. Amos said harshly. "I'm glad of that."

"If the boy dies, we will hang the man who killed him." The

muffled voice was strained, vengeful. "We will hang him high as Haman."

Dr. Amos hefted the saddlebags. "So it's up to me to keep him from dying, then," he said.

The masked figures followed him, to lurk in the shadows while he entered the livery stable to saddle his mare. The two o'clock town lay dark about them as they clattered through the streets. Dr. Amos found it strange that these masked men could move with impunity within the limits of Jamestown itself. If they were discovered, whoever saw them did not show himself.

Once in the country, they rode hard through the darkness, Dr. Amos flanked on either side by the masked figures. Except for the masks, made of black cloth and topped by black slouch hats pulled down over their eyes, they were dressed in nondescript clothing of everyday appearance. One of the men had a white piece of cloth, probably a handkerchief, tied about his upper arm. Dr. Amos wondered what that meant; probably that he was an officer of the Night Riders . . . perhaps even the supreme leader.

Dr. Amos occupied himself with trying to identify his two companions. They were both big men. They did not speak; the one who had spoken before had kept his voice muffled. Dr. Amos transferred his attention to the horses. He did not recognize them either.

He gave up the attempt, yielding himself to the ride. He did not think about what he was doing; he could not have done otherwise. He remained a doctor in spite of all; when a doctor is called, he must answer. This, at least, was clear-cut.

In the beginning, his allegiance to the Association had been quite as easy to understand. To Dr. Amos, the Association had been an entity as real as the entity that is an individual human being. He had, with others, created the Association and he was responsible for its growth and well-being as he was responsible for his patients. He was a rational, scientifically trained man, accustomed to considering mind and body, knowing the power of each yet considering each within the reach of his skill and knowledge.

Yet, as a doctor, he had known at least one case of possession; not possession by means of witchcraft, but possession by some element deep within the human soul, rising up to take command of both thought and action. Vividly he remembered the patient; a stolid elderly gentleman of substantial means, who on the nights of full moons had crawled howling on all fours, doing everything but sprouting the teeth and claws of a wolf. There was no curing him; because he became sexually aroused, it was necessary to chain him in the corn crib during the time of the full moon in order to prevent assault upon his wife, his daughter, upon any female within reach. Yet at all other times he was a grave and sober man.

The incurable case had disturbed Dr. Amos. What was it within the man that could rise out of the deeper reaches of his being with the advent of the full moon, turning him into an animal; yet blanking his memory afterward so that he had no recollection of his ravenous actions? Dr. Amos, though he had assiduously studied the scant literature on the subject, had never learned the answer; but he knew that the cause, the effect, was as real as the touch of one hand upon another.

On this long night ride, flanked by the masked Night Riders, with the memory of that patient rising involuntarily into his mind, Dr. Amos had a sudden vision of the relationship of the Night Riders to the Association. The Association was the staid and respectable man; the Night Riders were the mad werewolf of the full moon.

He had thought of the Night Riders, in medical terms, as a festering sore within the body of the Association. He had been wrong; it was nothing so passive. Not diseased cells, but wild cells, like cancer possessed of their own life. Within the body of the Association, they were a savage and autonomous werewolf, rising up in the darkness to possess the thoughts and actions of the Association. The Night Riders are not merely our brothers, he thought. They are *us*. The Night Riders are the embodiment of our own devil-possession.

He bowed his head under the emotional impact of his vision. He understood far better than he wished its ultimate meaning.

He had seen it, before now, but had not understood it. Many an Association member, who would never have donned a mask to ride the dark roads, manifested a tacit acceptance of the Night Riders. The Association officers blandly enrolled those Hillbillies who were frightened into joining. If a Night Rider were wounded, Dr. Amos would ride to give him medical aid.

In the moment when John Thomas had put the bland lie of his signature to that first proclamation, Dr. Amos Haines had known the beginning of anger. Now—out of anger and understanding, out of the profound impact of his moment of vision—he knew the beginning of decision.

The masked man with the white armband motioned them to a halt. The horses stamped in the packed dirt of the road. The leader peered into the darkness.

"Here," he said.

He rode ahead to a grassed side road that cut away toward a cluster of trees, motioning for them to follow. A hundred yards from the trees, he stopped. He whistled three times, sharply, the first sound long drawn out, the following two sounds shorter. He was answered in the same manner.

They entered the greater darkness of the trees. A figure rose before them. "Who comes there?"

"The silent brigade," the leader answered.

The guard relaxed. "Pass, brother," he said. Then, eagerly, "Did you git him?"

"I got him," the leader said.

They penetrated deeper into the trees. A light flickered, a circle of men parted to let them through. The dim lantern rested beside a figure stretched on a crude stretcher made of two saplings thrust through the sleeves of several coats. Dr. Amos stepped down from his mare and unfastened his saddlebags. He did not look at the masked faces. He leaned over the casualty, stripped to the waist, to look at the bullet hole in his side.

After his preliminary examination, Dr. Amos lifted his head. "I'm going to have to probe," he said. "Can you stand it?"

The boy, teeth clenched, nodded.

"Hold his arms and legs," Dr. Amos said impartially to the masked group.

After a moment's hesitation, four men obeyed. Dr. Amos began to work patiently with the probe. The wounded boy gasped at the pain, his body arching. Imperturbably, Dr. Amos proceeded with the task. He found the bullet, gripped it, extracted it as the boy let forth a ragged sigh of anguish.

"All right," Dr. Amos said briskly. "That's the worst of it."

He cleaned the wound, bandaged it deftly, his hands moving with quick certainty in the uncertain light of the lantern. Only when he had finished did he glance at his patient's revealed face. He recognized the son of a prominent Association member named Harris Clark. The boy's name was William.

"You were lucky, Bill," he said. "The bullet glanced off the rib cage and buried itself in flesh instead of passing through vital organs. You want the bullet for a keepsake?"

The palefaced boy nodded feebly. Dr. Amos put the bullet into his hand. "Hold onto it, now," he said. "Don't lose it."

He rose from his squatting position, looked into the masked faces.

"He can't ride. He'll be getting fever. You'd better be taking him home to his daddy, where he can be looked after."

"Go to my place and get the surrey," a mask said. "It's not far."

Another mask said, "Hurry. It'll be daylight before you know it. Whistle when you're down there at the road and we'll carry him there."

"We can't take him home, Dr. Amos," another mask said. "The whole community will know he's been shot, and why."

"He must be got into bed," Dr. Amos said. "A gunshot wound must be looked after. If infection sets in . . . I must see him every day for a few days."

A small man stepped forward. "We will take him to the camp," he said. "We have a tent there. We'll put out that he left the country for reasons of his own. Will you come to the camp to tend him?"

"Will someone be there to look after him?" Dr. Amos asked.

"We will see to it," the short man answered.

Dr. Amos stared at this new figure who stepped forward now into the flickering light of the lantern. He wore a white mask, and a white sash was crossed like bandoleers on his chest. Abruptly, Dr. Amos reached him in two steps and snatched the hat from his head. The mask came with it. John Thomas smiled sardonically.

"I thought I recognized you," Dr. Amos said sharply.

"That's one of the handicaps of being a little feller, I reckon," Mr. Thomas said.

"It was you all the time," Dr. Amos said.

"Did you really believe anything else?" John Thomas said.

Dr. Amos shook his head. "No," he said. He stared about the circle of men. "I'm sure I would know most of you, too," he said.

John Thomas chuckled. "I wouldn't keep on snatching masks, if I was you," he said. "Hit would be one surprise after another."

Dr. Amos turned on him. "I would like to hear you say why you felt it necessary, Mr. Thomas," he said stiffly.

"We knew you weren't the kind of man to do what had to be done," John Thomas said. "So we took it upon ourselves. Why, Dr. Amos, I won't even ask you to join us now, now that you know something about us. You just go your way, being president of the Association and all. We'll take care of the rest of it."

"What did you do tonight to get this boy shot? Whose tobacco barn did you burn? Who did you take out of his house and horsewhip?"

"Now, what you don't know won't hurt you," Mr. Thomas said. "How many new members has the Association enrolled this month, Dr. Amos? And how many of them answered to your sweet reason?"

Dr. Amos could hear the triumph in John Thomas' voice. He has wanted to face me like this, he thought. He's wanted me to truly know him. He had no need to answer; he needed only an answer to his own anger, his own decision. He turned away.

"I will go now," he said. "I have done all I can do here."

"Will you look after William Clark?" John Thomas said. There was a touch of anxiety in his voice.

"Yes," Dr. Amos said. "Of course I will tend him. You will have to let me know where to find him."

"A man will come to guide you," John Thomas said. He hesitated. "I cannot reveal the signs of our order, because you have not taken the oath. I will give you a private sign. A man will say to you, 'Do you believe in what we are doing?' You will acknowledge that you have recognized him by replying, 'Yes, I do believe truly.' That man will lead you to your patient." John Thomas grinned. "Maybe, if you say it often enough, you'll come to believe it."

Without reply, Dr. Amos threw the saddlebags over the mare's back and fastened them. A whistle sounded far below, one long and two short, and was answered by one of the sentries.

"Take him up now," John Thomas said. "We will ride him in the surrey to the secret place."

Masked men stooped to the stretcher poles. The wounded boy groaned with the movement.

"You will be escorted back to Jamestown," John Thomas said.

"I want no escort," Dr. Amos said. "I need no guide."

He left the group, riding down the hill through the trees. Once clear of the dark woods, he flogged the mare and when he passed the waiting surrey he was riding in a dead run. He had never before stretched his mare to the limit.

It was daylight by the time he reached Jamestown. He walked the winded mare down the street, sitting erect in the saddle, paying no heed to the people watching his return. He knew the conviction that lay within their minds.

Before the livery stable, he stepped down stiffly from the mare. "Rub her down good and give her a feed of corn," he said to the Negro boy.

Roscoe Barnes sauntered forward from the group of early birds clustered along the lot fence. "Well, well, the good doctor returns at dawn," he said. "You're rather belated, aren't you?"

Dr. Amos ignored him, busying himself with taking down the saddlebags.

Roscoe cast a critical eye at the mare, her flanks dusty, spume drying on her shoulders. She had obviously been hard-ridden during the night.

"I don't reckon you've heard the news," Mr. Barnes said. "Two Trust warehouses were burned last night, just over the line in Kentucky." He assumed a solicitous expression. "I reckon you been up all night with a patient, Dr. Amos. Mighty handy, being a doctor. Nobody can question your comings and your goings."

Dr. Amos, the saddlebags draped over one arm, turned on Roscoe Barnes. "Mr. Barnes," he said. "If you, now or at any time in the future, speak another word directly to me, I will call you out."

The expression on Dr. Amos' face gave a halt to Roscoe. Dr. Amos stared into his face for a full minute, waiting. Roscoe Barnes did not speak. Dr. Amos turned away and, carrying the saddlebags, plodded up the street toward his office.

"I wonder would he come alone, or with a bunch of Night Riders at his back?" Roscoe Barnes said in a voice that attempted to be jaunty.

He was careful to speak softly enough that Dr. Amos Haines could not hear.

VISTA: VII

Oren Knox: The Black Patch

OREN KNOX had sat still, his cold blue eyes fixed on Roscoe Barnes' face, letting Barnes talk on without comment until Barnes had run down into silence. He watched the uncertainty creep into Barnes' face, listened to Barnes' voice beginning to falter until at last he fell silent. He remained silent a moment longer, studying the man.

"Mr. Barnes," he said then. "When I hire a man to do a job, I expect that job to get done. Why have you found it necessary to come to me with your troubles?"

Mr. Barnes' face was sweating. "I felt . . . I thought you ought to know what's going on," he said. "Personally, I mean. I've sent in my reports but, as far as I could tell, they never reached you."

His cold blue eyes still held Roscoe Barnes nailed to his chair. "They reached me, all right. But you had to tell me in person that the job is too big for you."

Roscoe licked his lips. "No sir," he said. "I . . ." He fought for control of his voice. "I wanted you to know how dangerous the situation is in the Black Patch, sir. I . . . I felt it was my duty to bring it to your attention . . ."

"Mr. Barnes," Oren said. "I make decisions every day involving millions of dollars and thousands of people. Yet it's your opinion that your little corner of the world merits my undivided attention because you're having a little trouble with the planters."

Mr. Barnes had found his handkerchief. He wiped his face with it, looked at it absently, stowed it away.

"Mr. Knox, those people are trying to tear down the Trust," he said. "They've gone to Washington, they've . . ." he was sweating again. "They've got these Night Riders burning our warehouses and threatening and whipping people who sell to the Trust. They . . ."

"You have told me all that already," Oren said coldly. "But you haven't told me what you're doing about it. Are you doing anything at all?"

"What can we do?" Mr. Barnes said. "With the whole Black Patch against us? We encouraged the Hillbillies by paying them high prices. That was working pretty good. The members began to quit the Association to get the kind of prices we were paying. That's when the Night Riders got started. We . . ."

Oren Knox rose abruptly. He walked to the window of his office, stared out unseeingly for a moment. He turned back to Mr. Barnes. He was tired of the man.

"To break the Association, you must break the Night Riders," he said. "Do you understand that, Mr. Barnes?"

Mr. Barnes nodded, though his face displayed no understanding at all. Oren watched him for a moment.

"The Night Riders are the backbone of the Association," he said patiently. "Your first task is to break them. Expose their membership, bring them to trial, prosecute them. Destroy the Night Riders and you will destroy the Association."

"It's a very secret organization," Mr. Barnes said. "Nobody knows who's a member and who isn't. They say Dr. Amos Haines is the head—but nobody knows for sure." He lifted his head. "Mr. Knox, it's not just the Association. It's not just the Night Riders. Everybody in the Black Patch, outside the towns, at least, is against us. That's why the Night Riders can ride far and wide. They've got the support of so many of the people that there's no finding out anything."

"Could outside detectives help you?" Oren asked.

"No sir, I don't think so," Barnes said. "They'd stick out like sore thumbs."

"The thing to do, then, is to discredit the Night Riders with the Black Patch people," Oren said briskly. "Can't you think of ways to do that, Mr. Barnes?"

"How do you mean . . ."

"Start your own little band of Night Riders," Oren said. "Find some men you can depend on and pay them well. Hire the kind of man who likes to tear up things—you've got them, I know, because there's always people like that." Mr. Barnes nodded. "Since the Night Riders are a secret organization, they'll be blamed for everything your people do. Do you know what I mean?"

Roscoe Barnes was watching Oren Knox's face. "There's a woman there, who's been talking against the Night Riders," he said. "They've never laid a hand on her, because she's a woman, I guess. If she was taken out and whipped . . ."

"Now you're getting the idea," Oren Knox said. He looked at the man distastefully. "I'm sure you can think up some more ideas along those lines. Remember, you're fighting fire with fire." He paused. "Your next move is to show everybody you can protect the farmers who sell to us. Take delivery of the tobacco at the barn. Haul it under armed guard to our warehouses. You can organize caravans of wagons moving in force and under arms across the countryside. The Night Riders will not dare attack them in daylight, against armed and determined men."

"Yes sir, that's a good idea," Mr. Barnes said. "Thank you, sir."

The subservient words brought Oren Knox's annoyance to full flood. He stared down at Roscoe Barnes.

"Now that you have brought this matter to my attention, I want you to make a daily report directly to me," he said. "I want to know every detail that's going on. I want to know all about the men involved . . . this Dr. Amos Haines, those others you mentioned earlier. Do you understand?"

Roscoe Barnes rose, sensing the moment of dismissal. "Yes sir," he said. He made an effort to recover himself. "I knew you would understand just how important it is to the whole Tobacco Trust. I am gratified that you have seen fit to place me under your direct supervision . . ."

"Mr. Barnes," Oren said. "I also want to know the name of the man who hired you."

Mr. Barnes wilted. He gave Oren Knox the name with great hesitation.

"Mr. Barnes, I am giving you an opportunity to show what you can do," Oren Knox said. "You have let this situation get out of hand. I hope you can take control once again, and very quickly. If you cannot . . ."

"Yes sir," Mr. Barnes said. "I'm sure I can. I just needed to know that I had your support, and your ideas."

"Kill the Night Riders and you kill the Association," Oren Knox said. "To kill the Night Riders, you must turn the community against them. Penetrate the Night Riders if you can, find a traitor. Encourage your Hillbillies, guard and protect them." He paused. "If this does not serve, I will come to the Black Patch myself." He paused. "I do not want to take the time to come to the Black Patch personally, Mr. Barnes."

"That won't be necessary," Mr. Barnes said hastily. "I'm sure that'll never be necessary."

"Good day, Mr. Barnes."

Oren watched him leave the office. He shook his head in exasperation and annoyance and sat down to the papers whose study had been interrupted.

Chapter Eighteen

TO HIS own surprise, Dr. Amos Haines did nothing to carry out the decision he had already made in his own mind. It was as though, reluctant to become the man he must become, he were clinging to the man he had aways been. He knew his own mind; somehow, he could not translate that knowledge into the necessary action.

The period of withdrawal lasted for months, during which he went about his duties with an undue absorption in the day-to-day detail of his life, seeming to deny even to himself the significance of the events taking place about him. It was a time stranger than any he had known before, in which he seemed disembodied from reality, or in which reality was disembodied from him.

It did not seem to matter that the activities of the Night Riders were gaining increasing attention from the press. It was only an annoyance to have his footsteps dogged by reporters and feature writers from the big newspapers, from the national magazines like *Harper's Weekly*. The published stories depicting him as the sinister leader of the secret organization called the Night Riders had no more nor no less reality than the true state of affairs.

He applied himself to the practice of medicine more assiduously than he had done for a year past. There was a comfort in devoting himself to the physical ills, though a part of him knew that it was not a true dedication but rather a denial of his own anger, his own decision that had been formed within the fire of that anger.

Every day for a week he had made the long trip to the secret camp of the Night Riders in order to attend William Clark's wound. He performed this task in the same detached mood with which he did everything else, from putting on his shoes in the morning to presiding over a meeting of the Association directors.

The first time a man approached him with the password, he was not even surprised. It happened just as a director's meeting was breaking up; at the doorway, one of the directors said to him casually, "Do you believe in what we are doing?"

Dr. Amos turned his head, regarding the man with a frank curiosity. Mr. Carnett was a quiet man, who seldom spoke in open meeting. He was serious and slow in his thinking, careful with his words. He was also a Night Rider.

"Yes, I do believe truly," Dr. Amos said.

The director brushed by him, went on down the stairs. Dr. Amos followed him to the livery stable, where the man mounted his horse. On the edge of town Dr. Amos caught up with him.

"So you are a Night Rider, too," Dr. Amos said, after they had ridden silently for a time. "Tell me, Mr. Carnett. How does it feel to whip a man?"

Mr. Carnett did not turn in his saddle. "It ain't nothing to talk about," he said.

They rode a while longer. "Do you believe night riding is the way to solve our problems?" Dr. Amos said. The question was almost idle in its curiosity.

"I don't know a better way," Mr. Carnett said in his stolid, careful voice.

Dr. Amos did not pursue the thought any further. It was as though his mind shied away from it, like a saddle horse shying from a leaf blowing across the road. And yet the decision had already been made.

The camp had a long-established air. It was sited in a reasonably inaccessible place, far from the nearest road, hidden in the midst of an uninhabited cluster of high hills. One could approach it only from two directions and they were challenged while more than a mile away.

Two shabby tents were pitched beside a spring that boiled from the edge of a huge boulder. Beyond, Dr. Amos could see a rope corral, holding horses and saddle mules. Seeing them, Dr. Amos could understand why, on that first occasion, he had been unable to recognize the mounts of the Night Riders. A man was often known by his mount; if a Night Rider felt a risk of recognition, he could ride his own horse here and exchange to another for the raid.

No more than half a dozen men were in sight. Forewarned of his arrival, they wore their masks, even then remaining at a distance except for the man who was looking after William Clark.

William was recuperating well. Dr. Amos dressed the wound, warned him to remain quiet, for he had a touch of fever and there was still the danger of infection.

The complement of the camp seemed to change on each of his succeeding visits. In spite of their precautions, Dr. Amos recognized several of the men. One man walked with a limp; fifteen years ago Dr. Amos had set the broken hip that had given him his distinctive walk. Other characteristics betrayed other men to his eyes. He was beyond surprise; he had no wish to challenge them.

On the last trip, Dr. Amos told William he was well enough now to get along without further medical care. Dr. Amos could see that, with the return of health, William was beginning to be restless in his confinement. "Just take it easy," he said. "Give it a chance to heal, and you'll be all right."

The boy smiled and thanked him for his trouble. He was an open-faced young man, friendly and embarrassed by the trouble he had caused.

Dr. Amos received the thanks in silence, busily repacking his saddlebags. He rose, lifting the bags.

"Why are you a Night Rider, Bill?" he asked.

A sullen expression came over the boy's face. "I reckon it's the only way we'll ever sell our tobacco for a decent price," he said. "Put a stop to these Hillbillies, we . . ."

"Does your daddy know what you're doing?"

The boy's sullenness turned into belligerence. "My daddy was riding right by my side," he said. "He was one of the men who went to fetch you."

Dr. Amos turned away.

While Dr. Amos pursued his weirdly detached existence, uncommitted even to his own decision, the night riding continued. Throughout the planting season it occurred in spasms of activity, a week of quiet, then a raid here and a raid there. Another man was whipped. Trust warehouses were burned. A train was stopped and a Regie buyer taken from it, warned, and sent back in the direction he had come. Tobacco was destroyed in the fields. Lone Night Riders left warnings on gateposts, requiring a particular man to join the Association within a specified period of time, requiring him also to publish an announcement of his new-found allegiance in the newspapers. Most men so singled out took the way of discretion and joined the Association.

Though he knew, and did not seem to care, that the real decisions were being made elsewhere, Dr. Amos continued to preside over the meetings of the directors; he continued, with Mr. Wingo and the lawyer, to press for the anti-trust action; he went through all the motions of leadership without greatly caring one way or the other. He knew that nothing he did had anything to do with the numbers of Hillbillies flocking into the Association—a movement so extensive that, by the fall, when the smoke of curing fires hung once more over the countryside, the Association had doubled its strength to thirty thousand members, with practically the entire tobacco crop pledged.

It was a short crop, because so many plant beds had been scraped in the spring. Fields were left unplanted because there were no plants available. Many tenants and sharecroppers had left the country, both because of the Night Riders and because, with the shortage of tobacco plants, there was no work for them.

Substantial landowners, disturbed by the Night Riders but not wishing to oppose them—especially Hillbilly landowners who had been threatened—also left the Black Patch. Houses stood empty, fields remained untended, as though the countryside lay under the blight of war. As, indeed, it did.

With the tobacco in the barns, the Night Riders began to flourish once again. Hillbilly barns, full with the curing crop, were burned, sending new, destructive smoke into the night sky to mingle with the smoke of the curing fires. Resistance, under the tutelage of Roscoe Barnes, became more common than before; many a Hillbilly farmer spent the nights guarding his tobacco barn, his shotgun by his side, often assisted by town toughs paid by Roscoe Barnes. Roscoe Barnes organized caravans of wagons to haul the tobacco to the Trust warehouses, passing through the countryside in an armed state. Most of these organized caravans got through; a few were attacked by the Night Riders, the wagons overturned, the cured tobacco dumped into creeks or trampled into the dust of the road.

None of these sensations seemed to disturb Dr. Amos' mood of detached equanimity. He moved alone, not because most of the men about him belonged to the Night Riders and therefore left him isolated, but because his state of mind insulated him against them. He no longer speculated how many directors, in the meetings over which he presided, were members of the Night Riders. He no longer challenged John Thomas, who lolled insolently in his place at the table, his occasional words or speeches charged with secret amusement and open arrogance.

Not until the great Gurley raid did Dr. Amos find an impetus to jolt his long-held decision into motion. Shortly after midnight, one September Saturday, two hundred and fifty armed men took possession of the city of Gurley, Kentucky. They erupted into the town with a massive firing of pistols and shotguns. Masked men on horses milled in the streets, firing wildly in every direction while the citizens cowered in their houses. If a townsman showed himself, a bullet splacked against a wall nearby, or shattered a windowpane above his head. Half-a-dozen people were wounded by the random gunfire. The J. G. Ormsby and the Stiner & Dunker stemming factories were dynamited and burned, along with four hundred thousand pounds of tobacco. Several residences also caught fire and burned to the ground. The destruction completed, to the extent of more than a hundred thousand dollars, the wild, yelling mob of Night Riders swept out of town.

Three nights later, in Jamestown, a regular meeting of the Board of Directors of the Association was scheduled.

Dr. Amos entered the room after the other men were all in their places. The expression on his face stopped their conversation about the great events that had taken place in Gurley. In silence, they watched as he walked to his place at the table.

For so long, now, he had not known how to react to events. Or, rather, he had known; but something within him had refused to take the gambit. It had been a last lingering resistance to the sweep of events. That resistance had now broken and in breaking it had changed Dr. Amos Haines so profoundly that his new appearance held the directors enthralled.

He stood at the head of the table, staring straight at John Thomas. "Mr. Thomas, have you taken up war against women and children?" he said.

Mr. Thomas, in his present sly combination of secret amusement and open arrogance, laughed. "Me?" he said in mock surprise. "You think I had anything to do with the Gurley raid, Dr. Amos?" He shifted in his chair. "You know what I heard?" he said with gusto. "I was told that them Night Riders sent word beforehand to the insurance companies that the two factories would be burned. The Capitol Underwriters Agency and the Kingrow Insurance Company took the wind and cancelled their policies. It's a total loss for the folks owning them stemming factories."

Dr. Amos stared at him. "You actually enjoy burning and destroying, don't you?" he said. "Most men belonging to the Night Riders do it because they believe there's no other way to fight the Tobacco Trust. But you enjoy it—you thrive on anarchy and lawlessness."

The open contempt in his voice spurred John Thomas out of his chair.

"Are you agin them stemming factories getting what they deserved?" John Thomas said. "It's about time you chose up, Dr. Amos. Do you even have any idea of what's going on?" He paused, taking a deep breath, forcibly calming himself. "After he got his notice of insurance cancellation, Old Man Ormsby still had the nerve to run an advertisement in the Gurley paper saying he'd pay a bonus of twenty dollars in gold to the man who delivered him the best crop of tobacco this season. He bragged about the high Trust prices he was paying, and he even had the nerve to state that the planter didn't have to wait a year for his money, he'd be paid on the spot. Now you know, Dr. Amos, that was a direct slap at the Association."

"Sit down, Mr. Thomas," Dr. Amos said coldly. He waited until John Thomas had resumed his seat. He took a piece of paper from his inside pocket. "I will read," he said calmly. " 'Whereas, the city of Gurley has been recently visited by a calamity which we very much regret and for which we are in no wise responsible, and we deplore the public sentiment excited by the press, which has cast reflection upon our organization. Be it resolved by this meeting of tobacco growers that we condemn all lawlessness, riot and destruction of property.' " He stopped, surveying the table. "I presume that each of you will agree that the Association should issue this statement."

John Thomas chuckled. He had quite recovered his good humor. "Pitch it down here," he said. "I'll be the first to sign it."

Dr. Amos placed the paper before Mr. Wingo. Mr. Wingo signed. With bleak eyes, Dr. Amos watched the paper progress around the table. John Thomas signed with a flourish; Mr. Carnett affixed his signature with grave care. Dr. Amos received the paper, bearing the signature of every man in the room.

He stared down at the paper for a moment. He lifted his head. "I don't doubt that half or more of those signing this paper took part in the Gurley raid," he said.

He folded the paper once, with precise care. Then, in a sudden savage movement, his blunt fingers took the edge of the paper and ripped it in two. He turned the paper, ripped it again, and dropped the torn fragments to the table before him.

"I want to join the Night Riders," he said.

They were startled. They stared at him, motionless, speechless. He returned their gaze unflinchingly.

"I am ready to take my oath," he said.

John Thomas started to stand up, changed his mind, sank again into his seat. "Do you think that's a good idea, Dr. Amos?" he said. "You, the president of the Association, an actual active member of the Night Riders? You can do a lot more good, standing up in public able to deny in all honesty that you know anything about it."

"If I cannot join the Night Riders," Dr. Amos said harshly. "I will publicly resign from the Association. I will publicly give my reasons."

He watched their faces. "Let a man come to me," he said slowly. "I will follow wherever he leads. I will take whatever oath is required. I will discharge whatever duties are imposed upon me as a Night Rider as conscientiously as I have discharged my duties as the head of the Association."

He walked around the table. No one moved as he reached the door, paused, and turned to face them again.

"The original purpose of this meeting was to hear the report of our lawyer in Washington," he said. "On the progress of the investigation by the United States Department of Justice. He reports that within a year, at least, the Federal Government will file an anti-trust action against the Tobacco Trust." A short burst of heavy laughter rattled in his throat. "Within a year."

He left the room. He stalked through the streets to his office without looking to the right or to the left. He sat behind his desk, his back rigid, his head high, and waited.

It was midnight before the call came. In those four hours, he did not move from his posture of waiting. He knew that they would come; he did not even consider what he would have to do to make them accept his oath if he had not already succeeded in doing so. Nor did he think about the road he had chosen. That decision had been made so far the other side of that curious time of denial that it had become by now a part, the major part, of the man that was Dr. Amos Haines.

Upon the stroke of midnight, the knock sounded on the door. He sat alertly in his chair unstartled by the expected sound; but he could not prevent the hair from rising on the back of his neck as though indeed the devil were calling upon him at this witching hour, as he had called upon Faust, to bargain for his soul.

"Yes?" he said sharply.

The door opened. Two masked men stood in it, as they had stood once before. That time, the summons had been a summons to mercy. This time . . .

"Are you prepared to take the oath?" one of the masked men said.

"I am ready," Dr. Amos said.

"Follow us."

He picked up his hat, resting on a corner of the desk, and followed. As before, they lurked in the shadows while he saddled his mare in the livery stable. As before, he followed the masked men through the silent streets of sleeping Jamestown, moved up to join them when they struck the country road.

They rode silently, Dr. Amos flanked by the masked figures, and there was no conversation. The moon was shining brightly. About them the countryside was sleeping. Occasionally they passed a house, or a cluster of houses, near the road, and dogs would bark at them. Not a light showed, there was not even the lift of a curtain at a window. Those people in the houses knew that Night Riders must be abroad.

Just beyond such a settlement, the guides turned into a narrow lane leading to a schoolhouse. Dr. Amos knew the place; two-roomed, made of pine siding that had once been painted white, it gleamed with a ghostlike luminosity, picked up from the moon, among the darkness of the surrounding trees. The guides halted the horses and gave the three whistles. They were answered, went on, were challenged with the same password and response Dr. Amos had heard before.

A few men were clustered near the front door. One came forward to take the reins as the three men stepped down.

"Go right on in, Dr. Amos," one of the guides said. "They're waiting."

Dr. Amos, alone, mounted the three steps, worn by the countless feet of children, and opened the door. The room was dark; he knew he was silhouetted against the lighter darkness of outside.

"Advance to the center of the room," a voice said out of the blackness.

He moved forward. In the center of the the room, the children's desks, mounted single-file on long wooden runners, had been pushed aside in order to make a space. Masked men surrounded this open space. They moved aside in order that Dr. Amos might advance into the center of the group.

"Kneel down," the voice said sharply.

Dr. Amos took off his hat, holding it in his hand, and knelt in the center of the circle. His eyes were adjusting to the darkness. It did not help; there was nothing to see.

"Dr. Amos Haines, you have expressed a desire to join the secret organization of the Silent Brigade, known as the Night Riders. Do you still carry this desire in your heart?"

"Yes," Dr. Amos said.

"Do you understand the duties and the obligations you are taking upon yourself if you answer to this oath in this place on this night?"

"I think I do," Dr. Amos said.

"When you take the oath of the Silent Brigade, it is an oath you will carry until the day of your death," the voice said. "It is a vow committing your heart, your hand, and your mind to the Silent Brigade. You are swearing, upon your life, that you will never betray any member of this secret order. You are swearing, upon your life, that you will carry out any order given to you by any duly constituted officer of the Silent Brigade, whether or not you understand why that order is given. There are no exceptions to this obligation, even to the point of committing murder. Do you understand?"

"I understand," Dr. Amos said.

"We will now stand silent for five minutes while you consider your decision for the last time. Until that five minutes is over, you may arise from your knees, leave this room, and return to the man you once were. If you do not so arise and depart, you will become another man entirely—you will become a sworn member of the Silent Brigade."

The men about him fell silent. Dr. Amos, kneeling, began to feel the strain on his knees. The dusty floor seemed made of stone. He did not shift his weight, though the time seemed eternally endless. He did not reconsider the question of his affiliation, as he had been commanded to do. His mind was an empty space, as filled with eternity as the time. Not a thought moved within him, not a feeling. He merely waited forever, until the voice spoke once again.

"Dr. Amos Haines, repeat after me. I do solemnly swear, in the presence of God and these witnesses, that I desire to become a Night Rider."

"I do solemnly swear, in the presence of God and these witnesses, that I desire to become a Night Rider."

"That I will not write, talk or tell, to anyone, of the secrets of this order of the Silent Brigade, known as the Night Riders . . ."

"That I will not write, talk or tell, to anyone, of the secrets of this order of the Silent Brigade, known as the Night Riders . . ."

"That if I do write, talk or tell to any person any of the secrets of this order, they are permitted to do with me as they see fit . . ."

"That if I do write, talk or tell to any person any of the secrets of this order, they are permitted to do with me as they see fit . . ."

"For I know that death, hell and destruction will be my portion, and that my body will not be buried in a graveyard."

"For I know that death, hell and destruction will be my portion, and that my body will not be buried in a graveyard."

"I do willingly and freely submit to all this, so help me God."

"I do willingly and freely submit to all this, so help me God," Dr. Amos said.

"Rise from your knees, Dr. Amos Haines. A member of the Silent Brigade kneels before no man."

Dr. Amos rose. His knees were stiff and the circulation had stopped in his lower legs, so that he felt a tingle in his feet.

"Strike a light, goddamn it," a voice said. "I'm sweating like a pig inside this damned mask."

A match was struck, applied to a lantern. The light came startlingly into the room, making shadows where before there had been only darkness. The men were taking off their masks, moving toward Dr. Amos, surrounding him, their hands reaching for his hand.

"By God, I'm glad you come to the point," John Thomas said out of a sweaty, grinning face. He shook Dr. Amos' hand vigorously. "I was beginning to think you never would."

Dr. Amos felt unreal in this sudden illumination after the long darkness, at the sight of open, friendly faces emerging from behind the blankness of the masks.

He shook Walter Wingo's hand. "Why, Mr. Wingo, you're the one man I'm surprised to see here," he said.

Mr. Wingo chuckled. "No more surprised than I am. But, hell, the thing's working, Dr. Amos. I came to that conclusion a month ago."

"Were you in the Gurley raid?"

"Of course," Mr. Wingo said. "I put the torch to the first factory we burned that night."

John Thomas laughed. "Talk about a man sweating," he said. "He took a satchel with some dynamite in it to the factory. He got in a sort of a hurry to leave and forgot the satchel. It had his name written inside. Mr. Wingo was a mighty nervous man, I tell you, till he found out that the factory had burned all the way to the ground."

Dr. Amos shook the hand of the Association lawyer. The lawyer smiled.

"Surprised, Dr. Amos? I don't do any riding, but I'm a member right on. You'll find that a lot of people belong, even in the middle of Jamestown. Any Night Rider cases ever come to court, they'll come in handy for jury material."

Among the milling, smiling men, he saw all the members of the Board of Directors, except for two. He saw the face of Charlie Blake, who had been the first Negro to join the Association.

They crowded about, happy to welcome him. They told him how difficult it had been to maintain the secrecy against him, how they had talked about how to persuade him to join. The decision had been reached that he could not be persuaded, he would have to find his own path.

"We need you, Dr. Amos," they told him, one after the other. "We've felt the need of you all along."

Dr. Amos smiled and shook hands. A great sense of relief dwelt in his soul; he had taken the most difficult decision of his life. Now, for better or for worse, in spite of his own soul-deep resistance, it was made. He smiled and shook hands and felt himself among friends.

Yet, beneath the surface relief, the surface feeling of being among friends, he had to conceal that new man he had become in response to the demand of events. He did not know what the future would hold. For the moment, he did not care to look beyond this hour of unity and comradeship.

Chapter Nineteen

For months the woman had been talking loudly against the Night Riders. Her husband was afraid to make a plant bed because he had been warned by a note tied to his gatepost, so the woman singlehandedly made the plant bed and guarded it each night. She had made no secret of her contempt for the Silent Brigade. She was a loud-mouthed, high-headed woman, handsome in her wrath, with a feeling of inviolability in her femininity. She had been a school teacher, resigning under pressure the year before her marriage because of groundless talk about her moral character.

The Night Riders surrounded the house at midnight and called for her to come forth. The husband presented himself at the door in fear and trembling.

"We don't want you. We want her," the leader said.

"You'll have to settle for me," the timid husband said in a determined, shaky voice. "Helen Kate ain't coming out to you all."

"We gonna kill us a man or whup us a woman," the leader said, shouting the words. "Which you rather it be, Helen Kate? Have your tail whupped, or your man killed?"

Helen Kate pushed her husband out of the way. "I'm not afraid of you," she said disdainfully.

"Get in the house, Helen Kate," her husband said frantically. "Ain't no telling what . . ."

She stood high-headed in the doorway. Her hair was long, black. She wore a plain cotton house dress. Her feet were bare. She was a tall woman, with bold features.

"You put a man behind a mask, he's a man right on," she said. "You can't scare me. Any man who'll beat on a woman ain't no man, anyhow."

"We aim to shut your mouth, Helen Kate," the leader said. "Get in the house, Mr. Roberts, and shut that door."

"I ain't going," Mr. Roberts said.

The guns came up, leveled themselves.

"Get on in the house," Helen Kate said. She pushed her husband inside and closed the door. "What do you want with me?" she said to the group of masked men.

"Walk to yonder gatepost."

She stepped down into the yard, walked between the mounted men to the gatepost, stopped.

"Take off that flimsy dress."

She hesitated for a perceptible moment. Then, slowly, she leaned to catch the hem of the dress, stripped it over her head in one long slow reluctant movement. A sigh swept through the masked men at the sight of her body. A full moon floated serenely among white clouds in the sky, lighting the scene brightly.

"I'God, ain't she something!" a voice said.

The door of the house slammed open. "Helen Kate!" her husband yelled in a despairing voice.

A mounted man whirled, fired at the house. The bullet thunked within a foot of Mr. Roberts' head. He ducked inside.

"Walk," the leader said to Helen Kate.

Barefooted, naked in the moonlight, her head high, she walked ahead of the mounted men. In spite of herself, her body swayed with the walking and she could feel the hidden eyes of the masked men fixed upon her luminous flesh.

At the crossroads, she was halted. The men dismounted, leaving one to hold the horses.

"Form a double line," the leader said.

The men formed up, jostling for places. The leader stood beside Helen Kate, holding a quirt in his hand. "All right, Helen Kate," he said. "You just run down between them two rows of men, now. Run real slow."

She turned, her eyes flashing. "What kind of man are you?" she cried out in contempt.

He slashed her with the whip across the buttocks. She screamed, jumping with the pain, and began running the gantlet. The men lashed at her with their whips. She ran slowly, stumbling, almost bemused, her face hidden by the long black hair. The men flailed at her moonlit flesh with a strange tenderness, as though they were making love. When she reached the end, blood showed on her back.

She stumbled, falling into the crossroads dust. The men rushed to lay hands upon her. She rolled and twisted against their intimate handling, demanding her right to rise unaided. Eager to touch her, they insisted upon helping her to her feet.

She stood, swaying. "Are you through now?" she said.

"Form the double line again," the leader said. "She's still as sassy as a jaybird."

"Let's cut that long hair first," one of the men suggested. "Anybody got a sharp knife?"

Two men held her arms, holding her tenderly, gently, while another man hacked at her black hair with the long blade of a pocketknife. When he was finished, it stood only inches long, straying in ragged lengths. One of the men stooped to gather up a handful of the black hair and put it into his pocket.

She ran the gantlet again, more slowly this time, her breath gasping with each blow, her voice making tiny impacted screams. She paused at the end, wavering, and collapsed in upon herself, sinking down to the earth where she stood.

"Reckon she's had enough?" a masked voice said.

"One more time," the leader said. "Third time's charm. Maybe then she'll keep her mouth offen the Night Riders."

At the words, she staggered to her feet, began the tedious, interminable progress. She made it only halfway down the line before she collapsed once more. She fell forward, slowly, measuring her length against the earth.

"Turn her over," the leader said.

Hands rolled her in the dust. Her body, that had been luminous in the moonlight, was stained by dust and blood and sweat. They had made her ugly by extracting the lovely femininity from her flesh.

"Bring her out of it," the leader said.

They slapped her face, turning her head from side to side. She was weeping, the tears streaking the dust on her face.

"Kill me," she said in a voice that was proud Helen Kate's voice no longer. "Do . . . do anything to me. Just don't whip me. I can't stand being whipped no more."

The leader stood over her. "I reckon she knows now," he said. "Helen Kate!" She did not respond. He raised his voice. "Helen Kate! Do you hear me?"

She lifted her head.

"You gonna lay the weight of your tongue agin the Night Riders one more time?"

"No," she said, her voice moaning, her head turning from side to side in a frenzy of hurt. "No. No."

"I reckon she's had her lesson," the leader said. "Let's get out of here."

They mounted and rode away, leaving her lying in the dust of the crossroads. The moon sailed serenely among the high white clouds. Its luminous light was no longer kind to her body as she got to her feet and staggered toward home.

It was later, nearing daylight, when the body of men encircled another house.

"Come on out, nigger," the leader's voice called.

There was silence, stillness. The leader called again, without response. He made a gesture and a single bullet thudded into the house. The door opened.

"Why, Mister Night Rider, what you want around here?" Charlie Blake said.

"We want you."

Charlie Blake stood on the edge of the porch, shivering with fear, with before-dawn chill. He wore only a pair of jeans britches, slipped on hastily to answer the call.

"I been in the Association right along," he said. "Why, I was the first nigger in this county to put my name down."

"You figure you're might' nigh good as a white man, belonging to the Association, don't you?" a voice said. "You're getting to be a mighty uppity nigger. It's time you got showed your place."

"Ain't nobody holding nothing against me," Charlie said with dignity. "I'm a good Association member. You just ask Dr. Amos. Why, Dr. Amos was the very one signed me up . . ."

Two men dismounted, went up the steps. One of them pushed him off the porch. Charlie fell down the steps, landing on his hands and knees in the yard. They jerked him up, handling him roughly, and dragged him to a tree in the yard. They tied his hands around the tree.

He twisted his head over his shoulder, his eyes white with fear. "I have been there," he said. "On my bended knees."

"Listen to him. He's even been allowed to take the oath."

They had thorn bushes for the whipping. The thorns pierced and mangled his flesh with each blow, Charlie saying each time they paused, until he could say it no longer, "But I belong to the Association. You ask Dr. Amos. And I have been there, on my bended knees . . ."

They rode away, leaving him unconscious from the brutal whipping, the shattered thorn bushes lying against the base of the tree. A bird began to sing lustily in the predawn light.

Charlie lay on his stomach on the bed while Dr. Amos snipped away ragged edges of skin and cleaned the inflamed flesh. Charlie grunted with the pain. His words hurt Dr. Amos more than Dr. Amos was hurting Charlie with his ministering.

"Why did they want to come after me?" Charlie kept saying. "Just tell me why, Dr. Amos. I ain't done nothing out of the way. You know that. Why did they want to come after me?"

"Charlie," Dr. Amos said at last. "All I can figure, somebody had a grudge against you. Maybe because you got a black skin, no other reason. But, Charlie, those weren't Night Riders. Not true Night Riders, anyway."

Charlie grunted with the pain. "How's a man going to separate the true Night Riders from the other kind?" he said. "One mask is like unto another, Dr. Amos. True or not, they took to me with them thorn bushes."

"I know, Charlie," Dr. Amos said, not showing his anger. "I know."

"If they don't make no difference between friend and enemy, what's a man gonna do?" Charlie said. "You know I was the first black man made his signature in the Association. You know that, Dr. Amos. You know I taken the oath of the Silent Brigade."

"Yes, Charlie, I know."

"I'll tell you this, too," Charlie said. "They knew the secret words. They recognized the secret words when I used them."

"I'll find out who did it," Dr Amos promised out of his anger.

He was not called to the bedside of Helen Kate Roberts. But he heard about it. Jamestown was indignant with the news when he returned from treating Charlie, though a deep vein of gleeful speculation underran the indignation, for Helen Kate Roberts did not enjoy a good reputation.

"Wonder what else them Night Riders done to her?" Dr. Amos heard a man say in a sniggering voice.

"Hell, they couldn't force her," another man said. "Can't force a high-headed woman like that."

"Whupped her buck-naked in the high road," one man told another with horrified satisfaction. "Them night-riding folks do have their fun, don't they?"

The eyes watched Dr. Amos passing through the street, the faces wondering almost openly if Dr. Amos had looked upon the proud woman's flesh in the moonlight.

The following night, in the schoolhouse where he had taken the oath, there was a meeting.

"I want to know something," Dr. Amos said. "Who ordered Mrs. Roberts and Charlie Blake to be whipped?"

"You heard about that, did you?" Mr. Wingo said. "That's all I've heard talk of today myself."

"I don't know that anybody ordered it," John Thomas said. "Any of you fellers in on it?"

There was a general denial.

"Maybe somebody come in from the next county," Mr. Thomas said indifferently. "Maybe it was Hillbillies, trying to make us look bad. Who knows?"

"Charlie Blake is a good Association man," Dr. Amos said stiffly. "A member of the Silent Brigade, though he hasn't done any riding."

"He's a nigger, ain't he?" a man said. "Sometimes you got to lay it on a nigger just on general principles. If he ain't doing something, he's thinking about it."

Several of the men laughed. Dr. Amos' temper flared. It felt good to let himself go. He had never allowed himself a full flow of anger, as other men so often did. He stood up, recklessly sure of himself. He stared around at the men.

"So now we start night-riding against our own," he said in a tight voice.

"Hell, Dr. Amos, these mistakes are bound to happen sometimes," John Thomas said. "It takes hot-blooded folks to make Night Riders in the first place. Sometimes they're just bound to get out of hand."

Dr. Amos fixed his gaze on John Thomas. "You don't care whether it was true Night Riders, or somebody who wants to give us a bad name," he said. "It really makes no difference to you, does it?"

"I was thinking something ought to be done about Helen Kate," John Thomas said. "They just beat us to it, that's all. I don't reckon I'd've stripped her buck-naked to do it. But maybe it taken that to put the fear of God into her."

"And what about Charlie?" Dr. Amos said. "He told me they recognized the secret words."

"If it was our men, it was a mistake," Mr. Thomas said.

Dr. Amos tightened his lips. "If it was a mistake, it'll be the last one in the Silent Brigade, if I have anything to say about it," he said. "The organization of the Night Riders is too loose, Mr. Thomas. That's why it was a mob scene, when you raided Gurley, where it should have been a military operation."

John Thomas, alert now, lifted his head to look at Dr. Amos.

"It's hard to control the kind of folks who are willing to do this kind of job," Mr. Wingo said gravely. "We admit the problem, Dr. Amos. We haven't been able to solve it."

Dr. Amos kept looking at John Thomas. "The solution is military discipline," he said. "Every man must be totally responsible to a man over him, that man to a man over him, that man to the leader. Not a move must be made without orders. Offenders must be severely punished. Then we'll *know* what our men are up to."

"I suppose you know all about how to set up that kind of military organization," Mr. Thomas said.

"Yes," Dr. Amos said. "In fact, I demand that I be given the authority to begin its establishment immediately."

"We are not a parliamentary organization," John Thomas drawled. "I'll think about it. I'll let you know. After all, Dr. Amos, you're just about our newest member."

"I've been a member long enough to see what's needed," Dr. Amos snapped. "I've been on raids, as you know. I've seen how haphazard it all is."

"You ought to listen to Dr. Amos, Mr. Thomas," Mr. Wingo said. "You said all along you wanted him in the Silent Brigade. Now that's he's in, listen to him."

John Thomas wheeled on this new attack. "In a secret organization, there's room for only one leader," he said. "I am that leader, Mr. Wingo. I make the decisions."

"I agree with you about that," Dr. Amos said quietly. "There is room for only one leader."

"That doesn't mean you can't listen to good advice," Mr. Wingo said. "Or does it?"

Mr. Thomas paused, baffled. Mr. Wingo turned to Dr. Amos. "What have you got in mind, Dr. Amos?"

Dr. Amos, feeling a sense of triumph, sketched out the plan he had formed before the meeting. He had schemed for this moment; he had used his own anger to shape these men in the direction he wanted to go.

For so long, now, he had been the reasonable man; reluctant, hesitant, anxious to see all sides, to be sure of justice and honor and understanding. It was good to push ahead recklessly, erecting his willfulness against the willfulness of other men and sustaining it until they did as he wanted.

John Thomas, as Dr. Amos was well aware, sensed the change in Dr. Amos far more keenly than the others. He was wary, keyed to resist. As he talked, Dr. Amos, with shrewd calculation, ignored John Thomas, focusing the weight of his argument upon the others.

When he was finished, Mr. Wingo said, "Why, that seems like just what we need, Mr. Thomas."

The other men nodded in agreement. Mr. Thomas, trapped, stared about him.

"I'm the leader," he said, coming to his feet. "I started the Night Riders in the first place, while some people we know were still dragging back, preaching law and order." He glared at Dr. Amos. "I want to know who's the leader around here?"

"You are, Mr. Thomas," Dr. Amos said softly. "I'm just making suggestions. I'm willing to carry out the plan under your direction."

"There's nothing more reasonable than that," Mr. Meacham said. "What are you getting your bowels in an uproar about, Mr. Thomas?"

Dr. Amos watched John Thomas, knowing exactly what was going through his mind. He waited to see whether Mr. Thomas would make his stand here, on this issue.

There was a tense moment. Then John Thomas said, "All right. As long as it's clearly understood that I am the man who issues the orders."

"Why, we wouldn't think of doing it any other way, Mr.

Thomas," Dr. Amos said soothingly. Secretly, he was elated. For the first time he had put John Thomas on the run. It would not be the last.

The imposition of a military structure upon the Night Riders gave Dr. Amos an opportunity to become intimately acquainted with most of the membership. He visited group after group to inform them of the new plan, he even traveled to distant counties in order to establish the same organization, each with its district colonel.

The Night Riders took eagerly to Dr. Amos' plan. The basic unit was eight men, a lieutenant and seven privates. Each group was a cell unto itself, knowing only its own members. The lieutenant reported to a captain of five groups, receiving his orders only from him. The captain of each five groups reported to the colonel commanding the district, receiving orders only from him. The colonels reported to John Thomas, the supreme commander.

A raiding squad would be made up of a number of groups, brought together as convenience and necessity dictated, with one of the lieutenants chosen as captain for the squad. If the raid required five groups or more, it was led by a group captain or by the district colonel, depending on its importance.

An auxiliary organization, consisting of those men belonging to the Silent Brigade who were not expected to take part in Night Rider activities, was set up. These were the judges, the lawyers, the merchants and lawmen, who were in sympathy with the Night Riders. They were organized on a military footing also, though their duties were of a less definite nature.

In secret meeting after secret meeting, Dr. Amos, pursuing his private purpose, electioneered as shamelessly as if he were running for public office. He saw how the men's faces brightened when they realized that Dr. Amos Haines was one of them, and high enough in authority to be sent on this mission. He was taking upon his shoulders, so far as the members were concerned, the weight of the whole organization. It was he who settled the disputes that inevitably arose as the major problem of the new military structure. It was he who ruthlessly settled these disputes by setting down men who had been mistakenly elevated. Often it had not been a mistake at all, only a feeling in Dr. Amos that the man he chose to demote was a particular adherent of John Thomas.

Nor did he allow himself the easy comfort of auxiliary membership; he saddled a horse and rode forth with the others, his face masked. He looked upon men's welted backs, he watched their terrified faces in the light of their burning barns, he heard the screams of the women as their men were led out into the darkness. He would deny himself no participation, he would withhold himself from nothing. Only in this way could he sustain and justify himself in his larger plan. He had committed himself to the task of taking control of this evil of the night. He could not hope to keep his hands clean in doing so . . . no more than a doctor of medicine can keep the blood, the juices, of suffering human flesh from staining his own flesh.

There came a night when Dr. Amos Haines rose to his feet during another meeting of the leaders of the Night Riders.

"I have bad news," he said calmly. "There is a traitor in our midst."

Their faces stared blankly toward him. He knew these were dread words; he had chosen them deliberately for their shock effect, with no attempt to minimize their bluntness.

"What . . . what do you mean?" John Thomas said in a blustering voice.

"You mean to tell me you don't know what's going on?" Dr. Amos said. "I thought you were the Supreme Commander."

"I am," Mr. Thomas said belligerently. "What are you talking about . . ."

"I'm talking about that affair of Helen Kate Roberts," Dr. Amos said. "I have been conducting a quiet investigation, in the midst of my other activities, trying to find out who whipped Helen Kate Roberts and Charlie Blake."

"I told you. I think it was done by outsiders," Mr. Thomas said.

"It was. All except one. One of them was a true Night Rider."

Mr. Wingo shifted in his chair. "What are you driving at, Dr. Amos?"

Dr. Amos turned his attention to Mr. Wingo, leaving John Thomas alone for the moment.

"That raid, as nearly as I can find out, was organized and carried out by Roscoe Barnes," he said. "It was done by a bunch of toughs he had recruited for the purpose of impersonating Night Riders. Except for one man. I learned that Roscoe Barnes had quietly spread the word that he would pay five thousand dollars to any Night Rider who would reveal his identity. Several men told me they had been discreetly approached. One man took the offer."

He paused. The group was silent. These words struck fear to their hearts. Their strength lay in secrecy and silence. If their secrecy were betrayed, their silence ruptured . . .

"He gave Roscoe Barnes all he needed to know to have his men act and talk like authentic Night Riders," Dr. Amos continued.

"We'll read him out of the Silent Brigade," Mr. Thomas said. "We'll put a scotch to him, all right. If necessary, we will publish his name far and wide as a traitor. That'll take care of *him!*"

"I'm afraid the raid itself is not the end of it," Dr. Amos said gravely. "I was informed just this morning that Mrs. Roberts has decided that she recognized faces and voices. She named this man, this traitor. She also named you, Mr. Wingo, and me, and Mr. Meacham. Lewis Carnett is on the list, as well as several others. Today they arrested the traitor. He will be the star witness. He will confess his guilt and he will name the names that Roscoe Barnes wants named."

"My God," Mr. Wingo said softly. "How much can you buy for five thousand dollars? Who is this man?"

Dr. Amos shifted his eyes to John Thomas. He named the man, saw John Thomas' head jerk. The others simultaneously turned their heads to look at John Thomas. Dr. Amos had named a close friend of John Thomas', who lived only two miles from John Thomas' house, who had been one of the earliest

Night Rider recruits, though he had never taken a high place in the secret order.

"You will note that John Thomas was not accused," Dr. Amos said softly.

"Now, wait a minute!" John Thomas said.

"I'm not doubting you, Mr. Thomas," Dr. Amos said. "I don't think you're a traitor. But what are you going to do about your friend who is?"

"Roscoe Barnes won't be able to make it stick," Mr. Thomas said. "Every man that's indicted will have a parade of witnesses to prove they were elsewhere at the time. We'll flood the stand with witnesses." His voice rose. "Why, they won't even be having to lie."

"If we wait until this thing comes to an open trial, it'll be too late to save the Silent Brigade," Dr. Amos said calmly. "The traitor must be executed."

They stopped. John Thomas' mouth was open to speak more words. For a moment he forgot to close it. He stared at Dr Amos as the other men were staring. The room was deathly still.

"We've . . . we've never killed anybody," John Thomas said. "We've never had to go that far."

Dr. Amos' voice mocked him. "Where's all your anger, Mr. Thomas? Where's all that raw daring? You are our Supreme Commander, Mr. Thomas. Give the order for this man to be put to death."

Mr. Thomas' face was as white as paper as he fought to recover himself. Instinctively, he knew that he must oppose this new side of Dr. Haines. He sensed a danger that he did not yet understand. He had always been able to batter down Dr. Haines' appeals to reason and moderation. But this . . . this . . .

"There ought to be some other way," he said, muttering the words rapidly, feeling around in his mind for firm ground on which to stand. "We never planned to go as far as murder . . ."

"Remember the oath of The Silent Brigade?" Dr. Amos said relentlessly. *"That if I do write, talk or tell to any person any of the secrets of this order, they are permitted to do with me as they see fit, for I know that death, hell and destruction will be my portion, and that my body will not be buried in a graveyard."*

He waited a long moment. No one spoke. Mr. Thomas' fires had been put out; he was again the little man he had been, stripped of his aggressiveness and his authority.

"I will see to it that the execution is carried out," Dr. Amos said in a quiet voice. "I have had men dogging his footsteps. He has been allowed to go home, for they believe no one knows about his traitor's deed. We will take him tonight."

He waited again. He could read the mixture of emotions on their faces. Fear; pleasure that someone else would do something; fascination at his willingness to shoulder the task.

"Mr. Thomas," Dr. Amos said. "You are the Supreme Commander. Do you have different orders for me?"

"No . . . no," John Thomas said, his voice stuttering. "No . . ."

Dr. Amos smiled at him. He knew what he had done. John Thomas knew what he had done. For this reason Dr. Amos smiled, before turning on his heel to leave the meeting.

Late that night, the silent band of Night Riders surrounded the traitor's house. The defector knew he could not find salvation in submission. They had to enter his home and pull him from beneath his bed, where he had hidden during the small gun battle between the Night Riders and the deputy sheriffs assigned to guard him.

They mounted the man on a horse and took him away. Dr. Amos led the squad deep into the foothills, to a cliff potholed by deep caves.

"Stand him against a tree," he ordered.

The man was tied to a tree. He sagged in the ropes, half dead with fear. Dr. Amos took five bullets from his pocket.

"I will load the rifles," he said.

He took the five rifles in turn, one by one inserting the bullets. He himself did not know which bullet was a dummy, which four were real.

"Every man shoot for the heart," he said.

He lined up the firing squad. He sat his horse, tall in the darkness, while the others watched. There was only silence; no talking, scarcely any breathing except that of the horses, the clink of saddle gear, the creak of leather.

"Fire," he said.

They fired.

The body was dumped into one of the numerous potholes that went untold depths into the cliff. There was no conversation on the long ride home.

Dr. Amos rode in the van. Though waves of depression battered at his new center of being, he could not allow it to show. Nor could he allow it to conquer. He was not a doctor any longer; his given task was far greater. He focused his mind upon John Thomas. He must pull down John Thomas, as surely as he had pulled down the traitor, and elevate himself in his place. The execution, though serving its own vital purpose of protecting the Silent Brigade, had deliberately served Dr. Amos' purpose also. The men of the execution squad followed behind his erect figure; not one ventured to speak to him during the long ride.

He was greatly weary when he stepped down from the horse and surrendered the reins. A figure came toward him in the darkness.

"The meeting of the leaders is waiting for you," he was told.

Dr. Amos nodded and walked toward his own mare saddled and waiting. He rode away from the hidden camp toward the meeting place, in a church house ten miles from Jamestown. He entered the church and stood before the leaders.

Their waiting faces were lifted toward him.

"It is done," Dr. Amos said.

John Thomas cleared his throat. "Good," he said. "Good. We have other business to tend to, of greater importance." John Thomas paused. "I have decided that we must now move against the very center of Trust power. I am going to order a raid on Jamestown."

Dr. Amos had anticipated that John Thomas would make a major effort to reassert his dominance. Dr. Amos was tired. But, listening to Mr. Thomas, he knew he must muster up his forces. The long night had not yet ended.

"Why do you feel such a move is necessary at this time?" he asked.

"We need to show Roscoe Barnes and the Trust they can't count themselves safe in their own stronghold," John Thomas said. He bared his teeth in a grin. The mildness of Dr. Amos' reaction had emboldened him and he was quite his old self. "We'll pay Mr. Barnes a little visit while we're in town. After the . . . execution . . . it ought to scare the pants off of him."

"You'll be risking the loss of sympathizers," Dr. Amos said. "Especially if you conduct a wild raid like the one on Gurley. The governors of Tennessee and Kentucky have never really moved against us. A raid on Jamestown might force them to do so."

John Thomas became surer of himself. He had heard this tone of reasonableness from Dr. Amos before. It had never stopped him.

His voice sharpened. "I want to remind you, Dr. Amos, that the Silent Brigade is not a parliamentary organization." His voice became shrewder. "I suppose you want to wait until the Department of Justice decides what they're going to do."

Dr. Amos took a deep breath. The time had come. There could be no better time. He had just returned from the sternest mission any Night Rider could be expected to perform; the aura of his deed hung still about him.

"No," he said. "I agree with you. It may well be necessary to raid Jamestown. But why now, at this particular time? Why did you decide *tonight* to order the raid?"

John Thomas rose to his feet. The two men faced each other in the dim light of the lantern.

"Because I have decided," John Thomas said in his heavy, driving voice. "Because *I* am giving the order."

Dr. Amos was no longer aware of the other men in the room.

He faced John Thomas, as John Thomas faced him. He did not try to match John Thomas' voice in fire and drive. He did not need to; the words alone carried the burden.

"No," he said. "The Jamestown raid will take place when I decide it should. I say the time is not yet."

"What do you mean?" John Thomas said, his voice crying out in astonishment. "You're forgetting something, Dr. Amos. I am the Supreme Commander. I give the orders around here."

"You gave the orders until tonight. You do so no longer."

"Now wait a minute . . ."

Dr. Amos drove on. "You surrendered command, Mr. Thomas, when you refused to take the responsibility of ordering me to kill that traitor. I gave that command. From now on, I will give all the commands."

"Now wait a minute," John Thomas said, the words rapid in his mouth.

Dr. Amos waited until John Thomas had run down. He was, most surprising to himself, finding a certain exhilaration in the battle of wills. For the first time in his life, without fear or guilt, he was unleashing his whole self. He had always disliked John Thomas; now, as he lashed him with his tongue, throwing in John Thomas' face the fact of a willful ambition as bold and ruthless as his own, Dr. Amos felt like laughing out loud. He was tired no longer; his body, his mind, surged with a youthful energy he had not known for years.

Coldbloodedly he waited until it was amply demonstrated that John Thomas had no real answer to his challenge. Though ignoring the listeners, Dr. Amos knew they were important. He gave them a quick glance to see how they were taking it. They sat quietly, looking almost embarrassed.

The silence had lengthened. Dr. Amos took a step forward.

"Mr. Thomas, if you insist on ordering the raid on Jamestown, I will carry the issue of leadership to the rank and file. I will ask that you be taken down and that I be elevated in your place."

"But you can't do that!"

"The hell I can't! I'll tell you the fact of the matter, Mr.

Thomas. I'm tired of watching you strut around like a little Caesar. You're about as equipped to give orders as a blind mule. Now, if you think you can win against me, you're welcome to try. In fact, I wish you would."

John Thomas had flushed a deep red. His eyes were white-balled in their sockets. There was a sound in the room; Dr. Amos realized it was John Thomas' breathing.

John Thomas was in a murderous rage. The doctor in Dr. Amos, watching, was fearful of apoplexy; the man in Dr. Amos realized, with a thrill of wariness in the back of his neck, that John Thomas was on the edge of physical assault.

John Thomas moved one step toward Dr. Amos, two steps. His hands were curled, not into fists, but into a throttling hold. Dr. Amos braced himself.

John Thomas' voice was strangled in his throat. Hoarsely he said, "I'll kill you. I'll . . ."

His hands began reaching. In the same instant, Mr. Wingo loomed beside Mr. Thomas, a heavy hand on his shoulder.

"If you touch Dr. Haines, I'll shoot you where you stand," he said. "Sit down, Mr. Thomas."

Mr. Thomas sat down. He looked about him, his tongue running over his dry lips. The murderous anger had left him as quickly as it had come. This stern opposition from another quarter had unnerved him.

"What's going on around here, anyway?" he said.

"If you will agree to take orders, Mr. Thomas, this . . . discussion . . . tonight need not go beyond the four walls of this room," Dr. Amos said. "If you want the trappings of power, you're welcome to them. As far as the rank and file are concerned, you will still be the Supreme Commander. I have no desire for titles."

Jerkily, John Thomas looked about him at the other men. He found no comfort there. He looked at his hands lying in his lap.

"Well, of course, you know I'm always ready to listen to advice," he said. He lifted one hand, wiped the palm across his dry mouth. "You can depend on it, Dr. Amos. I'll always be ready to listen to you, at any time."

It should have been enough. Dr. Amos had gained all that he had determined to gain when he had made the decision to join the Night Riders. The Silent Brigade had become his instrument, to wield as he saw fit. It had resulted exactly as he had planned, including the temptation to John Thomas to retain the semblance of command by giving up its substance.

It was not enough. Dr. Amos stared down at the broken little man, knowing the appetite, not just for total dominance, but for its open acknowledgement.

"It's not advice I'll be giving you," he said. "It will be orders. I want you to understand that clearly. *Do* you understand it?"

There was a final resistance within John Thomas. He had not expected to suffer this ultimate humiliation. He bounced to his feet under the stress of the struggle.

"What do you want?" he cried out against Dr. Amos. "You want me to crawl and lick your boots? Will that satisfy you?"

"I want your clear understanding," Dr. Amos said coldly.

John Thomas collapsed. "All right," he said. "All right. You give the orders." He looked pleadingly at Dr. Amos. "But remember . . . you promised it wouldn't go beyond these four walls. You promised that nobody else . . ."

Dr. Amos turned away from him. "I'll keep my promise," he said in a voice that did not even trouble to show his contempt. "You don't have to be afraid of that."

"Now that you've settled that, what about the raid on Jamestown?" Mr. Wingo asked Dr. Amos.

There was a deeper respect in Mr. Wingo, this man who had always liked and respected Dr. Amos Haines. Dr. Amos surveyed the other leaders, saw the respect in their eyes, knew they were glad he had taken the reins of power from John Thomas' hands.

"The Jamestown raid?" he said. "Maybe the time will have to come. But not yet."

Dr. Amos rode his mare toward town. The weariness of the long night had come back upon him. But within the core of tiredness he had found a remarkable contentment and within the contentment lay the strength to banish the old feelings of guilt he had always known.

The truth was, in these days a new man had been born. Behind him were all the old needs and hungers and guilts that had gnawed at him. He had exercised the power of his will over other men and had found that power good. Within it was unleashed the angers and the disappointments—yes, even the evil—he had never found a way to harness before. The knowledge of command, of ultimate responsibility, rode lightly within him—even the responsibility he had taken tonight of ordering a man killed.

It was just daylight. The air was cold, for it was getting toward winter. Soon frost would grip the land, so that even Night Riders would no longer be abroad. The winds would sweep down out of the north, freezing the earth, killing the lush growth of the year, fastening an iron grip that would yield eventually to the insidious warmth of spring.

As he neared the livery stable, a train chuffed its way slowly across the street. It stopped with the Pullman cars before the station. One or two men came out of the station and boarded the train, four or five got off. The train pulled out of the station. Dr. Amos was sitting his horse, waiting for the train to clear the street.

The train, instead of departing on its run, began to back. Dr. Amos lingered, his curiosity aroused. The train backed onto the spur, uncoupled the last car on the siding fifty yards beyond the depot, and departed. Dr. Amos stared at the car that had been left behind. It was a long Pullman, black, its green curtains drawn; unmarked except by a discreet numeral near the rear steps. There was not even a railroad name to distinguish it.

While he watched, a man in a white jacket emerged and shook a table cloth over the railing. Idly, without curiosity, he looked at Dr. Amos sitting his mare. The man vanished inside and Dr. Amos went on to the livery stable.

Inside the station, the night telegraph operator finished his stint of messages in connection with the arrival of the train. He came out into the waiting room to put fresh coal into the potbellied stove against the chill of the morning.

He was a tall, lean man, with a nightside face. He wore a green eyeshade, pushed up above his hairline now, and a white shirt with sateen sleeve protectors. Against the chill he had retained the vest to his suit when he had removed his coat.

"You see that car the train dropped here?" he said to the two or three men sitting around the stove. "That's a private railroad car. Don't see many of them in this part of the country."

"You mean some feller got his own private car so he can just hitch on behind a train?"

"All them bigshots got 'em," the telegrapher said scornfully. "Carnegie, Vanderbilt, Astor . . ." He leaned forward. "You want to know who that one belongs to, setting right yonder?"

One of the men yawned. "I reckon you gonna tell us," he said.

"Well now, I don't know about that," the telegrapher said, walking toward the ticket office.

"Come on, Jake," the man pleaded quickly. "I didn't mean I wasn't interested."

The telegraph operator returned closer, leaned forward. "That's old O.K. Knox's very own private car," he said. "I got the word on the wire he was hitched onto the morning train."

"I'll be damned," one of the men breathed. "I'll be double-dog-damned."

He walked to a window, stared out at the blank sides of the railroad car. The other men followed, staring over his shoulder.

"He's in there right now," the telegrapher breathed. "Sound asleep and dreaming of money, more than likely."

"I wonder what he wants in Jamestown?" someone said.

"I reckon them Night Riders and that Tobacco Association gonna get their dues," another said. "Old O.K. Knox has done come to take care of his little Black Patch problem."

The blank-windowed, black-sided car waited on the siding. Dr. Amos, in his rooms behind the office, yielded himself to a sound and dreamless sleep.

Chapter Twenty

THE black railroad car was a presence on the edge of the town. It brooded in the cheerful sunlight, couched discreetly on its siding, the heavy window curtains drawn, showing no signs of life except for the occasional appearance of the white-jacketed man on the rear platform. Once he descended to inquire of the stationmaster where he could order ice. Occasionally he lounged in an angle of the wrought-iron railing to smoke a cigarette, gazing indifferently down upon the steady stream of townsfolk who made it their business to walk idly along the street, their faces turned toward the mysterious car. No man could even claim a glimpse of O.K. Knox himself.

In the middle of the morning, Roscoe Barnes paced importantly down the street and walked up the siding. Watched avidly by the loitering passersby, he disappeared behind the mysterious door.

Inside the car, he advanced toward Oren Knox, holding out his hand. "Why, Mr. Knox, welcome to Jamestown," he said. "The minute I heard you were here, I asked the sheriff to send one of his deputies."

Oren Knox ignored the outstretched hand. "Why did you do that?"

Roscoe laughed uncertainly. "Well, I don't think for a minute you're in any danger of having a call paid on you by the Night Riders. They've got better sense than that. It was just . . ."

"I was urged to bring a guard of Pinkerton men when I announced my decision to come here," Oren Knox said calmly. "I didn't think they were needed. I won't need your deputy sheriff, either."

"He will keep curiosity-seekers at a distance, anyway," Roscoe said. "Haven't you seen the crowd out there on the street?"

"All right," Oren said indifferently. "Post your deputy sheriff."

Mr. Barnes nodded importantly. "I would advise it," he said. "I know local conditions. I can advise you on the local people, too. Anything you want to know . . ."

"I want to know just one thing," Oren Knox said. "What are you doing to carry out your orders?"

Roscoe tried to laugh. "Didn't you read my daily reports?" he said. "Of course, there were certain things I didn't think it was wise to put on paper . . ." His voice ran down. He was beginning to sweat. Fumbling for his handkerchief, he said, "I sure was surprised to hear that you were here, Mr. Knox. I remember you said you didn't want to come to Jamestown unless you had to, so it didn't cross my mind . . ."

"I kept thinking about our conversation, Mr. Barnes," Oren said coldly. "The more I thought about it, the more I knew I had to come." He fixed Roscoe Barnes with his cold blue eyes. "The United States Government, Mr. Barnes, is snooping around the edges of our operations all over this country. It's been going on for some time, but we've just learned about it. My director for retail sales turned up a Department of Justice man working for him."

"I told you these Black Patch people were going to the government," Mr. Barnes said. "I reported that a long time ago."

"We knew that. But nothing happened. Whatever the Department of Justice was up to, they kept well covered."

Roscoe Barnes was gratified to be discussing such high-level matters with O.K. Knox. "Do you think they can do us any harm, sir?" he said.

"They can't touch us," Oren said. "That anti-trust law is unconstitutional, my best lawyers tell me. But they can cause us a lot of trouble and a lot of expense. I keep thinking that that trouble and expense has originated here, Mr. Barnes, where you were supposed to keep matters under control. Now tell me those things you didn't think it wise to put on paper."

Mr. Barnes was sweating again. "Well, things were going good, Mr. Knox. I found a Night Rider willing to talk for money. That woman I told you about, and a nigger, got whipped. The woman decided she recognized some of the leaders of the Night Riders. The Night Rider who came over to our side was ready to confess his own part, and implicate the others. It would have busted the Night Riders wide open, Mr. Knox. Wide open."

"*Would* have?" Oren said, picking up the revealing construction of the sentence. "What happened, Mr. Barnes?"

Mr. Barnes wiped his face with the handkerchief. "It's hot in this car," he said apologetically. "Well, I'll tell you, Mr. Knox. It was a terrible disappointment to us. Terrible. Not only that—it's going to make it harder to find another Night Rider willing to take our money and turn . . ."

"What happened, Mr. Barnes?"

Mr. Barnes looked away. "A band of Night Riders came and took him last night," he said. "Nobody knows for sure what happened." He looked at Mr. Knox, then, because he couldn't help himself. "I reckon he's dead by now. They'd kill him for sure, once they had their hands on him."

"So you have failed," Oren said in his most remote voice. "Our best chance to put a quick stop to the anti-trust investigation lay in completely discrediting the men who got it started." He stared unblinkingly at Roscoe Barnes. "The more I thought about you, the better I knew you would fail. I just hoped I'd get here in time. Why didn't you surround your witness with protection? I would have sent you Pinkerton men . . ."

"He was guarded by three deputy sheriffs," Roscoe said.

"They shot their way in, Mr. Knox. One of the deputies was wounded in the arm . . ."

"Mr. Barnes," Oren Knox said. "You are fired."

Mr. Barnes opened his mouth. "I . . ." he said.

"Good day, Mr. Barnes. You no longer work for Allied Tobacco."

"But . . . local conditions. I know the people you can trust, I . . ."

"I don't need to know about local conditions. I came for two purposes. The first purpose is now accomplished."

"But the other one. I can . . ."

"Good day, Mr. Barnes."

Mr. Barnes, flustered, unable to protest further, walked to the door. He paused to look back, hopefully, but Oren Knox had already resumed his seat to study a thick sheaf of papers.

When Roscoe Barnes emerged from the railroad car, jauntiness was an effort. He stood on the rear platform for a moment, wiping his face. Then, slowly, he descended and crunched through the ballast of the roadbed to the street.

"Did ya see old O.K. Knox his own self?" someone asked eagerly.

Roscoe Barnes did not satisfy the curiosity. Tight-lipped, he went on. Half an hour after his departure a deputy sheriff stationed himself beside the car. He stood for a time, shifting from foot to foot. At last he emboldened himself to sit on the bottom step.

Jamestown was bemused by the presence. O.K. Knox was the sole topic of conversation, displacing the previous concern about an imminent Night Rider raid upon Jamestown that had been the principal topic ever since the episode at Gurley. Even the disappearance and presumable murder of a man reputed to be an apostate Night Rider did not overshadow Oren Knox's presence, simply because few people knew about it. The Sheriff's Office had decided to keep their connection with the affair as quiet as possible, leaving it as one of those mysterious disappearances not too uncommon in these turbulent years. The other men who had vanished had almost invariably turned up alive and well in other states after a time, having fled danger rather than succumbed to it.

At one time or another during the day, every adult individual physically able to do so, and most of the juvenile population as well, took occasion to walk along the street beside the railroad station. The young men had set up a loitering station at one end of the depot platform, abandoning their usual haunts for this more interesting spectacle.

No one approached the car. A sacrosanct distance was maintained; not for fear of the deputy but because of the hidden presence within the car. There was only one violation of this respectful distance; a twelve-year-old boy, double-dog-dared by his contemporaries, crept timorously up the siding, moving inch by inch as though at any moment he might be discovered and destroyed, though he moved in broad daylight with at least a hundred people watching. At last, on hands and knees, he crouched alongside the car. Rising slowly, he reached up to touch the sides of the car with both hands.

The deputy sheriff on guard did not move, did not speak warningly. Nevertheless the boy whirled in a sudden panic and pelted scrambling toward the street. He had not taken more than a dozen steps before he tripped over his own haste and fell sprawling in the ballast. He recovered himself, the heels of his hands and his knees bruised, and scampered into safety. He was a hero for the day; grown men patted his shoulders and gave him dimes for a refreshing treat; but no one attempted to emulate his example.

Dr. Amos learned about the presence of Oren Knox soon after awakening, from Walter Wingo and John Thomas, who had come to tell him the news. Dr. Amos told about having seen the car being uncoupled from the early morning train, though he had not realized its significance.

"I wonder what O.K. Knox wants to come to Jamestown for?" Mr. Wingo said in a fretful voice.

"I doubt if anyone knows that but Knox himself," Dr. Amos said. "But I imagine he has in mind doing something about the situation here."

"Dr. Amos, can I make a suggestion?" John Thomas said.

Dr. Amos glanced at him. John Thomas was quite a different man this morning. His voice was subdued, even obsequious.

"Of course," Dr. Amos said generously.

John Thomas went to the door, opened it cautiously, and looked out into the hallway. He returned to his chair and leaned forward.

"I think the time is ripe for the raid on Jamestown. It would rattle old O.K. Knox to his eyeteeth." Heartened by Dr. Amos' acceptance, he grinned the mean grin that Dr. Amos had never liked. "We might even call him out for a little dose of Night Rider medicine."

"Don't be stupid," Dr. Amos said sharply. "Let one hand be laid on Oren Knox, you'll have Federal troops in here before you could bat an eye." He paused, thoughtfully. "You may be right about the raid, though. You have an instinct for spectacular violence, Mr. Thomas. This may be the time to indulge it."

John Thomas leaned forward eagerly. "We'll come swooping in, take the town, burn the Trust warehouses, and not even make a pass at his railroad car. He'll think—and nobody else could help from thinking—that, if we had so desired, we could have called *him* out as well." He stood up in his excitement. "That's the ticket, all right."

Dr. Amos was determined to keep him in check. "I suppose you'd like to see another raid like the one on Gurley," he said in a withering voice. "Wild firing and complete anarchy, with an excellent chance for getting some people killed. Just kill one woman, one child—you'll turn the whole state against us . . . the whole nation." He shook his head. "No sir, Mr. Thomas. If we have a raid, we won't have *your* kind of raid. You will not be in command, Mr. Thomas. I will be in command."

"Well, of course," Mr. Thomas said. He tried to laugh. "I wasn't thinking of anything else."

Dr. Amos turned to Mr. Wingo. "What do you think, Mr. Wingo?"

"It would be a show of strength, all right," Mr. Wingo said thoughtfully. "Show O.K. Knox that the Night Riders own this country, by raiding the center of Trust power and influence whilst he himself is in the town. Of course, it could easily turn into a pitched battle—they've been expecting us ever since the Gurley raid."

"Let us come swooping in here with a volley of gunfire and you'll see all them big talkers heading for the tall timber," John Thomas said scornfully.

Dr. Amos, ignoring him, thought for a moment. "There is one thing we have not considered," he said in a quiet voice. "We have felt the presence of Oren Knox, hidden down there in his private railroad car, purely as a menace. Perhaps we're overlooking an opportunity he's trying to give us for discussing our differences. He might be sitting down there right now, waiting for a responsible leader of the opposition to the Trust to make the first move."

"Do we have anything to say to the man?" Mr. Wingo said.

"I wouldn't speak word one—I'd just spit in his face," John Thomas said flatly.

Dr. Amos ignored him. He sat staring thoughtfully at the floor for a time before he raised his head to look at the other two.

"Mr. Thomas, I want you to go to the secret camp immediately," he said. "Send out a call for all squads that are close enough to reach the camp by midnight tonight."

John Thomas bounced to his feet. "Then we are raiding!" he said in a high, excited voice.

"Keep your voice down," Dr. Amos snapped. "Do you want to inform the whole of Jamestown?"

Chastened, John Thomas resumed his seat. In a lower voice he said, "But we are raiding, aren't we?"

"We are organizing a raid," Dr. Amos corrected him. "While you're sending out the call, I will see if I can talk to Oren Knox." He looked directly into John Thomas' face. "You are not to set one foot outside that camp until I give the order," he said. "Is that perfectly clear?"

"Yes sir," John Thomas said.

"Perhaps Mr. Knox and I can thresh out a solution," Dr.

Amos said slowly. "Perhaps the raid will not be necessary, after all. I hope so." He rose. "Let's get about it," he said.

It was the supper hour before Dr. Amos approached the railroad car. The crowd had disappeared toward home and evening meal, the children called in off the street, even the young men vanished from their station at the end of the platform. The sun lay low on the horizon, its rays slanting long shadows omening the coming night. The light lay flatly against the black sides of the railroad car. The deputy sheriff sat on the bottom step, his feet ringed by shredded stubs where he had smoked countless cigarettes.

Dr. Amos walked steadily upon the ballasted right-of-way. He paused before the deputy. "I have come to see Oren Knox," he said.

"Sorry, Dr. Amos," the deputy said. "My orders are that nobody is to get in."

"I am the president of the Tobacco Growers' Association," Dr. Amos said. "I have business with Mr. Knox."

The deputy shook his head. "Sorry," he said. "Orders."

Dr. Amos stood still. Absently, it seemed, he put both hands to the lapels of his coat, his thumbs under the lapels, and rubbed them down, then up. The deputy's eyes widened. He scrambled to his feet, tugged at his left ear lobe with his right hand.

"I see you have been there," Dr. Amos said.

"Yes," the deputy said. "On my bended knees."

There was a pause. The deputy then said, under his breath. "I'll be double-dog-damned. You really are in it. I'd heard it said, but . . ."

"I must go in," Dr. Amos said.

The deputy glanced about with a harried eye. "If I let you in there, it'll cost me my job. Right out here in broad open daylight like this . . ."

Dr. Amos lowered his voice. "In the service of the Silent Brigade," he said. "I must go in."

"You're not going to . . ."

"I'm going to *talk* to Mr. Knox," Dr. Amos said, emphasizing the word.

The deputy stood aside. Dr. Amos mounted the three steps. He knocked on the door. It was opened immediately by a young man in a discreet black suit.

"Yes?" he said, in a voice ready for dismissal.

"I am Dr. Amos Haines," he said. "I am here to see Mr. Oren Knox."

It was obvious that the young man had heard his name.

"Just a minute," the young man said hastily. He disappeared inside the car, returned momentarily. "Will you come in?"

Dr. Amos stepped through the door into the interior of the car. Oren Knox rose from a plush chair. Dr. Amos advanced to shake hands with him.

"Mr. Knox, I have come for a talk. Will you grant me a few minutes of your time?"

"I don't see why not," Oren said. "You are one of the reasons why I came to Jamestown, Dr. Haines."

He motioned for Dr. Amos to sit. Dr. Amos did so. The interior of the car belied the austerity of its outside appearance. It was decorated in ornate red plush, with deep green hangings. Over his head Dr. Amos saw a crystal chandelier. The railroad car seemed as crowded as a fashionable parlor with comfortable furniture; two chairs, a sofa with scrolled wings. The light was dim and grateful after the glare of outside. The air was warm, the car having been closed all through the heat of the day.

It seemed a proper setting for O.K. Knox. Dr. Amos sat in one of the plush chairs, studying the man who had been his distant opponent for so long.

Oren Knox was stocky, heavy, in his expensive suit. Under the suit coat he wore a vest with white piping on the edges. His shoes were made of black, supple leather, wrinkled to the shape of his feet. His hair, still luxuriant, had turned gray, almost white along the temples. He wore it brushed straight back, as though, impatient with appearances, he took the simplest way with such necessities.

His heavy face bore the accustomed authority of will and caprice. The face owned weight, but not fat; it was firm and controlled, the lips lying flatly against each other. There were deep lines that, as a doctor, Dr. Amos could tell were the lines of suffering, not of age. Not physical suffering; an inner hurt that had stamped his flesh irrevocably. Here was a man who had seldom smiled, a man unaware of how life had marked his face to a discerning eye; yet, withal, a man of weight and authority, who knew his mind, who exercised his will.

"John," Oren Knox said to his young secretary. "Take these messages to the railroad station and ask the operator to send them to our New York office. Show him our authority from the railroad's central offices to use their wires. Wait for any answers that might be needful."

He shuffled the mass of papers together and handed them to the young man, who disappeared. He resumed his own chair and looked at Dr. Amos.

It was the first time that Dr. Amos had been subjected to the clear gaze of his cold blue eyes. He sat still, feeling his own features peeled and exposed. Dr. Amos had never in his life seen a man with such coldness in his gaze. In spite of himself, he was intimidated. The face, perhaps, was a mask; the eyes were the true man, as cold and blue and final as the steel of a gun barrel.

For his part, Oren Knox saw a tall man sitting uncomfortably in the plush chair, his big hands, with the broad, blunt fingers, resting tensely on his thighs. Dr. Amos wore a stern face, the lines all running downward. His thick hair remained black and long, carelessly cut, carelessly combed, pressed down where the weight of his hat had rested. As Dr. Amos answered the challenge of his gaze, Oren Knox saw that his eyes were large and brown, clear-seeing but compassionate eyes.

Here before Oren was the man who was president of the Association, who was reputed to be the creator and leader of the Night Riders; a man who had ordered burnings and whippings and even, if tales were true, more than one killing. Oren Knox, studying his man as he studied all men who set themselves to oppose him, saw a tough but questioning soul. Here was a man with no more illusions than himself, who had looked at himself quite as thoroughly, who knew his strengths and weaknesses better than any opponent could know them. Oren wondered what had marked the sadness into so tough a soul. Perhaps it was the very compassion that showed itself so plainly in his eyes. They were eyes that could look unflinchingly upon pain; the more unflinchingly because behind them the mind would suffer the full impact of the seeing.

For the space of a minute, then, the two men measured themselves, one against the other, as wary as animals; seeing clearly, cautiously, respecting what they saw.

Oren Knox broke the deadlock of the pause. "May I offer you a drink?" he said. "A good cigar?"

"No," Dr. Amos said. "We will not be disturbed?"

"John knows from the manner in which I gave him his orders not to return until you have departed," Oren said. "Now, what do we have to talk about?"

"It seems to me that we have a great deal."

Oren nodded. "Yes. A great deal indeed."

The moment for mutual assessment had passed. They were feeling each other cautiously, now, with tentative words.

Oren abruptly leaned forward. He stabbed a forefinger at Dr. Amos. "I'm here to break your organizations," he said. "Both of them—the one above ground and the one below ground."

"It can't be done," Dr. Amos said quietly.

"Why not?"

"Because the Association is rooted in the people of the countryside. When this is true, there's no wiping it out. You may cut off the heads, but the roots will sprout new branches. It's like trying to kill Johnson grass in a field, Mr. Knox." He paused. "Why can't you try to live with the Association? We are not unreasonable men, Mr. Knox."

Oren leaned back in his chair. "Because the Association is costing me money," he said. "It's as simple as that."

Dr. Amos spread his hands. "From all I hear, you're from farming stock yourself," he said. "You know what it is to crawl through a tobacco patch on a hot day, worming it. You know what it's like to stand on tier poles in a tobacco barn and lift tobacco sticks high over your head to another tier pole you can barely reach."

Oren nodded. "I have done it."

"You know, as a man who has not done it cannot know, that growing tobacco deserves a living wage. Yet you want to deny the tobacco planter that living wage."

"If a man ain't got gumption enough to make a living at it, let him go to something else," Oren said. His voice had thickened to a drawl, the words dropping into a colloquialism that Dr. Amos found surprising in this expensive private railroad car.

He does that deliberately, he thought. Listen to him and not look at him, you'd think he was a plain old country feller.

"I ain't done nothing to the tobacco planter," Oren said. "There's a law I reckon you've heard about, Dr. Haines. The law of supply and demand. I rely on that simple law."

"You deny having rewritten that law to suit yourself?"

"I do the best I can for myself. So does every other man. That's a bedrock law, too."

Dr. Amos, watching his man, realized that on this level he could not hope to combat Oren Knox. He was facing the fighting mechanism that had shaped the Tobacco Trust, battling other men as well equipped, as ready to do battle. He must go beneath the armor against which his words were blunting themselves, find where the man truly lived.

"I wish you could have seen the suffering, the deprivation, that I have seen in this Black Patch," Dr. Amos said slowly. "I wish you could have stood at my side while I've tried to treat the diseases of malnutrition, while I have helplessly watched people die because they could not afford medicines, not even the proper food. I wish you could have seen what I have seen in these past five years."

"Suffering and hunger are nothing new in the world," Oren Knox said. "I didn't invent them."

Dr. Amos leaned forward in his turn. "There's something in you that wishes to do evil in this world," he said.

He did not say the words as he would once have said them, gravely and gently and with due consideration of their weight. He used them as a bright weapon, deliberately, to slice deeply into his opponent. Blindly, not at all with the skill of a surgeon, he struck as ruthlessly as he knew how and, watching Oren Knox, he knew he had slashed through to the meat beneath the armor-plating of the man's mind. Oren Knox stiffened. His face hardened. His voice lost the easy drawl.

"Evil?" he said. "I? Do evil?" He paused for a moment, gathering himself. "I have built a great business empire," he said. "From nothing. Yes, literally, from nothing. I began in business with one thin dime in my pocket. I still have that dime."

He reached into a pocket of his vest, laid a dime on the arm of his chair. The dime was polished smooth, it glowed with a dull sheen on the red plush.

"I had two things in this world. This dime was one of them. Here is the other." He rose from his chair, took down a Sharps rifle from a bracket on the wall behind Dr. Amos. "My father carried this old rifle in the War. It took me a while to find it, because it was sold off. I bought it for a hundred dollars, many years ago, and I have kept it since. A dime and a gun. I had to earn the gun."

He held the heavy, long-barreled rifle in his hands, hefting its balanced weight. He looked down at it, bemused. He had himself forgotten, long since, that he had been unable to search out the identical rifle that had belonged to his father. To his mind, the rifle he had purchased and the rifle belonging to his father had merged into one. He would not have believed, if he had been told, that the rifle in his hands was a lie that he had shaped for himself.

He returned the gun carefully to its place, resumed his seat.

"I built it all myself," he said. "With my hands, with my mind, with my energy. World-wide. Can you imagine how many people are employed in my enterprises? Can you imagine how much pleasure and enjoyment I have given to the working classes, as well as the rich? I've put a pack of cigarettes into the hands of every man who wants one, at a price he can afford to pay. You take away this great instrument of business that I have built—*then* you will see suffering in the world. Yet you come here to say that I have created evil."

"An instrument is neither good nor evil in itself," Dr. Amos said. "Good and evil is within the human soul. The instrument is good if it is used for good, evil if it is used for evil."

"What about your Night Riders?" Oren Knox demanded. "Putting masks on their faces, even taking women out and whipping them in the high road. Burning and destroying—and killing. Just last night they murdered a man in cold blood, I'm told. What about *your* instrument, Dr. Haines?"

His voice was bold, forceful. Dr. Amos could find within himself no answer for the blunt attack. Oren Knox stared triumphantly into his face.

"Let's forget about the Night Riders. Maybe they got out of hand on you . . . I can see how it could happen. I wouldn't sit in this chair and blame you personally for everything that's been done. Let's just consider your Association. I want you to tell me the difference between your Tobacco Association and my Tobacco Trust. The Trust is a monopoly for buying, processing and distributing tobacco products. The Association is trying to be a monopoly for the growth and sale of raw tobacco. It is a combination, just as the Trust is a combination. So tell me the difference between them."

Dr. Amos firmed himself. "The Association was formed to combat the clear and present evil of the Trust," he said. "It did not come into existence of its own accord. The Association was not created by me; it was made by the planters themselves. It grew out of their need. The Trust was oppressing them beyond the point where a man cannot be oppressed without fighting back. You cannot equate the Association with the Trust, Mr. Knox. The Trust is force. The Association is counterforce."

Oren Knox smiled. He was not a man to smile often. The cold blue eyes watched Dr. Amos while the face smiled, moving the lines about his eyes but not changing the eyes themselves.

"The Association is your creature, is it not?" he said gently. "You created it, you shaped and guided it because it was there to be created and shaped and guided. That's the sole reason, isn't it? You were you, and the opportunity lay ready to your hand. You took the opportunity—not for the good of anything in the world but your own self."

"No," Dr. Amos said. "No. I wanted only . . ."

Oren Knox leaned forward once more. He stretched forth one hand and gripped Dr. Amos' knee. Dr. Amos wanted to jerk his knee away. He could not do so.

"You and I, we are the same," Oren Knox said. "Don't you see that, Dr. Haines? We stood in a barnyard in a pair of ragged jeans britches, with mud between our toes, and we looked out into the world. And we said to ourselves, 'I'm going to make myself something out yonder. I'm going to make me a place to stand on.' "

They stared at each other. Oren Knox released his grip and leaned back.

"I know a man when I see one," he said quietly. "It's my job to know men. When I looked at you, I might as well have been looking at my twin brother. You think I'm hard and ruthless? Where you see hardness in me, it is in you also. You look at me, you are looking into a mirror of yourself."

Dr. Amos stared at Oren Knox, feeling within his guts the truth of his words. They flooded a bitter light into his soul. He is right, he told himself in words harsh with clarity. He is right, while I have sat here talking about good and evil, about moral judgements. I didn't argue right and wrong once I had decided to take command of the Night Riders. When I became the man who could chop down John Thomas in his high place, I became the brother that Oren Knox recognizes.

He thought of himself, in this moment, as murdering at last that boy who had yielded the wounded bird into the destroying hands of his blood brother; perhaps he was only, at last, bringing that boy into his birthright. Whatever it was, he was not only liberated from the great burden he had carried all his life; he recognized his liberation. He remembered the pleasure he had discovered in unleashing himself in the battle for control of the

Night Riders. He had done it because of hard necessity; at the same time he had enjoyed it. He marveled that such a simple truth had been undiscoverable for so long.

Sitting back easily in the comfortable chair, he smiled at Oren Knox, ready to do battle. "I guess you're right, at that," he said.

Oren Knox laughed. Dr. Amos laughed also. For this brief moment in the midst of battle, they were friends, with the thorough understanding and acceptance of true friendship. Along with the warmth there was a profound respect, which only enhanced the warmth.

"I wish I'd run into you fifteen years ago," Oren said. "I could have used a man like you on my side."

Dr. Amos shook his head. "We'd never have been on the same side," he said. "We would have had to fight each other. You would not have followed me, no more than I would have followed you."

Oren chuckled. "I reckon that's the truth, too."

Dr. Amos frowned. "I will grant all that you have said," he said slowly. "With one difference. You put your foot to one road, I put mine to another. That can make all the difference in the world."

He paused again, thinking. He had been challenged in the very depths of himself. He must answer Oren Knox on the same level. He lifted his eyes to Oren Knox's face.

"Most men want to believe that they are seeking the right," he said. "Once in a while they even have to tell themselves that they have found it. Have you ever, consciously, thought of yourself as seeking the right? Where is your monument, Oren Knox? Where can people look, after you are gone, and say, 'This is where Oren Knox built?' The Trust is not a monument, it is an instrument of your will and your power. Where is your monument?"

Seeing Oren Knox's eyes flinch, he knew that he had struck deep into the man's soul. He could not know that his words were echoing in Oren with the accents of Trenholm.

"You have built a Trust," Dr. Amos said, pursuing his

advantage as ruthlessly as Oren, a few minutes ago, had pursued his. "You have built a great estate over there in North Carolina. Are these, to your mind, monuments for a man to be proud of?"

Oren rubbed the palms of his hands against his thighs, making the continual gesture unaware that he was doing so. In an altered voice, he found himself speaking words he would have believed himself incapable of speaking to any man. He could not have spoken them to anyone, now or at any time in the past, if he had not found a soul that was brother to his own.

"I just went along from day to day," he said. "It was the only way I could do. I started with a dime, Dr. Haines. One thin dime, with the year of my birth stamped on it, 1858."

"I was born in 1858, too," Dr. Amos said.

"I looked up one day and I saw my wife. Dr. Haines, it's a most strange thing in this world, but I loved my wife. My wife could not love me, she could not allow my love. She brought me a son, but I had nothing left for a son. She gave me the son out of duty; once I had the son I no longer had my wife. I hated my son." He looked up into Dr. Amos' face. "My son is worthless, Dr. Haines," he said. "Once, just for a little while, I thought he'd be at least a going-on. But he is nothing."

He spoke the words calmly, dispassionately, without hurt.

"I put my mind on the Trust. I worked day to day and when I looked ahead it was for the Trust, not for me. Then—I built my estate. I did not build it as a monument. I built it for my wife. My wife did not want it, and she died."

He spoke simply. But these words had pain in them, as those before had not.

"But I have found a monument. It took me a long time to get to it and I reckon I wouldn't ever have thought of it by myself. It was my wife who put it in my mind."

He looked into Dr. Amos' face. "When my wife died, I buried her on that great estate where she had never once set foot. Right in the middle of it, in the center of the lawn in front of the great mansion. I put up a marble tomb and on it I put the words, *Trenholm Knox, beloved wife of Oren Knox.*"

He suddenly lifted his hands from his thighs and looked at the palms.

"My palms always sweat," he said. "Ever since I was a little boy."

He put his hands together, clasping each one strongly with the other.

"That stone is only a marker. The whole estate will be her monument. I intend to take the riches I have gathered and build a college there. The present buildings, the present grounds, can be adapted, and others will be added. There are twenty-five hundred acres to be made into a campus. It will be a great school by the time I am through."

"What will you call the college?"

"Knox College. It is my monument, as well as hers. It will be the one thing we will have found a way of sharing."

Dr. Amos nodded. "It is a noble thing to do," he said.

"That's what I'm working for now," Oren Knox said. "Not just for myself any more. I'm looking on ahead, Dr. Haines. Every penny of my fortune, except just enough to maintain my son in the idleness he enjoys, will go into Knox College." He paused, watching Dr. Amos. He said abruptly, "Do you want a medical school there, as part of the college?"

"Me?" Dr. Amos said. He was overwhelmed by the casual remark.

"I thought of a medical school," Oren said. "I've never had much love for doctors, though, since they couldn't do anything to help my wife. But if you want a medical school, I'll build one for you." He smiled.

"I can't say," Dr. Amos said, his voice stammering over the words. "It's not a thing I can . . ."

Oren nodded. "All right. I will decide. If I do build it, it will be a monument for you, too."

Dr. Amos smiled. "You can't give another man his monuments," he said.

"Of course," Oren said. "Of course, you are right." He did not move through the small silence that followed.

"So there it is," he said at last. "We began the same. You

thought of yourself as seeking the good. I sought nothing, beyond the simple performance, until mighty late. Out of your good, if you want to call it that, has come forth the Night Riders, violence and killing and destruction. Out of my evil, if you want to call it that, comes forth Knox College."

He spoke the words in a simple, musing fashion that brooked no reply.

"So there we are," he said. "But where are we? I reckon, when you get right down to it, we've both still got mud between our toes."

"We have lived in the world as men," Dr. Amos said. "Imperfect men, in an imperfect world. We have done the best we can." He raised his voice. "I am your enemy. You are mine. I will destroy your Trust if I can, and you will destroy my Association."

"What did you come here to say?"

Dr. Amos gathered his thoughts. "The Trust will eventually be destroyed," he said. "The weight of the Federal Government, the whole nation, will be brought against you."

"They may think to destroy it. They cannot do so. And how long do you expect to continue with the Night Riders before you bring down the wrath upon you?"

"The Night Riders will vanish when the reason for their existence has vanished," Dr. Amos said. He paused, wondering how far he should go in revealment. "There is a great danger facing us," he said. "I cannot tell you what it is. But if I leave this railroad car without a solution, I cannot take the responsibility for events."

"Jamestown will be raided, like Gurley was," Oren Knox said shrewdly. "That is what you are saying."

Dr. Amos did not confirm or deny the statement.

"How far can you speak for the Night Riders?" Oren asked. "Are you their leader? Do you control them? Can you guarantee their conduct, in the event of an agreement?"

"Let us say that I have lines of communication," Dr. Amos said cautiously. "You can talk to me, Mr. Knox."

Oren nodded. "The Night Riders are engaged in criminal

activities," he said. "You cannot acknowledge even to me your control of them."

He waited. Dr. Amos did not reply.

"All right. Let me hear your proposition."

"You have . . . the Trust has . . . desired to control the supply of raw tobacco," Dr. Amos said. "To be the sole buyer, to pay the price it chooses to pay. Each year of its increasing control the price of tobacco has been lowered, until the planter has found himself driven to the wall."

"Whereas, your Association desires to control the supply, in order to demand its price and receive it from all comers," Oren said. "As I said, there is no difference. It's just who's got the sword in his hand."

"Except the Trust came first. It created the situation. That is a big difference."

"It does not answer to the present," Oren said in a hard voice. "We must deal with the present."

"The situation must be changed," Dr. Amos said. "The Black Patch has never used the auction system to the extent that the bright leaf districts have. The Trust completely abolished the auction system as soon as it had the power to do so. I think our solution lies in that direction, Mr. Knox. The Association will agree, I am sure, to make open auction the standard method of sale for their tobacco, if the Trust will only agree to allow independent buyers and processors to enter the auction floor, bidding on the same level with the Trust buyers."

Oren promptly shook his head. "I grew up under the auction system," he said. "I have seen the abuses to which it is subject. The warehouse men are often a bunch of crooks. The pinhookers swarm like bees after honey, taking the farmer for every penny they can. I'm no friend of the auction system, Dr. Haines."

"It is a compromise," Dr. Amos said. "Many of the planters are dubious of it. But the auction system, established as a standard method, will give both Trust and Association a little room in which to move."

"I don't like it," Oren said abruptly. "I won't have it. If you don't have any other ideas . . ."

"What other idea is there?" Dr. Amos said. "We cooperate or we compete. You fight for total dominance, we fight for total dominance."

"Do you really think the farmer would be better off under the auction system?"

"Yes. I am sure of it, admitting the abuses you speak of. I don't think you know just how far down they've been pushed."

Oren shook his head. "I can't see it, Dr. Haines."

Dr. Amos gathered himself. "You and I . . . we met only an hour ago. We have spoken as friends. We have found, in one short hour, a kinship I have known with no other man in my lifetime. Surely between us we can do something to prevent . . ."

Oren's eyes were cold. "I cannot yield to you simply because I respect you as a man," he said. "If I did so, I could respect neither myself nor you."

"But surely . . . not yield. Compromise. With good will . . ."

Oren rose from his chair. "I have my task," he said. "You have yours. Show me my advantage in the auction system, and I will agree to it. Otherwise . . ."

"The Trust will enter the auction on precisely the same footing as all others who wish to buy. No advantage—no disadvantage. You will pay a price according to the competition, the quality, the quantity of tobacco. You will . . ."

"Some businessmen give lip service to competition," Oren said. "I've never seen one who wouldn't rather do without it. I am in the position to do without it. Besides, the auction system imposes middlemen in the chain of tobacco from farm to finished product. I'm no lover of middlemen, either. I have made it my lifework to eliminate the middleman."

Dr. Amos rose also. "There is nothing to be done, then?" he said.

"I am afraid so."

Oren thrust out his hand. Dr. Amos took it. They shook hands, looking into each other's faces.

"I wish it would be possible for us to talk more," Oren said.

"Perhaps we may," Dr. Amos said gravely. "And under better skies."

He walked toward the rear of the car. Oren went with him. At the door, Oren shook his hand again.

"Will you listen to a counter-proposal?" he said abruptly.

Dr. Amos paused.

"Dissolve the Association," Oren said. "Let the farmer deal individually with the Trust, as in the past. The Trust will make every effort to give him a decent price. Of course, the Trust will have to take world conditions into consideration, the law of supply and demand . . ."

He was well within his armor once again. Dr. Amos smiled, sadly.

"I cannot yield to you, no more than you can yield to me," he said.

Oren Knox laughed an abrupt laugh. "I guess not," he said. "Goodbye, Dr. Haines. I won't wish you good luck."

Dr. Amos rode through the mass of men toward the tent where the officers of the Night Riders would be gathered. Men turned to stare after him as he passed. Several spoke to him but he did not answer. He kept his eyes straight ahead. He dismounted and entered the tent where he had treated a gunshot wound on his first visits.

"I have talked to Oren Knox," he announced.

The assembled leaders lifted their heads to stare expectantly at him.

"What did he say?" Mr. Wingo asked eagerly.

Dr. Amos stood still for a moment, remembering the words spoken in that quiet and fatal conversation.

"We will carry out the raid on Jamestown," he said.

Chapter Twenty-One

JAMESTOWN lay dark upon the earth. The few street lights were always turned out at nine o'clock. Lights showed at the railroad station, the fire and police stations, and in the second-story windows of the telephone office. Another light hung over the door of the livery stable. Except for these five lights, marking the essential services, the town was sleeping. For weeks, now, there had been rumors of a Night Rider raid and the people had talked with worry and excitement among themselves. No one really believed in his own heart that it could happen.

The body of men, led by Dr. Amos, came in military formation up the railroad tracks from the south. They rode quietly, with only the creak of leather and the jingle of bits. Dr. Amos had formed the two hundred and fifty men into six squads, each squad entrusted with a definite task. The six squads traveled in one body toward the town.

The strange horse, big and rawboned, that Dr. Amos was riding was restive. He kept tossing his head, not liking the uncertain terrain of the railroad bed beneath his feet. Dr. Amos had to hold a tight rein to restrain him.

He rode in the vanguard, the white bandoleers of the leader

crossed on his chest. The night was cool, but he was sweating under his white mask.

A half mile from town, he turned his horse and whistled sharply three times, the signal for a halt. The squads halted, waiting in their double files.

"Squad leaders forward," Dr. Amos barked.

He moved a few yards ahead and turned his mount, watching the squad leaders detach themselves. These six men, under his command, would direct the raid.

"Do all of you fully understand your orders?" he said. "If anything is not clear, let's hear it now."

There was no reply, except John Thomas saying, "Let's get on with it."

His voice was edged with impatience and excitement. Dr. Amos looked at the dark figure that was John Thomas.

"I want to warn you again," he said slowly. "There must be no bloodshed. There will be shooting, of course. But your fire must be carefully directed, into the air as much as possible. Don't let your men get out of hand. If one of your men gets excited and will not obey orders, arrest that man and disarm him. Is that clear?"

"Yes," Mr. Wingo said. "I think we are all agreed that the raid must be a military operation."

"Then don't forget it." Dr. Amos paused. "Let us step down from our horses for a moment."

There was a rustle of surprise among the leaders. They dismounted, their feet sliding on the railroad embankment as they sought standing places.

"Reverend, will you lead us in a prayer?" Dr. Amos said.

He knelt, holding the reins of his horse in his left hand. The squad leaders did likewise and one of them lifted up his voice.

"O Lord, we seek Thy favor upon the necessity that brings us riding tonight. We ask Thee, O Lord, to lead us in righteousness and not in wrath. We ask that blood shall not be on our hands and on our souls after this night's work is done. It is our plea, also, that the eyes of men shall be opened, so that we will never again have to do what we are doing on this dark night. We ride in the darkness, but the light of Thy salvation is within our souls. Knowing that our cause is just, we ask Thy blessing upon it. In the name of Jesus Christ, Thy son, who died upon the cross for all our sins. Amen."

Dr. Amos rose to his feet. He stood quietly for a moment, head down. The agony was approaching.

Dr. Amos had understood the consequences of his decision. When man uses that most solemn thing, death, it seems as though he has lost faith in his own rightness, in his own irresistible and incorruptible strength. He is forever accused of striking terror; by taking up violence his ideas are incriminated, his aims suspected, his conscience denounced. He is reproached for raising up against the community a mound of miseries, of sorrows, of iniquities, of despairs, with tearing up blocks of darkness from the lower depths of the human soul.

Dr. Amos had hoped that no such violent remedy would be necessary. He had hoped to conquer evil, control it, study it lovingly, cure it as he had so often cured physical disease. It had not been possible; perhaps it had never been possible, and he had deceived himself. Now he could only force the election of violence upon the people, and abide by the decision.

He had committed himself; there could be no turning back. He put his foot into the stirrup, grasped the saddle horn with one hand, and swung himself into the saddle. The squad leaders mounted with him.

"Return to your squads," he said quietly.

He sat watching while the leaders moved away, to merge with the darker body of the mass. He sat his horse, thinking of the near two hundred and fifty men—others had entered Jamestown singly during the evening, in order to send warning of unusual activity or preparations—grouped into that darkened mass. The direction of these massed individuals lay solely in his hands. Whatever each one did, Dr. Amos Haines would do also.

He lifted his voice. "Let's go."

He turned his horse, moved him at a controlled trot toward Jamestown.

The first light they saw was that of the railroad station. It glimmered in the distance, drawing steadily nearer. Dr. Amos quickened the pace. He passed the railroad station in a steady trot, the squads moving in military files of two by two behind him. Dr. Amos saw the face of the night telegrapher peering out a window. It was the first Jamestown face he saw that night. Squad Number One peeled off from the formation, moving rapidly, three men dismounting and entering the station in order to prevent the telegrapher from sending news of the raid over his lines.

Dr. Amos had also seen, in the same sweeping glance, the black railroad car on the siding. He had hoped that Oren Knox would have taken warning and left by now. The railroad car remained dark, showing no signs of life. Squad Number One had its orders concerning Oren Knox's private car. The deputy sheriff did not attempt to resist their presence.

Dr. Amos turned into the street crossed by the railroad tracks and moved toward the center of town, followed by the main body of troops. He halted at the intersection of the two main streets.

"Follow your orders," he shouted.

In a sudden rush of movement, Squad Number Two detached itself to the left, galloping up Main Street toward the police station, alongside the courthouse. They made the three blocks in a fast rush.

Inside the police station, the telephone had just jangled harshly, startlingly, in the stillness. Three night officers were in the room. They looked at each other, each waiting for the other to take the call, for it undoubtedly meant leaving the cozy office. Finally, on the third ring, one of them reached for the telephone.

"The Night Riders are here!" the telephone operator screamed into his ear. "I just looked out the window and . . ."

The policeman turned, his mouth open. "Well, I'll be goddam," he said.

"What is it?" another officer said.

He put down the phone and crossed quickly to the door. He opened it, stepping outside. He saw the riders in the street and in the same instant bullets splacked against the front of the police station.

"Get back inside," one of the masked men shouted.

The order was unnecessary.

Squad Number Three, in the meantime, had galloped straight on across Main Street to the telephone office. Six men dismounted, ran up the stairs. The leader knocked on the door with his gun butt, then tried to open it. It was locked. They charged the door, broke it down in one furious wave. They halted inside the splintered door, looking at the three night operators.

The women sat on their high stools, their hands frozen in the movement of duty, their faces turned toward the door. They were pale.

"All right, ladies," one of the men said. "You're off duty for the night now. Just climb down off them stools."

The three girls, stiff with fright, obeyed. A steady fusillade of firing had started in the streets below. One of the Night Riders approached the switchboard, peering inquisitively. Several lights showed on the board, others were popping into activity.

"How do you work this goddamned thing, anyway?" the curious Night Rider said.

"Cut out the cursing," the squad leader said. "Remember, you are in the presence of ladies."

"Well, how do you work the doggoned thing?" the Night Rider said in an aggrieved voice. "I ain't never seen one before."

The head night operator said, "You put the plug in the little hole under the light. Then you listen in the headset."

The Night Rider did as he had been instructed. He listened to the voice on the line with evident delight.

"You want to know what all the shooting is about?" he said into the mouthpiece. "Lady, the Night Riders are in town."

He listened with satisfaction to the scream on the other end of the line.

"All right, no more fooling around," the squad leader snapped. "Ladies, you'll have to come downstairs."

The head operator was emboldened by the recent admonition against cursing. After all, she was still a woman; these persons, though wearing masks, were still men.

"We cannot leave our posts," she said. "There may be people calling for help, for doctors, for . . ."

"Lady, you want me to pick you up and tote you down them stairs?" the squad leader said.

She stared at him for a moment. Then, with a toss of her head and a twitch of her long skirt, she marched toward the door, followed by her sister operators.

Dr. Amos sat his horse at the main intersection of town, listening to the shots, watching the swirling activity about him. The men had been instructed to be careful in their shooting. They were following orders, though they seemed to take particular delight in aiming at windows rather than walls. That could be dangerous. But they were doing well.

Squad Number Four had already captured the fire station, he saw as he rode up that way to reconnoiter. The fire chief was arguing furiously with the leader of that squad.

Dr. Amos had by now received reports from each squad telling him that the town's communications were secure. They held the railroad station, the police and fire stations, the telephone office.

"What was the fire chief so mad about?" he asked the messenger from Squad Number Four.

"He was claiming the right to fight any private fires that might get started," the messenger said. "He's afraid some houses will catch fire when we burn the warehouses and the stemming factory."

"What did the squad leader tell him?"

"Told him not a fireman was to put his head outside the fire station."

Dr. Amos nodded. He turned to the two remaining squad leaders.

"Do your duty," he told them.

The fifth and sixth squads departed on their missions to burn the warehouses and the stemming factory. Dr. Amos occupied his time by riding up and down the familiar streets. The streets were being patrolled by masked men, their faces turned upward to the windows. Steady firing continued, dying into lulls and then spurting forth again. Some of the Night Riders shouted, riding back and forth and firing into the air.

It looked like turmoil and anarchy, but Dr. Amos could see clearly how well the discipline was holding. It was not like the Gurley affair. The noise was designed to intimidate, not to kill or wound. A few citizens had ventured into the streets, through foolhardiness or curiosity. They were being herded into a rope corral established at the intersection below the fire station. They stood huddled together under guard, their trousers pulled on hastily over pajamas or night shirts, their long underwear showing, their feet thrust into sockless shoes.

A messenger hastened to his side. "They're breaking into the newspaper offices," he said.

Dr. Amos paused, considering. The newspaper office had not been on the agenda. "Let 'em go," he said. "The newspaper has written enough against us, God knows."

He rode down the street to watch. They were enjoying smashing the furniture, tossing it into the street through the broken windows. Dr. Amos smiled under his mask, watching.

There was no doubt; a certain joy could be found in destruction. It was this in men to which John Thomas had appealed so successfully. Dr. Amos was channeling the destruction, holding it within bounds. It was the reason he had wrested control of the Night Riders.

A dull boom echoed. One of the men near him pointed and shouted, "Looky yonder. My god, just looky yonder!"

Dr. Amos turned his horse. Flame was blossoming against the night sky, billowing up in great sheets. The sight of the flames swept a boiling excitement into the Night Riders. They began spurring their horses up and down the streets like drunken men, shouting and firing into the air with a frightening randomness.

Dr. Amos spurred his horse, galloping back to the intersection. "Hold your squads," he shouted. "Remember your orders, now. Hold your squads."

His presence had a quieting effect in his immediate vicinity. Suddenly another flame sprouted like an evil flower, then another. They were so high and bright the masked faces were illuminated. The sides of the sweating horses seemed to be streaming blood under the lurid glow.

Dr. Amos gathered his messengers about him. "Find your squad leaders," he said. "Tell them to hold their men in check. We're nearly through, now. The big work is done."

A distant boom sounded and the stemming factory went up in flames. Four great fires now burned in the warehouse district.

"Hurry now," he said to the messengers.

Watching the activity around him, he could feel satisfaction. It was going well; better than he had expected. He wondered, suddenly, what Oren Knox was thinking, down there in his railroad car guarded by Night Riders against the exuberance of the Night Riders. Dr. Amos had given instructions that no one was to approach nearer than fifty yards.

A messenger came pelting back toward him. "They're calling out Roscoe Barnes," he shouted.

Dr. Amos spurred his horse in the direction of the Barnes home. He cursed under his breath with every lunge the horse made. This was just the sort of thing he had warned against. There would be no calling out, no whipping, no activities directed against any individual. It was to be a purely impersonal assault upon the presence of the Trust within the hostile town.

A group of Night Riders moiled in the street before the Barnes home. It was a long, low house, with shortened white columns spaced along the deep porch.

"What's going on?" Dr. Amos called.

A dismounted man turned his mask up toward him. "They're inside the house now, fetching him out," he said, shouting in his excitement. "They called on him to come out, but he shot out of the house. Hit one of the men."

Dr. Amos saw the man sitting on the ground. He rode to him, the big horse parting the masked men like waves.

"Are you all right?" he said, leaning down.

The man looked up. His mask was pulled awry. There was blood on his chest. "I reckon I'll live," he grunted. "The son of a bitch."

Inside the house, a woman screamed. Dr. Amos jerked the horse around to face the house. The Night Riders emerged, surrounding Roscoe Barnes. He walked in their midst, moving with reluctance, urged on by harsh hands.

"Whip the Trust bastard," a voice yelled. "He just killed one of ours."

A roar went up from the throng of masked men. They surged forward, Roscoe Barnes trying to scramble toward the house but prevented by his guards.

"Kill him!" another voice yelled.

The mob took up the cry until it echoed in the street. They surrounded Roscoe Barnes. One of the men closest to him clubbed him on the side of the head with a pistol barrel, knocking Barnes to his knees.

The men formed a circle, Barnes kneeling in the center, his head down, before the masked man with the long-barreled pistol clenched in one fist. He lifted the pistol, struck again, and again.

Dr. Amos sat his horse, unable to move. He was frozen by the hate boiling within him. This man kneeling beneath brutal punishment had ruined Virginia Temple, had saddled Dr. Amos with the guilt of that long-ago ruin. This man had been the head of opposition to the Association, glorying in his lucrative adherence to the Trust, strutting arrogantly in the streets on his fine horses.

Dr. Amos had, with the first blow, recognized the executioner of all their wrath. By his shortness, by the squad-leader insignia on his arm, by the white mask, Dr. Amos knew it was John Thomas, the man forever ready to do the dirty work, who actually enjoyed doing it.

For the space of three blows, Dr. Amos was held motionless by the suddenly discovered desire for a revenge executed by another, more willing, hand. He had only to watch while the bitterness was expiated. For the space of three blows; then, recovering volition, he spurred the horse through the ring of men. Drawing his own pistol, he leaned to strike John Thomas with surgeonly precision along the temple.

John Thomas dropped like a poleaxed steer. Dr. Amos had used exactly the force necessary to knock him out.

The men around him stopped in their turmoil, startled into motionlessness by Dr. Amos' sudden move. Their masked faces were turned accusingly toward him.

He spoke the bitter truth. "I chopped him down because he was disobeying orders," he said. "I'll do the same to the next man." He motioned to Roscoe Barnes. "Now take this man up and get him out of here."

Four men hastened to do his bidding. Dr. Amos looked down at Roscoe Barnes.

"Can you make it into the house?" he asked.

Roscoe Barnes wavered to his feet. He stared up at the tall man on horseback in the white mask, with the white bandoleers crossed on his chest. Barnes' face was covered with blood streaming from his scalp wounds. He stood shakily, his knees buckling, and stared at Dr. Amos.

"I can't . . ." he mumbled. He sagged to his knees again.

"Lift him up," Dr. Amos ordered.

Two men seized him under the armpits, stood him on his feet.

"Take him into his house and leave him," Dr. Amos said.

Roscoe Barnes lifted his head. "I know you," he said. "Don't think I don't recognize . . ."

"Take him on," Dr. Amos said.

The two men half-carried, half-dragged him through the yard. They eased him up on the porch, his legs dangling down the steps. The woman who was his wife rushed out of the house to crouch by his side.

"He'll be all right now," Dr. Amos said.

The masked men clustered about Dr. Amos' horse. They were sober now, quietened by the bloody events, by Dr. Amos' chastisement.

"He recognized you," a man said in an even-toned voice. "He had better be done away with. He showed that he recognized you."

Dr. Amos glanced toward Roscoe Barnes and the woman crouching over him, wiping the blood from his face.

"If there is any man here who can walk up to Roscoe Barnes and put a bullet through his head, let him do so," he said.

No one stirred. Dr. Amos sat his horse grimly, staring down at their masked faces. It was an individual deed to which he had challenged them. He had known he would find no response; the darkness within their souls was no longer stirred.

"He just thought he recognized someone," he said. "There's nothing to fear." He lifted his voice. "Mount your horses. Form into files of two and follow me."

He rode toward the main intersection, followed by the men, so recently a mob, now formed into military ranks. There he met the returning squads who had fired the warehouses and the stemming factory.

"All done?" he asked Mr. Wingo.

"All done," Mr. Wingo said. He put his horse alongside that of Dr. Amos. In a sober voice, he said, "We had to kill a man."

"What happened?" Dr. Amos said.

"He was a switchman," Mr. Wingo said. "He kept on trying to move some boxcars away from the warehouse, in spite of being ordered to leave them alone. One of my men shot to warn him away. His aim was bad—or too good, whichever way you want to look at it. He was killed instantly."

"I hoped nothing like that would happen," Dr. Amos said. "I prayed that it wouldn't. And I'm not a praying man, in the natural order of things."

The death had marked itself in him with the fatal words, quite as though he had himself fired the shot. For a moment he slumped in the saddle, overridden by sadness and fatigue, by a fatal feeling that he could not shake out of his mind.

It was only for an instant. He was still in command. He stirred himself, reached for his watch, looked at it by the light of the distant flames. It was three o'clock; for nearly two hours they had held the town at bay, accomplishing their destruction.

"It is finished," Dr. Amos said. "Let us go."

He motioned to one of his messengers. The messenger unbreeched his shotgun, began blowing into the barrel. The hollow, imperious sound echoed against the walls. It was the signal for withdrawal. The men began coming from the side streets and forming up. Those who would make up the rear guard hastened to take their places.

Dr. Amos formed the main body and led them the way they had entered, down the street to the railroad tracks, turning to the left upon the railroad right-of-way itself. At the station, Dr. Amos halted his horse to let the main body go by. Armed Night Riders sat their horses before the private railroad car resting on the siding.

Until now, the retreat had been orderly. The men, sobered by news of the death, that had swept through the ranks as rapidly as fire had swept through the warehouses, rode quietly, almost without talking. Sporadic shooting continued in the town, the small rear guard keeping up the illusion of many men. Behind them the sky was lighted redly by the still-burning fires. Here, the men were quiet, the horses were tired.

Suddenly, in the anonymity of the masked files, one man lifted up his voice. "By God, let's don't leave town without saying howdy to old O.K. Knox," he shouted.

With the words, he fired his rifle toward the railroad car. The bullet spanged against the metal, whined in a richochet. Dr. Amos spurred his horse to restore discipline. He was too late; the files were halting, breaking out of discipline into individual movement. They moiled, the men beginning to shout, firing into the air. The lines broke and men spurred their horses up the siding toward the railroad car.

The Night Riders guarding the car stood their ground for a tense moment. They yelled and waved their arms, but they could not stop the sudden wave of angry anarchy.

Dr. Amos, a heavy feeling of futility in his chest, cursed and shouted, riding forward. The men stopped their horses, sitting in a dark mass within a few yards of the blank-sided car. The scene was lighted dimly by the lights from the railway station, by the distant fires.

Dr. Amos pushed his big rawboned horse to the fore, turned to face them.

"If a man moves one step nearer, if a man fires one shot, I will kill him in his tracks," he said. His voice was deadly in its intent.

He sat his horse, holding his pistol ready in his hand. They stared at him. For a moment he was sure they intended to dare his challenge.

He lifted his voice. "Are you fools?" he said. "We have done what we came to do. We have done it, in the main, in discipline and in order. Are you going to throw it all away now?"

He would never know whether his voice would have turned them from this final focus of their discontent. As he finished, a sound came forth from the body of masked men. It was a wordless sound, thrilling, irresistible.

Dr. Amos turned his head. Oren Knox stood on the platform at the rear of his car. In the dim glow of light he appeared bulky, thick-bodied, wrapped in a velvet dressing gown, the tasseled ends of the belt tied neatly. It was his abrupt appearance that had evoked the wordless sound.

"I am Oren Knox," he said. "Do you have business with me?"

Dr. Amos turned his horse, rode toward Oren. He made no attempt to disguise his voice, though he knew that Oren Knox would recognize him when he spoke, if he had not done so already.

"Our business is not with any man," he said. "Our business is with the Trust. We have now finished, and we are leaving."

They looked at each other across the intervening space; Dr. Amos, white-masked, on his big horse, a pistol in his right hand; Oren Knox in his expensive dressing gown, standing erect on the platform of the railroad car.

Oren Knox lifted his gaze to the distant fires. "What kind of men does it take to destroy the property of others?" he said.

"Men of substance and good will," Dr. Amos answered his scornful voice. "Who have been driven to desperate measures by the Trust." He lifted his arm, pointing to the flames mounting against the sky. "You started those fires, Mr. Knox, just as much as we did."

They stared, each challenging the other. Behind Dr. Amos the mounted men sat quietly, the urge to destroy taken away, under discipline once more. Dr. Amos did not know whether it was himself, or the commanding appearance of Oren Knox, who had stopped them. He did not care, so long as they were stopped.

"We are through now," he said. "I would advise you to go inside. Our rear guard will be passing soon. There will be men to guard your private car until the last."

He touched his horse with a spur, moved him toward the men. "Form files!" he barked.

The men shifted into their semblance of military formation. The squad leaders took up their positions and the Night Riders began departing down the railroad tracks. Dr. Amos moved toward the station to wait for the rear guard to disengage and pass through.

Mr. Wingo joined him. "I turned my squad over to my deputy," he said. "I will stay with you."

"Good," Dr. Amos said.

It was fifteen minutes before the rear guard passed. During that time, Dr. Amos did not look again toward Oren Knox's railroad car. He did not want to know whether or not Oren Knox was still visible.

The rear guard came swiftly when they did come, clattering in a turn onto the railroad tracks, moving smartly in a double file. It did Dr. Amos' heart good to see them. He motioned for the guards at the railroad car to join them.

He turned to Mr. Wingo. "Let's go," he said.

Mr. Wingo chuckled. "It was a good night's work."

The horses were moving under them. "Yes," Dr. Amos said soberly. "It threatened to get out of hand once or twice. We killed a man, and Roscoe Barnes was pistol-whipped by John Thomas. But, all in all, it was a good night's work."

Ahead of them, a whoop sounded, along with a scattering of shots as the departing rear guard fired back at the town. Dr. Amos was knocked abruptly from the saddle by a random bullet. The big horse shied away.

He was jarred, his breath shaken out of him by the unexpected fall. He sat on the ground, feeling only the jarring at first. Then he knew the wound within his flesh.

Mr. Wingo hurried to dismount. "What's the matter?" he said. "Did your horse throw you?"

Dr. Amos gritted his teeth. "I'm shot," he said. "Those damned idiots . . ."

Mr. Wingo knelt by his side. "Bad?"

"I can't tell. I'm bleeding . . . help me up. We can't stay here."

With Mr. Wingo's help, Dr. Amos managed to straddle his horse. Leaning over, his hand pressing his body to control the bleeding as much as possible, he hung on grimly as the horse plodded down the railroad track into the country darkness away from the burning light of the town.

He lasted for a mile in this manner. His head was swimming and he often swayed in the saddle, so that Mr. Wingo had to ride close, steadying him. Ahead, they could hear men shouting and singing, with an occasional shot fired. They caught up with a slower portion of the rear guard.

"I can't last this way," Dr. Amos finally said, gasping the words. "The bleeding is pretty bad."

Mr. Wingo called to the men ahead. "Two of you go back," he said. "Steal the first horse and buggy you can find. We will leave the tracks and go to the road over there, about half a mile. Come along that road."

Two men hurried toward town.

"Can you ride to the road?" Mr. Wingo asked anxiously.

"I guess I'll have to," Dr. Amos said.

They cut away from the railroad right-of-way, riding across country. The horses moved slowly but the rough ground jarred Dr. Amos so that he moaned occasionally. Once on the road, Mr. Wingo eased Dr. Amos down from the horse.

They uncovered the wound and Mr. Wingo struck matches while Dr. Amos examined himself as best he could.

"A small artery has been severed, I think," he said. "I'll bleed to death unless it can be stopped. Get my saddlebags."

Mr. Wingo brought the saddlebags and upon instructions searched out the materials for a compress. Dr. Amos sat upon the ground, tending his wound by the flickering light of matches. He made a compress, his hands following the sure knowledge of his yesterdays.

"Will that stop the bleeding?" Mr. Wingo asked when he had finished.

"Maybe," Dr. Amos said. "It ought to be ligated."

"I'll bring a doctor," Mr. Wingo said. "We can't just let you bleed to death."

"No," Dr. Amos said. He smiled, grimly. "I'm the only doctor that's a Night Rider. We can't trust anybody else."

He lay back, resting, until the men arrived with a stolen carryall. Lifted into the back, lying on the jolting floor, he felt easier, though light-headed with the movement. It was a long journey to the secret camp. He was taken out of the carryall into the tent, while Mr. Wingo gave orders for the carryall to be abandoned close to Jamestown, where it might be found by the owner.

Dr. Amos slept off and on through the morning. He became weaker with the constant loss of blood. Outside the tent, though he did not know it, men clustered in silent concern, talking quietly among themselves about the events of the raid. Men rode away, returned with the news of Jamestown recovering in the light of day.

Mr. Wingo had long since given up urging the necessity of a doctor upon Dr. Amos. Dr. Amos would not admit of the risk, to himself and to the other men.

At eleven o'clock, Walter Wingo, with John Thomas, his head bandaged, entered the tent once more. Dr. Amos lifted his head feebly.

"Any news from Jamestown?" he said.

"They've brought in the troops," John Thomas said with

his wicked grin. "There's soldier boys all over the place, they tell me. I wish I could see it, but with my bandaged head . . ."

"It's like a beehive," Mr. Wingo said.

"I reckon we stirred them up," Dr. Amos said in his weakened voice. "Has there been any announcement by Oren Knox? I thought maybe he'd . . ."

"His private car was hitched to the midmorning train," Mr. Wingo said. "He didn't open his mouth, as far as I know, before he left town."

"I hoped," Dr. Amos said. "I hoped . . ."

He let his head fall back, unable to support it any longer. Mr. Wingo kneeled beside him.

"Is it still bleeding?" he said.

"Yes," Dr. Amos said.

"Let me bring a doctor. We'll abduct him, blindfold him . . ."

"I am an outlaw," Dr. Amos said. "Outside the pale." His voice was very weak. A smile showed itself on his lips. "Physician, heal thyself," he murmured.

He died at three o'clock in the afternoon. Before death he was as pale as death, for he had lost much blood. He died alone, for the man set to watch him had stepped momentarily outside the tent to relieve himself.

Dr. Amos Haines was buried in an unmarked grave.

VISTA: VIII
Oren Knox:
1923

TWO DAYS before the dedication ceremonies for Knox College, the reporters found Oren Knox in his New York town house. Wrapped in their overcoats, their hands gloved, for it was a bitter winter day, they clamored for an interview. Once, twice, three times, they were denied entrance. They persisted. At last, when it was obvious that they would not depart otherwise, they were admitted.

Oren Knox sat before a fire in his drawing room. He lifted his head as the reporters, suddenly quiet and respectful, were admitted to his presence.

"What do you want?" he said in a grumbling voice. "You well know I do not make statements to the press."

"But, sir, day after tomorrow your college will be formally dedicated. Surely, upon this great occasion . . ."

"I have nothing to say," Oren said.

"You have poured your entire fortune into Knox College. Do you intend to be present for the dedication ceremonies?"

"I hoped to. But I don't know. This terrible weather . . ."

They pressed forward, eager at the first breaking of his lifelong silence.

"Sir, there are so many things the world does not know about you. They know only the bad things, none of the good."

"For instance, why did you suddenly decide to add ten million dollars to the endowment for a medical college?"

"I have nothing to say."

"Why did you yield so suddenly after the great Jamestown raid and agree to an auction system of buying and selling tobacco?"

"I have nothing to say."

"Why did you ever agree to help break up the Tobacco Trust after the Supreme Court decision went against you in 1911? The judges themselves said, afterward, only you could have carried out the dictates of the court. Why did you agree to do it?"

"I have nothing to say."

A reporter pressed forward. "What about the old story that you held a secret conference with the infamous leader of the Night Riders, Dr. Amos Haines? What is your opinion of the man? Is it true that he is dead, or did he only disappear?"

Oren Knox mumbled words under his breath. The reporters pressed forward eagerly. Not one of them could understand that he said, "He was shot by one of his own. I stood there and watched it happen, while he was shot by one of his own."

"Will you repeat that statement, sir?"

Oren Knox turned angrily in his chair. "I've told you and told you, I have nothing to say," he said. His voice lessened, and he turned away from them. "Why won't you leave me alone? I am only an old man, trying to keep warm."

He huddled closer to the fire, rubbing his hands over each other with a dry rasp of flesh against flesh. They watched him for a moment before the secretary ushered them from the room.

ACKNOWLEDGMENTS: A novel such as this cannot be written without the assistance of many people. For access to research materials my thanks are due to: Dr. Wm. Stanley Hoole, University Librarian, Amelia Gayle Gorgas Library, University of Alabama; Mrs. Mary Ella Terrill, Reference Librarian, Rare Book Room, Amelia Gayle Gorgas Library, University of Alabama; Kenda C. Wise, Reference Librarian, University of Alabama Business Library; Miss Katie Ezell, Head Librarian, Hopkinsville Public Library, Hopkinsville, Kentucky; William S. Powell, Curator, North Carolina Collection, Wilson Library, University of North Carolina; and Richard Brough. My thanks are also due to Wallace W. Henderson, Hopkinsville, Kentucky; A. W. Wood, Publisher, *Kentucky New Era,* Hopkinsville, Kentucky; H. V. H. Stoever, Jr., Manager, The American Tobacco Company, Durham, North Carolina; and Ted Howard, County Agent, Christian County, Hopkinsville, Kentucky, for their courteous cooperation in many ways. Eva McKenna and John Ehle, of Chapel Hill, North Carolina, gave generously of their own time and knowledge of the region and research resources. Not to be forgotten is my able secretary, Mrs. Nancie Carnes, whose secretarial *expertise* made this book so much easier to write.

Borden Deal
September, 1964